W

Jenny Colgan was born in 1972 in Ayrshire. After Edinburgh University, she worked for six years in the health service, moonlighting as a cartoonist and stand-up comic. She is the author of three previous bestselling novels: *Amanda's Wedding*, *Talking to Addison* and *Looking for Andrew McCarthy*, all of which are in development for film and TV. Jenny Colgan lives in London and is working on her fifth novel, *Sixteen Again*, to be published in 2004, and a TV series. For more information about Jenny Colgan, visit her website at www.jennycolgan.co.uk.

Acclaim for *Working Wonders*

'In this witty and clever story, Colgan combines the mundane with the magical to create a memorable tale. The characters grow more loveable as the adventure progresses, and it's impossible not to root for them. Funny, magical and moving, this is a rewarding read.'   *Time Out*

'We laughed a lot'   *Heat*

of admirers. Fast-paced, funny, poignant and well-observed it reads as a pastiche of the movies she loved . . . If a time capsule were buried to capture the world at the turn of the 21st century, this would be a candidate for inclusion: her sense of time and place are that authentic.' *Daily Mail*

'*Looking for Andrew McCarthy* will strike a chord with anyone who did their growing up in the 80s. Wonderful, warm and resonant for anyone who ever wondered what happened to teenage dreams.' *Hello*

'*That's Life* meets *This Life*, with *Once in a Lifetime* thrown in, all talking heads, witty one-liners and angst-ridden relationships . . . Did I like this book? Well, d'uh! Do hedgehogs have quills? A pure belter of a novel.' *Glasgow Herald*

'Colgan's enjoyable new bestseller investigates the notion that having it all can sometimes mean having precisely nothing at all.' *Marie Claire*

'Colgan's *Looking for Andrew McCarthy* is sharp, well-observed and hilarious.' *New Statesman*

'Colgan's got an ear for sarky dialogue and a humour that gives her more options . . . retro-irony, perfect for a conscientious objector's beach holiday.' *ID*

JENNY COLGAN

Working Wonders

HarperCollins*Publishers*

HarperCollins*Publishers*
77–85 Fulham Palace Road,
Hammersmith, London W6 8JB

www.harpercollins.co.uk

This paperback edition 2003
3

First published in Great Britain
by HarperCollins*Publishers* 2003

Copyright © Jenny Colgan 2003

Jenny Colgan asserts the moral right to
be identified as the author of this work

A catalogue record for this book
is available from the British Library

ISBN 0 00 710555 X

Typeset in Garamond 3 by
Palimpsest Book Production Limited,
Polmont, Stirlingshire

Printed in Great Britain by
Clays Ltd, St Ives plc

Acknowledgements

Thanks to Ali 'the stun' Gunn, Rachel Hore, Lynne Drew, Nick Marston, Nick Sayers, Deborah Schneider, Jennifer Parr, Fiona McIntosh, Amanda Ridout, John Bond, Jane Harris, Martin Palmer, Venetia Butterfield, Esther Taylor and all at Curtis Brown and HarperCollins.

Also: Museum of London, Adrian Fisher at www.mazemaker.com, Sam Kennedy for not getting your name in – I just couldn't write a character as fantastic as you deserve, I'm sorry. Andrew Mueller – yes, he's half-bred, ho ho; Ronita Dutta (WLX!!!), Martin Quinn and James Crawford for their support and encouragement at particularly crucial moments.

Another book written listening to a fantastic Chris Hoban album: www.chrishoban.com

And: Katrina McCormack, Karen Murphy, Salty

Sandra, Shappi & Susan, Dan Rhodes, Ben Hatch, Mum and Dad, and the Writer's Blockettes.

I'd also like to take this opportunity to apologize for any suspect geography in this book. Sorry, Mrs Barr (who is in fact a very good geography teacher).

SAVE THE BEDLAM!

To Robin Colgan and Dominic Colgan,
for all the reading I got in as a child while you
were playing First World War/sailing boats/
digging enormous holes for no apparent reason.
As annoying brothers go, you're absolutely
the best a girl could wish for.

Chapter One

'Stop kicking me.'

Arthur had been dreaming of thundering hooves, when suddenly the hooves came to life. Fay hadn't been dreaming of anything, and redoubled her efforts.

'I have to keep kicking you! Otherwise you don't get up and go make the tea.'

'Why don't you use the energy you're expending on hurting my legs to get up and go make the tea?'

'What are you, a time and motion expert?'

'Yes, actually!'

Arthur sighed. An argumentative approach to mornings with Fay had never benefited him before and seemed unlikely to start now. He rolled out of bed, wincing. Outside it was still dark.

'There's no milk!'

There was no reply, either. Fay had rolled over and grabbed the pillow, luxuriating in a few extra seconds of warmth – *his* warmth, Arthur thought crossly.

'Do you want juice, water or ketchup on your cornflakes?'

Fay eyed him balefully. 'I want you to remember to buy milk.'

Arthur moved into the bathroom impatiently, as usual knocking over several of the ornamental starfish and candles with which Fay insisted on cluttering up the place. The house was a boring estate semi in Coventry, not a New England beach house. No-one would ever, ever walk into their little bathroom and think – ah! Grooved wood! Perhaps I have been magically transported to a world of fresh lobster and windswept sands. Arthur had never been to New England. He briefly wished himself there, if only because the time difference would give him another five hours of delicious sleep.

Groaning, he stared sticky-eyed into the mirror and splashed water on his face. It was normally a nice affable face, although right now it looked cross and tired. He looked at his hair and resisted the urge to measure it. His floppy brown hair was one of his favourite things about himself and he was terrified of the day it would finally desert him, although it was bearing up all right (his forehead was just getting a bit longer, that was all). At thirty-two years old, the confused vertical groove line between his eyes was becoming permanent but his smile was lovely, which he would have known if he ever smiled at the mirror or in photographs, which he never did.

'Hurry up in the bathroom!'

For God's sake!

'You're not allowed to hurry someone out of the bathroom and still be functionally asleep, okay?'

He took off his pyjamas to get in the shower. When had he started wearing pyjamas? When had he and Fay stopped diving into bed naked as piglets all the time?

He briefly considered a quick Kevin Spacey in the shower but he had to get to work . . . oh, Christ, work. Arthur hit the plain white tiling with his fist. He'd forgotten.

'Shit. SHIT!'

'Well, that's nice,' said Fay, wandering past the shower curtain. She was wearing a hideous dressing gown. When you thought about it, he supposed, all dressing gowns were hideous. Why had he never noticed that before? The pattern had not yet been invented that didn't render them staggeringly unattractive. Nighties were sexy and nudie was beautiful, but dressing gowns were like dating a sausage roll.

'Why don't you take off your dressing gown and get in the shower with me?' he said impulsively. He suddenly wanted to do something cute and fun and detract from the fact that he had just remembered that today he was due to be interviewed about his job by some people who had the power to take it away.

'I thought you were busy with all the tile hitting and cursing,' said Fay, brushing her teeth.

'I was, then I saw you, a vision of loveliness in acrylic.'

'Uh huh. Well, personnel issues won't just sort themselves out, you know.'

I bet they would, thought Arthur mutinously to himself. He'd been with Fay for five years and still wasn't a lot closer to understanding what a recruitment adviser did now than when they first got together.

'And don't you have that survey thing?'

He groaned again. 'Please, don't remind me. And it's not just a survey, it's a total strategic review of our entire function.'

'What, playing Sim City?'

'Yes, that's right, Fay. That's what I do. I play computer games all day and deliberately make the traffic go slowly.'

He felt her raising her eyebrows at him.

'Well, you're incredibly successful at that. Anyway, the condoms are downstairs.'

Arthur stood in the shower and let the water cascade over him. This was new. He had a sneaking suspicion Fay wanted to throw away the contraception and get on with the business of having babies. She was thirty-one. He thought that might be it. Anyway, she'd taken to hiding the condoms in unconventional places, possibly in the hope that he'd be so carried away he would say not to bother. It wasn't working, particularly not when she was wearing a dressing gown that rendered her nicely curvy body practically bovine.

He closed his eyes, wondering whether to risk shaving in the warmth (which would earn him a lecture and a bottle of Cif shoved into his hands). Suddenly he got a strong sense again of last night's dream. The hoofbeats were pounding on snow. He could almost remember the smell of the sweating body of the mare . . . That was odd. How did he know it was a mare? Well, dreams were the most peculiar things; he'd never met a horse in his life.

'Can you ride a horse?' he asked Fay downstairs. She was now unattractively done out in a purple business suit with accenting scarf.

'Why, would it be quicker getting me to work

than the Mondeo? Is this your new scheme for the town centre?'

'Never mind,' he said. 'What are we doing this weekend?'

'The Hunters on Friday night and some cheese and wine thing on Saturday.'

His face fell. 'But the Hunters are very *very* boring.'

'Well, they live in our street. And, you know. So are we.'

She pecked him on the cheek and disappeared out of the door, shutting it a little too forcefully.

* * *

The clouds were as heavy over Arthur's head as the bedclothes had been. The traffic was a heaving mass stretching out in front of him as far as he could see. When the system had been designed by Arthur's office in the 1960s, the concept of even every house having a car was completely ridiculous. Now everyone felt it was their basic human right to keep two, though it meant that, in practice, nobody could move. And at least half of the cars were as large as vans and fitted out so that if you had to take a quick detour through the jungle, they'd be ready. Mind you, driving via the jungle and up through Borneo might be quicker than most trips on the A405 to Coventry. But this morning, the A405 suited Arthur fine. Anything that kept him as far away from work as possible whilst letting him listen to Radio 2 was a good thing as far as he was concerned.

The man in the white jeep next to him managed to pick his nose, scream into his mobile and make a rude gesture at a lorry simultaneously. Arthur shook his head. Days like this had been getting more frequent recently. He might be only thirty-two, but he felt fifty-five. When he looked ahead, he didn't seem to see anything – just more of the same, with less hair. This is just Tuesday mornings, he thought to himself. The grey road and the grey horizon and the long monotonous journey ahead were conspiring to make him maudlin. This wasn't new. And today's forthcoming inquisition was merely serving to remind him that he'd been feeling this way for a long time.

* * *

Fay slammed the door on the way out of the house that morning, then winced at herself. Very mature, she thought, that will definitely make him love you. Of course, he wouldn't have noticed – probably wouldn't even have cared if he had.

She got into the little Peugeot and slumped forward onto the wheel, wincing as she felt the roll of fat press over the waistband of her skirt.

It was just . . . God, *Arthur*. What was it going to take? He seemed to be going directly from student to mid-life crisis with no intermittent period of, you know, adulthood. She loved him so much. And it felt that she just got nothing, absolutely nothing in return. She couldn't leave him. She loved him. And did she really want to be single again? And not twenty-five-and-living-in-London single – thirty-one-and-buried-in-Coventry single. That really didn't bear thinking about. Prey to the cream of dandruffed middle management. And it would be divorcés or nothing and you'd get their horribly whiny brats with E-numbers smeared all over their greedy maws . . .

I want a horrible whiny brat, she thought to herself, pulling out into the already incredibly heavy traffic. Only mine would be sweet and interesting and well-behaved and only eat organic vegetables and actually like them.

Maybe I should just tell Arthur straight out. I do love him, and the timing is right. There's never a good time to go for it. He's never thought about it for a second, but if I just said, 'Hey, why don't we have a baby?' then maybe he'd just say, 'Oh yeah, wow. I never thought of that before. I love you, darling.'

Or he might not look up from *Integrated Transport Today*.

I really have to tell him tonight.

* * *

The large dingy lobby in the grim, low-rise public sector building – barely brightened by some amateur executive artwork depicting what might have been Lady Godiva or a camel and a bear having a fight – was humming. Arthur realized that subconsciously he had put on his smartest suit and tie.

'Yo,' said the temp on main reception. She had arrived as a temp – a particularly surly one – in about 1983 and never left. Unfortunately Arthur had never got around to learning her name and felt it was a little too late to ask now.

'Hey,' he said. 'What's going on?'

'Some bunch of wankers turned up and took over the management offices.'

'What did they look like?'

'Wankers, I just told you.'

'Scary wankers, or the normal sort?'

'What, like you, you mean?'

'Um, yeah.'

The temp pondered for a moment. 'No, I would say they were more arseholey than you.'

Arthur smiled. 'Do you know, that's the nicest thing anyone's said to me for ages.'

She looked at him. 'I could believe that.'

Arthur grimaced and sidled past her, into the

open-plan space beyond. The office was cunningly done out in various shades of grey on grey which blended into the background outside, so that it rendered the world in black and white, punctuated occasionally by a particularly jolly stapler and purportedly humorous Garfield posters peeling from the walls.

His nearest colleague grunted, from behind his partition. Sven was a Neanderthal umbilically connected to his computer. He had convinced himself that in traffic patterns lay the ultimate sequence of truth: the perfect number, the end of pi and the key to universal harmony, or so he explained the hours a day he spent staring at the screen and plotting wildly complicated graphs in the further reaches of Excel.

Arthur could smell something. Part of it was Sven – if you're looking for the ultimate sequence of truth, as Sven often pointed out, personal hygiene is not a priority. Also, Sven liked to think that really he worked in Silicon Valley in California, or Clerkenwell, which meant a surfeit of slogan t-shirts, trainers, and a diet consisting entirely of junk food, none of which helped the hygiene issue particularly.

The office of course smelled the way it normally did – of ink, dirty computer keyboards, bad food and a general low-lying depression. Under that smell, though, there was something else — something different, Arthur thought. Something reminiscent of wet school blazers and drool. He navigated the last few identical grey desks — newcomers could often be found scurrying around here like panicking rats before they gave up and simply became resigned rats.

Oh God, this was all he needed. Sure enough, now he thought about it, he could hear the heavy panting. He stood up and peered over the partition. There was Sven in all his normal early-morning sweatiness, munching his way loudly through a breakfast bun, but today — yet again — with the help of Sandwiches, his small, droopy-eared, stubby-legged, dribbly, stinky basset/sausage/God-knows-what of a dog.

'Bloody hell!' said Arthur, all the frustrations of the morning welling up. 'Sven, I thought you were supposed to stop bringing that fucking dog in. Today of all days!'

Sven grunted, entirely unconcerned. 'Are you my boss?'

'That's not the point. Your dog is so dirty he's a fire hazard. It's health and safety.'

'It's "Bring Your Dog to Work Day", innit?'

'It is *not*,' said Arthur fiercely, although a faint glimmering of doubt crept into his mind. *Was* it?

'Yeah, it is. It said so in the *Guardian*.'

'What? What on earth could a dog *possibly* do in an office? Well, yours could lick all the stamps.'

Sven snorted. 'Yeah. And he could probably do your job. With one paw tied behind his back.'

'Oh, don't start.'

'Who started? You started, you doggist bigot.'

Sandwiches reached up and carefully ate the end of Sven's malodorous bun.

'And if you fed your dog properly he wouldn't fart all over the place.'

'He doesn't fart all over the place!'

'Yes, he does, actually. You just don't notice because you, too, fart all over the place.'

'Why are you so fucking grumpy this morning then? Not getting any?'

Arthur wondered if job stress might make him impotent for the rest of his life. 'NO!'

'I reckon Sandwiches gets more than you, and I chopped his bollocks off five years ago.'

'Nyeaarrgh,' said Sandwiches.

'Coffee?! Anyone? Who wants coffee!?'

A woman in a bright pink mohair sweater popped her tidy, short-white-haired head round the other side of Sven's desk. This was Cathy who administrated the planners, oiled the troubled waters, did far too much of everyone else's boring

12

jobs and gave off an aura of complete desperation. She had a horrible husband and two horrible teenage boys, and coming to work was just about the most fun she ever had. Arthur tried not to think about this too often.

Sven and Arthur stopped sparring for a moment and grunted back at Cathy. Sandwiches's tail wagged sturdily: he was the only person in the office, and possibly the world, who loved her unconditionally.

In fact, Arthur didn't mind fixing coffee in the morning: it deferred the ultimate computer switching-on moment when the jolly day's crap would begin.

'No, it's okay, I'll manage.'

'Ooh, I'll come with you. But we can't be too long, or people will start to talk!'

Cathy tried to look flirtatiously at Sven, who gave a groan of disgust and ignored them.

'Do you like my new brooch?' Cathy showed off the diamanté panda bear incongruously fastened to where her nipple must be underneath her shapeless sweater. 'It was a birthday present!'

'Oh, that's nice,' said Arthur. 'From Ken?'

'No.' She looked at the floor, then jollied up again. 'I got it for myself. Well, you know, the boys are *soo* forgetful. Which is actually better, you know, because I get to choose what I want!'

'It is,' said Arthur, trying to nod as if this were true.

'So . . . it all starts today . . .' Cathy offered tentatively as she pottered around the urn.

'Don't worry,' said Arthur, 'I'm sure you'll be fine.' In fact, he reckoned mousey work-horses were almost always the first to go; they complained less about redundancy.

'Is it really a good idea to make us reapply for our own jobs, do you think? I mean, management must be right, but . . .'

Arthur nodded. 'Absolutely. The fact that we're in these jobs to begin with, of course, must be sheer chance. I got mine through my lottery numbers, in fact.'

Cathy perked up as she spotted someone on the horizon.

Great, thought Arthur, as Ross, his Tosspot Boss, came striding towards them in his cheap suit, with a big grin on his face implying that, whatever might happen to the rest of them – destitution, poverty, depression – he, mate, was going to be just fine, alright, mate? Yeah.

'Art. Cath.' Ross the Tosspot Boss was a year younger than Arthur and liked to point it out. His shirts were always on the wrong side of shiny, his voice on the grating edge of bonhomie and his actions mean as a snake. Arthur half-suspected that this strategic review thing was his idea. It meant Ross got rid of people with no direct route to himself: the consultants made him do it. Perfect. Although on reflection, Ross would probably have absolutely no trouble telling people to go by himself. He'd like it, in fact. A lot.

'What are you getting up to in here then, yeah? Hanky panky!'

Cathy grinned and blushed. She had a hopeless crush on Ross – she clearly had a type. 'Oh no!' she fluttered.

'Unlucky, eh Art?'

'Yeah,' said Arthur, as if yearning for nothing more than to be banging a sad-looking fifty-year-old woman on top of a coffee machine. Every time he let Ross call him Art, he reflected, a little bit of his soul died. He suspected (correctly) that Ross knew this. 'I was doing alright until you came along.'

'Oh!' Cathy blushed again and waved her hands. This was possibly the most wonderful time she'd had in years.

'Never mind, eh, pet?' Ross leaned in chummily. 'If you get made redundant today we'll just go and cruise round the world, eh?'

Cathy smiled happily. Arthur shut his eyes. This was awful. Why didn't he just punch him? He'd seen the picture of the ex-page-three model Ross claimed to be going out with, and she didn't share much in common with Cathy apart from a certain look of resignation around the eyes. He should defend Cathy and punch Ross and . . . thrust a sword through his heart.

He opened his eyes. A sword? That was a bit much, surely. Offensive weapons weren't really his style: he was a Labour voter and an inveterate spider freer.

'Worried, Art?' said Ross.

'No,' said Arthur, panicking.

Ross sniffed, looked as if he knew something the others didn't, and walked away.

Can I feel my blood pressure rise? thought Arthur. Ooh. If I had a heart attack I'd get three months off to recover. Then: I am thirty-two years old and wishing for a heart attack. That cannot be good. Perhaps a mildly painless form of cancer, that got lots of sympathy. Or if he jumped out of the window here, made it look like an accident . . .

He wandered back to his desk, ostentatiously holding his nose as he passed Sven. 'You've got mail!' said a smarmy American voice. Arthur was surprised to see he'd automatically turned on his computer. Oh God. This, as well as a tendency to dial 'nine' before making a phone call at home was starting to make him think that his brain was

16

gradually melding with the office. Soon, he would have no independent thoughts left of his own. His computer would beep 'You've got thoughts!' and then proceed to delete them, one by one.

Eighteen messages, almost all involving the project he was currently working on – the mooted bid for a new hypermarket near the town centre which involved knocking down substantial bits of old houses and creating a six-hundred-space multi-storey car park which would obscure the view of the marshland. It would also create fifteen hundred jobs and, on the whole, people tended to like handy hypermarkets. As a government worker charged with reviewing the viability of such projects, he often figured it would, in the long run, be quicker for him just to pull down his trousers and pull open his butt cheeks for the mega-grocers.

The e-mail he was looking for, however, was about a third of the way down the screen.

re: Strategic review job reassessment schedule.

In his head, he heard them mispronounce 'schedule'.

Please report to conference room B at 10.10 a.m . . .

Ah hah, he thought. Not even doing it in half-hour cycles. They must already know who they wanted in or out.

. . . for your psychometric testing.

Oh crap. The last time Arthur had done any psychometric testing, it had recommended he join the army. Although, on balance, how could that possibly be any worse than what he was doing now? Well, he could be shot to death, he supposed.

I would like to remind all staff that this is simply a cost-benefit-efficiency exercise devised to see how we can get the best out of all public service environments – a goal with which we're all in agreement!

Yes, thought Arthur. I would gladly let my family starve and my house get repossessed if it benefited public service environments.

So, don't worry and you never know – you might even enjoy taking the test!

Yours, Ross.

Cathy leaned over from the next booth, twisting her brooch nervously.

'I get three twenty-five,' she said. 'You know, I'm not sure if I will enjoy taking the test.'

Arthur wanted to be reassuring, but couldn't think of a way. 'I'm not so sure, either. Otherwise they'd call it a "party". Although not one of our Christmas parties. Which are also misleadingly titled.'

Cathy's face fell even further. 'I organize those.'

'Of course you do! Just being . . .' he groped for a word. 'Um, "wacky".'

Cathy, not normally a good judge of wacky behaviour (eg: having more than two piercings would count as wacky, as did being gay; filling your house full of china dolls bought on a monthly payment plan however would have crossed her radar as perfectly normal), narrowed her eyes at this travesty of the Trade Descriptions Act.

'It'll be a piece of piss,' said Sven, standing up for his twice-hourly trip to the vending machine. He normally timed them for whenever his phone was ringing, which drove everybody crazy. 'Just tell them you're not doing it!'

'Yes, well, the only way someone could get away with that,' said Arthur, realizing he was sounding peevish and exactly like his father, 'would be to do a job so incomprehensible that no-one understands it, so they can't fire you. Or your dog.'

Sven nodded with satisfaction, taking the compliment. His phone started to ring. He ignored it and walked away.

'Yeah. I'm so happy I'm not some generic paper pusher – ooh, sorry,' was his parting shot.

'I am NOT . . .' Arthur took a deep breath, conscious that Sven was always trying to rile him and that it always worked. Also, that whoever the evil consultants might be, they would probably choose a good moment to walk past while he was getting involved in a yelling match. And also, that it was true.

He sighed and turned back to his computer. Sven came back slopping coffee, and took an enormous bite out of his second roll, spluttering crumbs all over Arthur's in-tray. Management had discouraged the habit of going out to lunch by situating the offices seventeen miles from the nearest conurbation, so the entire room had a patina of other people's pot noodles and Marmite.

Arthur sat in purgatory for the next forty minutes, unable to concentrate. How had he got here, struggling to hold on to a shitty job he didn't want, on a wet Tuesday in Coventry? School had been alright, hadn't it? College – fine, fun. Geography, the world's easiest option in the days when universities had still been fairly exclusive organizations that didn't include degrees in Star Trek and Cutlery. And, 'There'll always be a need for town planners,' his dad had said, pointing out with unarguable logic that people did, indeed, continue to be born. And now he was thirty-two and wanted to kill someone for accidentally spilling small pieces of bread into a black plastic container that didn't belong to him, filled with crappy bits of paper he didn't give a flying rat's fart about. Hmm.

At four minutes past ten, he got up as casually

as he dared without pondering too much on the fact that if he was absolutely spot-on for time, this could mean something on the psychometric testing. Cathy looked up at him with wide-eyed fear.

'I'll write the answers down on the back of my hand for you,' he said.

'Will you?'

'No right answers, mate,' said Sven. 'Ooh no. Just wrong ones. Then they escort you out of the building and lock you up for life.'

'He's kidding,' said Arthur. 'Leave her alone.'

'Woo, back off Sir Galahad.'

Cathy giggled and blushed again. Arthur wondered how much he would mind starting his working life all over again as a lonely shepherd on a hillside.

* * *

'Sheep is to shepherd as goats are to . . . banker-shepherd-goatherd-banana.'

Arthur sighed and ploughed on with his pen. These were unbelievably crap, but he knew in the way of these things that they might suddenly get really hard in about fifteen seconds. At this point they were still checking his ability to read, which didn't exactly reflect well on their hiring strategies in the first place.

'Pig is to sty as dog is to . . . house-sty-kennel-banana.'

What was the fascination with farm animals, anyway? Was it an additional measure of stress, to conjure up bucolic fantasies whilst being held prisoner in a room without any windows? Arthur suddenly felt a desire to draw one of those adolescent penises, with enormous teardrops coming out the top, all over the paper.

'Monkey is to banana as polar bear is to bamboo-banana-fish-asteroid.'

Hmm. Perhaps being a town planner was marginally better than being the guy who had to make up questions about polar bears.

'Sword is to truth as horses are to . . . loyalty-dreams-journeys-bananas.'

Arthur started and sat back from the table. He looked at the question again and remembered his dream suddenly. Well, that was a strange one. Horses again. Then he ticked 'journeys', even though it wasn't the least bit the same at all.

* * *

It was ten forty-five and he'd barely made a dent in the piles of paper. Now he was doing stupid maths questions along the lines of squares of things and whether or not two is a prime number, just because it really doesn't look like one. He dispatched these quickly enough — one doesn't become an expert on suburban bus ratios without being able to do long division — and reached the largest section of the test. Stretching, he realized how incredibly hot it was in the room. His shirt was sticking to his back.

'There are no right or wrong answers on this test,' it said at the top of the paper. Arthur snorted, then instinctively looked around for a security camera. 'Please answer questions as quickly and honestly as you can and give the first answer that comes into your head.' I would do, thought Arthur, if there was a box that said, 'Augh! Christ, get me out of here!'

Please tick whichever you feel _most_ applies to you.
I want everyone to like me
I want to be successful
I want time to read my book

Hmm, thought Arthur. It's like a haiku. And I want all of these things. Let me see: like me means weak, read my book means slacker — he ticked successful.

I want to travel in my life
I want to be successful
I carefully finish projects

23

Ooh, getting tricky. Let me see: slacker, successful, anal. Okay. If there was a 'I want to be successful' line in every question, then he was home free.

Only your mother really knows what is best
   for you
I want time to read my book
I want to be the leader

Okay. Hmm. Between all the successes and leaders, he was coming out a bit too type-A-heart-attacks-risk. The mother thing was a nightmare waiting to happen. Books are good.

Four hundred identical ones of these later, Arthur was going stir-crazy. The same lines, repeated in seemingly infinite patterns of stupidity, designed to gradate just in whichever direction, given that you were already going to lie, you would prefer to lie. Would he rather come out as the teacher's anal sneak or the crazed ambition seeker? The joiner-inner or the workaholic? What was more important – the good name of the company or getting every detail finished? Working yourself into an early grave or keeping up the good name of the company? Arthur groaned and let his head sink forward onto his arms, then pulled it up again in his ongoing hidden camera paranoia. He stared at the paper, distraught. This was meaningless. Useless. And if he didn't pass . . . well, he was a town planner without much of a life and absolutely sod all he cared about. His body boiled with fury and he was very close to crumpling up the papers and storming out when the last question caught his eye.

I was made to gallop through the trees
I miss my sword
This is not my time

He stared at it, then swirled round in confusion as the door opened behind him. A tall, elegant-looking woman walked in.

'Are you finished?'

He looked at her. She was a very pale blonde, slender without being skinny, and had a high forehead and quite a long nose. Not exactly beautiful, but undeniably striking.

'Um . . . Just about . . .'

She swept the papers away from in front of him. 'I'm afraid we have a strict time limit.'

'Can I just see the last page . . .'

'Sorry.' She didn't smile. 'I'm Gwyneth Morgan. CFC consultancy.'

'Ah, the Crazy Frightening Company,' said Arthur, and immediately wished he hadn't. 'I'm joking. You know, I'm sure our excellent chief executive Sir Eglamore would agree that humour in the workplace and . . .' He was starting to stammer.

She stared at him coldly. 'Yes, I take your point, except of course that humour is normally funny.'

Arthur was stung. 'Well, very little is funny when you've been chained to a desk in a windowless room for ninety minutes.'

She raised her eyebrow. 'Perhaps you'd rather be excluded from the process.'

Arthur stood there for a minute, feeling the adrenalin rush through him. Suddenly, he felt furious. What the hell was he doing here and why was she treating him like this? Shaking, he pushed back his chair and stood up. She was offering to sack him and he was swallowing it like chocolate. He hated himself.

'Am I done?'

'For now.'

He almost pushed past her into the corridor.

* * *

Open-plan offices don't have anywhere to hide. Well, the solitary cubicle in the men's toilets, but that isn't a pleasant place to be at the best of times and this was emphatically not the best of times. Unconsciously loosening his tie and wiping his forehead – Jesus, why couldn't that bitch have given him two fucking minutes to read the last fucking question – he strode back to his rat hole, hot and furious.

'How was it?' asked Cathy anxiously.

'It's fine,' he said, almost spitting the words out. 'Nothing to worry about.'

'Why are you such a funny colour, then?' Sven said, picking his nose behind a magazine.

'I am not.'

Sven looked over pointedly, still exploring with his finger. 'Nah, you're right. You look incredibly casual and relaxed.'

Cathy stroked him on the sleeve. 'Don't worry,' she said. 'I'm sure you'll be fine.'

Her pitying kindness was worse than Sven's predictable indifference, and left Arthur shaking off her arm, half wanting to scream and half wanting to cry.

'It's *okay*.'

Ross stopped past. 'Hey guys!' He smiled unconvincingly. 'You know, just because it's a special day doesn't mean there isn't work to be done, hey?'

Arthur briefly closed his eyes, as Sven's phone started ringing. Sven ignored it for the eighteenth time that morning and Ross made himself scarce.

'Sven, answer the phone.'

'I *can't*, I'm engaged in an important creative mission.'

'ANSWER THE PHONE!'

'You answer it! It's two feet away.'

This was true. Didn't prisoners get ten feet by twelve?

Ross may have moved on, but the other office monkeys looked up, sensing something interesting.

'I am NOT answering your phone, Sven. It'll be some Danish roofing contractor who wants to know British tiling serial numbers again.'

'How? How can I create a city if I'm being constantly distracted?'

'Answer the phone!'

'No!'

'ANSWER THE BLOODY PHONE!'

'NO!'

People who had blended in against the grey background and the aura of coffee breath were openly watching now; signs of animation and interest were showing in weary eyes long-sighted from reading consultancy proposals.

Arthur unplugged the phone, picked it up and walked to the window of the office, which overlooked the business 'park'. His mind a blank, he had only a very vague idea that he was planning on throwing it out when he got there. Of course, the windows weren't designed to open, and he hurt his fingers tugging at them.

'FUCK!' he said, out loud. Somebody in the office – probably Cathy – gasped. Everyone was silent now.

He put the phone down on the photocopier, still clutching it furiously, his knuckles white with anger, blood flowing like acid through his veins. Suddenly, all he wanted to do was smash the window with the phone, sending it hurtling to the ground and sending Sven right after it.

It's only a phone, he thought to himself. Calm down. You're having a bad day. What the hell are you doing? For fuck's sake, it's only a fucking phone. That was right. He couldn't. He should pull himself together, walk back over to Sven's desk and plug it back in. When it started ringing again he would calmly pick it up and say, 'Sven isn't here. He got a bit of a fright from a hole-punch this morning and accidentally crapped himself. He's gone home and is never coming back again, the shame was so much. You wouldn't believe how bad it still smells in . . .'

And then Sven would grab the phone off him and everything would be okay.

Instead, Arthur stepped back from the window, picked up the industrial-sized photocopier with the phone on top, and hurled with all his might.

The photocopier flew through the air and broke through the bullet-proof glass like a flying hippopotamus, gracelessly soaring out onto the grass below. The phone bounced back off the window-frame and knocked him out.

Chapter Two

Arthur looked around. It felt like sun on his face. Where was he? What about a window? Was he outside? He risked opening an eye, and instantly staggered backwards. He was on the edge of a forest and there wasn't another building in sight. It was dark and icy, and he caught a glimpse of something white through the trees. Then he woke up.

He couldn't tell where he was. His face was pointing upwards towards some light, which could either be good, as he wasn't face down in a gutter, or bad, if he were dead. He realized how ironic this would be after wishing himself dead all morning, then realized that if he really were dead irony probably wouldn't come into it. He tentatively opened his eyes.

'Well, hello.' A warm voice sounded in his head. He focused. He was lying on a sofa. A woman in her mid-fifties, with long grey hair tied back, was sitting opposite him, regarding him calmly. She was staring at him without blinking, and her eyes were an odd shade of yellowish hazel.

Arthur blinked twice. 'Um . . . Where am I?' he sputtered, in the traditional way.

'You're . . . just here,' said the voice.

He became aware of the throbbing in his head, as the faint memory of what had happened started to crystallize. He didn't think it was going to be good.

Arthur sat up a little way and looked around. He was in a heavily furnished room. The room was full of things: sticks, models, pipes; every available surface was covered in clutter. There was a familiar noise which he realized was the whistle of an old-fashioned kettle. The furniture was old – dark wood mostly, including a long desk. There was even a window, which looked out onto a small sunny garden – it must have been round the back of the building, away from the car park. That was odd; the rain must have cleared up. Then in a flash, he remembered the whole thing.

'Oh, God. Oh no. Oh no.'

'Sssh.' She smiled and leaned forward. 'Don't worry about it. It appears a telephone jumped up and attacked you.'

'Oh,' said Arthur. He was feeling it deeply. 'Oh,

my God. Did I really throw a *photocopier* . . .'

The woman nodded. 'Yes, you did. That's why we thought you had probably better go somewhere quiet for a little while.'

Arthur tentatively fingered the impressive bump on his head. 'Where am I?' he asked again.

'Oh, you're still in the building. You're just in my office, that's all.'

'Who are you?'

'I'm Lynne,' she said, reaching out to shake his hand. 'I'm the company psychotherapist.'

Arthur lay back and exhaled. 'I was afraid of that,' he said ruefully.

'What?'

'When I saw, you know, the non-office soft furnishings and stuff. Company shrink. Today of all days.'

Lynne smiled. 'And that is so terrible?'

'I would say me turning into an official, rubber-stamped nutjob on the day the consultants come in is, on the whole, pretty terrible, yes.'

'Nobody is saying you're a nutjob.'

'Well, I just did. Oh, hang on, if you think you're a nutjob, doesn't that mean you're not one? Or maybe it's the other way around. In which case I'm really in trouble.' He sat up again.

'Calm down,' said Lynne. 'Relax. I'm a doctor, you know. And it's not every day someone throws a photocopier through a window then knocks themselves unconscious. We had to look you over. You're going to be fine.'

'Oh, God.' Arthur winced at the memory. 'I am so not going to be fine. I'm going to get fired for this, aren't I? That's why I'm down here with you. You're to calm me down with yoga or something so I don't run upstairs and strangle Ross's pimply little carcass. Great. This day could not possibly get any worse.'

'Ssh,' said Lynne. They sat in silence for fifteen seconds.

* * *

'So this is treatment, is it?' said Arthur eventually, as it became clear that she wasn't thinking of saying anything to follow up 'Ssh'.

She stared him down until he went quiet again, lay back, then finally began to relax. After five minutes – and as Arthur was on the point of dozing off – she leaned over slightly.

'That's better.'

Arthur blinked up at her through sleepy eyes.

'Am I in serious trouble?'

She shrugged. 'No. I don't think so. You may have to see a bit of me, though.'

'But why not? I mean, I destroyed half the office and could have killed someone.'

'I know,' said Lynne. 'And when that copier went through the window I could hear the cheers and applause all the way down here.'

'*Really?*'

'Oh, yes. You've become something of a folk hero.'

'Good God.'

'Well, possibly not amongst the professional photocopier repairman fraternity. And yes, you certainly sparked some excitement upstairs.'

Arthur couldn't quite take this in. 'You mean, they're not going to fire me?'

Lynne permitted herself a quiet smile. 'Who'd dare escort you out of the door?'

He blinked. 'Doctor . . .'

'Lynne is fine.'

'Lynne . . .' He turned and looked straight at her. 'Lynne, I can't lift a sack of potatoes. How on earth did I do that?'

She looked right back at him. Her gaze was penetrating, and he noticed again that her eyes had a curious, almost yellow cast to the iris.

'Well, maybe if you keep coming to see me we'll find out.'

* * *

Arthur crept slowly out of the building – he'd been given the rest of the day off. From the corner of his eye, he saw something burning. A horrid acrid smell was being given off and as he went closer he saw that someone had set fire to the photocopier, which had landed in a mangled heap on a patch of landscaped grass. A small crowd of people were standing round it, watching it burn from either end, the paper igniting and the plastic melting.

Fumes, he thought, slinking his way to the car. But one of his colleagues saw him and peeled off from the group.

'Hey! Hey everyone, it's Arthur!' The crowd of people gathered round, then all began to clap and cheer. Arthur took a step backwards, touching his bump again. Marcus, the accounts manager, came running up to him.

'Hey, well done, mate!'

'Yeah!' shouted one of the secretarial staff. 'Won't be getting any more paper jams from this bloody thing, will we?' She kicked the smouldering mass with her shoe.

'Yeah! Collate THIS!' yelled someone else, kicking it again.

'That was great, what you did,' said Marcus, clapping Arthur on the shoulder. 'Much respect.'

'Yes, well, um, good,' said Arthur. 'Well, I'm off.' And he wandered slowly towards his car. As he reached it, he turned and looked up at the offices. He could see Ross, eyeing him up from behind the glass. When Ross noticed him, he very slowly drew a line across his throat.

Cock, Arthur thought to himself. That tosser's going to sack me after all.

* * *

The house was quiet when he got in. Unused to being around during the day, he padded up and down, looking for something to do. The semi looked gloomy and dark – immaculate but somehow unpleasant. Arthur didn't like the relentless tidiness; it implied a panic that anyone should ever smell anything or see anything not entirely bland and lemon-scented. He picked up the TV remote control, then threw it back on the sofa in fear. His life may be going to the absolute shits, but nothing would make him watch daytime television.

He knew he should phone Fay, but he was putting it off for as long as possible.

Putting what off? he suddenly thought. How much with Fay was he really putting off?

He went over to the mantelpiece and pushed aside a prominently displayed christening invitation. Fay had left next to it a Baby Gap catalogue, with a note for him to look through and choose the 'cutest' pair of dungarees for some sprog or other.

I'm not ready for a baby he thought, for the millionth time since he'd been . . . well, a baby.

I'm not ready for a baby with *Fay* he thought, more honestly. Oh well, if I'm about to lose my job for being a nutcase, it's hardly going to be an issue. I'll have to tell her tonight.

* * *

'Do you want to watch *West Wing*?'

'Yeah, all right. Nice dinner, by the way.'

'Thanks. It's called pasta – apparently the Italians invented it. Not bad, eh? Shall we have it again sometime?'

'Give us the remote.'

'Are you all right?'

'Fine. Why – are you?'

'No, no, I'm fine.'

'Okay.'

* * *

Well, she'll find out soon enough, thought Arthur, crawling through the next morning's traffic. When I get given my cards . . . do they still give cards? Well, P45. Whatever. I hope I get redundancy. Ooh. What if I get redundancy? Maybe I should go round the world. On my OWN. Maybe I should go to Brazil and get plastic surgery and a fake passport and become a diamond smuggler.

He parked, for possibly the last time, and looked up at the grey building. Its boundless conformity scared him; always had. Whoever designed this building – what were they, a robot? Did they really despise people so much? To go through thousands of years of civilization and end up with a big grey portaloo with windows that didn't open and flat roofs without gardens?

The office actually went quiet when he walked in. People would kind of half look at him, then pretend to be incredibly busy with something else as he approached. Ooh, the walk of shame. Any doubts he might have had about whether or not throwing a photocopier out of a window was quite as cool a feat as Lynne had implied were immediately confirmed. He could feel the tension in the air. He was going down.

And sure enough, when he got to his desk, there was that consultant bitch Gwyneth standing imperiously over it, her back to him. He felt his face colour. She'd bloody better not have been going through his stuff. He wished he'd had time to scribble 'Gwyneth is a big nosy cow' all over his papers, which had always done the trick at school.

She straightened up slowly, her back still to him. 'Wonder what crappy power management weekend she learned that on?' he muttered to himself.

'Arthur,' she said, turning round and extending a long hand. He didn't take it.

'Yeah?'

'Would you mind stepping into my office?'

'Is that really necessary?' He'd decided to say this on the way in, as he reckoned it would sound rather cool and suave.

'Yes, I think it is.'

'Um, yeah, all right.'

Dammit, he thought. And, I wouldn't be that rude to people, even if I did have fabulous legs . . . Arthur shook his head. Infidelity, unprofessionalism and favouring someone he despised all in one scoop. Dammit.

Gwyneth closed the office door.

'Well, we've studied your tests, and everything that happened yesterday,' she began.

Arthur attempted to jut out his jaw. 'And?'

She sat down on the edge of the desk. 'We're making you – the new head of department.'

* * *

'How soon can I leave?'

Gwyneth looked at him curiously.

'Oh,' said Arthur. He looked embarrassed. He had been expecting the phrase so much, he actually thought she'd said, 'We're making you redundant.'

Then he fell silent. 'No diamonds, then,' he muttered to himself.

'I *beg* your pardon?'

'But what about . . .' he started up again. 'You know, the whole . . .'

'The photocopier?'

He nodded, glumly.

'Don't worry about it. We'd like you to keep seeing that therapist, if that's okay, but apart from that, we think you're the man to take on our new project.'

'What project?'

Gwyneth stood up with a theatrical flourish and unleashed a flattering picture of Coventry (taken from quite far away). Overarching it was the European flag. One particularly big star hovered over the top of the town hall.

'What I'm about to tell you is extremely important,' she said. 'It's entirely confidential for now, and is going to change your life.'

Arthur raised an eyebrow at her. 'Don't tell me, they want me to retime the traffic lights in the pedestrian precinct.'

She ignored him. 'Right,' she started again, indicating the picture. 'We, with the help of you,' she said proudly, 'are going to make Coventry . . . "European City of Culture 2005"!'

Arthur stared at the picture for a long time. Then he looked at Gwyneth to see if this was some terribly unfunny office prank, which would eventually lead to him losing his job after all. She wasn't smiling – smiling did not seem to be a Gwyneth attribute so far – but was looking at him expectantly. He winced. The silence lengthened until he realized he had to say *something*.

'Um . . .' He coughed. 'Why would they choose us and not, say, Birmingham?'

'Exactly!' said Gwyneth dramatically. 'We have an epic fight ahead and many strong competitors!'

Arthur shook his head. 'Gwyneth, I don't know what this has to do with me but, you have to admit, we are generally considered to be the ugliest town in the entire world. Well, we're running a very close thing with the dung heap shanty towns of Rio de Janeiro.'

'That's why it's such a great challenge! We need someone strong and motivated and unafraid to make this happen – we need you, Arthur.'

Arthur was stunned. 'But . . . This'll never work. I don't even think there are that many hanging baskets in existence.'

''Course it will. Glasgow was a slum.'

'A slum with a working infrastructure and thousands of beautiful Victorian sandstone buildings.'

'Grab this!' said Gwyneth, dramatically leaning in close and looking straight into his eyes. 'This is your great opportunity, Arthur. Seize it with both hands!'

'Oof, hang on.' Arthur leaned backwards to reclaim some personal space.

'Oh, sorry.' Gwyneth immediately retreated and dusted herself down. 'I knew that weekend assertiveness course was a bad idea.'

They looked at each other.

'It's completely impossible,' said Arthur.

'You get your own office,' she replied. 'And a budget. Your own team. And access to corporate catering.'

'Access to *what*?'

'You know, those mini prawn thingies. And sausages and stuff like that.'

'When would I get those?'

'Whenever you like. Every day.'

* * *

Arthur stared into space and said a brief farewell to the diamond mines of southern Brazil.

'Well, I guess I'm your man.'

'I know.'

She stood up and held out her hand. He shook it. It was soft and warm and . . . oh crap. He fancied her.

'We'll be working together quite a bit,' she said.

I was afraid of that, thought Arthur.

'Great!' said Arthur.

'Oh, and by the way,' she called out to him when he was nearly free, 'I'm afraid you have to tell Ross.'

'Tell Ross . . . ?'

'That you've taken over his job.'

Arthur marched back into the middle of the room.

'I've *what*?'

'Well, how did you think it was going to work? It was you or him. It's you. Now, tell him.'

'I have to *fire* him?'

'No, you have to give him some sweets. Yes, you have to fire him. You're in charge.'

Arthur backed out, feeling white in the face, with deep and profound misgivings as to what he'd just agreed to do.

'Right . . . Yeah . . . I'm in charge.'

* * *

Being in charge, Arthur decided the best thing to do straight away would be to take a quick slip through the side door, drive into town and go for a little walk. This was going to take a while to sink in, and he fancied a quick look at the size of the problem he was going to be dealing with. Plus, wandering through towns and cities, reading their infrastructure and examining how they were put together had had a calming influence on him for years.

It was a chilly grey morning, and now most people were locked into their offices for the day it was incredibly quiet around the shopping precinct. He walked across the pedestrianized street. This had been meant to improve the city. Instead, it had provided a good ground for people to fight each other, and hanging-out areas for the local youths. Dilapidated brick stands of pot plants filled with phlegm and cigarette butts stood forlornly at intervals, and the garish shopfronts told their own story: 'Everything for ninety-nine pence', 'Pricesavers', 'Remnant Kings'. Plastic products nobody wanted spilled out of their fronts. Two hulking teenagers in sports gear were kicking around a tin can, watched appreciatively by four or five others. One just sat on the ground, eyes glazed with cheap cider, or worse. Underneath the centre were miles of deserted, dank underpasses that most people were too scared to use.

Arthur circumvented the youths carefully and wandered into the run-down shopping centre to ponder what to do. It felt . . . This was what he was supposed to want, wasn't it? To run things his way. More money. Power. Responsibility. Surely he should be more excited than this?

Truthfully, all his life Arthur had waited for

things to come to him. It saved too much boat-rocking. God, Fay had practically had to jump him the first few times they'd met. And this . . . what were they expecting? After all, he hadn't meant the thing with the photocopier. What if they expected him to be that macho all the time? And how the hell was he going to fire Ross? He scratched the back of his neck. Christ! Maybe he should just stick to this leaving idea. He'd almost got his head around it, after all. In fact, the very thought of having to run this project was bringing him out in a cold sweat. It would be bad for him. Bad for his health. Bad for everyone. It would end in ruins and they'd shunt him to the back office and . . .

Deep in thought and staring at the ground, he didn't even notice Lynne until he walked right into her as she came out of a shop.

'Argh!'

Lynne dropped several packages on the ground whilst Arthur started a long litany of apologies.

'God, I'm so sorry . . . Let me help you with . . . Wasn't looking . . .'

Scrabbling around on the pavement, he couldn't help noticing that some of the packages were quite peculiarly shaped. Looking up, he realized Lynne had been coming out of the pet shop. A fat man, obviously the shopkeeper, came out behind her.

'Look,' he said, 'I'm sorry. We just can't get

crocodiles, okay? They're illegal.'

'*Illegal*? How on earth does anyone make soup?'

Lynne raised an eyebrow at Arthur as the man retreated inside. 'Hello, Arthur. Well met.'

Arthur swallowed. 'Em, hello there.'

'Are you going this way? Let's walk a while.' It sounded more like a command than a query.

'Why . . .' Arthur stumbled for something to say. He didn't really know any therapists and was slightly worried about being misinterpreted in some way that would mean he was a terrible person. 'Why do you want a crocodile?'

'Who wouldn't want a crocodile?'

Arthur shrugged. 'Yeah, I guess.'

'What's the matter?'

Arthur looked at her kind face. Today, her hair, decorated with pendants that looked like leaves, was loosely pinned back in a bun with tendrils escaping.

'Well . . .' He explained about his conversation with Gwyneth. She was meant to be his counsellor, after all.

'Hum.' Lynne stared straight ahead. 'That was quick.'

'What? You knew they were going to do this?'

'No, of course not. Not as such,' said Lynne, twisting up her face. 'Office grapevine, you know.'

Arthur nodded.

47

'So. How are you going to begin?'

Arthur shrugged. 'I was actually just considering . . . that I might not.'

'Might not? Don't be ridiculous.'

'What's ridiculous? Do I have the look of the man who's going to spend the rest of his life stuck in an office?'

'Around the mouth . . . and the nose, yes.'

Arthur grimaced and walked on. Lynne caught up with him.

'I think it is time, don't you?'

'What?' He turned round. 'It's not my time.'

'It is,' said Lynne urgently. She looked at him, and he felt something odd pass between them. He shook his head.

'Sorry – I don't quite know what I meant by that. I mean – well, what do you mean? Time for what?'

'Time for you to take all this energy and . . .' Lynne cast her hand around the desolate parking garage where they found themselves. It was puddled with oil and cigarette ends. 'Ssh,' she said.

Arthur followed her gaze. In the far corner, three white faces were huddled round a brazier, staring at them like ghosts out of the darkness. Not an unfamiliar sight in the back roads of the town. Arthur and Lynne quickly hurried on through the car park.

'Who's going to change all this if you don't?'

'What, now you want me to tackle the *drugs* problem?'

'Environment matters, you know that. Pride, Arthur. It's time to pick up your sword and go for it.'

'Pick up my what?'

'It's just an expression.'

'Oh. Only I seem to have been hearing about swords rather a lot recently.'

'Yes, well unfortunately I'm not a Freudian type of analyst, so I can't help you with that one.'

'What sort of analyst are you?'

'Oh, I don't know. Let's just see how it goes along, eh?'

'You are a real therapist, aren't you?'

'Yes,' she patted him on the arm. 'Yes, I am. Now, what have they asked you to do? Fire someone?'

Arthur gave her a sharp look. 'Do you do everyone's therapy or just mine?'

'I can't tell you that, I'm afraid.'

'Well, then. Obviously you already know. Yes, they have.'

'Then do it quickly. Show who's in charge. Don't mess around. If you're going to run this thing, Arthur, you're going to need respect.'

'I know. But even though I hate the guy, I don't want to ruin his . . .'

'Week, perhaps? Month, maybe? His type always bounces back. Look over there.'

Arthur followed where her finger was pointing. Two nine-year-old boys were bent over a rain puddle in the cracked concrete. They should have been at school. Instead they were mindlessly, repetitively, picking up pieces of rubbish, setting them on fire with a lighter and dropping them in the water.

'You don't have long,' said Lynne. Arthur watched the two boys for a moment more.

'But I . . .' He turned round. In the darkness of the car park, Lynne had gone.

* * *

Ross was sitting alone in the canteen, a place made up of hideous plastic furniture that somebody believed would be made to look like the Dorchester by the addition of some wickerwork and some pathetically touching pot plants. He was rocking on the edge of his chair and prodding a pencil at a glutinous piece of Danish pastry. Arthur stood in the doorway and looked at him. Suddenly, he didn't look much of a tosspot any more. He looked like an ordinary young man, already running to fat, anxious and insecure.

'Ross,' said Arthur softly. He'd felt nervous about doing this, but seeing him, he couldn't be.

Ross blinked and let his chair fall back to the table with a start. He couldn't quite look at Arthur but stared straight ahead.

'Hey Art!' he said, forcing the jocularity into his voice.

'Do you want a coffee or something?' As soon as he'd said that, Arthur realized it was cruel. Why prolong the uncertainty while he buggered about getting a cup of coffee? He might as well have said, 'Would you like an extra four and a half minutes of excruciating torture?'

'No, thanks,' said Ross.

'Ross . . .'

'Yeah? What? Good news, is it?' He coughed a cynical laugh.

'No,' said Arthur. He wondered if Ross would punch him, but he still felt all right; quite under control.

'Ross, they're doing something different. I'm afraid you're going to have to leave.'

Ross stood up, as if he couldn't bear to be any closer in airspace to Arthur. 'God, God, I bloody *knew* it.'

'I understand you'll be feeling upset . . .'

'Might have known they'd get some namby

51

pamby PC non-car bloody saddo who just happens to be good at fucking poofter tests . . .'

'Okay . . . maybe not quite that upset.'

'I told 'em. Sort out the roads. Build more. Don't hire some soft wanker who can't even get laid.'

'Yes, well, we seem to be moving from upset to offensive . . .'

'And now they've got you running the whole bloody town! Well, God help them, that's all I can say.'

Ross stood up and kicked his plastic chair crossly, his heavily gelled ginger hair sticking straight up from his forehead. He advanced on Arthur.

'I don't give a fuck, you know. You're not the first guy in here. Some bloke walked in and offered me a job in Slough. You just bloody watch me. I'll sort out that place and we'll be using your fucking pedestrianized precincts as car parks.'

Arthur got riled. 'That will be great. Why have just one town hating you when there are so many more opportunities out there?'

Ross leaned into him menacingly. The room was eerily silent, it still being out of lunch-hour time. Arthur suddenly found himself thinking back to his first and only fight ever. He was ten years old and, after kicking the shit out of everyone in the class in ascending order of size, McGuire had finally got round to him. The time had been pre-ordained. The class had encircled them. Arthur had taken a deep breath, trying to remember what his stepfather had told him – 'Don't worry, son, you only have to square up to the bullies once, then they'll leave you alone. Run at him as fast as you can and try and hit him on the nose.' Of course McGuire had held out one arm, held him by the forehead and pounded him into the ground – on that day and so many days after that, it long ceased to be a spectator sport. Arthur's nerves were not, at the moment, at their boldest.

Without warning, Ross's left arm shot out and smashed him on the ear. It felt like being stung by an extremely large bee. Arthur was dimly aware of a buzzing noise, then realized there wasn't a bee, it was the rest of the office, attracted to the open door of the restaurant. Before he could stop to think, the adrenalin kicked in, and he threw up his arms like he was playing volleyball. He caught Ross a glancing blow on the underside of the nose. Ross grunted and staggered backwards a few feet. Whilst Arthur was taking this in, Ross threw out a foot and cracked it into his gut. Arthur squealed – it was as undignified as that – but, finding it in him to ignore the pain, came charging forward, yelling and letting fly with an erratic punch which landed straight in Ross's eye socket.

Ross was roaring now, like a giant bear, lunging around with his hand to his eye. Furiously, he dragged up one of the plastic chairs which, Arthur dully noted somewhere in the bottom of his mind, were normally bolted to the floor, and brandished it in the air across the canteen.

And Arthur, noted coward, who had never done anything even vaguely out of step in his life before yesterday, who had balked at everything that came his way, who was ready to get soft and old in his middle age, said something he'd never said before in his life, not even in fun. Instead of clenching his body and waiting for the blow or trying to make himself as small as possible, he pushed out his shoulders and opened his body wide, like a gorilla, or Russell Crowe. He stood, legs apart, eyeing up the other man with as much ferocity as he could muster.

'BRING IT ON!!!' he roared.

The sound bellowed and bounced off the walls. Then – silence.

Ross and Arthur stared at each other. The crowd of people by the door were completely silent. Nobody dared breathe. Then, with a crash, Ross hurled the chair across the room, but away from Arthur. It split through a picture frame hung from the raffia.

'Fuck you! This will come around,' said Ross, his

54

face purple and red to bursting. He pointed his finger at Arthur. 'THIS WILL COME AROUND!!'

And he stormed out of the room, leaving Arthur and the rest of the office staring in his wake.

* * *

'How was your day?' Fay asked carefully.

'Oh, oh, it was fine, you know. Usual.'

This was becoming a nightmare. He used to share everything with her. Now he could barely talk to her beyond politeness, before she'd sigh and start mentioning somebody or other's toddler who had done something which was supposedly cute but in fact just sounded incredibly annoying.

Fay was well aware of this. She flicked quickly through *Heat* magazine, elaborately casual.

'So the black eye . . .'

Arthur winced. Okay, that was stupid. Perhaps he should have double-checked for the visual evidence.

Fay let out a long sigh. She remembered what the book had said – never nag, never burrow into his affairs. She tried to do her best. But he was late, tired, distracted, he'd hardly said a word to her for what felt like months – ooh, and, by the way, there was blood on his collar and he had a black eye. Her man – the sweet, gentle man she'd fallen in love with five years ago at a training conference in

Peterborough – couldn't even tell her why he was dripping blood. She set aside her magazine.

'Arthur, we have to talk.'

He grunted into his newspaper. Yes, he knew they did. He looked up at her. His eyes were hollow.

'What's going on?' she asked.

'Well . . .' Arthur did a quick summary in his head.

Hmm not that bit . . . No, maybe not that . . .

'I got promoted.'

Fay's face lit up. 'Really?'

He nodded. 'Yes, really.'

'But this is brilliant!' Her eyes shone. 'I mean . . . we'll have enough money to – hang on.'

She ran to the fridge and came back with a bottle of champagne they'd been keeping for good news.

'This is so fantastic!' She kissed him on the top of his head. 'You're so clever, darling! And think what we can do now . . .' She straightened up for a second and smiled at him. 'And the black eye is, what – the official entry token to the executive washroom?'

'I had to fire Ross,' said Arthur matter-of-factly, uncorking the bottle.

'Oh! God, well, that's even *more* brilliant. Isn't he the one you thought was a bit of a tosspot?'

Arthur nodded. 'With a good tossy right hook.'

'Ooh!' She sat by his knees, hugging her own, and lifted up her glass to be filled. This was it. This was the moment. No wonder he'd been so quiet, if he'd been working up to such a wonderful surprise!

'So, there'll be a bit more money coming in, won't there?'

'Um, we didn't discuss it . . . Probably.'

Oh God, thought Arthur. He suddenly had an inkling as to where this was heading. Thank God his eye was already black. Although of course she could still scratch it out.

'So, you know, maybe we could . . .' She twirled her manicured finger around the top of her glass. Looking at it, Arthur realized for the first time that he didn't really like manicures. He didn't say anything. He didn't want to sound like he was encouraging her. The pause grew longer. She looked up at him, firstly with hope, then, as the silence continued, almost as he watched, the light in her eyes slowly dimmed.

She stared at the seagrass carpet for an even longer time. It was killing Arthur to keep quiet, but he didn't know what else to do. He felt a lump in his throat. The wait grew interminable. Finally, and very slowly, she raised her head back up to look at him. Her eyes were full of tears, quivering, hovering and waiting to fall.

'Are we . . .' She was attempting to sound dignified, but there was an immediate wobble to her voice. 'Are we – are *you* . . .' She shook her head to get a grip, and managed to steady herself. 'Do you really want to be with me, Arthur? Properly? To settle down and have a – a family and everything?' Immediately her eyes flicked away. A ten-ton weight settled on Arthur's ribcage. He had to say something soon. He had to.

He couldn't think of anything. He was failing.

'Aren't you even going to *talk* to me?' The tears were falling now.

'Aren't you going to even deign to . . . Am I really worth that little to you?'

Fay's voice was angry now, and hard.

'Look at me, Arthur.'

Slowly, Arthur lifted his head. Her face was white, and her hands were gripping the wine glass so hard it was frightening. Neither of them spoke. Arthur loathed himself, and his cowardice.

'Are you – are you talking about having a baby?' Arthur managed to force out, quietly.

'No!' said Fay, indignant. 'Can't I ask a perfectly reasonable question about where our relationship's headed without it turning into a big fuss about . . . *babies*.'

'Oh. Only, I thought you were talking about babies.'

'Yes, of *course* I'm talking about babies.'

She attempted to laugh and half choked, loudly in the quiet room. Arthur reached out his hand to her but she shook it off.

'Fay, – I'm not sure I'm ready.'

Her face creased with disappointment, then she took a breath. 'How . . . How . . . When would you be ready? We have three bedrooms and two cars, for fuck's sake!'

'I know.'

'We chose this place together!'

'You chose it, Fay,' he said, as gently as he could, realizing of course that this wasn't fair.

'I chose it because . . . because we're going out and you're thirty bloody two years old! And so am I, nearly! We're not fifteen! You don't fuck about with someone just to go out with them!'

'I – I'm not fucking about with you.'

'I'm thirty-one years old. If you don't want to get married and have a family with me, you're fucking about.'

Arthur felt disgruntled. 'Who invented that rule? I thought we were having a perfectly nice time.'

'Did you?'

He ignored the obvious truth in her statement.

'I don't see why, just because we're seeing each other . . . I mean, I don't owe you anything.'

59

As soon as he said this he realized how awful it was. She blinked twice rapidly and edged away from him. 'You . . . you . . .'

'Listen, Fay, I didn't mean that. You know I didn't. It's just . . . I've had a really tough day and you've just started in on this and . . .'

But she had already stood up and was backing away across the room.

'Look, Fay.'

But she didn't even look like Fay any more. She looked like some strange person he'd never met before in his life. Her eyes frightened him.

'You don't owe me anything,' she echoed.

'Oh, come on, let's talk about it.'

'No, no need for that. You don't owe me a thing.'

'*Fa-ay*.'

Now she looked around, bewildered. She stopped herself. 'Well,' she said.

'What?'

'Well, I guess I'll be back to pick up my stuff . . . whenever . . .' She cast an eye round the tasteful living room that they'd gone down to London to furnish – the brown leather sofa, the Habitat rug, the widescreen TV. Suddenly she had pulled herself together, and was eerily calm.

'You owe me that sofa,' she said. Arthur was standing now, casting his arms around, trying to say something, anything, but realizing as he did so that somewhere, underneath all of this, there was a definite feeling of relief – and that this was the biggest betrayal of all.

'You . . . you betrayed me,' she said, unnervingly voicing exactly what was going through his head. 'Maybe not with another woman – but then, of course, I don't know you at all, do I?'

'There aren't any other women,' said Arthur dully, although he couldn't help wondering – it was a flash, nothing more – about Gwyneth's set up.

'But you betrayed me, nonetheless. You saw me every day and you knew absolutely what I was in for, and absolutely what I was after and you spat on it and pissed it out the window the whole damn time. Did you laugh as the years went by, Arthur? Did you laugh every day because I still hadn't cottoned on that nothing – *nothing* I did was any use? That there was nothing I could do? You stole that time from me, Arthur Pendleton. You stole it, and you know you did.'

'I . . .' Arthur exclaimed helplessly.

'You absolute *wretch*. Well, fuck you! That's my curse on you. Fuck you and everything that will ever happen to you.'

'I wish people would stop saying that today.'

'Fuck you,' she said again, and it echoed around

61

the room as she slammed the door. Arthur stood there for a second, until she marched back in, scooped up the television remote control, her bag, her dressing gown, then stood in front of him where he was frozen to the carpet and calmly blacked his other eye.

Chapter Three

'I think I'd maybe . . . I'd quite like to come in and see you.'

Lynne regarded the strange purple-eyed apparition peering round her doorway coolly. Arthur had driven in at five miles an hour.

'*Can* you see?'

'Ha ha. Is this a good time?'

'Time . . .' mused Lynne. 'What a funny question. All times are exactly the same.'

She stared out of the window. Today she was wearing six layers of different colours of brown. They floated all over her chair. One layer looked like it might be made out of a piece of sacking.

'Er, yes they are,' averred Arthur. 'Except you know, they're not. When you're doing something or, you know, waiting for black eyes to heal.'

'Is that what those are? I thought you were turning into a panda. I saw that happen once . . .'

Arthur threw up his hands in defeat. 'Fine, I'll come back later.'

'No, no, come in.'

Arthur mooched in and slouched onto the sofa. There was an expectant silence.

'Well?' said Lynne.

'I don't know . . . Can you give me some therapy or something?'

'What, just like that?'

Arthur shrugged. 'I don't know.'

'Jolly good,' said Lynne. 'Right. You get confused between umbrellas and your penis.'

'I do not!'

They both looked out of Lynne's windows, where it was raining.

'Just as well,' said Arthur.

'Quite,' said Lynne. 'Well, you get that kind of thing with off the peg therapy.'

Arthur sighed. Lynne peered over her spectacles.

'Do you want to talk about it or do you want me to psychically guess that Ross took a swing at you and you've split up with your girlfriend?'

'That's creepy,' said Arthur. 'Well, what do you recommend, seeing as I'm supposed to be starting the most difficult job of my career this morning and I look like George Dubya eating a pretzel.'

'Talk to your girlfriend,' said Lynne. 'That's probably better than talking to me.'

'What! That's the most useless advice I've ever heard! You're the worst therapist ever!'

'What do you want me to say? Well done for betraying your girlfriend?'

'I didn't *betray* her. She bloody said that too. It's not like I did anything.'

But his face gave him away.

'Well, exactly. You should have done something. You should have split up with her years ago.'

'Okay, well, thank you Germaine Greer but I happen to completely disagree. All she ever had to do was ask, then she did ask and I told her.'

Lynne shook her head. 'You're going to regret that.'

'What? I thought I could say anything in here!'

'Not what you said. What you did.'

'Yes, I'm sure I will regret it, if I lose the sight in one eye.'

They were quiet. Arthur was seething. This was a hard time for him, goddammit. Didn't he deserve a bit of sympathy?

'You'll be late,' said Lynne.

* * *

The huge cubicle room was not just quiet, it was completely, utterly silent. It was hard to believe there was anyone in there at all. From the second Arthur stepped through the door, heads disappeared into files, up close against computer screens, probably even in some cases straight under the desks, using the 'if he can't see me he can't fire me' technique. Arthur went forward gingerly.

'Hello!' he said as usual to the grumpy temp at the front of the office. But instead of grinning and giving him some cheeky answer, she looked up, startled.

'Er, hello Mr Pendleton.'

He squinted at her. 'Um . . .' Of course he still couldn't remember her name. 'You don't have to call me Mr Pendleton.'

She looked at him. 'What, do you want me to go back to calling you "Not Too Much of a Wanker"?'

From somewhere he could be sure he heard a very quiet giggle.

'No, I stay away from my Native American name when I'm working,' he said, heading past her.

'Sorry,' she said. 'I just didn't recognize you with your sunglasses on.'

'I'm not wearing . . . oh, forget it.'

He was conscious of her eyes on him as he started to make his way through the maze. And everyone else's, for that matter. As he was nearly at his desk, he realized with a cold shock of horror that of course this wouldn't be his desk any more – he'd be expected to go to Ross's old office. But he was already too far along in the opposite direction. Oh crap. He felt his face go puce and the back of his collar felt damp. He decided to try and pretend that he was just on his way to pick up a few things and actually said, 'Huh, just going to pick up a few things,' tentatively out loud as he was going along, feeling more and more that he should just carry a sign saying 'Dickhead! Hate me forever!'

Of course, as usual, the smell hit him first. No. Of all the cruel tricks to play on him. Sandwiches was sitting lugubriously in *his* chair – or rather, what had been his chair – stinking the place out and looking up at him with a mildly quizzical air. He was wearing one of Arthur's ties. Sven was nowhere to be seen.

'Sven!' Arthur yelled, breaking the silence in the room.

The fat blond head raised itself incrementally over the partition, like a *Wot*! cartoon. 'Oh . . . Hi, Arthur!' he said, with elaborate unconcern.

'Sven, you know how we had that talk the other day about who was the boss?'

Sven nodded.

'And I couldn't ask you to remove your dog?'

'Uh huh.'

'Remove the fucking dog.'

Cathy put her head round the cubicle. 'Arthur . . . Mr Pendleton . . . Hello!'

'Hi, Cathy. You don't need to call me Mr anything.'

Cathy came round the side of the partition. 'Um . . . Arthur . . .'

'Yes?'

'Um, it was just . . . Well, I spoke to the girls in the typing pool and . . . well, we just wondered if there was any way we could keep Sandwiches. You know, for therapeutic value.'

'What? What's therapeutic about a methane machine who eats staplers?'

Sandwiches obligingly spat out the stapler he'd been attempting to maul. A long trail of drool still connected him to it, and he regarded it closely.

'We thought,' Cathy shrugged, 'seeing as you'll have a new office, you won't be near enough to smell him.'

Arthur shook his head. 'You're telling me you actually *want* that thing in here?'

Sven regarded the scene carefully.

Cathy snapped her fingers. Sandwiches took a careful glance at Arthur to make sure he was watching, then shuffled on his stubby legs off the chair and rounded the partition – his bottom disappearing last, like the slinky dog in *Toy Story*. Arthur stood back so he could see. Sandwiches was fawning up against Cathy's legs, rubbing his head and giving his best pathetic dog eyes. Cathy leaned down and scratched his head.

'It's more affection than I get from my husband,' she said, trying to laugh, although the statement was so obviously true it was painful. She knelt down and gave the dog a scratch.

'Happy workers, innit?' said Sven. 'Lowers aggression in the office and all that.'

Well, he'd rather got him there. More aggression in the office was something he could definitely do without for the moment.

Arthur sighed and looked at Sven. 'Will you change what he eats? So he doesn't fart so much?'

'Charcoal biscuits only,' said Sven solemnly. Sandwiches coughed and deposited four loose staples on the carpet. Cathy rubbed him as if he'd done something clever and unwrapped him a Fox's glacier mint.

'Oh God,' said Arthur. 'My first executive decision and I've let the place be overrun by wild animals.' He headed off towards Ross's old domain.

'Marcus, I believe you're goin' to have to set up

a new expense account,' he could hear Sven say, grandly.

* * *

Ross's office still smelled of him – Lynx deodorant, sweaty hair and air freshener. Even the boss's windows didn't open. Arthur paced around the room, picking things up and putting them down again. There was a long, standard issue pine desk facing the door right in the middle of the room – Ross liked to play the part of Blofeld, and sit with his back to the hapless visitor in his office (it didn't matter what they'd done: the fact that they were in a room with Ross at all already made them pretty hapless). He hadn't even left time to pick up his personal possessions. Arthur looked at them now, vowing to pack them up and send them on to Slough. On the desk there was the framed picture of Ross, trying to smile, with the very attractive woman he called his girlfriend scowling. Arthur wondered idly if this was his girlfriend or some woman he'd sidled up to at a motor trade fair. There was also a model of his car (a ridiculously over-customized silver-blue Audi that positively screamed 'dickwad'.) Well, maybe he wouldn't return *all* the stuff. On a whim he threw the model in the air and kicked it as it came back down to earth. The plastic shattered with a satisfying noise.

He caught the main part of the chassis with his foot and kicked it into the air again. It flew across the desk and knocked the framed photograph onto the floor. Goal!

'Oh, *whoops*!' he said out loud.

'You know, your destructive skills weren't the only reason we hired you,' said the cool voice.

Gwyneth, wearing a peppermint-green suit, was cool and unruffled-looking. She had been standing in the corner behind the door and was now pretending to examine the files against the far wall.

'Oh!' said Arthur in a high-pitched voice, which annoyed him. He cast around for some excuse for wilful destruction of somebody else's property, but couldn't come up with one. He tried to change the subject. 'Nice . . . breakfast?' he asked, then winced at the pathetic question.

Gwyneth looked to the side. 'I don't eat breakfast,' she said.

'No, of course not, otherwise how would you keep your slim . . .' Oh God, he said to himself, shape up, you're starting to sound like Vic Reeves.

'Well.' She turned and stepped forward to confront him. 'Your first day. Welcome.'

'Thanks,' said Arthur, mumbling and looking at the floor.

'What did *you* have for breakfast? Or rather . . .' She looked at his bruised face. 'What had you?'

'Ah, yes,' said Arthur, pawing his face. 'Um . . .' Well, he wasn't going to get into this. 'Did it myself . . . You know, to even things up. Don't you think it looks better?'

Rather than answering him, Gwyneth snapped her fingers and a scared-looking secretary marched in, carrying three tons of files. The secretary dropped them onto the table with an exhausted sigh.

'Thanks, Miriam. You can go home now.'

'That doesn't seem bad for a day's work,' mused Arthur. It was still nine thirty.

'Night shift,' snapped Gwyneth. 'Efficiency drive.'

'Of course,' said Arthur, sitting down gingerly.

'Okay. Here we have financial projections, budgetary restraints, minutes from the working party, the futures committee, the town council, the planning board, the county council, the department of the environment – oh, here's the white paper. Over here are the application guidelines, the tendering process, the likelihood graphs. Plus studies from Glasgow, Manchester, Amsterdam, Prague and Budapest. I wouldn't bother with that last one, depending on how good your Hungarian is . . .'

'Bit rusty, actually.'

'Fine.'

She eyed him over the wall of paper that now divided them.

'Why don't you get started?'

'Sure,' said Arthur, as if having to read fourteen thousand pages of the most mind-numbing
information ever committed to paper was exactly
the kind of thing he'd been dreaming about all
these years.

'Ehem, what will you be doing exactly?'

Gwyneth stared at him. 'Right,' she said. 'I
think it's best if you call a team meeting. Then
we can outline all our roles. I'm going to be
working on the bid with you. Get your best
people.'

Arthur stared at the pile of papers. He picked
some up. He smelled them. He did not have a
clue what to do with them. But, casting around,
he noticed one thing – he had an intercom!

He reached over and pressed a button. As soon
as he started speaking, his voice boomed right
back at him – he could hear it out on the main
floor. Oh, this was cool. Resisting the immediate
temptation to sing 'Angels', he coughed – nearly
bursting the eardrums of anyone on the floor – and
leaned forward to the speaker. Who were his best
people? He chose to make a management decision
and simply ask anyone he knew.

'Er . . . Hello, everyone. This is Arthur . . .
Um, could I see . . . Sven, Cathy . . . er . . .
Gwyneth . . .'

'I'm only in here,' said Gwyneth, crossly opening the connecting door.

'Marcus . . . Marcus . . . Um, if I think of anyone else I'll say in a minute.' There was a long pause. 'Um, sorry. Can you come and see me in the conference room, please?'

With trepidation, they filed in.

'Sit down, everyone.'

The group bustled around, looking at the table.

'Anywhere special you want us to sit?' asked Gwyneth.

Arthur looked up, startled. 'No, of course not. Sit wherever you like.'

They seated themselves around Marcus, the finance director, whom they found safe, being the only person in the office who knew how to add up. He lived in a world of fake friendship and promises, as girls gave him lascivious winks if he promised to help them out with their expenses, and many pints were bought for him round about the March mark. Sandwiches sat at the end of the table.

Looking round the room for the first time, Arthur realized, suddenly, that he didn't care in the slightest. Whatever he did, this was it now. He was in charge. He was the boss. They were going to like him or – well, who liked their boss? Forget it. They were going to hate him, but they might respect him or they might not. He took a deep breath and began.

'Well,' he said. 'Things have changed a bit round here.'

Yes, that was obvious enough. He decided just to get down to it.

'Okay . . . team. Here's what we're going to be doing.'

He revealed the graphic overhead just as Gwyneth had done, and tried to garner the same level of dramatic enthusiasm.

'Our new project,' he announced, 'is to take Coventry all the way to becoming European City of Culture!'

There was dead silence round the table.

'What's that then?' said Marcus.

'Ehem . . . It's whatever you want it to be,' said Arthur. 'We're going to create the city of our imagination!'

Gwyneth coughed discreetly.

'Within certain highly defined boundaries, of course.'

'It's an urban rejuvenation project,' said Gwyneth. Immediately, the eyelids of the entire room began to droop.

'This . . . I cannot imagine the amount of money it would take to transform Coventry,' said Marcus, wonderingly. 'All of it?'

'It's to bring out the beauty of the city, make it a tourist attraction. Show its true colours.'

'Those being what – grey, grey and dark-grey?' joined in Sven.

'What's the slogan going to be?' added Marcus. '"Coventry's Crappily Better"?'

'Come to Coventry . . . if you're a cu—'

'Is anyone else really missing Ross?' said Cathy.

'Yes, yes, okay, okay, calm down,' said Arthur, the tips of his ears going red. This wasn't starting well.

'Gwyneth and I . . .' This felt very odd to be saying, almost like 'my wife and I'. 'Gwyneth and I think you are the best team to take the project forward. I know it seems a huge, huge mountain to climb, but I really think we are in with a chance.'

The room went silent as they all looked at him.

'Any questions?'

'Yes, one. Very important,' said Marcus. 'Are we going to get access to those executive snacks?'

* * *

'Tea,' said Gwyneth brightly. 'Let's all take a break for tea.' And smiling like a primary school teacher, she hustled everyone out of the room towards a table which had been set up specially – with chocolate biscuits. The group fell on them with gusto. Gwyneth came back into the room, where Arthur was still standing.

'They're . . . they're absolutely *dreadful*,' she said, her face like thunder.

'What?' said Arthur. This woman was completely incomprehensible. 'What is?'

'Your so-called *staff*.' She practically spat. 'Is that bunch of work-shy cynics the best this office can do?'

'That lot?' Arthur looked at them. 'But you've just given them all chocolate biscuits.' He sat down. 'I don't think that will work particularly well as staff aversion training. Here – annoy Gwyneth. Have a biscuit!'

'They're like a bunch of children. And that Sven – he's just a pig!'

'Yeah, he is a pig,' agreed Arthur. 'A strange, ugly pig with superior logistical ability.'

'For a man or a pig? That's an important distinction.'

'Go easy on him, Gwyneth – do you know he's never had sex? 'Fessed up to the temp at the Christmas party, poor bastard. He's a virgin.'

'I'm not surprised.' She shuddered. 'Can you imagine . . .'

'No,' said Arthur quickly, trying very hard not to think about sex and Gwyneth in the same context at all.

'And you're meant to be leading this bunch of reprobates – look at them. They're slagging you off right now.'

'They are not,' said Arthur, looking out of the door nonetheless.

Sven was holding up his chocolate biscuit plate and saying, 'Please sir, I'm little orphan Arthur. Please can I have a European City of Culture?'

The others were laughing.

'I'm never going to get them to do anything, am I?' said Arthur.

'You just have to get tough with them.'

'That will never work.'

Gwyneth turned round and stalked into the open area outside the meeting room. She stood before them with her hands on her hips.

'Right, you've had your chocolate biscuits. Now fuck off, and Arthur wants two-page memos from each of you on your preliminary ideas for the bid, on his desk, Friday morning. Here are copies of the guidelines, budget not an issue, just brainstorm.'

'Yes, ma'am,' said Marcus, and the rest of them shuffled off obediently.

Gwyneth turned round again to Arthur, who tried not to show how impressed he was. God, but this woman was annoying.

* * *

Arthur was stretched over the empty bed, one of the few pieces of furniture Fay had left behind. It still smelled, faintly, of her conditioner. There was a long brown hair lying across the pillow. He picked it up. It felt for a moment like a trap – like she had left it there to see if her bed would be disturbed; to see what would happen.

Later, he was dreaming of horses again. He was pounding over the land. It was winter again, and the frosted wind caught against his throat. This time, he wasn't alone. He looked down and realized his arm was around a girl. She was cowering into him and holding him tight, but oddly, he felt no emotion towards her. Suddenly he realized it was Gwyneth. Her fair hair was blowing over the cowl of her cloak. He groaned once, in his sleep, and turned over.

* * *

'I can't believe they're actually all here,' said Gwyneth that Friday. 'And they're all pretty much legible. Sven's has something on it . . .'

'I think that's dog slobber,' said Arthur.

'Oh, God,' said Gwyneth, dropping it as if it were acid. Arthur watched her, remembering the fragile creature he had held in his dream three nights before, not this smartly dressed efficiency machine standing before him.

'Why do you do this?' he asked suddenly.

'What? Pick up pieces of paper typed by dogs with dirty paws? I have absolutely no idea, I assure you.'

'No, I mean, your job. How did you get into it?'

Gwyneth looked at him. 'Well, at university, I spent my summers working for . . .'

'I don't mean your job interview answer. Just . . . why?'

She shrugged. 'Well, why does anyone become a management consultant?'

Arthur sat back.

Gwyneth was looking at him like the answer was obvious.

'I genuinely don't know.'

'I think it was . . . the travel, the glamour . . . meeting new people . . .' Gwyneth looked around the office.

'Oh, yeah.'

Gwyneth flopped into a chair. 'You know, I used to believe that, and now – look. Trapped in sunny Coventry.'

Suddenly, something in her face shifted. She looked like she was having an internal battle within herself. She glanced around as if she'd forgotten where she was, she looked at Arthur, she looked at the floor. Then, in almost a whisper, she leaned over and said, 'Oh, God, sometimes I *hate* it.' Then, she kind of shook herself. 'Gosh, I'm sorry. I don't know what came over me. I didn't mean that. It's just, you know, sometimes I think maybe I should have become a vet after all.'

'A *vet*. You wanted to be a *vet*?'

'What's so funny about that?'

Arthur looked at her immaculate suit. 'Gwyneth, all you do is complain about dog slobber.'

'That is *not* all I do.'

'Have you any *idea* what the slobber ratio is like in being a vet? And not just dog slobber, either. Ohhh, no. Elephant slobber. Yuk. And have you ever seen a lizard slobber?'

She shrugged. 'No. Have you?'

Arthur considered. 'Well, no, but I'd bet it's revolting, wouldn't you?'

There it was again . . . almost a smile. 'What kind of a lizard?'

'Oh, geckos. They're filthy.'

She nodded. 'Or limpodos.'

'You're right. Even a gecko wouldn't give house-room to a limpodo – bleargh!'

Arthur could have sworn she nearly giggled. Then she pulled herself together and stood up, ner-vously tugging on her immaculately ironed blouse.

'Give me those papers,' she said. '*Not* Sven's, thank you.'

* * *

Arthur picked up Sven's and started to read. On the page was a picture of a large neutron bomb with an arrow pointing downwards towards Coventry. Oh, very funny, Arthur thought to himself. He looked over to the outside area. Gwyneth was standing next to the coffee machine, leafing through the unexpected submission from the temp, which seemed mostly to concern the amount of temporary staff required for the new-look town (lots, apparently). It was the first indication that this project might be of some interest to people outside their own small circle.

'Is that about the temps?' yelled Arthur. 'How many?'

'Everybody,' said Gwyneth, without looking up. 'Everyone should do their job on a temporary basis so that anyone can just move on when they feel like it. Makes everyone a lot happier when they feel footloose and fancy free, and apparently happy people don't litter.'

'Is that true?'

'There's no evidence provided.'

'I'd have thought you'd have been more likely to litter when you were happy – you know, tra la la, dum de dum; I'm so comfortable with myself today I don't even care what I throw around, la la . . . Wouldn't you think?'

'I don't litter.'

'Well, there you are. You're an unhappy non-vet, and you don't litter, so maybe the theorem is true.'

'I'm *not* unhappy.'

Silence fell as they skimmed through the other proposals.

'Sven wants an internet connection on every park bench.' Arthur examined it closely as Gwyneth wandered over to take a look.

'Oh yes,' said Gwyneth, 'some other council tried that.'

'What on earth for? So the flashers could get quicker access to their internet porn?'

'No, to show their interconnectivity in the world. To let people get out, smell the roses, enjoy the trees. Work in different environments; experience nature.'

'What happened?'

'Oh, you know. There was a whole flasher internet porn incident and they discontinued it.'

'Uh huh.'

They continued leafing.

'Marcus has laid out how much money we can spend,' said Arthur, holding up a densely typed wad of Excel spreadsheets.

'How much?'

'Well, judging by these calculations here . . . and this table over here . . .'

'Yeah?'

'God, hang on . . .' He paused for a minute, his brow furrowing with concern. 'Well, it seems to say here – no, it can't be. It looks like absolutely nothing at all. In fact, he seems to have gone into the realm of imaginary negative numbers.'

Gwyneth squinted over at him. 'Like how?'

'Well, apparently if we did anything – *anything at all*, including moving from *these seats, right now*, we'd have to cull every lollipop lady within an eleven-mile radius.'

'That can't be right.'

'God, but look at the figures. It adds up.'

'We'll get an extra budget. It's been approved.'

'It's been spent.' Arthur held up a second sheet. 'It says here . . . "extraneous disbursements". There you go. That's our entire budget.'

'Sixteen million pounds?'

'Sixteen million pounds. I wonder what extraneous disbursements are?'

Gwyneth stared at the paper in disbelief. 'So you bloody should.'

She picked up the phone. 'Marcus?'

The voice on the other end was timid.

'What the hell are these figures?' She switched on the speaker phone.

'Um . . . yes, I had a funny feeling those might come up,' said Marcus.

'Did you, now? Then what the hell are they?'

Marcus mumbled something incomprehensible.

'What? Speak up, for God's sake.'

Then he spoke up, and Arthur turned white.

* * *

'I don't understand,' Arthur was saying for the sixth time, standing over Marcus's desk. Marcus was cowering and concentrating on the paper in front of him.

'How the hell can it cost sixteen million pounds to fix a photocopier?'

'It was a weekend. Call-out charges.'

* * *

Oh, God. This place was disastrous. Gwyneth came round into the grey car park and fished in her handbag for her car keys, with a half-hearted plan to go back to her main office and think this through. Across the motorway, the sun was setting over a field. If you could ignore the town, this really was a most beautiful part of the world. She looked back at the office.

Suddenly she remembered the look on Arthur's

face that morning when he'd got the photocopying bill and almost laughed. The way his soft brown hair had flipped over his face . . .

Oh no, she thought, fumbling with her key in the lock. No, no no no. She couldn't possibly fancy the guy she was working with. She couldn't. For a start, it was forbidden in company policy (until you reached director level, at which stage you could shag the pope and it would be discreetly ignored).

Not only that, it was obscenely unprofessional and Gwyneth was nothing if not a paradigm of professionalism.

'I am a paradigm of professionalism,' she said to herself, looking in her car mirror and trying to make it sound like a positive reinforcement statement.

Oh, but his hair's so cute, she thought to herself.

No, no no no no no no, she also thought to herself.

But she wondered what would happen if the project got cancelled and there was nothing in the way.

Chapter Four

Fay shivered and pulled her coat further around her. The November air was chilly, even if it wasn't raining this morning. She'd driven all the way from Birmingham, where she was staying with her mother. They spent most of their time together slagging off men – Fay had never known her father – and even the very concept of maleness. It wasn't as much fun as it sounded. Fay could hear the vinegar creeping into her voice as they spoke.

Arthur hadn't phoned since she'd left. Not even once. It wasn't as though she expected vast bouquets watered with tears, although they wouldn't have gone amiss. She didn't require marching bands although how come, when Bono fell out with his wife, he'd recorded a single about how she was the sweetest thing he'd ever known and got all her favourite stars like Boyzone to be in

the video and it worked and *they* had a baby —
why couldn't she have been going out with an
international rock star instead of a bloody useless
bloody town planner?

With Arthur there'd been nothing, absolutely
nothing at all. It was as if he'd just popped out
to take the video back. It was as if she *was* the
video. How could he? How could he just waltz
on so very bloody quickly? This wasn't *Men are
from Mars, Woman are from Venus*. This was 'Men
are From Mars, Arthur is an evil demon from the
pits of HELL'.

There aren't many places to go in Coventry if
you're single and not fourteen years old. That's
how Fay found herself in Cork's wine bar, nursing
a solitary glass of wine and trying to look as if she
was engrossed in her copy of *Red* magazine. Why,
she was wondering, does the time from *Jackie* to
Red go so fast? Next stop *Woman's Own*. She was
reflecting on the fact that the age ranges of maga-
zines appeared to be in alphabetical order when
someone, who'd obviously been nursing slightly
more than a simple glass of wine, heaved himself
onto the next stool along.

'In't you,' — he screwed up one of his eyes —
'don'tcha know Arthur Pendleton?'

Fay regarded the rumpled chunky mess in front
of her with some alarm. 'Um, yes, but . . .'

''E's a bastard.'

Fay looked closer.

'Is me!' he expostulated.

'Rósh, you know! Arthur's bloody boss. Well, Arthur's bloody *ex* bloody boss, bloody bastard, bloody . . .'

Oh, yes. Fantastic.

'Bloody ex-bastard,' said Fay, allowing herself a tight little grin.

'I recognize you . . . from the Christmas party . . . always fancied you . . .'

What were you doing in the stationery cupboard with that poor Cathy woman then, thought Fay, but decided not to mention it.

'Yes, of course I remember,' she said, using the brisk tone one reserves for children and drunks.

'Do you know . . . he bloody sacked me . . . bastard.'

'Me too,' said Fay with a half-smile. 'I know how you feel.'

'Really?' He moved forward across the stool.

'Not that much.' She promptly removed his hand from the top of her thigh, where he'd landed to steady himself.

'Can I buy you a drink?'

'No, thank you.'

'Oh, go on.'

Fay arched her eyebrows, hoping he'd continue

on over to the bar and forget he was ever talking to her. On the other hand, the article in *Red* was 'Baby Massage With You, Your Baby and Your Ever-Loving Partner – First, pick your largest, sunniest reception room . . .'

'You know,' said Ross, trying to be conversational, 'they've offered me the other job.'

'What other job?'

'*His* job. In Slough. Same deal. BUT! Only one city gets to be European City Culsha.'

She looked at him. 'Slough's a city?'

'Yeah, it's – it's got an IKEA and six polyversities. Yeah.'

'Oh. Right.' But inside she was thinking that this might be rather interesting.

'What do you do again?' he said.

'Personnel management.'

He pointed a beefy finger at her. 'We NEED one of those.'

'What are you talking about?'

Ross became momentarily distracted by a passing waitress. 'Oh, she's gorgeous, eh? I bet I could have her. I had this page three girl once. Well, I met this page three girl once . . .'

Fay sighed and went to finish her drink.

'No, no, right, you'd be perfect for the job.'

'What job?'

'Coming to be in my team, thass wha job.'

'What, you'd give me a job just because I hate Arthur Pendleton?'

'*Precishely.*'

'I'll have a white wine spritzer, please.'

* * *

And that was how, a week later, she found herself on secondment from the recruitment firm ('*City of Culture*' her boss had twittered, '*such* an exciting opportunity for the firm . . . all those heads! . . . all that hunting!') driving to start her first day's work for Ross, a man whose tosspot qualities had been expounded on at such length and in such detail by Arthur, she was warming to him already.

* * *

There was a summons.

Arthur would be meeting the chairman for the first time, to have a discussion about the delicate financial situation.

He hadn't been able to chat to Gwyneth before he'd left the night before. Weighing up the balance of the evidence, he reckoned she was going to grass him up. He sighed. Sixteen million quid, and he'd be back to where he started. Or worse: they might sack him. Or he'd go to prison, maybe. No, surely not prison. Still. Nowhere good.

Arthur looked at his forehead in the bathroom

mirror. Was there more hair there or less? And where was the soap? By utter coincidence, ever since Fay had left he'd run out of soap, toilet roll, razorblades and clean towels.

That *is* a coincidence, he thought to himself. He stomped out of the bathroom to iron a shirt, and immediately forgot all about it when he realized he was going to have to be eating cooking chocolate for breakfast again. At least something good was happening.

There were a million other things to do. Or, of course, none, he reflected.

For the first time, realizing that he might lose this job, he became aware of how much he wanted to do it.

* * *

When he entered the main boardroom – distinguishable from the rest of the plastic grey building only by a singularly incongruous stag's head attached to the wall – Gwyneth was already there in a pale grey trouser suit with a lilac coloured top. He didn't know anything about women's clothing, but he noticed there was a subtle difference in the suit she had on and the dumpy two-pieces Fay used to wear. He bet she smelled nice. Right before she grassed him up of course, the cow.

Gwyneth was sitting next to the chairman, so it looked like they were in it together already, Arthur thought glumly, taking a seat across the table. There was another, younger man, sitting at one end, obviously there to take minutes. Nobody said good morning.

The chairman, Sir Eglamore, seemed an amiable enough old buff. He studied his notes, then glared at them incredulously.

'Is this in shillings or – drat it, what are those blasted things called?'

His softly spoken PA leaned in. 'Euros, sir.'

'That's right. Blast their eyes. That Tony Blair, you know. Should be hanged.' He sneezed. 'Who's in charge of this affair, anyway?'

'Me,' said Arthur.

'Ah, young Arthur, am I right?'

Arthur nodded, already surprised. Well, he was one up if the top brass could bother to find out his name.

Eglamore pulled his half-moon spectacles further down his long nose. 'You've got a long way to go, then.'

Arthur nodded vehemently. 'Yes, sir.'

'Not the best of starts, is it?'

'No.'

'Hrumph.' Eglamore turned his attention to Gwyneth. Arthur looked at her curiously.

'And we thought this was the best man for the job, did we?'

'Um, yes.'

'On the basis of . . . ?'

'Um.' She looked embarrassed. 'Many reasons, sir.'

Sir Eglamore made a noise like an angry horse. 'Photocopier incident, wasn't it?'

'Um, yes.'

'So what do you think now, hey?'

Gwyneth looked at Arthur, then straight at Sir Eglamore.

There was a pause. Then she said, 'He's still the best man for the job, sir.'

Both Sir Eglamore and Arthur's eyebrows shot up in the air.

'What's that, what?'

'And he fits candidate requirements.'

'And accidentally losing sixteen million pounds is a candidate requirement, is it?'

'It seemed the right thing to do at the time,' said Arthur and Gwyneth simultaneously. Then they looked at each other.

Sir Eglamore studied his papers for what seemed like a month. Then he looked at them from under his craggy eyebrows.

'Well, I don't approve . . . but I don't know how we can back out now. I've told all my friends at the

– well, yes, you don't need to know about that.'
He plumped up the papers on his desk, slightly
embarrassed. 'Of course, it won't be happening
again, you understand? Or even anything like
it. I don't know what all this modern fuss is
with photocopiers, anyway. Just get a couple of
the boys to copy them out by hand. Keeps them
quiet and out of mischief.'

Arthur could have wept with relief. 'I'll try and
stay away from all heavy office equipment, sir.'

'I'm going to put someone in place to watch
out for you. In fact, my nephew is looking for
a job. He can come and cast an eye over your
figures, what?'

He looked rather dodgily at Gwyneth for a second,
who effortlessly ignored him. 'Yes, yes, I'll send Rafe
along to you. Heard he's the best man for the job,
what.' He turned to his PA. 'Right, right, next? And
do hurry it along – it's venison for lunch.'

* * *

'Rafe? Who the hell is Rafe?' said Arthur, once
they'd got back to his office. 'It sounds like Sir
Eglamore's helping out the local orphanage! Who
asked him to interfere, anyway?'

Gwyneth shrugged. 'No clue,' she said. 'Presumably one of Sir Bufton Tufton's useless inbred
Cyclops children.'

95

'Yeah,' said Arthur. 'He'll be a complete burden. And anyway . . .' He knew this much from countless boring personnel conference evenings with Fay. 'We can't just take someone on. We have to advertise it and then interview all the one-legged people who apply or something.'

'No, really? God, yeah. I forget this is a public service organization.'

'That's cos we hate serving the public and what we do is actually invisible.'

'And what's he going to do?'

Arthur scratched his head. 'Well, now we've got our money back, I'm sure we'll find something . . . yes?'

Marcus put his head round the crack in the door. 'It's here!' he said excitedly.

'What?'

'What are we waiting for?' said Gwyneth.

'I don't know – what's up, Marcus? Have they just announced that they want all the accounting in base thirteen?'

'No, no, look.'

He entered the room, and brought out from behind his back a long roll of paper. 'The mighty scroll,' he announced with some reverence and placed it in front of them on the table.

'The *what*?' said Arthur and Gwyneth, simultaneously.

Marcus looked around. 'Um, I mean the official European application form.' He looked slightly embarrassed. 'It just came by fax. So I just thought it would be – you know, more fun – if I delivered it in the form of a mighty scroll.'

'It's okay.' Arthur picked up the scroll and unrolled it flat. It covered the entire length of the table and dropped onto the floor. 'We already know your job is boring.'

Gwyneth looked over his shoulder. 'Good God, it's immense.'

'That's because it's in fifteen different languages.'

'God, so it is. Look, it's in Welsh! Who on earth thinks Swansea would be made European City of Culture?'

'I'm from Wales,' said Gwyneth.

'Most beautiful countryside in the world, isn't it?' said Arthur hurriedly.

'Wow, this goes to the European Parliament,' said Marcus, reading the small print.

'That's the least exciting parliament ever, though,' said Arthur. 'It's like the Saturday superstore of parliaments.'

'This is going to take a lot of serious work, even just in English,' said Gwyneth, looking worriedly at it.

'I don't think putting porn plugs in park benches

is going to pass for the required "Three Major Cultural Events", do you?'

'Just the one,' said Marcus.

'No, *none*.'

Marcus looked at it again. 'Ooh, look, we have to support and develop creative work, which is an essential element in any cultural policy. Like, Sven's expenses.'

'Is that someone taking our name in vain?' asked Sven, walking in eating a hot dog with Sandwiches at his heels.

'Can't you knock?' said Arthur, still sitting slumped in his chair.

'Cool down, el power-crazed Nazio.'

Sandwiches, meanwhile, had scrambled in ungainly fashion onto the meeting table and was clacking across it, looking for custard cream traces.

'You should get that dog's toenails trimmed,' observed Gwyneth.

'What? *What*?' Arthur turned round to look at her. 'Is that really your first reaction? Maybe you should have been a vet. Why didn't you say, you should get that dog out of the office – or, you shouldn't let your dog onto other people's tables . . .'

'Or, you shouldn't let your dog eat the mighty scroll,' said Marcus in horror, staring at where Sandwiches was happily tearing away at the edges. Drool advanced down the paper.

'Nooo!' Arthur lunged for it, causing Sandwiches to slide backwards across the polished wood and disappear, ears last, over the end, giving an anguished yelp.

Sven rushed to his aid and Sandwiches – wounded only in pride – hid his head in Sven's meaty armpit. Rather him than me, Arthur found himself thinking.

'Don't shout at Sandwiches,' said Sven.

'I'm sorry, but I reserve the right to shout at anyone who eats the proposal guidelines,' said Arthur.

'It was only that we have to "exploit the historic heritage, urban architecture and . . . something about life in the city",' said Gwyneth, unravelling the slobbery bundle. 'And by the way, how come I've only been here a fortnight and I've already become an expert in dog kablooie?'

Marcus and Sven started an argument about expenses as Gwyneth and Arthur bickered over who was going to pick up the scroll, and it took them a while to notice the shadow in the doorway.

The man standing there nearly filled the doorway. Tall and fine-boned, with a mop of long, curly blond hair, he looked, as the light fell upon him, like a pre-Raphaelite painting caught in a frame.

It was as if a spell had been cast over the room.

As Gwyneth stared at him, Sven and Marcus fell quiet. Sandwiches dropped like a rock out of Sven's arms and went over to explore.

'Hey,' said the man, smiling suddenly. It lit up his features and broke the mood immediately. He dropped a long arm to scratch the dog. 'Is this Festival City?'

'That depends,' said Gwyneth. 'Who are you?'

He looked around the room. 'You know, you're all so lucky.'

'We're *what?*'

'I mean,' he gestured to the scroll, 'you've got this blank canvas, right? And this town . . . Man, anything you do to this town is going to make it better, isn't it? You could put up a picture of this dog taking a leak and it would be more attractive than ninety-five per cent of the town centre.'

'I like you,' said Sven, coming forward.

'But you could make it – God, absolutely fantastic! And that's your job description, isn't it? I mean, you've got so much potential. So much fun! Fairs and parties, and celebrations and flowers and . . .' He stopped and collected himself for a moment. 'Sorry. I'm getting carried away.'

'No, go on,' said Gwyneth, finding herself doing something uncharacteristic. Smiling.

'Well, you can basically plan for anything – one town had a new tram network. One place made an entire square blue — the stones, the walls, everything. You take the money you have and find out what you can do, then Brussels puts up some more money, then lots of people come and bring money into the town and it all works brilliantly . . .'

Arthur turned round slowly from the window. 'Sorry, but — who are you?'

'Oh, sorry, hi — I'm Rafe.'

* * *

Arthur couldn't sleep that night. Something felt wrong. Something wrong in the world . . . Of course all insomnia is melodramatic, he thought, staring at the flashing LED of his alarm clock. Three thirty-two a.m. Insomnia makes you feel you are the only person awake in the entire world. Of course, he could have got up and phoned his half-brother Kay, who lived in Australia and would be more than happy to hear from him in the middle of the afternoon . . . but no. He felt pinned to the bed, and even thinking nice thoughts about Gwyneth wouldn't help him drift off.

Finally, in a fit of exasperation, he threw the covers off, got up and stared out of the window. All the windows in the executive estate were dark, every single one. Somebody must be up, he thought. Somebody, anybody, doing something.

No babies? No parties? Yet there was nothing but the sodium lights of the tall street-lamps, and the distant hum of the motorway. Nobody moved. Nobody stirred. Arthur looked up to the stars, and imagined the world this quiet a thousand years ago, with everyone asleep when it got dark and up with the sun.

He shivered in the early morning cold, but didn't go back to bed – now he was up, he actually felt rather peaceful. He liked the idea of the world quiet; full of possibilities and opportunities. Everyone asleep, optimistic about tomorrow – or at least, optimistic enough to sleep. A thought struck him. This would be a good time to see the place, see the absolute raw material he was dealing with – what the streets looked like empty. If this was going to be his town he should go out, take a look around it, examine it from the beginning with no hordes of teenagers or gangs of lads getting in the way, and no cars to block the view across the road. The more he thought about it, the more he felt it was a good idea. Even if, he realized, somewhere not too far away, it sounded like something was howling.

Ten miles away in her mother's house, Fay had felt pulled awake at the same time as Arthur. Her first day at work hadn't gone so bad . . . well, Ross hadn't groped her. As such. But this was all going to be worth it for the look on Arthur's face when she and Ross won the bid and left him crying on the street. Yeah. Her face took on a grim satisfaction and she turned over again on the single bed and fell asleep.

The darkness was hinting at dawn. Arthur looked at his own reflection in the window. God, yeah. That really was something howling. It did it again. Arthur reminded himself that wolves no longer roamed the countryside.

Sounded bloody weird, though.

* * *

'We're all going out at *what* time in the morning?' said Gwyneth.

'No sodding way,' said Sven.

'Listen to me,' said Arthur, then realized he was begging, and that he was trying to remember about this whole respect issue, and took a breath.

'Look,' he said. 'This came to me last night. It's a great idea. We're going to go out into the city when there's nobody else there, and take a good long look at it. See what we've got to work with. It's the only time of day we can do it — after the drunks and before the milkman. Plus, it'll be fun. Maybe. No, yes it will. It'll be like an expedition.'

'Fine by me,' said Cathy.

'Great, that's great!' said Arthur. 'Well done.'

'I usually get up at that time to start the boys' breakfast. And do the ironing, you know.'

'I can't, anyway,' said Sven. 'It would interfere with Sandwiches' digestion.'

'Yeah – might make it work,' retorted Arthur.

'Couldn't you come without your dog?' said Gwyneth.

'No. He sleeps right across me.'

As if to demonstrate, Sandwiches crawled up and lay in the most ungainly fashion across Sven's lap, a forlorn stubby pair of legs and a single ear hanging down either side.

'That's *disgusting*,' said Gwyneth, committed vet.

'I think it would be nice to have something to cuddle at night,' said Cathy. Then everyone – including her – remembered she was actually married and already shared a bed with her husband and she blushed.

'Yes, well,' said Arthur briskly, 'we're going to take a look at a blank canvas; imagine what we could do if we set our minds to it. Too late for the drunks and too early for the milkman,' he repeated. 'Do milkmen still exist?'

'You're thinking of the bogeyman,' said Gwyneth practically. 'Milk, yes, bogeys, no.'

'Speak for yourself,' said Sven, with one finger up his nose.

Just then Rafe walked in, the only fresh-looking person in the room. Gwyneth had invited him along for the day to 'see how the department works' and he, amazingly, still seemed quite enthusiastic in the moments he could join them between hurrying to the toilet to cope with Cathy's near-endless coffee provision.

Cathy looked at Rafe with that strange mixture of lust and motherly devotion only women teetering on the brink of menopause can conjure up for fresh-faced young men. 'Hello, Rafe. More coffee?'

'No, I'm fine thanks, Mrs P. What's up?'

'He's trying to make us go out in the cold and dark.'

'Why?'

Sven explained, and Arthur hovered in a corner feeling stupid. He'd planned to get them all whipped up with his enthusiastic oratory. Sven was making it sound as if he was transporting them all to prison ships. Rafe listened closely, nodding his head. The whole room was watching them. Finally, he straightened up.

'Well – that's a brilliant idea!' he said. There was something about his open handsome face that made it look permanently smiling, and it was infectious.

Sven wrinkled up his nose in confusion. 'Is it?'

'Yes, don't you see? Arthur, you're absolutely right – we can get an idea of how the whole place *could* be. It will be mystical, magical – the city will be dead, but we – we can bring it alive, through knowing what people miss every day, through the power of our free imaginations – don't you see?'

Arthur was half pleased, half slightly grumpy. 'Well, yes – that's exactly what I was . . .'

'Ooh, and I can make soup,' said Cathy.

'Not potato soup,' said Sven. 'That's rank.'

'How rank can a potato be?' asked Marcus. 'It's a potato. That's like calling bread offensive.'

Arthur stood at the back of the room, quite amazed. Gwyneth looked over to him.

'They're arguing about the soup,' said Arthur quietly to Gwyneth. 'I think Rafe's won on points.'

'Well, it was your idea,' said Gwyneth. 'But, incidentally, he didn't convince me. I don't want to clatter about on my own in the pitch dark to meet you lot.'

'Oh, please come,' said Arthur, realizing suddenly that he was gazing at her.

Marcus, Sven and Cathy had gathered round Rafe, who was pointing things out on a map.

'I mean,' he was saying, 'have you ever looked at the top of the high street? I mean, *really* looked at it?'

'I'm usually too busy trying to avoid the syringes,' said Gwyneth.

'I'll pick you up if you like,' said Arthur.

Gwyneth glanced sideways to avoid his eyes. 'Um . . . yeah. Okay.'

'I mean, just, you know, in my car. You know, just to take you to this work thing!'

'I know,' she said. 'I know.' And she sounded as anxious to correct the misunderstanding as he was.

* * *

It was freezing. Properly, unbelievably freezing. After his broken sleep the night before, Arthur found tearing himself from his bed before four a.m. was a near impossibility, managed only by the warming thought of Gwyneth in bed – possibly naked – right now. Groaning, he stumbled into the kitchen, boiled some hot water and fumbled around for something to put into it. Let's see – Marmite, toadstools (growing, sadly, rather than handwrapped) or an old bottle of Grand Marnier. His stomach rumbled warningly and he decided instead just to brush his teeth fifteen times.

Gwyneth's house was actually rather charming – set back from the road, it formed the top two floors of one of Coventry's not terribly widespread Edwardian villas. Arthur was just debating how much he cared about waking up the whole street by sounding the horn, as opposed to stepping out of the car and losing all feeling in his extremities, when the front door opened and a slight figure slipped out.

Arthur had never seen her out of a strict, well-cut work suit before. She was wearing thick rolled up khaki trousers, walking boots, and a huge man's jumper that made her look incredibly young and cute. A little red hat jammed on top of her blonde hair finished the effect.

'It's my lucky red hat,' she said when she caught him staring.

'What?'

'Nothing. It's not lucky – I live here after all. But this is definitely a night which requires a hat.'

Arthur checked to see if the heating was turned all the way up and started the car.

'There's no way anyone else is even going to get out of bed for this,' she said. 'Nobody is stupid enough.'

Arthur found himself thinking this wouldn't be the worst thing in the world. Maybe they could just keep warm in the car and . . . er, chat.

''Course they will. It'll be fun.'

She stared straight ahead. 'Getting out of this

car is not going to be fun. It's going to be like jumping off the *Titanic*.'

'But think how nice it will be to get back to bed.'

Gwyneth grimaced. 'Yes – two minutes later, I reckon. Nobody's going to stand for this. If they're here at all.' But she stopped as Arthur swung onto Greyfriar's Lane and both of them realized three things simultaneously: one, that it was amazing to drive at night and be able to cut through without a single piece of contending traffic; two, there were the others, and three, the two of them were about to step out of the same car in what, if you had a mind like Sven, might be construed as a mildly interesting way.

They both stopped talking normally. 'Rightyho!' said Arthur. 'Here we are!' like some children's entertainer. 'Uh huh!' said Gwyneth. They sat for a second, then Gwyneth took a deep breath and opened the door.

Cathy was standing clutching a large bag to her chest and smiled helpfully when they walked over.

'Hullo there! Isn't it . . .'

'HEEEEy!' shouted Sven, who was unaccompanied for once. 'What's this, then?'

Gwyneth looked at him with her best haughty stare, which was very haughty indeed. 'Oh, *shut up*, Sven.'

Arthur looked round the market square.

'Ooh, there's Rafe,' said Cathy. 'Now, who wants soup?'

'I think if I put out my hand to pick up the cup it might stick in the position forever,' said Marcus, who was barely visible between three layers of scarf – only his eyes could be seen.

'I'm glad that, as the most sophisticated planner in the country, I'm being pulled out of my bed in the middle of the night to watch people's arms fall off,' said Sven.

'Isn't this great!' said Rafe, striding up, looking pink-cheeked, his curly hair also crammed under a hat. He should be less tall, Arthur found himself thinking.

'So – what's the plan?' said Rafe. 'Is that soup?'

Cathy poured him a cup, beaming.

'Well,' said Arthur vaguely, and indicated the area. 'This is our city, our home. I want us all to see it from different angles, in a new way. We're just going to walk through, observing and taking notes, and get as many ideas as possible. Then we just pick out all the good ideas and hey, we're on the way.'

'Sort of, "chip off everything that doesn't look like a tiger"?' said Gwyneth.

'Exactly! Here.' He doled out the little disposable cameras he'd bought for everyone. 'Let's go!'

And they set off towards Market Street, a

funny little group, completely isolated, huddling together for warmth under the ever burning fierceness of the sodium lamps, and the ring road still thundering overhead.

* * *

At first they didn't know what to say or what they were looking for, apart from Rafe, who immediately started snapping all over the place. But as they looked longer, they started to notice all sorts of things impossible to see during the day when trying to avoid the uncollected rubbish.

'Do you get much wildlife round here?' said Rafe, taking a picture of a spider's web spanning a bypass.

'I don't know,' said Arthur. 'We get foxes, I suppose. Spiders, obviously. Um . . . has anyone ever heard of there being wolves?'

The others looked at him.

'Perhaps a hundred years ago,' said Gwyneth.

'Or in a country that actually has wolves,' said Sven. 'Denmark has them. They're cool.'

'Well, just a rumour then, obviously,' said Arthur, looking at his toes.

'God, look at that,' said Gwyneth, pointing to the ring road overhead. 'When there's no cars in the way . . . That cluster of lamp-posts looks like a forest.'

They wandered over to catch the best angle.

Cathy looked around on the other side. 'How far have we come? I've completely lost my bearings. It's weird at night, isn't it?'

'That's all right,' said Arthur. 'Lose your bearings. We're in the car park – there's just no cars.'

'Oh, yeah.'

They wandered through the bylanes behind the cathedral. 'It's like a maze round here,' grunted Marcus.

'Oh, I love mazes, I do,' said Cathy. 'Have you ever been to . . .'

'A maze!' said Gwyneth and Rafe at the same time.

'That'd be *brilliant*,' said Rafe.

'Yes,' said Arthur as they turned a cobbled corner.

'People do like mazes, don't they?'

'You could do it the same shape as these back streets,' said Marcus.

'That'd be stupid, wouldn't it?' said Sven. 'It'd be obvious and dead easy.'

'Well, it's not really obvious in the dark. Without names on the streets, I bet it'd be harder than you thought. I bet you couldn't do it.'

'I bet I could,' said Sven, covering his eyes. He immediately walked into a wall. 'Well,' he said, going overboard to recover his dignity. 'You'd need a flat surface for a start. And a *lot* of calculations of people flows and timing and stuff.' He became thoughtful. 'It'd be really hard sums.'

Arthur looked at Gwyneth and she half-smiled back at him. In fact, he'd found it hard to take his eyes off her in her red cap, and was trying to keep a safe distance behind her.

'It would need the application of some kind of . . . superbrain . . .' the Dane continued. Then he paused expectantly.

'Oh, Sven,' said Cathy. 'Maybe *you* could do it.'

Sven looked thoughtful. 'Do you reckon?'

'Oh, it would require a *lot* of computer modelling, though – possibly on superfast equipment,' said Gwyneth. 'Maybe that's not your kind of thing.'

Sven's eyes were wide. 'Uh, I, uh –'

'Where would we put it?' asked Rafe, walking in circles across the cobbles as if he were crossing a labyrinth. 'It's got to be huge, otherwise it's rubbish and only fun for four-year-olds.'

'Chapel Fields,' said Arthur. 'Or Hearsall Common.'

'Or you could take over the pedestrian precinct and make it a maze to get from one shop to the next. Given that it's already a pain in the neck, you know, add a bit of fun to it,' put in Marcus.

'Yeah, maybe that wouldn't be quite so popular,'

said Arthur. 'Hard to get through without tripping over the triple buggies.'

'Or as easy to grow,' said Gwyneth.

'Oh yeah – they take years, don't they?' said Rafe. 'Can we still have one?'

'I'm sure you can import them,' said Arthur, as five middle management brains tried to get their heads round what a job involving real things moving around might conceivably entail.

They walked on. Some crows flew above the electric wires and instantly disappeared into the blackness as the little group strode down Salt Lane, pointing out the less hideous buildings to each other.

'We should focus on the tops of these buildings more,' mused Rafe. 'Nobody ever looks up here. They ought to. Look at that gable – it's absolutely beautiful. Might be Elizabethan. But because there's a Whittard's coffee shop underneath, nobody even gives it a second glance.'

'We could light them up,' said Sven. 'Put lights around the window frames.'

'Yes, well, I suppose we could ask them,' said Arthur.

'Is it just me or is it not quite so freezing around here?' said Gwyneth.

'That's cos we're busy, and working things out and, you know, getting things moving,' said Rafe, smiling and clapping a hand around Gwyneth's shoulders in a jovial manner. Arthur expected her to stiffen immediately and make some cutting remark, but she didn't – she smiled, and, after a moment, moved on and out of his near-embrace.

Arthur watched, quite surprised at the sudden stab this caused him. I reckoned one salty dog was quite enough for our office, he thought to himself crossly. This was ridiculous. He shouldn't fancy her, and he certainly shouldn't care about anyone else fancying her. Suddenly, out of the corner of his eye, he caught sight of a figure scurrying across the other corner of the square, about twenty yards away.

'Who's that, then?' said Sven, loudly enough to alert the person, who stood stock still as they strained to make him out.

'It's a burglar!' said Cathy. 'Ooh, I hope it's not my Ricky again.'

'I think, if it was a burglar, you'd hope he might be running away from us rather than . . . What's he doing, anyway?' said Gwyneth, sounding rather less scared than Arthur thought he might sound if he opened his mouth. Did burglars have guns? He wasn't sure.

They strained their eyes again. The person seemed to be sniffing the air. Then he set out towards their little group.

'Oh, that's all right – it'll be a policeman, eh?' said Sven. 'What's our cover story, then?'

'We don't need a cover story, Sven,' said Arthur. 'We aren't planning a heist.'

'Maybe we should tell him we're planning a heist.'

'We'll tell him the truth! That this is a management exercise.'

'Good luck with your cell mate,' sniffed Sven.

'Don't be ridiculous,' said Gwyneth. 'They can't arrest you for being outside. Unless there's a curfew . . . There's not a curfew, is there?'

They looked nervously at each other as the figure approached. Arthur couldn't help but be glad to see that Rafe and Gwyneth had moved apart entirely.

He looked across the square. As the figure came closer, he could see that this definitely wasn't a policeman. Too many layers for one thing – pieces of material flapped in the cold breeze, cloaks and sheets wrapped on top of one another.

'Oh, I think it's a homeless person,' said Cathy, her face full of concern. 'Here, everyone, give me the rest of that soup. What a terrible night to be out.'

'I'm not a homeless person!' said the bundle suddenly, although surely he must have been out of earshot. He arrived in front of them, and suddenly Arthur almost jumped in surprise.

'But I will take that lovely potato soup if you please,' said Lynne. 'It is *rather* a chilly night to be abroad.'

* * *

'Lynne!' Arthur was amazed. 'What on earth are you doing out here?'

Lynne looked around the group. 'Thought I heard wolves last night,' she said. 'Doesn't seem to be much sign of them tonight.'

'Who are you?' said Sven. Lynne put out her hand.

'Um, she's my . . .'

Arthur really didn't need Sven getting ammunition as to whether or not he was a mentalist.

'I'm a friend of Arthur's – I work at the office. I'm surprised you don't recognize me – you've got a dog, yes?'

Sven nodded guardedly. He was clearly thinking that he'd have remembered a crazy old lady wrapped up in fifteen layers of hessian. 'He's a lovely creature.'

. . . On the other hand thought Sven, maybe she's not too bad.

'This soup is still hot,' said Lynne, looking at it confusedly.

Nobody spoke.

'Um, yes, it's in a thermos,' said Cathy tentatively.

'A what?' She took it from Cathy and studied it closely. 'Whoever heard of such a thing?'

'Hi, I'm Rafe,' said Rafe, openly, breaking the slightly awkward silence.

Lynne eyed him for a second before taking his hand. She seemed almost . . . Arthur couldn't quite put his finger on it. Lynne had to be the least stand-offish person in the world, but he was sure he could detect a certain frisson.

'Yes.' She stood back and looked him up and down. Then she turned, abruptly.

'And you must be Gwyneth?'

Gwyneth raised her eyebrows. 'Hi?'

Lynne studied her. 'Yes, you really are very pretty,' she said, in an almost casual, objective fashion.

'What is it you're doing out here?' said Gwyneth. 'I didn't quite catch what you told Arthur.'

Lynne polished off the last of the soup. 'Oh, couldn't sleep, my dear. One rarely does at my age.'

'What's that, seven hundred and forty-two?' whispered Sven to Rafe. Lynne turned her bright eyes on him again.

'You're under-estimating, dear,' Lynne said. 'Now, let's go down to the river.' She was already

118

marching off down a side street. 'Seeing as it's such a beautiful night.' And it was, the morning star rising high, a promise of the dawn that was still a long way off, frost crackling at the coldest point of the morning.

'Why don't we take a walk down by the river?' Lynne said again, loudly. 'Rafe, walk with me,' she continued. 'I want to get to know you.'

Amazingly they all followed her, down the steeply sloping wynd, Gwyneth and Arthur at the rear.

'What a *peculiar* person,' said Gwyneth. 'How did you say you met her again?'

'Well, actually, it was your lot that sent me to her,' said Arthur.

Gwyneth whipped round, looked at Lynne then turned her attention back to Arthur. 'Oh, my God – *she's* the company *therapist?*'

'Well, yes.'

'Oh, ho, oh . . .' It took Arthur a while to realize she was laughing. 'Oh my God, no wonder the department's in such a state.'

'Now, hang on!' Arthur found himself getting cross. 'She's very good, actually. If a little unconventional. And we are planning to make the department rather better than a state, if you recall.'

Gwyneth couldn't stop laughing.

'Oh, ho, listen to you! Now you're properly

coming over all presidential, and we're out in the freezing cold at five o'clock in the morning!'

Despite himself, Arthur started to smile. 'What's funny about that?'

'Nothing! Every company should do this! Oh my God, Arthur, do you realize . . .'

He grinned, not knowing what she was going to say, but revelling in the way the cold wind had brought the red to her cheeks and her laugh brought a sparkle like the ice to her eyes.

'What?'

'By not being stupid enough to come out tonight, *Sandwiches* is a better project leader than we are!'

Finally Arthur caught the mood and started to laugh too, painfully as he pulled the freezing wind into his lungs.

As he laughed, he made to lunge for her. 'How dare you say that to your superior officer? Hey! Come back here!'

She had started to run from him, giggling incoherently and shouting over the wind. 'I'm sorry Sir couldn't understand any remarks vis-à-vis his managerial competence versus that of a *big slobbery dog.*'

'Right, that's it!' He chased her as she backed down the hill. 'It's going to be a bit more than a verbal warning for you, young lady.'

'What's that? Woof woof woof what?'

And, near hysterical, they didn't notice Lynne watching them curiously, almost sadly – didn't notice anything at all, until Gwyneth nearly fell into the river.

* * *

'Oh, watch it!' shouted Arthur, and reached out an arm to grab her as she tottered on the tow path. But before he could catch her hand, Lynne was there, grasping Gwyneth by the shoulders.

'*Look*,' she whispered very faintly into Gwyneth's ear.

'What?' said Gwyneth, turning around.

'Hi,' said Sven, coming through the passageway and onto the river bank. 'It can't be work if you're laughing.'

The others came through the passageway.

'Oh my God,' said Cathy. 'Oh my God,' said Gwyneth.

* * *

Cathy was exclaiming about the beauty of the scenery – a faraway glimmer of pink light had just started to catch over the top of the water, illuminating the canal boats moored on the far side, and the frost covering the trees and icing over the water at the edges.

Gwyneth was standing stock-still, peering into the dark, looking terrified.

'Is that . . . ?'

She turned round, her face full of fear, looking for Lynne.

'I thought I saw a hand – a white hand . . .'

'Is there someone in there?'

Arthur craned his neck. 'I don't see anything,' he said.

They stared and stared into the blackness.

'No,' said Gwyneth, still staring straight ahead. 'I must have imagined it.'

Arthur looked closely at the brightly-painted houseboats which seemed to rise out of the water – he'd caught the reflection of the new forming ice, and tried to work out how the houseboats could be moored in it. It had looked to his eyes as if there were buildings set on the ice.

'Wow,' he said.

'What?' demanded Sven impatiently.

Arthur turned round, but this time he was smiling and looked genuinely excited. 'Guys – imagine if this river were iced over completely? We could walk all the way to Warwick!'

'What would be the point of that?' said Sven.

'I don't know if you could do the whole thing,' said Rafe. 'I've lived near here all my life. The bridge . . . .' He indicated it further downstream over the Black River; 'Its arches are too close together or something. I don't quite understand.'

'Basic thermodynamics,' said Sven loftily, but declined to explain further.

'Wouldn't it be brilliant, though?' said Arthur, still caught in a reverie.

'We could have tents and stalls . . . and people could skate . . .'

'An ice carnival!' said Gwyneth. 'A big festival! All through the winter! That's what I'd call bloody culture!'

Arthur stared at her.

'Yeah, guys, I don't want to stick a spanner in anything, but this river doesn't necessarily ice,' said Rafe again.

Arthur looked round. 'There's fake ice, isn't there?'

Sven looked at him. 'To ice over a whole river?'

'I don't know – is it impossible?'

Sven looked like he was working something out in his head.

Meanwhile, Gwyneth moved towards Arthur, and touched him lightly on the elbow. He opened his arm slightly, and let her small hand slip inside the crook.

'Nothing's impossible, surely?' she said, softly.

Lynne was watching Gwyneth. 'Did you say you thought you saw a hand, my dear?'

Gwyneth turned. 'Yes, it must have just been the dark playing tricks.'

Lynne patted her on the arm. 'Watch out for things in rivers.'

'Er, yes, okay,' said Gwyneth, moving her arm away from the mad old lady.

Meanwhile, Arthur had closed his eyes. Surely nothing was impossible now, out here in this freezing night, all alone together? He turned to Sven.

'Well?' he said again, with a more commanding tone of voice this time. 'Is it impossible?'

'I'd need to work it out with Marcus. This amount of nitrogen, over a moving current – I mean, maybe it could cost, like, millions of pounds.'

'But it's *possible*,' said Arthur, eyes shining.

Sven shrugged. 'I guess.'

Arthur smiled and turned round. 'Did you hear that, Lynne? I think things are taking a turn for . . .'

'Where did the old lady go?' said Rafe.

Chapter Five

''Ere's what we're doing, right?'

It was another grey day in Slough. Sometimes Fay imagined that the rest of the world was bathed in sunlight, with just a canopy over this conurbation west of London where concrete came to die.

She'd been surprised that this job had happened at all. It had seemed so sudden. But she got a grim enjoyment from working long hours – it saved time spent at her mother's chopping up Arthur's CD collection. She didn't think he'd even noticed she'd taken it. It was as if, in his life, she'd been a mere passing cloud, come and gone in an afternoon. But as she looked at her thickening figure – too many G and Ts with her mother – in the full-length mirror of her bedroom, and grimaced close up at the tiny lines on her forehead, she still thought of him as a thief. A thief who was going to get what was coming to him.

Ross, though horrible, was at least efficient. As soon as they'd got the documentation from the European commission ('who know nothing,' he had pointed out. 'They should just have "England – Country of Culture" forever and shut the fuck up about it') he'd handed it to his idiotic and bouncer-like number two, Dave Gorman, who ran it through a computer programme so they could see what everyone else had done.

'Flower festival?' he'd grunted. 'Crap. International *craft* exhibition? What unbelievable crap is that? Beer hall? Well, that's not too bad, I suppose. Apart from being crap!'

He paced around the office. 'See, the thing is, Fay love, nobody – including your beloved Arfur Pafetic (he thought this was hilarious) – has got a bloody clue, right? I mean, what people actually *want*.'

He stared at her meaningfully, and she wasn't sure if it was a rhetorical question or not. 'Ah mean, what do you want?'

'I don't know . . . um, a baby?'

Ross clearly hadn't been expecting that.

'Eh – I mean . . . I didn't mean that. I meant, um, shoe shops open all night?' said Fay quickly.

'That's more like it! That's more getting in with what we're thinking, right, Dave?'

Dave shrugged. 'I don't care much about shoes, like.'

'No, not *shoes*, idiot. Consumer bloody choice, innit?'

'Oh, yeah,' said Dave.

'Consumer bloody choice. Bloody free market. Fat lot those bloody bloated Brussels bureaucrats know about that, eh darling?'

Fay nodded, her face still burning as she thought of how her mouth had betrayed her. 'Yes, definitely.'

'That's what we need here. Fun and Stuff to Buy. Makes sense, dunnit?' He opened up some files he'd been working on. 'Okay. Listen up.'

Fay and Dave sat attentively.

'Fay-ona.' She hated it when he called her this. She suspected he knew that. 'What do you think when I say to you – theme park?'

She shrugged. 'Um, vomiting . . . small children crying . . . danger . . . horrible hot dogs . . . immense queues in the midday sun or pouring rain . . .'

'Alright, alright, shut up a minute. Dave, what do you think?'

'Fun, boss,' mumbled Dave. 'Lots of people. Retail opportunities.'

'*That's right*,' said Ross. 'Do you see, Fay? *Fun. Retail opportunities.*'

Fay nodded, trying to look surprised by her own stupidity.

'What I really wanted to do . . .' Ross turned towards the window and sighed, in the manner of one forced to give up his life's dream of inoculating children in Africa, 'was to open the biggest casino this side of Las Vegas, Nevada, USA. Oh, it would have been fabulous. The Las Vegas of North-West of London, slightly East of Reading.' He stared into the middle distance. 'Twenty-four-hour licensing . . . people pouring money into machines like there's no tomorrow . . .'

'Organized crime,' said Dave wistfully.

'But do you know,' Ross whipped around, 'do you know those poxy bloody PC bureaucrats – they *don't fund casino start-ups*! Can you believe that?'

Fay shook her head.

'We give them our bloody sovereignty, our bloody queen's head on a bloody plate and they can't even help out with basic bloody fun. Bastards.'

'So . . . What are we going to . . .'

'FUN!' roared Ross. 'We are going to turn Slough into so much FUN you wouldn't believe. Look at this!'

He lit up the overhead projector and put a slide on it. It was a picture of Slough town centre, complete with the clock tower of the Arndale centre – which now had a roller coaster around it.

'Ever been on a roller coaster around a city, Fay-ona?'

'No.'

'Me neither! That'll drag the bloody culture punter in. Look, I've got pictures of John Betjeman on the cars.'

He pointed to the street level. 'There we go. Dodgems on the bus lanes. Who needs bloody bus lanes, anyway?'

'Buses?'

'Yeah, old people. But this is . . . A New Slough for a New Millennium. And it's going to be FUN.'

Fay looked more closely at the drawing. 'There seem to be an awful lot of hamburger outlets.'

'Sponsorship, innit? The Brussels Sprouts can't exactly argue with public private partnership, can they? They bloody invented it.'

'And what's that?' She pointed to a huge tent in the centre of the shopping area.

Ross leaned over the table. 'What,' he said, 'is the one thing that binds our world together through the eyes of the young? That moves us on, that keeps us together no matter what the colour of our skin, our religion, our dreams?'

'Sunny Delight?'

'Computer games,' he said proudly. 'We're going to have the best, most fuck-off, brand newest computer games festival in the world. If you can shoot it, punch it, blow it up or drive it off the road, we'll have it.'

He stood back as if expecting applause.

'So you're saying pretty much,' said Fay, 'that you're designing a European festival of culture entirely for fourteen-year-old boys.'

Ross grinned wolfishly. 'They're going to inherit the world, aren't they, pet? There's your babies.'

* * *

Marcus was staring at the spreadsheets in disbelief, as Arthur, Rafe, Cathy, Sven and Gwyneth sat across the table looking like guilty schoolchildren. Sandwiches was sitting on a chair looking martyred; whatever was going on here, this was nothing to do with him.

'But,' Marcus said in his pained way, 'I thought you meant – when you said "management exercise", I thought you really did mean that it was going to be just a "management exercise". "Concept" . . . "Direction". You know, for imaginations and brainstorming and stuff.' He said 'imaginations' as if he were pronouncing it in a foreign language. 'I didn't think we were actually planning to do any dumb idea someone shouted out just because they were cold and wanted to go home.'

The rest of the group looked at him impassively.

'What next? Do you want to build a wall around the city and dig a moat?'

'Yes!' said Arthur, Rafe and Sven simultaneously.

'I'm being sarcastic. I mean, have you any *idea* what these kinds of things cost? It's like, do you want *magic elves*?'

'Yes!' said Cathy and Gwyneth.

'I'm obviously going to have to work at this sarcasm thing,' said Marcus, patting his papers carefully. He sighed and sat back in his chair.

'I mean – it was fun going out and everything, but you've read the scroll . . . I mean, the guidelines. We have to provide sustainable achievable goals to attract people to our environment; to make them happy, and awe-inspired, and give them a sense of learning and wonder.'

'Do you know what happened the last time someone said that?' said Arthur, fiddling with his pencil.

'What – goals?'

'Yes – goals, targets, sense of learning, sustainable . . . all that bullshit. Do you know what you get with that?'

'Projects finished in time and on budget?'

'You get the bloody MILLENNIUM DOME!' said Arthur. 'We are going to have to think just a *teeny* bit beyond the spreadsheets for once.'

131

'I thought the Millennium Dome was quite good,' said Marcus, straightening his spectacles on his nose. 'But, I mean, what's instructive about building the biggest maze in the world?'

'What's instructive about having a festival of culture in the first place? We should just give the budget to the hospital to fund kidney machines!' said Arthur.

There was a long and uncomfortable pause around the table.

'Um,' said Gwyneth.

Everyone looked at each other.

'Well, it's not called the European City of Kidney Machines,' said Gwyneth.

'Maybe it should be,' said Marcus.

'Look,' said Arthur. 'If we write on our entry forms, "our plans to make Coventry the European City of Culture are . . . seventy-five kidney machines," we're all going to be back-stapled to our cubicles by the spring.'

'We need culture,' said Gwyneth. 'Have you ever driven past the Angel of the North? Doesn't it lift your heart when you see it?'

'Not as much as the sight of a kidney machine would if I was dying of . . .' began Sven.

'Okay, okay,' said Arthur. He looked around the table. 'I'm here because I believe in this project.'

'And to avoid getting made redundant,' said Sven quietly to Sandwiches.

'If anyone wants to go off and help the world in some other way, they can. But this is our way, right here. And it's the best we're trained for and the best we can do, so I think it's valid that we try and create something great and wondrous and just brilliant, without focus groups and desperate marketing specs and a million small-minded consultants – sorry, Gwyneth . . .'

'Did you mean me in there?' said Gwyneth. 'I didn't think you thought about me like that before. But *now* I do . . .'

'No, I didn't mean you at all . . .'

'Really? Cos it sounded like you did. Otherwise, you wouldn't have brought it up.'

'I really wish I hadn't brought it up.'

'Yeah, me too. But I guess that's just because I'm so small-minded.'

'Ooh, a lovers' spat,' said Sven. They shut up after that.

'We're going to make this thing work because we believe in it. And that's all I wanted to say,' said Arthur, and he sat down again. 'Now. Marcus. Help us.'

And, inside, he felt strangely excited.

* * *

'Ah, there you are.' Arthur popped his head round the door. Lynne looked like she was picking

133

something out of a large pile of soil on the floor, although it was hard to tell amongst the haphazard detritus. Outside the window, some beautiful red and gold leaves were gently falling, and there was a smell of bonfires in the air.

Lynne looked up and smiled kindly, taking off her half-moon spectacles and rubbing her nose tiredly.

'Oh, hello, Arthur.'

'You haven't been here when I've tried to see you the last couple of times,' said Arthur. 'If I wasn't such an obviously sane person I'd think that my therapist was rejecting me.'

Lynne smiled faintly as if she hadn't really heard and indicated for him to sit down. 'How are things?'

'Better, actually. Since we met you that night . . . people seem to have been getting more into the spirit of it. Well, apart from going on about the money being better spent on kidney machines.'

'What's a kidney machine?'

He squinted at her. 'You're joking, right?'

She shrugged.

'Umm . . . well, I don't know what it does. Filters the blood, kind of thing. Does the work of your kidneys if they don't work properly.'

'A humer cleanser,' mused Lynne. 'Very clever.'

She moved over to the table and started packing

away some very old books and some fish skeletons.

'Anyway, that's irrelevant. On the whole, apart from Sven's ongoing deodorant issues, it looks like we might be starting to pull it together.'

Lynne smiled and nodded.

'What?' said Arthur instantly when she didn't say anything.

'Nothing,' she said. 'Just . . .'

'Lynne, you're being almost coy. What is it?'

She lifted a stuffed mongoose down from a high shelf. 'Give me a hand with this, will you?'

Arthur looked around the office. 'You're not leaving, are you? You are. Where are you going?'

'Oh, Arthur.' She sighed. 'I'm not leaving. Well, not yet. But it's time.'

'Time for what? What are you talking about? Are you just tidying up and I've developed full-blown acute psychosis?'

Lynne sat down. 'I knew this wasn't going to be easy,' she said. 'You're all such smartarses these days, and nobody believes in anything.'

'Huh?'

'Much easier in the old days, you know. Much.' She shook her head.

'Lynne, you're going to have to tell me what you're talking about.'

She sighed deeply. 'Okay, here it comes. You may want to sit down.'

Arthur shrugged his shoulders and didn't sit down. Lynne prepared her face as if this was a speech she'd had to make dozens of times.

'Arthur Pendleton, you are a descendant of the once and future king.'

'I'm a what?'

'You're of Arthurian lineage.'

'Yes, my name's . . . What are you talking about?'

Lynne explained it again. 'You're a descendant of King Arthur. Pretty directly, in fact. And, as part of that lineage, sometimes you get called when you are needed.'

'Nope,' said Arthur. 'You've lost me completely.'

Lynne rubbed her head. 'Okay. Let's try this. Been having any strange dreams recently?'

'No, none at all . . . except, yes,' conceded Arthur.

'Hearing things? Feeling called in any way?'

'Um, I'm not sure.'

'But you've felt differently, though?'

'Well, yes, kind of. Yes.'

He was still staring at her. 'Is this why I think I can ride a horse?'

'That sounds about right.'

'So – what . . . Explain it again.'

'Well, you know who King Arthur was, don't you?'

'Yes.'

136

'Well, he's still King of Britain. Technically. And he is there in times of need. And you are a part of his blood, so you are here in a time of need. That's why I'm here, too. To make sure you realize that, and stay here, and do your duty.'

'My what?'

'Your duty — to this city.'

Arthur sat, looking as if he'd just been hit on the head with a heavy weight. His mouth tried to open, but nothing came out.

'But —' he said.

'Ah . . .' he said.

'This is *bull*shit,' he said.

Finally, he thought of something. He sat up straight and looked back at her. 'Do I . . . do I get any superpowers?' he said.

* * *

'No,' said Lynne.

'But I have got . . .'

'You've got a mission,' she said clearly.

'Really? What? Will I need a sword?'

She shook her head and smiled. 'You're on it, Arthur.'

'What . . . what do you mean?'

She spread her arms around. 'This is it.'

'What?' His face fell. 'Oh, you don't mean . . . you don't mean the City of Culture project?'

Lynne nodded.

'No. You don't.'

'It's your destiny, Arthur.'

'What? What! No. You're telling me I'm a member of this famous lineage and I come from this blood – which is very nice of you by the way, so thanks, although of course I don't believe you or anything – but if I did, I can't believe it would be to run a town planning unit on an industrial estate.'

Lynne patted him on the shoulder. 'You know, most people are very proud.'

'Yeah, that's probably because they've got dragons to slay and lots of beautiful maidens,' said Arthur petulantly.

Lynne raised her eyebrows.

'Are there a lot of us, then?'

'A few. Some have bigger tasks than others.'

'Are there any alive now?'

'I can't tell you that, I'm afraid.'

'Oh, go on. Just tell me one.'

She half-smiled. 'Well, John Lennon was one.'

'Get out!'

'No, seriously. Very nice chap.'

'My dad always said he was our second cousin or something.'

'Twice removed,' said Lynne. 'But yes, he was.'

'Who else?'

'It doesn't matter,' said Lynne. She put both hands on his shoulders. 'What matters is, you have a sacred trust. This city is crying out for beauty, and fairness, and change. And it's in your hands. This is your Camelot, Arthur. And you must shape it. It's your destiny.'

Arthur was shaking his head. 'Who are you?'

Lynne looked at him straight over her glasses. As he looked at her more closely, he finally realized what was so odd about her. Her eyes were hardly those of a person, but those of a hawk. Yellow surrounded an elongated iris.

'Who do you think?'

'Oh, this is PREPOSTEROUS!' Arthur shouted, leaping out of his chair. Lynne turned to pack away some parchment. By the time she turned back, her eyes were completely normal again.

'There will be dragons, Arthur,' she said. 'Just be careful what they look like.'

'What if I can't do it?'

'I'll be here to help you.'

She patted him once more on the arm. He thought of something.

'So, presumably, this is where I got my name from?'

Lynne blinked rapidly. 'No, that's just a coincidence.'

'Oh.'

He headed towards the door. Just as he left, Lynne called out, 'Speak to Fay.'

'What . . . Why should I? She's taken a set of compasses to all my Bruce Springsteen albums and left them on the doorstep.'

'I mean it, Arthur. You must speak to her.'

'And tell her what – to leave my albums alone because she's dealing with a friend of the once and future king?'

She smiled.

'Godspeed, Arthur.'

* * *

Arthur sat up in bed. Since he'd got home, every so often his head would twist around and he would almost feel like giggling. Perhaps this was one of those new management techniques he was always reading about. Convince your workers that it is their true destiny to work ridiculous hours and kill themselves in the process.

How did they ever employ such a nutter anyway? Surely if they really had a therapist he'd at least know something about it? She must be some crazy person. God, yeah, look at her office. She'd obviously walked off the streets and into the right office – after all, there, everything was always somebody else's job. They'd all just turn a blind eye, even if a crazy woman walked in off the streets with a dead mongoose and set up a fake therapy practice.

Yes, that must be it. He'd put in something about it tomorrow.

He shook his head again, then switched off the light and turned over to sleep.

* * *

This time he could feel the horse move under him, the muscles rippling against his skin, the bright cold of the frosted day. The twigs and icicles cracking above him on the trees, the sound of the crisp bracken under the mare's hooves. Sparks from her shoes bounced off rocks.

Gwyneth sat before him in the saddle. She twisted her head to look up at him. 'I'm so, so sorry,' she said.

He shook his head. 'What do you mean?'

But her face was a picture of cold and misery, and she merely stretched out a hand from under her cloak and lightly touched his face. Her hand was cold too, and as he clasped hers with his, she handed him a small white flower.

He woke up with the flower in his hand.

* * *

'Oh crap,' said Arthur to himself in the bathroom mirror.

* * *

He peered into the office, unusually late and still feeling distinctly odd in the head.

Everyone had moved into the boardroom by special permission of Sir Eglamore, and it was completely overrun. It looked like a war room. All the computers had come too so they could work with each other without having to pop their heads over cubicles, and it meant the conversation could run in a constant hum, or in Sven's case, humming and then shouting. There was paper everywhere: charts, graphs, and Marcus's tear-stained financial projections littered the floor. Sandwiches had built himself a tunnel out of the computer paper circling the table, so he could get from one pot noodle to another undetected, and with less chance of getting one of Gwyneth's stilettos in the ear.

Arthur looked in on them with, it struck him, a near parental air. It was strange to feel so separate from them, suddenly. And yet so concerned. He wandered over to where Sven was frantically typing.

'What are you doing?' Arthur asked, gently.

'Why? Nothing? Why? It's nothing. I haven't done anything!' said Sven, whizzing round.

'No, no, I was just interested . . . But it doesn't matter,' said Arthur.

'Oh.' Sven shrugged. 'Well, it's ice density ratios. Look.'

Arthur leaned over his shoulder as Sven pressed a button and initiated a moving graph. 'The ice moves in waves when you change the climate, just like real ice does.'

'That's really nice.'

'Thanks,' said Sven. 'Now, have you finished your bonding textbook bullshit or do we have to talk some more?'

'Never mind.'

Arthur looked over to where Gwyneth normally sat. There was so much to take in and organize that he had started coming in earlier and earlier. It was nice to get some peace and quiet in the morning and it meant he missed a lot of the traffic. Also, Gwyneth often came in early too, and he got a little happy feeling in his stomach when he saw her glide in with her bought-elsewhere coffee, perhaps a wisp of hair across her face if she'd been buffeted by the wind coming in from the car park. She would immediately head to the root of their latest problem – how to move people around the city, how to grant concessions, where to get the staff – with customary directness.

The submissions and presentations were, it seemed, still months away, but the team had to go up in front of the council in three weeks' time to humbly ask them that if, on the complete off chance they were to get some hypothetical money, then possibly, just asking, no harm in taking a punt, could they annex half a park and import the largest maze in the world? And illuminate the top halves of all the buildings? And make a forest out of lamp-posts? And the six hundred other crazy ideas various people popped up with every day — ooh, and by the way, they wanted to pump one hundred tons of frozen nitrogen into the river and freeze it, was that okay, Mr Health and Safety and persons in charge of not letting anyone fall through the ice or inhale poisonous gases?

Part of Arthur felt nervous, but part of him felt like he hadn't had so much fun in years, as he came in, tripped over the mess, shouted out projection figures and tried to get Sven to stop making the maze spell 'fuck off' from above in Danish.

As for Gwyneth, well, he tried (and, had he known it, failed utterly) to stay calm and professional around her, but he was definitely . . . Well, maybe he'd take the team out for a drink to celebrate all their hard work. He knew it was tacky, and that crapping on your own doorstep — even if she did allow him to, uh, crap — was a terrible idea and that it would upset the entire office and unbalance everything and everybody else would hate it (everybody else, actually, already thought something was going on) and it would be terrible . . . ooh, but even just the idea. Maybe a little business trip away . . . He found something extremely erotic about the idea of them knocking over the mini kettle in some three-star travel tavern and banging into the trouser press.

Suddenly, with a shock, Arthur realized he might almost be happy.

He quickly quashed any ideas of whatever the hell Lynne had been talking about, and decided to concentrate on the work in hand.

It was in this state of tired but pleasurable reverie at the end of the day that he parked the car outside the house, looked at the house and thought he really must put it on the market, give Fay some money and move somewhere he didn't hate, when he saw her. At first he thought he was imagining things: thinking about someone and seeing them at the same time. She looked very strange indeed. He watched her for a second, then with a sigh, his stomach plummeting like a runaway lift, he slowly unbuckled his seat belt and opened the car door.

* * *

'Hello, Fay.' Too late, he remembered what Lynne had told him. Dammit, he should have called her before. It was so stupid, and selfish.

He didn't even call me, thought Fay, her hands

clenching at her sides. He puts a bomb under my life and now he tootles up here looking . . . looking *happy*. She couldn't bear it. If she had had the slightest reservation about her plan, about what she'd come here to do, it evaporated. He really didn't give a shit and he'd proved it, every night, every hour she'd sat on her old single bed at her mother's house, crying and crying and waiting for the phone to ring.

'Hello Arthur!' she said gaily, pasting the smile onto her face and stepping forward. 'Just came to pick up the . . . um, coving.'

* * *

'I can't – I mean, you're being so good about this,' Arthur was saying. It was much later. Fay had brought two bottles of wine and he'd drunk most of them.

'Well, there's no point in being unreasonable,' said Fay. 'These things happen.'

They were dividing up what was left of the plants and small ornaments and finishing off a Chinese carryout. After he'd stepped out of the car, Arthur had been expecting almost anything – John Wayne Bobbitt had briefly come to mind – but a smile and a bottle of wine hadn't been on the list.

All the way into the house she'd apologized for

her behaviour before: talked about how shocked she was, but how she was getting on with life as usual.

'How's work?' he'd asked.

'Oh, same old, same old,' she'd replied. 'You know how it gets in that crazy old world of recruitment.'

'Yes,' he'd said, registering vaguely that he never really had.

And now they were lying on the rug, listening to one last unmauled Bruce Springsteen album to ascertain which one of them liked it the best so could take it home, and giggling.

'Well, you've certainly got this stripped down living fashion right,' said Fay, looking round the practically empty sitting room.

'Yes. But it's funny, things keep disappearing. Toilet roll, soap. That kind of stuff. I can't work it out.'

'Oh, it'll come to you eventually.'

Fay rolled herself over onto her stomach and manoeuvred herself towards him.

'What about . . . a little bit of old times' sake?' she said suddenly, sucking seductively on a noodle.

Arthur was drunk but not crazed. 'Look, Fay . . . I don't really think . . . you know I don't think we can get back together . . .'

'I know *that*, silly,' she said, playfully batting him on the nose. 'In fact I'm seeing someone else anyway.'

'Really?'

'Well, kind of. But that doesn't matter. This would just be by way of . . . you know, what do the Americans call it?'

'Don't have sex with your ex, Tex?'

She giggled, letting herself sound more carried away with the wine than she actually was. '*Closure*, stupid.'

'Oh. Is that that thing about the two psychiatrists in Seattle?'

'*No*.'

They were lying side by side on the rug now, their shoulders touching. She leaned her head on his shoulder. Arthur was thinking this was rather nice and odd, and how it really shouldn't be . . .

She kissed him.

It had been a long time since they'd really kissed, properly. Kissing is the first thing to go in a relationship. Everything else just drips down after that. He'd forgotten how nice it was. He'd forgotten what it was like to kiss *anybody*. It was very very nice. He was dimly aware that he was terribly drunk.

'Oh, don't stop,' he said, smiling at her when she pulled away.

'I won't,' she said, running a hand across her shirt and fingering her bra strap.

'But it's just . . . you know, we probably won't see each other again after tonight. Or, it won't be the same.'

She poured out the remainder of the wine. 'So. Tell me everything. Tell me about your life. Just so I know.'

Arthur looked puzzled. His hand followed hers to the bra strap, and she rubbed against it.

'What do you want to know?' he said, wondering when he'd forgotten how soft her skin was.

'Well, tell me about this new job. What are you doing?'

'You really want to know about that?'

She rolled over, unbuttoning her shirt. 'Tell me *everything*.'

And he told her everything.

* * *

'Where are you going?' Arthur was nearly asleep, but he could see her silhouette in the bedroom as she calmly dressed.

'I'm going home. This isn't my home.'

Arthur grimaced. He'd been expecting this, really. You don't just get free sex with someone you used to go out with. It was going to have to be an argument.

'Oh, come back to bed, pet,' he said. 'We'll talk about it in the morning, I promise.'

Fay switched on the overhead light. Arthur winced and stuffed his head under the bedclothes. There was a pause, as if she was gathering her thoughts. Then she began to speak.

'No, I will not come back to bed – look at me, Arthur. No, I am not coming back to bed. In fact, my last cervical smear test was more fun than anything that's ever taken place in there.'

Arthur's head whipped up. 'What?'

'You heard. Ugh, I am so glad I never have to go through *that* again.'

Arthur's head was starting to throb. 'Um . . . wasn't it your idea?'

She sniffed. 'Oh, boys are so susceptible.'

'What on earth are you talking about? What are you going to do – impregnate yourself from the condom and charge me child support? Clone me? Have you taken compromising pictures?'

'Your child! Your child! Ha. HA!'

She stood ready to go in front of the doorway where she knew he could see her. He was cowering under the bedclothes, looking confused and a little frightened of her. Good. If only she could have made him cry.

She took a deep breath. 'No, in fact, I did this for Ross.'

And she turned and walked downstairs and out of the house.

* * *

Arthur felt pinned to the bed. For who? For what? He couldn't even understand what she'd just said. It made no sense. She couldn't mean his ex-boss Ross, could she? She wouldn't. She couldn't . . .

Arthur jumped out of bed starkers and pounded down the stairs. Out on the street, Fay was already in her car, pulling away. He ran out after her before realizing that he was both naked and in absolutely no fit condition to drive, so merely had to content himself with staring angrily and shaking his fist at the departing car.

He turned around wearily, to retreat before the neighbours popped their heads out for a look, and wandered back into the house.

Listening carefully, he thought he could hear the cry of wolves again.

Chapter Six

'You look tired.'

'Thank you. I thought since I got made boss you were going to stop being so cheeky to me.'

'Why?' said the temp. 'Want to fire me?' She pulled a long string of gum out of her mouth and coiled it round her fingers.

'Can't this morning, too tired.'

And, he didn't add, guilt-ridden and ashamed and fearful of what he'd done.

* * *

He couldn't see anybody in the boardroom, even though it was after nine. Just mounds of paper and charts lining the walls and something that looked suspiciously like a model railway, with a small train rattling round the tracks.

Moving forward to examine it, Arthur tripped

over the prone forms of Sven, Marcus, Rafe and Sandwiches, landing rather heavily on his side.

'Oh, morning Mr P,' said Rafe.

'What the hell are you doing?' said Arthur, still spreadeagled on the floor. 'If you're hiding from me, I'll have to point out, it's not working terribly well.'

'It's Sven,' Rafe went on cheerfully. Arthur turned his head. Sven was indeed a horrible colour, and was making quiet groaning noises. In fact, he looked even worse than Arthur felt.

'I'm not well,' said Sven. 'I had a bad tortilla.'

'How many tortillas did you have in total?'

'Just, well, maybe twelve.'

'Uh huh.'

'Lying on the floor is going to help stop him being sick,' said Rafe. 'And we're helping by still discussing work down here. So, actually, it's good really, isn't it?'

'Actually I just fell,' confided Marcus, who was operating the train controls, 'but now I'm down here I quite like it.'

'And he's helping us brainstorm,' said Rafe. 'You know — horizontal thinking.'

'Well, while I'm here,' said Arthur, wondering if this was giving out the right message, but deciding in his extremely messed up universe it didn't really matter, 'is that a model railway?'

Marcus smiled happily. 'Yup.'

'And it belongs to . . .'

'I thought I should bring it in,' said Rafe. 'It'll give us a good idea of how to integrate, you know, the transport network.'

'Uh huh. And not so you can all play with it?'

'No,' said Marcus. Sven grunted his assent with a loud moan.

Arthur gazed at the ceiling. 'So, it's just coincidence that Sandwiches is wearing a guard's hat then, is it?'

Sven looked slightly embarrassed. 'Something like that. Ouch.'

'Sven, if you're not well, go home, or to your cave or wherever it is you live.'

'He can't,' explained Rafe. 'It's the maze guy today.'

Oh, crap. In the confusion of everything that had happened last night, Arthur had forgotten. A man who worked for a maze designing firm was coming up from the south coast to discuss what they were going to do here, and, more importantly, what it was going to cost and how long it was going to take.

'Have you got the swearwords out of it yet?'

Sven turned a jaundiced-looking eye to him. 'Yes.'

'In every language?'

'Unless there are any Sumerian speakers buzzing over the top in low-flying light aircraft, you're going to be fine.'

'Okay,' said Arthur. 'Great. If we can only get off the carpet, everything's going to be just wonderful.'

Gwyneth landed head first over the top of all five of them.

'Oh, Christ,' she said, and flopped, not moving while she caught her breath. Sven grunted, but possibly not with pain at this particular moment. 'Well, if this is the new way of working, can I just remind you, one, that the maze man probably doesn't know this, and two, Sandwiches is too heavy to be riding that goods van.'

'Yeah, all right,' muttered the guys, starting to make moves upwards.

Arthur, being at the end, had Gwyneth's head very close to his. She looked at him briefly.

'Morning,' she said, with a twinkle in her eye.

But Arthur was too ashamed of what had happened the night before to even look at her, and he half-smiled and looked away.

* * *

When he arrived late that afternoon, the first thing Arthur noticed was that the maze man was tall, very tall. He appeared at the door in a dark grey suit which looked like armour. He didn't smile, but stalked in, looking around him.

'The cubicles,' he said, gesturing at the open-plan space. 'Were they designed on labyrinthine principles?'

'Um, I don't think so,' said Arthur, indicating for him to sit down.

'Hum.' The man looked at his well-manicured hands. 'You know, it's a big responsibility, taking on a maze.'

Everyone nodded seriously.

'Do you know how they arrived in history?'

They looked at each other, unsure of his schoolmasterish tone.

'I do,' said Gwyneth suddenly. 'They're Welsh. Brought here from Troy.'

The maze man nodded solemnly, but the others just looked at her. Sven snorted.

'Welsh people think everything came from their country, even when it's bollocks.'

'No, right. Another thing that came out of Wales was rollmop herring. Or was that Denmark? I can't remember.'

Sven shrugged. 'I'm just saying, that's all. It's not all down to the Welsh, you know.'

'I don't know. Best king of England,' said Gwyneth sharply.

'Who's that then? The Prince of Wales? I don't think so.'

'King Arthur, actually,' said Gwyneth. 'If you know anything.'

'Was he Welsh?' said Arthur.

'Yup!'

Great, he thought to himself. I'm not only a Coventry town planner, I'm also Welsh.

* * *

The maze man regarded them without smiling and laid out some sheets of parchment on the table.

'Now, what do you want? A maze or a laby-rinth?'

They looked at him.

'What's the difference?'

'Dead ends. A labyrinth doesn't have any. It just takes you through, and it's the journey that's important. It's ritualistic. Whereas a maze is . . .'

'Actually fun,' said Sven.

'Labyrinths are quite fun, in fact,' said the man. 'They're often used in courting rituals, certain dances . . . often there's a prize of some sort at the centre. But, more frequently, they mean a journey. In a maze, you have to make a decision as to whether to travel left or right. With a labyrinth, your only decision is to begin your journey. That's why priests have used them for so long. They are reflection times.'

'So, basically, it's just walks that priests like to

do?' said Sven. 'Right, that sounds great.'

The man looked at him sadly, then turned around. 'I think perhaps my work is not for here,' he said. 'Excuse me, everyone.'

Arthur stepped forward. 'No, hang on a sec. Sven, go feed Sandwiches.'

Sandwiches immediately started hopping up and down excitedly on his stubby legs. He stumbled to the door and started jumping up and attempting to bite the door handle. Drool ran down the door. With a sigh, Sven lumbered off after him.

'I'm sorry,' said Arthur to the man. 'I think he wanted to design it himself.'

The man shrugged. 'It is not so easy as . . . drawing on paper.'

'No, I know. Please, don't go just yet.'

The man nodded, and pulled at his enormous briefcase. Out of it he drew some large, flat, cardboard packs. On the table in front of them, he slowly opened up the packs, one after another.

The whole room gasped. When the cardboard was unfolded, it revealed a series of 3D models of mazes and labyrinths. They were perfectly painted and designed, with hedgerows, flowers, fountains and small figures running through the high trees.

'They're so beautiful!' exclaimed Gwyneth,

lowering her face to the level of the table. 'I feel I could run inside them.'

From a table-height perspective, her eye line was completely suffused with green. Close up, she could differentiate between yew trees and rosebushes; high bushes, like the Sleeping Beauty's, or long avenues of straight planting. The figures were painted as if from a fairy tale; the women wore girdles and wimples and were being chased by tall noblemen. Gwyneth felt she could almost hear music; the power of the lute pursuing her as she ran, faster and faster towards the forbidden centre . . .

She shook herself and stood up again, to find the maze man looking at her curiously.

'You like?' he said, in his curious 'mittel' European accent.

'Very much.' She nodded.

'The power of the labyrinth,' he said. 'It's very strong.'

Rafe pulled down the enormous map of Coventry on the wall, and pointed out Chapel Fields. 'We wanted it for here.'

The man stepped up and examined the map carefully. 'Hmm, a Cretan of course would be no use . . .'

He studied the shape from several angles, then felt about in his breast pocket. Into the hexagonal edge of Chapel Fields, he slotted this:

It fitted perfectly. They all stared.

'That's just right,' breathed Gwyneth. The twists and turns seemed to reflect the trees of the park itself.

'It's perfect,' said Arthur.

'We're in,' said Rafe. 'Let's go to the pub.'

It was the fact that he said it so casually, Arthur reflected later, as if this would be the most natural thing to do in the world – bunch of people working together, going to the pub. But in fact, differently to every other office, possibly in the country, they had never drunk together. There were Christmas parties, obviously, and the occasional leaving bash, but to actually choose to spend time with each other outside of office hours did seem very strange indeed.

At first they all looked around.

'What's the matter?' said Rafe. 'Have I committed some kind of a big old weird office faux pas?'

They still stayed silent.

'Nooo,' said Arthur. 'Um, do we know where there's a pub round here?'

'There isn't one,' said Sven scornfully. 'This is a motorway. They don't put pubs on motorways. Although maybe we could start.'

'No, no – I think the whole not drinking/driving at ninety miles an hour is probably all right for now.'

Everyone stood around hesitantly, not quite knowing what to do.

'Well,' said Rafe. 'Why don't we all go home then meet in, say, the Lion Rampant at seven?'

Arthur waited for everyone to make lame excuses and sidle away, but people were nodding in agreement and picking up their coats.

Gwyneth raised her eyebrows. 'Okay,' she said, 'I'll see you all there.'

And she walked out.

'Do you know,' said Sven, as they picked up their bits and pieces and continued after, 'I thought she was going to be a completely stuck up cow.'

Yes, well, that makes two of us, thought Arthur ruefully.

'But now I think she might be all right. Pretty . . . *shaggable*, in fact.'

Oh crap, thought Arthur. that really *does* make two of us.

'You'd never get her,' said Marcus scornfully. 'Do you really think she'd go out with some backwater jerk from Coventry? She's probably got some famous London boyfriend or something. She wouldn't want to be slumming it here with you.'

The words felt like an awkward stabbing pain to Arthur.

'Sure she would,' said Sven. 'Have you never seen any porn? Everyone knows Danish people are sexy.'

'Yes, so slim, tall and unbald . . .' said Marcus. 'And they smell nice, too. And they're almost all dog-free . . .'

Sven was already heading towards the door. 'Come on, Sandwiches. Let's go get dolled up. I think tonight might be our lucky night.'

'I'd put my money on Sandwiches,' said Marcus.

* * *

The Lion Rampant was glowing like an island of warm light at the bottom of Station Road, and looked exactly the right place for a weary traveller. The eighteenth-century tavern still clung onto a residue of its original, wood-timbered charm and had managed to resist – so far – being turned into some terrifying theme bar, with matching casuals in shiny suits drinking Metz and boring pissed-up miniskirted teenagers about the engine models of their new cars.

Arthur was the last of the group to arrive out of the wind and the cold.

He stood at the door and looked in for a second, observing the group as they sat in a circle.

Rafe was in the centre, illustrating a story vividly with his hands. Cathy was sitting on his left, completely engrossed and watching him fondly. Arthur wondered how she'd got out of making dinner for her horrible family. She was sipping sherry and already looking faintly tipsy. On Rafe's other side was Gwyneth, then Sven and Marcus, who were arguing – probably about robot wars again. Sandwiches, wearing a rather dashing neckerchief, was sitting on Sven's lap.

They did, Arthur reflected, look like a group, finally; a team of people, together. They could have been any bunch of friends anywhere. And he found this rather reassuring as he started to shrug off his heavy mackintosh and walk into the welcoming circle of light.

* * *

'All I'm saying is,' Sven was pointing out, 'when we totally revolutionize this town, right, if they want to put us in charge, we should let them.'

'I don't quite think that's ever going to happen,' said Arthur, sitting down next to Gwyneth. 'Why are you talking about this?'

'Hello! HELLO!' Sven waved one of Sandwiches' paws in front of his face in a particularly annoying manner.

'What?' said Arthur. 'Don't do that with that dog. It's unhyg—' He noticed Sven was letting the dog sip from his pint. 'Never mind. What is it?'

'All I'm saying is, why not? If we make everything lovely and fun, right, I don't see why we can't be crowned kings or something.'

Rafe leaned over and giggled. 'What would you do if you were king, Sven?'

Sven shrugged. 'I don't know. Probably something about pet passports and herring import licences.'

'Well, that would be worth it.'

In deference to Sven, the table had a round of Skol, with a sherry for Cathy.

'What would you do, Rafe?' asked Gwyneth. She'd changed into a soft grey sweater with a red skirt and knee-length boots, and she knew she looked good. Plus, next to Cathy with her sweet, collapsing face, she knew she looked even better, and that this wasn't a particularly nice thing to be thinking, but that it was true nonetheless. She was chatting to Rafe to see how Arthur reacted, but he didn't seem to notice. It wasn't as if Rafe wasn't cute. Oof, perhaps the Skol was a little stronger than she was used to.

Rafe looked up for a minute as if this was the best question he'd ever been asked. 'Well, there's the wenches peeling grapes for you,' he mused. 'But that's just for starters.'

'Grapes!' said Gwyneth. 'That's really the first thing you'd think about if you were a king? What about world peace?'

'Ah, but you see, it's very hard to get world peace without grapes being involved. That, tragically, is what so many of our world leaders just don't understand.'

'Wenches, too?'

'Well, you know, women – the peace-making species.'

Sven snorted vigorously.

'Nah, I don't think I'd really want to be king,' said Rafe. 'All that responsibility. I mean, look at our Arthur here, and he's only the project manager.'

Arthur had in fact been miles away, thinking of Fay. What was she up to? What was she doing? He ran last night over and over in his head, but it never came to any better conclusion – she had been pumping him, quite literally, for information, and she was going to take it back to Ross.

That meant a couple of things: either that slimy little bastard was going to use it to rubbish him in front of – well, the committee, or the local papers – or he was going to rip everything off. Either way, it didn't bode well. How could he have been so stupid? Why hadn't he stood up to Fay in the first place? Or been nicer to her, as Lynne had suggested? Or . . . well, not just shagged her first chance he got. He winced. Dammit. He had got every single thing wrong.

'We're wondering what it would be like to be king,' said Gwyneth. 'And how you cope under such a heavy burden.'

'Er . . . I'm not king,' said Arthur, unsure if he was being wound up or not. Maybe he was giving off king vibes.

'No, we know that,' said Marcus, exaggeratedly slowly. 'We're just wondering what you would do if you were.'

Arthur furrowed his brow. What were they talking about? And if you were king, did you get to choose whoever you wanted to go out with you?

He shrugged, hundreds of things in his head. 'Well, I guess I'd start with the wenches.'

'So, that's settled,' said Rafe, getting up to buy another round.

* * *

'What's the gossip round this place anyway?' he asked, as he returned, putting down the tray of drinks. There was silence.

'You mean . . .'

Rafe looked around. 'I heard, when I left college, right . . . I mean people were always talking about what people in offices got up to. Behind the filing cabinets, right, and Christmas parties and . . .' He paused as the others looked at him. 'It was all a big con to make me go to college, wasn't it?'

They nodded slowly.

'What about . . . you know, creative fulfilment, self-direction, that kind of stuff?'

The table shouted with laughter.

'Don't worry,' said Arthur. 'It's not that bad. You know, this whole being trapped in an office for all the daylight hours of your natural life type thing.'

'Really? I mean, what would you rather be doing, if you could do anything?' said Rafe.

'I'd do this,' said Sven, decisively. The table looked at him. 'Aha! But at NASA.'

'Ooh, yes. That sounds good. Can I come with you?' said Marcus.

'Marcus, you have got the worst imagination of anyone I have ever met,' said Arthur.

'Show me an accountant with a good imagination and I'll show you a direct route to jail,' said Marcus. Arthur nodded. Rafe turned to him.

'What about you two? NASA related or not?'

'I'd rather be out riding,' said Gwyneth and Arthur instantaneously. They stared at each other.

'You ride!' said Gwyneth. 'What do you ride?'

'Um . . . er . . .' Oh God, thought Arthur. How could he tell her he'd never been on a horse in his life, and what on earth had he been thinking when he'd said it?

'I've got the most gorgeous mare out near Huntingdon,' she said. 'What stables do you use?'

'Oh, no, I hardly ever ride now,' he said, blustering slightly. 'But I miss it from, you know – the old days.'

'Oh, you must come up one weekend and have a shot.'

Arthur winced: the joy of spending the weekend with Gwyneth versus the fact that he didn't know the arse end of a horse from a tractor.

'Yeah, that would be great,' he said. He could sort out the other stuff later. Either learn to ride very very quickly or own up . . . No, no, he could learn quickly, surely. 'Don't worry, Rafe.'

He changed the subject. 'It's not too bad. Welcome aboard. We'll try not to make it just like any other boring old job.'

'No,' said the stocky figure who had suddenly planted himself in front of them, his face grim. 'We're about to make it much, much worse.'

* * *

The table stared in amazement. Arthur's stomach dropped through his boots.

It was Cathy who finally broke the silence. 'Ross!' she said, blushing and delighted. 'Come and have a drink.'

'I won't, thanks,' he said, surveying the room. All the fake smarminess he used to show around the office had gone. Instead, there was just a nasty cast to his eye and he gave off an aura of snarling. Of course, it helped that Dave Gorman was standing next to him, looking huge compared to Ross.

'But I've been hearing a lot about what you shower have been getting up to.'

Arthur felt his stomach turn into a plummeting lift. Gwyneth looked at Ross, completely unfazed.

'Really?' she said blandly. 'That's nice. Impossible, of course.'

Ross didn't budge. Seated half-hidden, a couple of tables away, Fay looked white. Inside she was furious. This information was meant to give them an advantage when it came to doing their jobs. Not to be used in some kind of pissing competition. But she couldn't leave now; she knew how unpleasant Ross could be and she didn't fancy risking it.

Gwyneth was looking entirely unimpressed by Ross. Fay glanced at her, then looked at how close she and Arthur were sitting together. Oh, bugger it. She looked again, realizing she was probably being paranoid, but couldn't help staring anyway, comparing Gwyneth's shiny hair to her own frizzy flop with the highlights growing out of it: Gwyneth's Jigsaw to her Jonelle.

Fay realized immediately why Arthur hadn't rung, and her bitterness and hatred reasserted itself. She couldn't compare. 'Go, Ross,' she whispered under her breath.

'Yes, well . . . of course,' said Ross, turning round as if he was going to go, then turning back. 'Oh, and good luck with getting planning permission for that maze, by the way.'

Gwyneth had been about to make some casual retort, but instead felt as if someone had punched her. 'How – how on earth . . .'

'Although,' Ross went on, lifting his pint to his lips, 'there won't be much left for bribing the planning committee after you start on your ridiculous ice magic programme. Cheers.'

He and Dave choked with laughter.

'Ice magic – yeah,' said Dave.

Arthur cringed in disbelief. He could throttle Fay. He could throttle himself. He could see her in the corner, not meeting his eye, focusing instead on Gwyneth, who had risen to her feet. White with rage, she towered over Ross with her heels on.

'I'm so sorry you got fired,' she said. 'Oh, no – hang on – I'm not at all.'

'Don't worry about it,' said Ross, directing a pitying look at Arthur. 'I'm just sorry you have to work with that piss-poor failure machine.'

Arthur jumped up immediately. 'If you want to talk like that to her, I recommend you remember the last time you and I met!'

Ross took a pace backwards, but Dave stood where he was. Ross wasn't finished. He looked pointedly at Fay, then back to Arthur.

'Nice to know you're still doing your ex-girlfriend. Have a good time on Tuesday night, then?'

Gwyneth stared at Arthur in horror, as Fay rose and stood next to Ross, who took her hand. 'Thanks for all the info, *mate*.'

'What . . . what are you talking about?' Arthur couldn't take in the unfolding nightmare.

'Took that job at Slough, didn't I? Me and Fay here. Or didn't she tell you?'

Arthur stood stock still.

'Magic ice!' Dave was still snorting as they left the bar.

* * *

'You see,' said Sven patiently, 'what you're supposed to do is sleep with them and get information from *them*. Haven't you ever seen any James Bond films?'

'But I didn't *know* she was working for him,' said Arthur in anguish, for the nineteenth time. It was much later. Everyone hated him. 'And anyway, it won't be too bad, will it? I mean, either he can copy us and we can tell people it was our idea first . . .'

'*Lame-oh*,' said Sven.

'Yeah, okay. Or, he can do something different so it doesn't matter.'

'No,' said Gwyneth, shaking her head. 'That's not it at all. He can tell the local newspapers. Launch a rubbishing campaign. Speak to local councillors and the people who are meant to be okaying the project. Misinform local environment-alists, so they start campaigning against us.'

Her face looked dull. Inside her head, neon lights were flashing: ALL MEN – THE SAME! ALL MEN – THE SAME! at her in a way that was hard to ignore. 'There's plenty he can do. We might as well just give up and go home.'

Suddenly, Rafe spoke up. 'You're telling me

we can't beat that delinquent dwarf prick? Just because he's heard one or two things we *might* be getting up to? Bullshit! We should hardly even worry about it. Actually, we should get Arthur to sleep with that girl again and this time feed her false information.'

'No, we shan't be doing that,' said Arthur.

'Well, okay. But for goodness' sake – this is only one tiny little problem. What's in Slough, for God's sake?'

Everyone shrugged.

'Exactly. If he had to make the trip all the way over here just to tell us that – they must be terrified, right?'

Sven shrugged.

'I mean, they haven't a clue what to do so all they can do is slag off and try and intimidate us.'

'I agree with Rafe,' said Cathy, unsurprisingly.

'What else is there to do?' said Marcus.

'Slowly try to resurrect the ashes of my career,' said Gwyneth. 'If I still have one. Night, everyone.'

And she got up and left the bar, nodding at everyone but ignoring Arthur blatantly. Arthur sighed. Well, at least he wouldn't have to pretend to know how to ride a horse.

'Another round?' he said.

'Yeah,' said Sven. 'But try not to sleep with anyone and spill all our secrets on the way over.'

Chapter Seven

The next morning, Arthur knew as soon as he stepped out of the car that it wasn't going to be good. Gwyneth swept past him across the windy tarmac without giving him as much as a glance.

'Look . . . Gwyneth . . . I'm really sorry.'

She turned round shortly. 'It doesn't matter. Only weeks of work down the drain, not to mention however much money and – God, even just to feel there was something going on in the office, in the world . . .' She shrugged.

'It's not over, okay? You heard what Rafe said last night. It's my project anyway, and I say it's not over.'

'You can say what you like.' Gwyneth marched past the temp. 'It doesn't change a thing. Look what you've done to morale, to motivation . . . Arthur, I can't even tell you how serious that is.'

Rafe came running up to them through the double doors. 'Come quickly!'

'What?'

'Just – just come!' He was smiling. Gwyneth squinted, but they both followed him into the boardroom. The others were standing around, also all grinning broadly.

'What is it?' Arthur reached the doorframe and saw what the others were looking at. He gasped too.

Gwyneth was already kneeling down in front of it. 'It's perfect,' she breathed.

It had arrived that morning from the maze man. It was the scaled mock-up of their maze, complete with little plastic – although amazingly realistic-looking – hedges, on the kind of grass that comes with model railway stations. You could take your fingers and run through it, and around it was everything there should be – the road, the car park. It was so realistic you could almost see the figures move.

'Oh, my goodness,' said Gwyneth. 'The paper model was something, but this . . .'

'This,' announced Sven proudly, 'is the absolute SHITS!'

'Nicely put,' said Arthur, but it was undeniable that the model was beautiful. If you caught sight of it out of the corner of your eye, you could swear the tiny bushes actually moved in the wind.

Gwyneth picked up the letter that had come with it. 'Oh,' she said. 'We still have to choose what to put in the middle of it.'

'What about Ross's head on a stake?' said Arthur.

'I think, a very large statue of Sandwiches,' said Sven. Sandwiches woofed appreciatively.

Marcus looked at the letter pensively. 'You could put an enormous pile of burning money. Then it would match the rest of the project.'

Gwyneth looked at it and shook her head. 'No, it needs something really special. Something beautiful. There aren't enough beautiful things in Coventry. But we'll find one.'

'And if that doesn't get us planning permission, I'll eat my pyjamas,' said Sven.

The model seemed to have lifted people into a positive mood again, even if it was temporary. Arthur tried to catch Gwyneth's eye, but she was having none of it.

'That's great,' he said. 'It feels like we're moving! Now, the ice festival – Sven, where are we with the nitrogen people?'

Sven grinned again. 'Good news. They won't say it's *impossible*.'

Arthur waited. '. . . And?'

'What do you mean, "and"? Isn't that brilliant?'

'Sven, pig heart transfusion is possible, but that doesn't mean it is in the *Yellow Pages*.'

'You are boring. Anyway, they told us to go visit them.'

'Where are they?'

'Milton Keynes. Largest indoor ski slope in the world. They do fake snow, ice, you name it.'

'As long as it's snow and ice,' said Gwyneth.

'Well, yeah. But they sounded excited.'

'I'm not surprised,' said Arthur. 'If the most they've ever done is an ice rink and a small ski slope, a river is going to be something of a challenge. Is this a big company, or two blokes in a hut drinking mugs of tea and shredding polystyrene really quickly?'

'They just said it was possible,' said Sven, 'that's all I know, okay? Right. Do you want me to go and investigate the pig heart thing now?'

'No,' said Arthur. 'Just leave all that for now. Rafe?'

Rafe was waving excitedly. 'Look,' he said. He brought out a series of photographs of the tops of the houses of Kingsland Avenue. 'I went and took these at the weekend. Here's what I thought we'd do – go to each household and ask them if they want to be a part of this thing.'

'Which of course they will,' said Gwyneth drily.

'Yeah, 'course they will. Anyway, when they've said yes, we do this.'

He took out another sheet of paper, onto which the outlines of the houses in the photographs had been carefully traced. Around the rooftop drainpipes of each house were large fairy lights, making it look as if a Christmas wreath had been stretched the length of the street, illuminating the unusual gabling, Tudor-panelled windows and intricate chimneys. In each window – one for each house – a lamp was gleaming.

'What's that?' said Gwyneth, looking at the picture.

'This is what I'm thinking,' said Rafe. We get everyone to string lights like this, right, so it doesn't go in their windows or anything.'

'Apart from the people who steal them,' said Arthur.

'And the people who have dogs and their dogs sometimes eat light bulbs if they're in a bad mood because they're not allowed to have chicken bones,' said Sven.

'Okay, well, let's worry about that in a minute,' said Rafe, uncharacteristically terse. 'Then, we ask them if they want to shine a light in their main windows too.'

'Why?'

'Well, first off, most people's bedrooms won't be facing the road, will they? That'd be stupid.'

Arthur nodded.

'Anyway, it's just a gentle light. Really soft lighting, like an oil lamp.'

'Why?' said Gwyneth.

'Well, because it's comforting, for starters. It feels welcoming. But also, if it's symmetrical – look. It will lead people's eyes up . . . here.'

He turned over the page, and it was rows of dark streets, all leading up to the same focal point – the ring road. At each junction, Rafe had drawn a little forest of lights – lamp-posts close together, giants, wrought-iron period pieces, normal street-sized ones – it looked like a bouquet of lamp-posts growing out of sheer concrete. It was bizarrely beautiful.

'Can you spell "crash risk"?' said Gwyneth.

'No, but look,' said Rafe. 'With the strings of lights along the tops of the houses . . . from the air . . .' He opened another page of his sketch book, '. . . The ring road will look like a star.'

It was true. In the shot from above, the clusters and delicate outward fronds looked like a giant star, or sun. Or jellyfish, thought Arthur, but he had to concede it was very pretty.

'So, it's what . . . a landing strip for birds?' said

Sven, studying the picture from several angles.

'No, it's just what people will see when they fly over. It'll be visible from planes. It'll be amazing! People will want to go up to high places just to see it! *And* it won't be that expensive.'

'See,' said Sven, 'if you'd let me have that swearword in the maze we could have killed two birds with one stone and just lifted people up on a big crane or something.'

'Yes, well, having even more cranes in Coventry might come across as counterproductive,' said Arthur. 'Rafe, it's great. And it looks like it might not be too dear. Check out it's not going to kill anyone in the manner of bogus lighthouses. Then some lucky team is going to get to start sounding out the residents . . .'

Rafe's face lit up like one of his thousands of light bulbs. 'Cool!'

Arthur couldn't help half-smiling to himself. He looked over at Gwyneth.

She sniffed at him, and stared furiously at the plans.

'Okay, well, great!' said Arthur, pretending he hadn't just been snubbed really badly. I guess the next thing we have to do is get ready for the planning committee . . . with this . . .'

You couldn't help but smile when you looked at the model of the maze.

* * *

Ross sighed as he rolled up his trouser leg. Going to these bloody meetings was bloody boring – let's face it, most of the Black Knights were hopeless bloody snobs, only joining their pathetic so-called secret society to get away from the wife, to try and make a few business contacts or to get their kids off minor drug offences by hanging out with the chief constable – but in this case, needs must. All senior councillors in the area, practically, were members. At least, the powerful ones were. Gave them a social life – no-one else would want to go anywhere near them, if they didn't have to by virtue of being blood and brotherhood.

For Ross, it was a good chance to get pissed up, have a bit of a chat with that chappy from the planning committee, and, more importantly, get the press on his side. However, he was utterly dreading tonight – tonight was initiation night, and it wasn't going to be pleasant. He walked into the room and looked round disdainfully. He was in the crypt-like cellar of a large hall in the centre of Slough. Men stood quietly in a circle, dressed in masks and ceremonial robes and holding up blazing torches. They were silent, waiting for him.

'Step forward the one they call Mawdryn,' said

the central figure, whose robe had slightly more fancy gold on it than the others.

Ross slouched forward.

'Kneel!'

Ross half-smirked and got down on one knee. The man, his eyes blazing – which was odd, thought Ross, as he secretly knew him to be the editor of the local paper, and a lazy fat old sod at the best of times – leaned forward, to impress the seriousness of the occasion on him.

'Do you, Ross Mawdryn, seek to enter the hallowed halls of the Black Knights?'

'Yeah,' said Ross.

'Yes, oh Grand Vizier,' said the editor, slightly brusquely.

'What?'

'You have to say, "yes, oh Grand Vizier".'

'Oh. Yes, oh Grand Vizi – blah blah blah.'

The men were circling him now, holding the torches high and mumbling incantations in low voices, their shadows high on the cellar walls.

'Do you promise to uphold our principles of loyalty and commerce, raging against the faceless, amoral bureaucracy of the blank, administrative world?'

'Does this mean you're all going to help me get squillions of quid for this town?' said Ross, looking round. The men in masks all nodded feverishly.

'Are you going to help me?' Ross asked the Grand Vizier pointedly.

'Yes,' said the editor.

'Cool,' said Ross. 'Let's go.'

'Now you must swear to keep this a secret or the hawks will claw out your tongue and the wolves will tear your heart.'

'Yeah, yeah,' said Ross, 'we're just putting off the cock-kicking, aren't we? Can we get a move on?'

The Grand Vizier stood up solemnly. 'Before we welcome our Brother Mawdryn – let the painful and difficult initiation commence.'

Ross blew the air out of his cheeks as thirty dressed up middle-aged Slough worthies grinned with glee under their masks and lined up to kick him in the crotch.

* * *

'Okay, the planning committee,' said Arthur. He knew it had been a mistake to call a breakfast meeting. Sven and Sandwiches kept nodding off at one end of the table, particularly unpleasant given the fate of the egg sandwich Sven was holding. Gwyneth had managed to keep up the silent treatment now for a week and a half, which was good going, even by Arthur's long experience with the huff medium. Only Rafe was raring to go, as ever, and Arthur was feeling very grateful to him. They'd even managed to fit in another pint together, just the two of them, although Arthur secretly suspected that discussing mazes with a male friend might be a bit – well – gay. But it was nice, though.

'We have to convince them to give us planning permission for something that's about the size of ninety kitchen extensions. It's not going to be easy. We're going to have to be mature, convincing, dedicated and, er, awake.'

'I'm awake,' said Sven. 'What are we doing today?'

'We're going to whup some ass!' said Rafe cheerfully.

'Oh. Cool,' said Sven. 'Will be there food?'

'Right!' said Arthur, feeling like some kind of ridiculous teacher. 'Remember, we have the total costings, contributions, profit margins, space . . . all on Marcus's super-charts! Gwyneth, you're handling aesthetics – why a maze is the true thing Coventry needs and how this is the only maze it can be.'

Gwyneth raised her head. 'Apart from this, when does the official proposal have to go in?'

'Nobody knows yet. They like to spring it on you, apparently. Sven, your job is to sit outside the meeting room and, er . . . guard us from any interlopers. Now, remember – this isn't just a planning bid. Really, this is us launching the town's bid and marking out what we think we want to do. So, think about that – okay! Let's go! Um . . . asses whup!'

* * *

'You'll be fine,' said Lynne.

'I'm not one of nature's ass whuppers,' said Arthur, fiddling with something he'd found on Lynne's couch. It looked like a fang. There was very little left in the room.

'Lynne?'

'Uh huh?'

'What's going to happen out there? I mean, are these City of Culture people . . . Do I have to fight them?'

Lynne smiled. 'Oh, no. They're not the enemy.'

'They're not?'

'Bureaucracy isn't evil, Arthur. It's neutral. It only seeks to preserve itself.'

'Uh huh,' said Arthur.

'You just have to watch out for people closer to home.'

'Sven?'

Lynne gave him a look. '*Slough.*'

Arthur sat up. 'Look, if you know all this stuff . . .'

'Yes . . .'

'I mean . . . okay, I don't know. Right. Do dragons exist? Who killed JFK? Ooh, what about Jesus?'

'There are many mysteries, Arthur.'

'Oh, don't be like that. That's rubbish! Unless of course you don't know.'

'I do know that the planning committee is somewhat obsessed with timekeeping.'

Arthur looked at his watch.

'But I'm not finished . . .'

'Alas, I'm afraid universal mysteries will just have to keep for today.'

'Bugger!'

* * *

The main council office was a terrible, late gothic monstrosity. Pigeon-stained gargoyles leaned over its dark red precipice-like walls, and, inside, mountains of steps led up to its long linoleum corridors. Everywhere hung curling pieces of paper, warning about things people walking into the chambers should not be doing, and giving their particularly baroque opening hours (9.22–11.15, 14.57–16.01, winter times). It smelled of old schools, chalk and damp overcoats, and Gwyneth's heels clicked loudly as they made their way down the endless corridors.

Arthur was nervous. This was the first fence. How he performed here was, on the whole, pretty important. He didn't know who was going to interview them, but he hoped they'd be sympathetic. He hugged his overheads closer to his body and smiled round at everyone. Everyone smiled back except Gwyneth.

* * *

'Come in.'

The voice that was calling out from the room did not sound friendly. They had been sitting there, drinking revolting coffee and waiting, for twenty-five minutes, getting increasingly agitated and worried. Marcus was feeling sick.

The group got up, and Arthur pushed open the heavy wooden door.

The room was large and panelled. Once smart, it now bore a patina of minutes and boredom – the tables, once ornate, were scratched and covered in coffee rings; the chairs were cheap plastic standard issue.

There was a long desk against the far wall. Behind it sat three figures, barely lit by the weak sunlight coming through the high windows. The whole place was dusty. The central figure was tall and forbidding-looking. Heavy eyebrows overshadowed his long face. He didn't smile when they entered. To his right was a woman dressed in a suit straight from Conservative Party central casting. She nodded her head formally. And to his left was a very quiet man who neither looked up nor spoke throughout the proceedings, but concentrated on scratching notes on paper with a fountain pen.

'Um, hi,' said Arthur, giving what he hoped was an open and confident smile. It wasn't returned.

'I'm Arthur Pendleton, from the district department to discuss . . .'

'We know why you are here,' said the man in the middle. His voice was low and ominous. 'Proceed.'

Arthur nodded in a way that attempted to convey that he didn't mind this little brushoff in the slightest, and started to outline the project, whilst Marcus distributed handouts and tried to get the overhead projector to work.

'Thank you for agreeing to look at our submission. Now, this is what we're planning . . .'

Ten minutes later, Arthur was struggling. He was getting no feedback from these people, none at all. No-one was smiling, not even when he made his patented hilarious lost children joke. They were scarcely glancing at their handouts. The woman kept looking at her watch. This was making Arthur angry, which didn't quite reconcile with the light, open approach he'd been aiming for.

'So you see, that's the space problem solved . . . car parking . . .' he stuttered, 'and, overall, it'll be good for families, and I see your granting permission as the first step on a much better road for Coventry. And . . .'

He ran out of words.

'And, that's it. Thank you for your time,' he concluded.

The panel sat back, still eerily silent. The man in the centre started leafing through the booklet of projections Marcus had put together, without noticeable interest. Arthur felt the palms of his hands begin to sweat.

The moments ticked on, the silence seeming to stretch out into some space of infinite time. He snuck a glance at Gwyneth, who was concentrating extremely hard on the cornicing.

Finally, at some secret sign, all three members of the committee sat back.

'We have recently decided to try out,' said the one in the centre ponderously, 'a new method of assigning credibility. We find the old style too . . . too . . .'

'When we used to ask questions about the project plans,' the stern-looking woman interjected –

she leaned forward on the desk — 'people *lied*.'

Arthur mimed shock and surprise, whilst feeling uncomfortably at the same time that she had just accused every single one of them of being a liar.

'Quite,' said the man in the middle. 'So, we've decided to ask . . . er, slightly different questions. To test your mettle, as it were. See what you're made of as a team. See if you can carry this thing,' — he held up the booklet — 'through.'

They looked nervously at each other. Marcus's eyebrows were raised. Arthur reckoned they were covered if arithmetic came up.

'I will ask you three questions,' said the dark man. 'You must answer them all. If you answer them all correctly, then you may go on your way and do as you wish.'

'What? What the hell is this?' hissed Gwyneth, but Arthur only shrugged.

'Go ahead,' he said.

The man blinked and went on. 'Very well. Ahem.

My first is in the arm but not the hand
My second can be found in both sea and sand
My third cannot be found in skies of blue or
     oceans deep
But locked close in its heart its secrets keeps
My fourth can die but never will be born
My whole is of the night but rules the morn.'

190

Marcus, Gwyneth and Arthur sat stock still.

'*What*?' said Gwyneth, to Arthur, not having recovered her composure.

'Ssh,' said Arthur. 'It's a riddle.'

'I know it's a riddle! What's it doing in a planning meeting?'

'Testing our initiative. Must be one of those new American management techniques. Don't look unsettled.'

'If the first is . . . x,' said Marcus, scribbling on a piece of paper, 'no, that's not going to work.'

'It's not algebra, Marcus.'

'Damn shame.'

Arthur scribbled some notes on his pad. 'My first is in the arm but not the hand . . .'

'A wristwatch,' said Marcus. 'Or, underarm hair.'

'Yes, that would work, if you didn't have hairy palms,' said Gwyneth crossly.

'Ssh. It's letters,' said Arthur. Gwyneth looked over his shoulder. 'Like R or M? Ooh, like the band.'

'Just the one letter. What's the second line?'

Gwyneth thought. 'Something about beaches.'

'A watch at the beach,' said Marcus pensively.

'You just don't get this, do you?' said Arthur. 'Both in sea and sand. That means either s or a . . .' He jotted them down on the piece of paper, then suddenly started. 'I know what it is.'

Gwyneth sniffed. 'What are you, some kind of genius?'

'No, that's me,' said Marcus.

'No . . . it's just – wow! I know what the puzzle means. I understand it.'

Gwyneth sniffed. 'Well, enlighten us, genius.'

He pointed it out. 'Say if the first two letters are "m" and "a".'

'Uh huh.'

'And it's "of the night" . . .'

'Margaret Thatcher.'

'It's a mare. It's a mare, isn't it?' Arthur said to the judges.

'You have *night*mares,' he explained to Marcus's uncomprehending look.

'I'm in one,' said Gwyneth,

'And mayors rule during the day!'

'Oh,' said Marcus. 'This is stupid. Well, the next one's *bound* to be maths.'

'Correct,' said the man.

'Yay!' said Marcus.

'I mean, your first answer was correct. I doubt you will find this one so simple.'

'Yeah?' said Arthur, feeling pleased with himself. 'Let's see, shall we?'

The man coughed quietly.

'I never was, am always to be,
No-one ever saw me, nor ever will
And yet I am the confidence of all
Who live and breathe on this terrestrial
ball.
How loved and feared am I, how short, how
long
Far longer than the night, beyond the reach
of every dawn.'

Now they were even quieter. Arthur felt tenser than ever. Lynne might be fairly sure that these guys weren't out to get him, but it didn't feel that way.

'It sounds like Sven's dog,' said Marcus.

'Yes, that's what they would give us a riddle on,' said Gwyneth crossly. 'Sandwiches. The next one will be about your mum.'

'Are you dissing my mum?' Sven interjected.

'Stop it, you two,' said Arthur. 'We have to concentrate.'

'But this is stupid!'

'I may want to point out at this moment that you are the ones wanting to take public money to build a labyrinth in a park,' said the woman. 'Oh. I just did.'

'I never was, yet always am to be . . .' said Arthur as he wrote out the words. He pondered on whether it might be his namesake and supposed ancestor. Just at that moment he caught the eye of the main judge and had the weirdest impression that he knew what he was thinking. Then he blinked and returned to his papers.

'A baby?' said Gwyneth.

'That never was? An abortion?'

'Thanks for that Marcus, that's disgusting. And how would that have the confidence of all?'

'If it was the baby Jesus, maybe.'

'The baby Jesus,' said Arthur. 'Is he both short and long?'

'Well, I suppose he started off short and got long . . . you know, as he grew up.'

'He doesn't have the confidence of all though, does he?' said Gwyneth. 'I mean, if you're Jewish or something.'

'Terrestrial balls,' said Marcus gravely.

'Oh, God, what's the second verse?' said Arthur. 'Can you repeat the poem?'

The old man did so.

'What's longer than the night?' pondered Arthur.

'Anything over eight hours,' said Gwyneth. 'Depending on the time of year. Oh GOD!' She stood up suddenly in exasperation. 'This is so stupid. I can't believe I'm even here. This is a total waste of everybody's time. This is a serious project to us and everyone involved and we're going to prat it up because of some stupid Gyles Brandreth tactic. Really, I just want to go home and wake up tomorrow and pretend this never happened.'

'What did you say?' said Arthur suddenly.

'I am surrounded by morons,' said Gwyneth. 'This is not good.'

'No, just that last bit again. What did you say you wanted to do?'

'I – I wanted to go home.'

'And?'

'And . . . go to bed . . .'

'And . . . forget all about it tomorrow . . .'

Arthur snapped his fingers.

'I never was and always am to be . . .
Nobody ever saw me nor ever will . . .'

Gwyneth held up her hands. 'I told you, I *don't know.* One of those really small cats?'

'No! It's "tomorrow"! I'm sure of it. Marcus, give me some of the other lines.'

'Far longer than the night, beyond the reach of every dawn . . .'

'It has to be. Don't you see?'

'Like, *Tomorrow Never Dies?*' said Marcus.

'No, like, "Tomorrow never comes",' said Gwyneth. She looked at Arthur, still hostile, but coming round to his point of view. 'That's what it means, isn't it? Yes, I think you're right. It must be.'

'*Tomorrow Never Dies* is a really good film, too,' mumbled Marcus. Arthur looked at them both for affirmation, then took a deep breath.

'It's tomorrow,' he said squarely to the three seated behind the desk. The old man paused for a moment, then, reluctantly nodded.

'Yes!' said Arthur, punching the air – although just the bit next to his hand, and quite quietly.

'Great,' said Gwyneth. 'Can we go now?'

'There is one further question,' intoned the woman. She looked excited. This was obviously her question, her big moment.

'Well, I'm sure Arthur can handle it. He knows everything,' said Gwyneth, shooting him a nasty look.

'Gwyn . . .' said Arthur imploringly.

She stared at him coldly. 'What, am I letting down the team?' she said pointedly.

'Don't go,' said Marcus, suddenly. Gwyneth looked at him. 'You're kind of handy.'

This was the first indication Gwyneth had had from any of the rest of them that she was any use to their office whatsoever. She was touched.

'You mean it?'

Marcus shrugged. Gwyneth sat back down.

'I'm staying for him,' she said to Arthur, in case it wasn't already completely obvious.

Arthur nodded and sighed. No wonder global warming hadn't quite arrived yet. Thawing icebergs actually took for bloody ever.

'Are you all . . . quite ready?' said the now slightly excited-looking woman.

'Yup,' said Arthur.

'Okay then,' said the woman. She leaned forward and asked the question.

* * *

Arthur was puce.

'You can't be serious,' he said loudly.

'Three questions, you were aware of the rules,' said the fussy man. 'We'd like an answer from you, please.'

'Oh, crap.'

Arthur stared at the floor. Marcus's face was burning just from the question. He was desperately hoping not to be asked for input. Only Gwyneth sat stock-still.

Finally, Arthur turned to her. 'Well? Can you?'

She shrugged. 'Why should I?'

'Oh, God, please.'

She still stared straight ahead.

'Please.'

'I'm so angry with you and what you did,' she said, almost despite herself.

'I know,' said Arthur, hoping that he did know; hoping that he knew why. Why would someone get so upset about him sleeping with someone else? Only if . . .

There was silence. Then, slowly, Gwyneth stood up once more.

'Um,' the man said, 'I'm afraid your leader has to answer this question.'

Gwyneth raised her eyebrows. 'Why is that?'

The man looked perturbed. 'Um, I'm . . . I'm sure it's in the rules.'

Everyone looked at the second man, who was still scratching the proceedings into a ledger. Finally realizing that all gazes were on him, he looked up. 'Er.' He started leafing through his scrolls of paper. A shaft of dull evening light breaking through the high windows illuminated the dust rising from the handwritten pages. 'I'm afraid . . . there's nothing *specifically* here.'

'Look again!' said the other man, in outrage. The rustling of the paper continued for several minutes.

'No . . . no, nothing, I'm afraid,' he said eventually.

'Well, this is preposterous.'

'Can she answer or not?' said Arthur.

There was a long silence.

'I . . .' The man cast around, as if looking for somewhere else to go. 'I suppose so.'

Arthur looked directly at Gwyneth.

'What women want?' she said. 'You want me to answer the question.'

'Please,' he pleaded.

'Yes,' she said. Then, calmly, with her usual grace, she approached the table. Without a backwards glance at either Arthur or Marcus, she rounded the table to the left until she came to the woman interviewer. Very carefully, she bent down and whispered in the woman's ear for several seconds, then stood back.

The old man looked at the woman. The whole room looked at her. Very slowly and reluctantly, she nodded. The old man sat back, shaking his head.

'Well,' he said. Arthur was staring at him very very hard.

'I suppose,' he sighed, 'the criteria have been fulfilled. You have your maze.'

* * *

Marcus and Arthur waltzed down the steps. Gwyneth followed them at a slightly disdainful distance.

'We RULE!' said Marcus, narrowly avoiding a large pink bus.

'That was brilliant. I am so happy,' said Arthur. 'Here.' He hailed a taxi. 'As a show of how much I appreciate our excellent work, I'll even stump for a cab.'

'Could this day *get* any better?' wondered Marcus. He jumped into the waiting car. Arthur turned back to let in Gwyneth, but she was just standing, listlessly, in front of the council building.

'Um, you go ahead,' Arthur said to Marcus. 'We'll catch you up.'

* * *

'Hey,' said Arthur, approaching her.

She shrugged.

'Thanks . . . thanks for your help in there.'

'Well.'

'We couldn't have done it without you.'

'No, you couldn't have.'

'What did you tell her?'

Gwyneth laughed. 'You don't expect me to tell you, do you?'

'Worth a shot.'

'If women told men what they wanted, you'd find some way of deliberately screwing it up. Although you seem to manage that perfectly well without any guidance at all.'

He looked straight at her, suddenly serious.

'Would I . . . could you see a way in which I

might be any part of what you wanted?'

Her eyes dropped from his to the ground and she didn't answer him. Her face was bright pink and white, either from embarrassment or rage, he couldn't say.

Suddenly, it felt like time. A feeling of calm went through him. He stepped forward. She didn't step away.

'Hey!' shouted Marcus. 'Am I waiting with this cab or what, only he's going to set the meter running fast.'

Chapter Eight

'It really smells in here,' said Sven, the following morning, as Sandwiches was sniffing round the skirting board of the boardroom.

'No, it smells *clean*,' said Arthur. 'I had the cleaners come in specially. It was getting revolting.'

'Or pleasantly familiar,' said Sven.

'Aorwhoo,' agreed Sandwiches.

Arthur ignored them both and wandered on towards his desk, feeling like humming, or perhaps rendering a couple of verses of 'It's a Wonderful World' – loudly, whilst tap dancing in a Fred Astaire manner over the coffee machine, backed by a hundred dancing girls and a thirty-piece orchestra.

This girl . . . wow, she was something else. He reckoned, if Marcus hadn't intervened, he'd have got a snog, definitely. Maybe his ancestral status was making him more attractive to women, and, if so, why couldn't it have kicked in at college?

'You've got your eyes shut,' said Sven.

'Can we all work like that please?'

* * *

Gwyneth looked at herself in the dressing table mirror. Oh God. What had *that* been about? She couldn't do this again. She'd been attracted to clients before – it was an occupational hazard – and she'd also seen what happened when other people gave into it. You were the talk of the company party. And wasn't it hard enough being a woman here in the first place? She shook her head as she brushed out her hair. This was a terrible idea.

But she still remembered the way his hand had felt on her face . . .

* * *

Arthur's euphoria was brief, slightly overshadowed by Rafe dragging in sixty feet of electrical cable to simulate what a forest of streetlights might look like (after it had been lightly chewed by a dog). But his warm glow carried on, even when Sven got into a complicated and personally insulting conversation with the ice makers, with whom they were due to meet, when Cathy brought in some homemade and completely inedible things which may have been cookies or muffins or slates, and when Marcus asked him to okay an enormous pile of figures, not a single one of which he understood. But where was she?

The glow remained, Arthur's attention constantly straying towards the door. It was torture. How would she be?

He tried to concentrate on the flurry around him, explaining to Rafe that he couldn't have a tram or a Japanese bullet train to ferry people around the exhibitions, and dealing with Sven, who thought his computer wasn't working because his fingers weren't sticking to the keys.

Finally, however, at about ten thirty, he saw a familiar shape make its way through the open-plan area. His heart leaped. Until he saw her face.

* * *

At first he assumed it was because of him. He had – or hadn't – done something. She was suing him for sexual harrassment. He'd been reading this all wrong.

Maybe she was just pretending! To show the others she didn't care . . . But one look at the pained set of her jaw disproved that theory. He looked at her, waiting for the secret sign to show she wasn't cross at *him*. It didn't come.

It must be about work. That must be it. There couldn't be another explanation. She must have got herself all het up about status and professional responsibilities. Well, he was sure he could talk her round that. He'd get a chance to speak to her in private later on. He wondered, seriously, what the possibility of ever getting off with her in the stationery cupboard might be . . .

Gwyneth, unbelievably relieved that nothing had happened yesterday, threw the newspaper down on the table.

Nobody said anything, but gradually, gingerly, edged towards the desk. Once there, they leaned over each other to see what it said.

'Ooh,' whistled Sven thoughtfully.

COVENTRY IN LAUGHING STOCK RACE

Councillors confirmed today that Coventry is being entered for the prestigious European City of Culture awards – previously held by Glasgow in 1991 – by a 'tin pot bunch of useless no-marks' a source high up in the local council revealed today.

'They're out to make us look stupid,' he continued, mentioning that the senior council was 'forced' to pass a motion to allow a maze to take over almost 20% of parkland.

'It's political correctness gone mad,' said the

source. 'Kiddies use this park. They don't want to have to look at some maze.'

Other plans for the submission are said to include 'light flowers' and 'a very large skating rink'.

Chairman of the council Sir Eglamore said today, 'We are aware that Coventry is considering entering a bid for the City of Culture award, however we're sure all entries will be taken purely on merit.'

The bid is said to be led by a low-level manager at the planning department, Arnold Pendleton, who has only recently taken over this post.

Sure enough, there was a blurry photograph of Arthur, taken from the annual report four years ago, looking slightly perturbed and absurdly young. Underneath it said, 'Arnold Pendleton – thinks extra skating rink will impress European bosses'.

Local skating rink manager Howard Franscombe said, 'Well, we know nothing about this. You'd think they might have the courtesy to have a word with us if they're building another rink. Plus, it's not like we're mobbed in here as it is. These are people's jobs they're talking about!'

Park manager Francis Onetapo had this to say:

'Yes, I hear this morning they are taking away half of my park. It's the kids I feel sorry for really.'

Silently, Gwyneth turned to page four.

THE COURIER SAYS

Coventry needs prestige. Of that there is no doubt. But is the right way to go about this really by letting us be held up as a laughing stock and depriving our kids of play areas?

Local government must stop this loony scheme (already tipped to be won by Slough, in Berkshire) and use the money for something really worthwhile in our community – like kidney machines, to name just one example!

The phone rang. Cathy picked it up, then looked rather frightened. 'Arthur,' she said. 'It's the *Sun*. They want to talk to you.'

* * *

Arthur couldn't sleep. It was just turning into dawn and he'd been awake for hours, staring out of his window and watching the frost form on the branches of the emaciated, plastic-looking trees. He had heard the wolves again tonight, and his heart was heavy. He cradled the white flower – he'd pressed it underneath some weights he'd bought six years ago and never got round to throwing away; this was the first time he'd ever used them.

It was no use. The last couple of days had been absolutely awful. They'd hit the red-top nationals: 'Crazy Coventry Cock up!' was one of the headlines. It was a quiet time for news, and any local council wackiness was welcome, it seemed. The letters pages had been full of complaints about money-wasting eejits. Arthur was waiting on a summons from Sir Eglamore which hadn't yet come, making the waiting worst of all. And that moment with Gwyneth . . . she had been so sweet, and so briefly. Now, she wasn't being deliberately hostile to him, but things were just too difficult to take any further.

He heaved a sigh and stood up. Light was just starting to break over the horizon. He'd take a walk. The wolves would disappear for daylight. Maybe he could tire himself out enough for a couple of hours' sleep before he had to go in . . . no. Still, he'd take a walk anyway. There wasn't much else to do.

It was a beautiful morning – frosty, but not freezing; bright and sharp. The town was just starting to stir – one of the few remaining milkmen clattered past on Feldane Road, an early starting postman stomped off in the direction of the high street.

The cars, of course, were still moving; were always moving. And the coming brightness of the morning showed up the damp seeping through the cheap, thrown-together, post-war buildings, the concrete, deliberately, it seemed, stamping ugliness on top of ugliness.

Arthur sighed and wandered on into Chapel Fields.

Here, dog walkers and joggers, wrapped in headscarves and Walkmans, and red in the face, pounded past him. He kept his head down, in case anyone recognized him from his picture in the paper. That was the last thing he needed – someone starting a fight.

His feet were getting muddy as he walked across the wet and crunchy grass in his Hush Puppies, but he didn't care. Let him be as cold and miserable as he could. Suddenly he missed the days when he was a bored drudge, blankly pushing his best days behind him and scarcely thinking beyond his next Chinese carryout.

'Arthur! Hey! Over here!'

He blinked, then walked on, in case it was someone as obnoxious as that overweight journalist who'd asked him why he hated sick children.

'ARTHUR!'

He turned at last. About twenty yards away, he could see Rafe waving wildly at him. His face was pink-cheeked from the cold and some exertion. As Arthur moved closer, he noticed Rafe was wearing mittens and looked not unlike a bouncing Jamie Oliver.

'Hi there!' said Arthur, confused but pleased to see him. 'What are you doing out here? T'ai Chi?'

Rafe looked slightly sheepish. 'Um, no.' He looked around him, slightly secretively, but still didn't say anything.

'You're . . . walking Sandwiches and he's fallen down a well and you're trying to leave the scene of the crime. Don't worry, I'm not going to report you for that.'

'No, Sven told me Sandwiches takes himself on walks. Won't let anyone come with him. Same time every day.' Rafe shook himself to keep warm. 'Er, I was just . . . looking, you know. Looking to see how much space the maze is going to take up, stuff like that.'

Arthur looked around. 'It would be here, wouldn't it?'

'It *will* be here,' said Rafe, sincerely. 'Don't worry about a few stupid newspapers.'

'I wouldn't mind a *few*,' grumbled Arthur. 'It's when it's all of them that it starts to piss me off.'

Rafe smiled, showing white teeth. 'Eh . . .' he said. 'It's only the press. Okay. Tell me now:

who got a doing in last week's *Coventry Advertiser*?'

Arthur shrugged. 'I've no idea . . . em . . . someone connected with the local farming community?'

'Who knows? Probably. Or, you know, could be anything. Naughty vicar. Busty barmaid.'

'Dodgy town planner.'

'See! You're even less memorable than that badger who had twins in a milk float!'

'Yeah,' said Arthur.

And as the two men briefly grinned at each other, he left Rafe tracing imaginary boundaries in the watery sunshine, and returned to his house to get changed. Examining his red-rimmed eyes in the mirror, he felt strangely cheered that someone, somewhere, seemed to be on his side. It seemed odd, given how he felt about Gwyneth, that it should be Rafe.

* * *

'Oh, I am so happy.'

Ross stamped around his office. 'Oh yes, yes, yes, I am. What a lovely day.'

'All you need,' observed Fay, 'is an evil cackle.'

'Bwa ha ha ha,' added Dave Gorman helpfully.

Spreads from the newspapers were plastered around the walls of the office, drawing attention away from the collection of model cars that seemed to be spilling across every available surface.

'It almost makes up for not getting your way with the committee,' said Dave.

'Yes, shut up,' said Ross. 'Who could have guessed they'd have had some stupid bird on their panel, anyway? Lucky fluke. *Won't* happen again.'

He sat down in front of the computer, then stood up once more. 'Ooh, no, let me see the *Courier* again. That is just so sweet.' He rubbed Fay under her chin.

'Well done, sweetheart. Clever piece of espionage.'

Fay twisted aside. She had felt worse and worse about it since it had come out, but she wasn't going to admit this to anyone. In fact, anytime it crept into her conscience at all, she deliberately hardened her heart against it and made herself tougher. Sometimes she caught sight of her mother reflected in her own mirror.

Well, he wasn't going to get the better of her. He deserved this. She squeezed her fingers into her palm and forced herself around with a smile.

'It wasn't exactly what I'd call fun . . .'

Ross and Dave both sniggered dirtily.

'She's a picky lady,' said Ross meaningfully.

She hadn't let him yet, but he was clearly and consistently trying to get into her knickers. At first she considered it, thinking how angry Arthur would be. Now, she didn't think Arthur would even care any more, so why put herself through something that would once have made her ill?

'Yeah,' she said. 'Now, where are we?'

Ross pulled some of his model cars closer towards him. 'Okay, we're going to take this churchyard here, right?' He pointed out a small square of green in the centre of his large map of west Slough. 'Okay, well, that's going to be the main car park, *here*. Then we're going to have moving walkways . . . with fruit machines lining them . . .'

'Moving walkways . . . that's great,' said Dave.

'Yeah – who likes walking? That's for losers who haven't got cars. Okay, have you spoken to the fruit machine guys?'

'Yes,' said Fay. 'He said he can take on fifteen extra men to get them finished in time.'

'Perfect,' said Ross. 'We can leak that to the papers – getting down the jobless totals. How's the planning going for the outdoor bingo?'

Fay shuffled her notes. 'It's going to need a louder public address system. But that's okay, it'll help with the broadcast adverts anyway.'

Ross nodded. 'Well, anything that helps bring in the dough. And it's not as if the town isn't noisy already. Right. How's it going on getting Laurence Llewelyn-Bowen to open it?'

'He says any day between . . . no, hang on, absolutely any day is fine.'

'Great, now, how about the local hunt?'

Dave nodded. 'Yeah, they're on. Apparently they think they've got a bit of an image problem.'

'Really? Well, they won't do after we let them ride through the town. And how about the *Daily Star*?'

'Hmm.' Dave paused. 'I don't think they're too keen on the wet t-shirt competition coming from here. I think they'd prefer Malaga or somewhere.'

'Then speak to them again. Slough is going to be *the* place for girls with big bazooms and wet clothing come next year. Got to get the punters in. Hey, Fay, maybe you could . . .'

'Yeah, no, I won't be doing that,' said Fay quickly.

'Well, they've got Lady Godiva,' pouted Ross.

'I don't care!'

'Huh. Okay, then. Right, and last item on our agenda – the live Robot Wars. Dave?'

'It's looking good.'

Ross stared into the middle distance in what he considered to be a statesman-like manner. 'This . . . it's just going to be so great. Give something back to the town, make an absolute fortune. I mean, live Robot Wars. How cultural is that?' He sighed with happiness. 'Do you know, I think we can treble the fast food concessions in this town in under a year. That's what I call achievement.'

Fay looked at the floor. 'This just gets better and better,' she said quietly.

* * *

Arthur looked at the fax and let it drop quietly onto the floor.

'Oh, well,' he said, attempting a 'don't care' voice.

The fake ice company had withdrawn their offer of help. They couldn't resist alienating their main area client, they explained. Particularly after the bad publicity and everything.

Marcus stood on one leg and scratched his head. 'They said . . . well, the other ice rink was threatening to take away their business.'

'It's not *another* ice rink, Marcus. It's an ice *festival*.'

'Yeah, uh huh,' said Marcus, who wasn't exactly sure of the difference himself, except for several noughts at the bottoms of invoices.

'Fine,' Arthur said. He was saying fine to everything at the moment. If the roof fell in on his office and they were overrun by a freak shower of scorpions, he was going to say fine to that too. Otherwise he had to stop long enough to think about things.

215

Sven leaned over and heaved a heavy sigh. Everyone ignored him. He did it again.

Cathy looked up, vaguely sympathetically. Sven confused her completely, but she was very fond of his dog.

'What is it?'

'Well,' said Sven, then raised his voice so Arthur could hear. 'WELL . . .'

'I'm right here,' said Arthur. 'If I'm ignoring you, it's on purpose.'

Sven ignored him right back and wheeled his impressive form round to face the room. Marcus and Cathy stood on the side. Sandwiches slunk over from where he'd been busy making friends with the curtains and scrabbled up onto his lap.

'Of course,' began Sven loftily, 'I do come from the land of perpetual ice and snow . . .'

'That's right,' said Arthur. 'So, you'd obviously know fuck all about the fake stuff.'

'Well,' said Sven. 'Perhaps there is a mysterious race far in the north of Jutland, who have studied the different formations of snow and ice all their lives and are the acknowledged experts at reproducing it.'

'Do you reach it on the back of a giant eagle?'

Sven ignored him. 'Perhaps they're the famous Skærgård "*Is og Sne Kontor*" renowned throughout the world.'

Sandwiches snuffled appreciatively, but nobody else made a sound.

'I wonder what people think when they hear the words "Seoul Winter Olympics" . . . ?'

'I wonder when the rhetorical questions stop?'

'Seoul,' went on Sven doggedly, 'is a very hot place.'

'. . . And . . .'

'And maybe this rather *high profile event* needed the most *high profile snow and ice makers* in the *world* . . .'

'What are you saying?'

Sven shrugged. 'Just, what do you expect from Mr Freddy Roller Rinks sitting in a shed in Milton Keynes anyway?'

Arthur shrugged. 'I don't know. You're the one who told me they could do pig heart transplants.'

Sven ignored him again and opened his hands. 'You know, this is an art we're talking here. I mean, do you want slush everywhere? Do you want grey ice? Do you want little kiddies falling through the ice?'

'Are you trying to blame the deaths of children on me not listening to your latest hairbrained scheme?'

'No, that was kidney machines,' said Marcus from the other end of the room.

'So, what's the point in doing this if you don't

do it right, yeah? And doing it right means going for the best. And the best is in Skærgård.'

'And you're related to how many of them?'

Sven shrugged. 'None of them. They're just the best in the world at what they do. It's a Danish thing. Like bacon.'

'Like horse porn,' said Arthur. 'What are you proposing?'

'We go there, and see what they do, then you can probably weigh up a decision between them – as artists – and some local Mr Watery-Molecules.'

'An overseas jolly,' said Arthur. 'That'll go down great in the papers.'

Sven turned to him. 'Look, it's not like you have a lot to lose at this point. And now the local boys won't do it, and I'm telling you how good these ones are . . . don't you even want to consider it?'

'Don't they have a catalogue?'

'You can't touch a catalogue! This is so good, it's like real. You can cover the river, decorate the bridges . . . I'm telling you!'

'Okay, okay, I'm listening.'

'We need to see it.'

'Who's we?'

'Well you, me – I speak the language . . .'

'I'm glad to hear it.'

'Gwyneth, Sandwiches.'

'You can't take Sandwiches!'

'Yes I can! He loves Denmark and he's got a pet passport.'

'They gave him a passport?' said Marcus. 'What did you two do, get married?'

Sven and Sandwiches sniffed, and Sven leaned over and ferreted around in his grubby rucksack. He passed over a smart royal blue plastic booklet. Arthur opened it. He looked at Sven, looked at the dog and shook his head.

'You're joking, right?'

Sven shook his head.

'Your dog has a *diplomatic* passport.'

Sven attempted false modesty. 'Yeah.'

* * *

London fell away beneath them, a dingy grey puddle. Arthur sighed and settled back in his seat.

To his right, Gwyneth was buried in a pile of papers. She couldn't understand Arthur at all. Ever since they had nearly . . . well . . . he had paid her no attention whatsoever. That was a good thing, of course, but . . . truth was, his stepping back had piqued her curiosity. She found herself thinking about him more and . . . but no. It was impossible. He was bonking his ex-girlfriend, for one thing, and for another he didn't seem that keen, and for another . . . dammit. She tried

219

to turn her attention back to the cost/benefit analysis.

Arthur looked at her bent-over profile and thought how gorgeous she was. But he'd fucked it up so badly. He sighed.

'What's the matter?' said Gwyneth.

For a moment he considered telling her how he felt . . . no. Being called a dick in public was always embarrassing.

'Nothing.'

'Oh,' said Gwyneth. 'Well, we've had a good response from the street residents,' she said, keeping it purely professional and passing over a sheaf of papers. 'Quite a lot of them want to get involved. Although they seem to think we're taking over their entire electricity bills.'

'Great, that's great,' said Arthur, taking the papers gingerly and making sure their hands didn't touch. 'What about the traders for the fair?'

'Fine. Although I think there's going to be a preponderance of people selling oversized jester's hats.'

'Well, that's traditional. Perhaps we should have a mediaeval dressing up day for the whole town?'

'Yes, maybe. Although the insurance is going to be terrifying as it is. I'm not sure about throwing unwieldy costumes and sharp blades into the mix.'

Arthur looked up. 'Nobody is going to fall under the ice, are they?'

'Just those few small children here and there I expect.'

Arthur looked at her again.

'I'm *kidding*.'

Sven leaned over from where he and Sandwiches were sitting behind them. 'No-one will fall through. I'm telling you, this stuff is more solid than rock.'

Gwyneth snapped her fingers. 'Hey – why don't we have it on some rock?'

'Yeah, yeah.' But Arthur was secretly smiling that she was even bothering to be sarcastic to him.

* * *

It was a plane trip, a taxi ride to the railway station and a long, long train ride through ever-thickening forest, and an ever-darkening sky. The country looked huge, and rather as Arthur had hoped for, he thought, pleased – like somewhere Santa Claus might live, or at least come on holiday from the North Pole. Snow lay thickly on the ground, and reindeer could be made out among the trees when the train slowed. Sandwiches leaped up at the window and gave them menacing looks, his paws scratching against the glass.

'I didn't know Sandwiches got violent,' said Gwyneth. 'I thought he just sicked up on things he didn't like.'

'Yes, that's his primary mode of self-defence,' said Sven. 'But he's always had a thing about reindeer. One antlered him as a pup. He went flying through the air and landed in . . .'

'Some sandwiches?' said Arthur.

'*No.*' Sven gave him a look as if this was the stupidest thing he'd ever heard. 'A bouncy castle. We were at a party.'

Gwyneth couldn't help smiling. 'What on *earth* did Sandwiches look like on a bouncy castle?'

'Oh, he loved it. Wouldn't come off it all afternoon. When he bounced higher than the wall he could see the reindeer. Woofed menacingly at them.'

'Woof,' said Sandwiches.

Arthur shook his head. 'I swear that dog understands everything we say.'

'I know,' said Sven mournfully. 'He's losing all his Danish.'

* * *

Day was turning into evening, and Arthur was starting to worry.

'They will see us, won't they?'

'Oh yes,' said Sven. 'I've spoken to them about it. They'll meet us and talk to us, then decide if they want the job or not.'

'They decide?' said Arthur. 'I thought it was

us who decided whether or not to give them the work.'

Sven huffed. 'Yeah, you wish.'

'I wonder what it was like when I controlled things in my life?' said Arthur. 'Oh yeah, I remember. I never did.'

* * *

Finally, the train drew into Skærgård station. It was pitch dark, and bitterly cold. Arthur absolutely had to put up the hood of his jacket, even though he knew it made him look like a dick.

'Wow, you look like such a dick,' said Sven, who was wearing an enormous fur hat.

'Thank you, Buzby. Now, where's the cab rank?'

Sven smiled at him. 'Oh, follow me, it's just over here.' He led them off through the steaming station waiting room and out into the forecourt, where both Arthur and Gwyneth stopped suddenly, their mouths hanging open.

In front of them was a row of large wooden sledges, lit by oil lamps swinging at the corners. The drivers were standing around chatting and stamping their feet, or rubbing down their horses. Bells attached to the horses' reins made a tinkling sound as they moved.

'Oh!' was all Gwyneth could say. She broke into a ridiculously wide smile. Arthur saw it, and

wanted to kiss her more than anything he'd ever
wanted in his life.

'*Kontoret for Is og Sne, så gerne.*' Sven hopped
up into the first sleigh and beckoned the others,
slipping Sandwiches under the blanket that was
handily provided.

'*Ja ja. Tyve minutter, OK?*'

'Okay,' said Sven.

Arthur leaped onto the sleigh immediately.
That's not terribly gallant, Gwyneth found herself
thinking, until she saw him turn round, crouch
and offer her his hand to help her climb up. Or
it is, she thought, pleased.

'Where did you go to sledge etiquette school?'
she asked, pulling her scarf tighter round her neck
and sitting down in the middle of the boys.

'My father always said it would come in handy –
and it has!' Arthur said. 'Not sure about the bongo
lessons, though. And the synchronized swimming
was a complete waste of time.'

'*Afgang!*' shouted the driver, and the two horses
moved away. Gwyneth looked around her in excitement. The town was small, and other sleighs passed
them up and down the white streets. People walked
in snow shoes. The houses were small and brightly
painted. Through the wooden shutters they looked
warm and cosy. Many had open fires. She saw a
mother read a bedtime story to a sleepy tow-headed

toddler wrapped in an elaborate sleep suit and wondered what it would be like to live here, in the frozen north. Her romantic fantasy lasted as long as it took for them to hit a massive rut in the road and for her to get snow down the collar of her jacket, but she still watched in wonder. The houses became more and more spaced out, and the whoosh of other vehicles – there were skidoos too, and the occasional Landrover – gradually died away as they passed into the open countryside. It was so dark now that all that could be seen were the haunting shapes of the forest around her, and the icicles hanging down over the pitted road. Occasionally she thought she saw movement through the trees, and she huddled down further under the blanket.

Arthur looked over her. To be so close – under the covers for goodness' sake – and not to be able to touch her was torture. He leaned in and rubbed his chin against her red hat in a way that could have just about looked accidental.

'Hey,' she said as soon as he touched her.

'Um, sorry . . .' He moved back.

Gwyneth raised her eyebrows. Then she looked at him. 'What?' she said.

'Nothing. Nothing. Sorry. It was an accident,' he said defensively.

'Okay, okay.' God, thought Gwyneth. This

bites. Maybe I just need something uncomplicated. Maybe with someone like Rafe . . .

The sleigh turned into what appeared in the dark to be an open field with a rutted trail across it. The horizon opened out. Gwyneth thought she could make out some lights at the far end of the field, and pointed them out to Sven, who nodded and leaned further over.

'What is it?' said Arthur. He couldn't believe Gwyneth was still ignoring him.

'Look! Do you think that's where we're going?'

As they strained their eyes, however, it suddenly felt as if morning had come. There was a definite, perceptible lightening in the air.

'*Se! Se!*' shouted the driver suddenly. He pointed straight up in the air, and they followed his finger.

'Oh, oh my goodness,' said Gwyneth, the breath knocked out of her.

Above them, the cloud cover had moved away and shimmering delicately in the night were strange, luminescent shades of green and pink, dotted with stars.

'*Nordlys*,' breathed Sven. 'I'm home.'

Arthur nearly stood up. 'I never . . . aurora borealis,' he said. He looked at the others in excitement. 'The northern lights . . . all my life . . .' He cleared his throat as his voice caught, and sat down again suddenly. 'Well. Um, it's very exciting to see it, I mean.'

It was so beautiful, thought Gwyneth suddenly, staring at it and trying to swallow it with her eyes – it made her want to cry. It could almost make you believe in anything; an older world. The smell of pine in the air, the quiet crunch of the snow under the runners, the light tinkle of the bells – and apart from that, silence, and their dazzling private light show.

And there, at the far end of the field, now spread before them, was what looked like a madman's playground.

* * *

A huge, towering castle loomed up in the murky dark – next to a statue of an elephant that was nearly the same size. Next to that was a huge Viking ship, sailing on to nowhere. The effect was extremely eerie. The sleigh proceeded towards it, as they pushed themselves forward.

'What are we looking at?' said Gwyneth.

'We're here,' said Sven. 'This is it.'

They passed slowly beneath the massive sculptures, looking around them in wonder, and feeling extremely small, holding the oil lanterns towards them to get a better view. The statues were at least thirty feet high, and close by, with the light of the lanterns and the stars above them, they could see they were made entirely of ice, so sharp and clean it looked like glass. Gwyneth realized that they weren't in a field any more; there were no ruts or bumps. The horses' hooves cracked and they slowed down measurably, and she realized they were passing over hard-packed snow on solid ice.

'My God,' said Arthur.

'Beats your little skating rink man, huh?' said Sven, but not nastily; he was as busy drinking in the view as the rest of them.

At the far end of the sculpture park – behind an enormous, impossible oak tree hewn entirely from frozen water – stood a small cottage made from logs. It looked isolated and lonely in the strange oversized landscape, but a warm glow came from its lighted windows.

'*Stands her*,' said Sven. The sleigh driver nodded. Then, gingerly, the party disembarked. Gwyneth expected to skid on the ice, but it felt surprisingly solid beneath her feet.

'Right,' said Arthur, and Gwyneth, looking at him, realized he was nervous. 'Um . . . let's go do the big ice thing.'

* * *

The man who answered the door looked infinitely old. He was tiny, and had a long beard, and privately Arthur wondered if he might be part dwarf. In fact, he was.

'Welcome,' he said, in English. 'Welcome – come in, come in.'

The room was sparsely furnished in wood as an office. Through a curtain, they could see a second room that may have been a bedroom.

'It is good when people make the trip,' he said, nodding his head. Then he extended his hand. 'I am Johann Vit.'

They shook it. Sven said something quietly to him in Danish, and Johann flapped his arms and said, no, no, he must not, he was a modest man. Then he knelt down and scratched Sandwiches behind the ear.

'Come, come. Sit by the fire. I will make hot chocolate and then we will talk, yes?'

He disappeared into the back room and they sat down in wooden chairs which were surprisingly comfortable. Gwyneth felt her cheeks turn red in the heat from the fire.

'So, we didn't need you to come after all to translate, eh Sven?' said Arthur, examining the pictures on the wall – scenes of great, vertiginous and beautifully made ski slopes, vast ice rinks and sculptures. Around the room were models and brochures.

'Yes that's right,' said Sven. 'You could easily have walked here.'

Johann re-entered the room with chocolate and small rolls. Gwyneth realized she was absolutely starving and took them gratefully.

'Now,' he said. 'You wish to enter my ice kingdom, *ja*? No, it is my joke,' he said when he saw Arthur's face. Arthur was a little sensitive to talk of kingdoms. 'Well. Tell me what you do.'

* * *

It took them much longer to explain than they'd thought. The man's bright-eyed, intelligent face encouraged confidences, and, before they were done, Arthur found himself explaining about Ross – not the sleeping with his ex bit, more the innate rivalry bit – and the planning committee. Gwyneth helped too, talking about what the ice festival would mean to the area, and why they even wanted to do it in the first place. Sven chipped in with what a good job he was doing with all the logistical programming on his new computer. Sandwiches went to sleep.

'Ah,' said Johann when they had finished. He sat back and steepled his fingers together. Gwyneth and Arthur looked at one another.

Johann sighed deeply. 'It will be difficult,' he said.

Arthur nodded. 'We know.'

'You will have to divert the path of the river.'

'We'll build a weir.'

He nodded and, very slowly, stood up. His bones creaked as he walked towards the bookcase. 'In your country,' he said, shaking his finger, 'in your country, you had the most magnificent ice festivals . . . ah . . .'

'When?' said Arthur.

'Oh, for years.' Johann squinted. 'Until quite late. The longest one was in 1684. Ooh, a very cold year, no doubt.'

'You speak like you were there!' said Gwyneth.

'Ha! Well, yes, however,' said Johann. He smiled. 'You know, they used to roast oxen on the ice. There were pedlars and minstrels and jugglers, and everyone used to come. You could smell it from miles away – all kinds of food and sweets,'

'Did they have skates?' said Sven. 'How could they have skates?'

'They did, actually. Wooden. But most people just walked. And the children ran and slid and fell over.'

'It sounds wonderful,' said Arthur.

'Oh, it was. Except, there was too much ale, so there was always a casualty or two. But, you know – life.'

'No licensing,' said Gwyneth, reaching for her notepad.

'It would be a wonderful thing to see it again in England,' the old man said meditatively. 'A wonderful thing.'

'Will you do it for us?' said Arthur.

The man looked at the floor, then back up at them.

'Yes,' he said. 'Yes, I will.'

* * *

After more chocolate – this time laced with brandy – they sat and listened as Johann explained exactly what was going to be required.

It was a massive project. They would have to pay seed money up ahead, whether or not they got the commission. Then it would take a month of diverting and setting up and cleaning and flattening, and trying to rope off anywhere likely to be of dangerous interest to two-year-olds. They would have to sort out disputes between traditional Morris dancers and endemic Peruvian pipe players. Did they want scary carnival rides or was the concept going to be enough in itself? Did they . . .

Suddenly Johann stood up and sniffed the air. The others looked at him. 'Oh, no' he said abruptly. 'I am afraid . . . it is late. You have to go now.' He had switched from being a charming, intelligent man to someone more brusque. 'I am sorry. The night comes on so quick . . .'

Arthur glanced at his watch. It was past ten o'clock.

'. . . and still I lose track of the hour. Please. If you are to get back to Skærgård . . .'

'We're sorry,' said Gwyneth, standing up. 'We lost track of the time.'

'No, no, it is not that.'

Johann was agitated now, pulling out their coats and hats from the pegs on the wall. 'Sometimes, out in the woods, late . . . it is not so safe. And not so good for your driver and his horse, yes? We talk soon, yes. I like you. I think we can work together. But for now . . .'

Gwyneth and Arthur looked at each other as they shrugged themselves into their coats. Arthur raised his eyebrows.

'Okay, then. No, wait!'

Johann scuttled back into the second room in the building and returned an instant later. 'A gift for you,' he said to Arthur, and handed him a long piece of what looked like crystal.

'It is bore ice,' he added, to Arthur's bemused expression. 'Taken from the very bottom of the lake. This ice has been in existence before the dinosaurs. It's encased in resin, but it was formed at the beginning of time.' He looked straight at Arthur suddenly. 'Many things are older than you know.'

Arthur swallowed. 'Thank you, sir. Thank you very much.'

Johann nodded. 'Not at all. We shall speak again. But now – hurry,' said the little man, pulling open the door and practically thrusting them into the freezing wind outside. 'You must hurry.'

There was a clatter of the door shutting, then the external light was switched off. Gwyneth, Sven, Arthur and Sandwiches found themselves looking out on the mysterious ice shapes looming into the midnight air.

'Where's the cab?' said Arthur. But the little bells of the sleigh were nowhere to be heard.

* * *

'Um,' said Sven, swallowing nervously after a few moments had passed. '*Chauffør*!?'

Silence. Just the wind whistling through the ice. Somewhere beneath them in the dark, Sandwiches made a cringing noise and tried to crawl, unsuccessfully, up Sven's trouser leg. There was a panicked scrabble and a quiet whine and he slipped back on to the ice.

'There there,' said Sven absent-mindedly. '*CHAUFFØR*!?'

'Er . . .' Gwyneth turned back to the little house. But all its lights were out now. If ever a house had tried to curl into a ball and pass unnoticed, it was this one.

'Crap!' said Arthur. 'Where is the guy with the horse?'

But, as if in answer to his question, there was only the sound of the wind whistling through the corridors of the sculpture park. Then suddenly, in the distance, came the sound of a long, low howl.

At once, Arthur knew what it was. It was the sound he had heard late at night, hundreds of miles away. It was the sound of his nightmares. It was the sound of a wolf.

'Wh – what was that?' said Gwyneth, pulling her arms around her.

'Um, an urban fox?' said Arthur, not expecting her to believe him.

'This . . .' She peered out over the glacier. 'This isn't urban, Arthur.'

'No.' He could feel the fear in her voice.

'Where's that bastard cabbie?' said Sven. 'They're all the same – no, I won't take you south of the river . . . no, I won't take you through the wolf-infested forest . . .'

'Oh God!' said Gwyneth. 'It's a WOLF?'

'Whooo!' came the sound again, as if in confirmation.

'Well, what are we waiting for? We're going back to hammer on the door.'

'I wouldn't do that,' said Sven. 'Northern people are very superstitious about their wolves. They believe a lot of the old stories.'

'What old stories? Like . . . werewolves?'

Gwyneth had intended this to come out as sneering and sarcastic, but at the last moment she absolutely couldn't pull it off.

'*Ja,*' said Sven. 'He probably wouldn't let you in, in case you'd been bitten. Or he might just blast you away with a silver bullet.'

'He wouldn't.'

The howling came again.

'Look,' said Arthur. 'The sleigh driver can't be far. We'll do better going to have a look for him than just standing around freezing our arses to death. Okay?' He looked at his phone. 'I've still got some power left in my battery. So if we can't find him you, Sven, can phone the Danish wilderness equivalent of *Yellow Pages* and get us out of here.'

'Yeah, in lots of little pieces,' said Sven sullenly.

'None of that, please. You're scaring Gwyneth.'

'Uh huh!' said Gwyneth.

'Me, I mean. You're scaring me.'

'No, me too,' said Gwyneth.

'Okay,' said Sven, 'it's just, I'm the one that has to drag this with me, that's all.'

Sandwiches was lying perfectly still on his back in the snow, with his legs pointing straight up in the air.

'Stop playing dead, Sandwiches,' said Sven. 'It's not going to help, you know.'

But Sandwiches point-blank refused to open his eyes, so Sven had to pick him up and put him round his neck like a snake.

'Actually, it's quite warming,' he said, patting the dog's ears. Sandwiches continued to refuse to react in any way.

'Amazing,' said Arthur. 'Okay. Off we go. *CHAUFFØR!*'

And they marched forward under the eerie-coloured starlight, and into the park of ice sculptures beyond.

* * *

The howling was definitely closer now. There was still no sign of the driver or the sleigh. They were huddling together underneath the Viking ship, some hundred yards or so ahead of where the house had now vanished into the darkness.

'Oh *crap*,' Gwyneth was saying.

'Ssh,' said Arthur. 'Just keep moving on. We'll find them.'

'Or die horribly!'

'No, I'm sure that won't happen.'

'I'm just going to play dead here like Sandwiches,' said Sven.

'Oh no you're not,' said Arthur. 'I am not hauling your carcass through the snow.'

The howling came again.

'Are there more than one of them?' said Gwyneth, feeling her heart jump.

'God, I hope not. Because if there's only one, then it'll get tired after the first throat . . .' Sven trailed off.

Arthur shut his eyes. What was coming? It was getting rapidly colder. They were going to have to go back to the old man, they had to. Sven was being ridiculous. But where the hell was the cabbie? Had he not understood and just up and left them? More than anything, Arthur wanted him and the horse to be standing round the next corner, looking relieved and asking them where they'd been.

Round the next corner was an odd sculpture which resembled a desert scene in ice – there was a cactus, and a palm tree, and a coyote.

It wasn't a coyote.

Arthur felt as if an enormous hand was squeezing his windpipe. The cold air he'd sucked in burned its way down his throat. It was every time he'd ever woken up in the night thinking he'd heard a burglar; every time he'd nearly walked in front of a moving vehicle. Simultaneously, it felt like he was being punched in the chest.

Gwyneth hadn't meant to punch him in the chest but – look!

'*Look*!' Her voice had petered out to a petrified squeak.

'Yes, I know,' said Arthur, whispering. The wolf was about twenty feet away, casually regarding them in the moonlight. The wind was gently ruffling its fur, and it was staring straight at them with ice-blue eyes, looking completely unperturbed. Its entire body gave off a power: heavily contained muscles under tight control.

Arthur's brain was working overtime. He couldn't think straight. Could they scramble up the side of the ship? Could wolves climb? Anyway, how could they climb up the side of something made of ice? Could they make it back to the cottage? Almost certainly not: the creature could outrun anything and it would definitely grab the one nearest the back. He glanced at Sven, who was carrying at least three extra stone in weight, not to mention a cowardly dog round his neck.

'If only we had a weapon or something,' he moaned.

'It's all in the sleigh,' said Sven mournfully. 'They have a plan for times like this. Flares and things.'

'Well, that would have been great,' said Arthur, 'if it hadn't eaten the sleigh.'

Slowly, as if relishing its status, the wolf started to pad from side to side, moving almost imperceptibly closer.

'Oh, Christ,' said Gwyneth. 'It's coming for us. I can't . . . I mean, we're not going to *die*, are we? I mean, on a business trip. It seems so stupid.'

'Don't be silly,' said Arthur. 'And deprive Marcus of his expenses claims? It would be against all natural laws.'

The wolf moved forward, slowly. It sniffed the air. The others backed away, pointlessly. The wall of ice that was the side of the ship was right behind them. There was nowhere to bolt.

In the full light of the moon, the wolf arched its back again and howled. In a shot Arthur saw why wolves had always been part of folklore, despite usually looking like grumpy oversized dogs. This was no dog. This was a pure wild animal, that could smell them from a mile away and wanted warm fresh meat. Its insides were as cold as the ice around them.

And still the creature advanced. Its eyes reflected the moon, and seemed to shine out of its head. It still took its time.

'Oh . . .' Gwyneth, Arthur vaguely realized

through the iron grip of fear that had taken control of his own head, was sobbing. He put his arm round her and patted her ineffectually on the shoulder.

'I can't believe . . . This is just so *stupid*.'

Sven was staring straight ahead, absolutely frozen to the spot. Arthur went through his possible options and couldn't for the life of him think of one. Sweat broke out on his forehead as the wolf stepped forward yet again. His hands, anxiously struggling in his pockets, hit against something. He drew it out. It was the bore ice Johann had given him. It was the nearest thing to a weapon he had.

'Oh God,' said Arthur. He darted a look at the others. 'Stay here.'

'What? What! What are you doing!' said Gwyneth hysterically. Sven remained in his catatonic state.

'Just stay here, okay? I think we might have one shot.'

'You've got a gun?'

'No. Look, I'm going to distract it, and you two have to run back to Johann's hut, okay?'

'But . . . but he'll chase us.'

'Not if I'm there.'

Arthur's face was grim, reflected Gwyneth, and his jaw was incredibly set.

'Get ready to run, okay? Sven?'

'Uh?'

'Run. With Gwyneth. When you hear me shout.'

'But . . .' Gwyneth held onto his arm. 'This is *madness.*'

'No,' he said. 'This is – we've got one shot at this, okay? You understand? There's nothing else to do.'

She nodded mutely. Sven stood there, not moving at all.

Arthur turned back again to face the beast, motioning the others to get behind him.

The animal turned its full attention to Arthur now. It seemed to know, somehow, that this was where the battle would be joined.

Arthur steeled himself and kept on walking forward. Part of his brain was screaming at him, 'What are you doing! What are you DOING!!!!!' But part of him was almost calm, accepting his fate. It was saying, 'Ah, almost certain death. So *this* is what it's like?'

When there were only ten feet between him and the wolf, he stopped and they eyed each other for five . . . ten seconds. It felt like forever under the freezing endless sky.

Arthur took a deep breath. 'OKAY,' he shouted suddenly. 'Run NOW!!!!! NOW!!!!!! AIIIIEEEE-EEEEEEE!'

And he screeched at the top of his lungs.

He'd expected the beast to be quick, but not this quick. The next thing he saw was the animal, seemingly far too high in the air, bearing down on him from nowhere with a blood-curdling howl.

As fast as he could, he raised the hard resin of the bore ice, remembering what you were supposed to do with dogs – grab their forepaws and move them as wide apart as you could. He had personally doubted his ability to ever perform such a grotesque act on an animal, but right at this moment . . .

Almost without thinking about it, he rammed the ice bore as hard as he could at the animal's head. With a whinnying shriek, the wolf wobbled slightly to the side, but was only deflected momentarily from its course, and its paws still knocked Arthur backwards onto the ice.

He could smell the creature's hot breath. For a second, Arthur and the wolf were eye to eye. Then the animal opened its enormous jaws, sparkling with saliva.

'HnNNurggh!'

Arthur didn't know where he found the strength, but he pushed himself up, unbalancing the wolf, who staggered backwards, growling.

Arthur thought . . . but before he had time to do anything, the wolf tackled him again, this time from his left side, and both of them were crashing down on the snow once more.

This at least gave him a chance to drag his right hand free from the wolf's paws. He was still clutching the ice bore. Scarcely thinking about it, he plunged it as far as he could into the wolf's ear.

'Grraaaa!' The wolf shook its head furiously and twisted out of Arthur's reach. The ice bore skittered away across the ice. Both their heads shot round to follow its progress. It was certainly too far away for Arthur to grab it. The wolf refocused its attention.

'Oh God,' Arthur breathed to himself dully. He tried to raise the strength for another almighty push, but there was no purchase on the ground beneath him. His fingers desperately scrabbled at nothing. And once again, the slavering jaws were moving down, ever closer. He closed his eyes . . .

* * *

He opened them again a second later, at a high-pitched yelping noise.

The wolf was buzzing in consternation, although his front paws were still firmly planted on Arthur's chest and arm.

Behind him, barking madly, and skittering

along the hard-packed snow towards the ice bore, was Sandwiches.

'Sandwiches!' shrieked Arthur. The wolf could scoop him up in one gulp, then come back to Arthur as a main course.

The dog picked up the bore and shuffled joyously up towards Arthur.

'NO, no, that's not what I meant!' said Arthur, cursing himself. 'Don't bring the stick to me. Don't fetch! Sandwiches, don't fetch!'

But the little dog trotted on towards him. The growls from the wolf came from deep down in his belly.

In the distance, he could hear Gwyneth and Sven screaming. So much for the brilliant running-away-to-get-help plan.

With a grunt, as Sandwiches dropped the bore at Arthur's hand, the wolf stretched out one paw and took a swipe at him. And blindly, instinctively, without even thinking, Arthur grabbed the ice bore and thrust it as hard as he could, deep as a sword, into the animal's chest.

* * *

A terrible groaning tore across the plain. It was a horrible, horrible sound: an animal in pain. Or, to be more correct, two animals in pain, as Sandwiches had taken a nasty clap to the head from an errant paw, and had skittered backwards, bouncing his head off the hard-packed snow. Arthur watched, dumbfounded, as the terrible weight came off his hand and chest, and the great creature arched up, roaring its agony.

Suddenly, as if from nowhere, a huge boulder came crashing out of the sky and hit the wolf square in the forehead. Immediately the howling stopped and the creature sank to the ground. Everything was still. Arthur found he was blinking rapidly.

'*For fanden*!'

The sleigh driver stepped out from the woods.

Arthur turned round in amazement to where Sven had dashed forward to cradle Sandwiches in the snow.

The driver came forward, gesticulating.

'Sven, what's he saying?'

Sven looked up, his face pale and strained.

'Um, he's saying, sorry, but he had to hide up a tree because . . . um . . . because a big wolf came.'

'Right,' said Arthur. 'Okay.'

And he wandered back to Gwyneth who was standing trembling violently, and enfolded her in his arms.

Chapter Nine

'Hey,' said the temp. 'Good trip?'

'Um . . . it was very interesting,' said Arthur. 'Actually, you won't believe what happened . . .'

'Yeah,' said the temp, chewing. 'Anyway. There's lots of messages for you. Ooh, is the dog wearing a new hat?'

Sandwiches stalked in proudly wearing his enormous white bandages. Sven followed him, still watching his every step nervously.

'Morning!' said Arthur cheerily. There really was nothing, he thought, quite as likely to buck you up as cheating death, fighting a wolf and getting to save a gorgeous woman you really fancied. She had held onto him all the way home. He was definitely getting somewhere. It didn't do to rush these things. Deep down, he was a bit worried. He hadn't felt like this about someone in . . . God, years. Fay had just been – well, he wasn't thinking about Fay any more. But she certainly hadn't been as calm and attractive and . . . Oh, yes. He wasn't going to move too quickly. That was best.

* * *

What did she have to do? Gwyneth was thinking mutinously. Strip naked and spreadeagle herself on his desk? All the way home he'd put his arm round her like a brother. Well, that was enough. She couldn't be bothered with all this. She decided to take a walk before going into work, to settle herself. After all, he wasn't the only bloody man in the office.

* * *

'Hey,' said Sven. He looked grey.

'Are you all right?'

'Yes, yes.'

He didn't look it, though. He looked like he'd stayed up all night worrying about a dog who, even now, was jauntily approaching the rubbish bin with an expectant look in his eye.

Oh, well. Everything was fine. Arthur buzzed on through to the boardroom. There was a chunky, badly-dressed man standing there in a cheap suit. He looked vaguely familiar.

'Hello?'

'Yeah, hi . . .'

The man stuck out one hand and used the other to scratch his nose. 'Hi – I'm Howard Phillips?'

'Howard?'

'I wrote the piece in the *Herald*?'

Now Arthur recognized the little snotrag. He'd broken the story Ross had leaked to him, and he was the journalist who'd approached Arthur in the park.

'Get out of my office, shithead.'

'No, no!' As the man moved towards him, Arthur noticed he had a slight limp. 'You don't understand! I have to get this story. I'm going to lose my job if I don't.'

The man sat down without being invited, heavily. Arthur noticed he was sweating and sticky strands of hair clung to his bald head.

'Yeah, sit down,' said Arthur sarcastically.

'Look, I'm sorry, but it's just my job, okay?'

'It's just your job to try and lose me my job. Right, yes, I sympathize. Coffee?'

'Yeah, that would be . . .'

'No! You're not having any coffee!'

'Oh.' The man looked mournfully at the floor, and rubbed his hand on his bald spot, which looked agitated and red. 'Can I have a glass of water, then?'

'No. Oh, yes okay, you can have a glass of water.'

Arthur cursed himself for getting up and betraying the weaker hand, but if he had a heart attack . . .

'Thank you,' said the man. 'I get a bit sweaty on assignments.'

'Thanks for sharing.'

'Look,' said the man. 'I just want to put your side of the story.'

'No, you don't. You want to dredge up evil insights into the spendthrifts at the planning office.'

'Yeah, yeah I do, yeah,' said the man sadly.

'Ooh, you gave in quickly.'

'I'm not a very good journalist.'

'Okay,' said Arthur. 'Go somewhere else please.'

'I can't,' said the man. 'I have to stay here and find out about Denmark or my boss is going to fire me.'

'What do you know about Denmark? Oh, bugger it.'

The man smiled greasily.

'Yes, I'm very naïve,' said Arthur. 'Was that actually a secret journalist trick, to make me cough by looking pathetic?'

There was a pause.

'No,' said the man. 'I got lucky.'

* * *

They walked out past the open-plan. Arthur noticed with half an eye that Sven had covered the area with

'I visited Denmark's Best Ice Shop 2002!' posters and made a mental note to have a quiet word about project confidentiality. He *didn't* notice Howard very quickly reading his post tray upside down, and extracting an envelope from it, sweating even harder as he slipped it into his pocket.

Arthur invited the journalist out for a walk, figuring if he was going to have this snivelling wretch following him around, it was probably best to do it in the open air.

'Why do you limp?' he asked him, curious, as they made their way across the car park and under the hideous piss-stained underpass, past the *Big Issue* sellers they no longer noticed.

'Huh,' said Howard. 'I dunno. For the last three weeks there's this bloody little sausage dog or something that comes past my house every day exactly when I'm leaving for work and bites me on the leg.'

* * *

'The thing is,' said Howard. 'The paper's out to get you.'

'Really?' said Arthur. He'd just picked up this week's edition. On the front page it said,

SCANDANAVIAN ROMP FOR EVIL 'CULTURE CITY' PROPOSERS

After unveiling plans to spend millions of pounds on a second ice rink for Conventry, planners from the city office have been off on their latest hairbrained scheme – to Denmark!

'What were they there for?' said random passer-by Miles Sampson. 'To see Santa Claus?'

'A random passer-by?' said Arthur.

'Yeah,' said Howard. 'It was late.'

'But why?' said Arthur. 'We're only trying to do something cool for the people – sorry, did I just sound really Tony Blair?'

'That's okay,' said Howard, rubbing his scaly head.

'So, what's the problem?'

'I dunno. Someone at the top's got it in for you. Maybe they reckon you're pulling Coventry down into the dirt or something.'

Arthur looked around at the hopeless expanse of grey concrete blocks.

'How could I possibly do that?'

Howard shrugged. 'Look, mate. You're the one who thinks you're going to beat Slough. You're making some dangerous enemies.'

'You're telling me – what, that municipal council officers make dangerous enemies?' said Arthur, trying to sound braver than he felt.

'You see a lot in this job, mate.'

Arthur wandered on, as ever, to the park.

'So, just give me the inside story and I'll leave you alone.'

'Yeah, you said that. And you also said you were going to twist it around and make it horrible.'

Howard sighed at the terrible contradictions his own life's work had led him to.

They entered the park.

'I mean,' Arthur was going on, 'the money won't even have to come from round here, anyway. Brussels will supply a lot of it. And look at all the jobs and visitors it'll create.'

'Yeah,' said Howard, unimpressed.

'We'll be the major tourist attraction of the West Midlands!'

'Yeah, you probably would be, if you got it. Unfortunately, I'm only allowed to slag you off.'

'Ah!' said Arthur in frustration. 'This is awful.'

Howard shrugged noncommitally. They neared the place where the maze was going to go.

'Is that . . .' Arthur squinted his eyes through an unlikely ray of December sunshine that had poked through the sky. Sure enough, Rafe was there again, the same place he'd been that other early morning, walking across the green, surrounded by . . .

'What the hell is going on!'

'Arthur! ARTHUR!' Rafe was yelling. 'Come and see this!'

Arthur took a sidelong look at Howard.

'Has something gone horribly wrong?' said Howard optimistically.

'Yeah! Arthur!'

'Gwyneth?' Arthur screwed up his eyes. Rafe and Gwyneth were running about the park in an uncharacteristically joyful manner for Coventry.

'G-W-I- . . .' said Howard laboriously, pouring over a notebook with a sticky pencil.

'Stop that,' said Arthur as they drew closer. Then he just stood back, shaking his head in disbelief.

Gwyneth and Rafe were surrounded by children, running around in the frosty sunshine. The children were dancing in strange, formulaic patterns. Arthur wondered why, until he noticed Rafe gesticulating wildly at his feet.

'What is that?'

'It's cress!' said Rafe proudly.

'It's *what*?'

'Don't you see?' said Gwyneth. 'Rafe's traced out the shape the maze is going to be with cress.'

'To make soup?'

'To see how it would look, and whether it would be fun.'

Arthur looked over to where Rafe had started a conga line with a crowd of children, all screaming merrily.

'And is it?'

Gwyneth nodded. 'They're *loving* it. I wonder where Rafe's put his camera?'

A six-inch hedge of the seed coiled in little lines for as far as the eye could see. Already, clumsy children were falling over it and – occasionally – hopping for good luck, but on the whole the lines were clean, and the shape a beautiful mish-mash of curlicues, elaborate curves and dead ends.

'Come on in and try it!' shouted Rafe. 'I'm going to take some photos to show people how much fun it is!'

'I don't think that'll be necessary,' said Arthur. 'By a lucky coincidence . . .'

Howard sweated and mopped his brow.

'Who's this?' said Gwyneth, reaching them.

'Um, I'm Howard Phillips . . .' said Howard, staring at the ground.

Gwyneth advanced. 'You mean that snivelling little . . .'

Howard snivelled and attempted to make himself look small.

'Gwyn –' said Arthur.

'You know who this is? The guy that stitched us up in the paper!'

'Yes, yes, I know. But look. I'm showing him some of the cool stuff we're doing now, like how the maze is going to work.'

Gwyneth narrowed her eyes. 'Are you going to write something decent, shithead?'

'Um, not sure,' said Howard.

'It's probably more likely if you stop calling him shithead,' said Arthur.

'Not necessarily,' said Howard.

'Huh. Right!' said Gwyneth. She was in an exceptionally capricious mood — happy from the trip, and happy to see the maze. 'Come on, we have to give it a try!'

Arthur followed her to the start of the maze. In his memory, from the beautiful model, he remembered there being a gate here, encrusted with roses. But of course there was just a space now. Rafe was somewhere in the distance, still playing Pied Piper, but Arthur was pleased to see other people — not just children — threading their way around in strange directions, staring hard at their feet.

'The trick is,' said Gwyneth, 'you have to stare at your feet and not look up. Otherwise you'll see other people and step over the walls and you'll be cheating.'

She looked so serious saying this Arthur wanted to kiss her immediately, but counted on this not being ideal in front of a journalist.

'Okay? Right, count to twenty after each person that goes and then set off.'

Arthur smiled, feeling happy nonetheless. Even Howard seemed to have perked up. Arthur put his head down and Gwyneth counted him off first.

* * *

He'd thought that it would be ridiculous – a maze with invisible walls was no game at all – and that it would finish briefly. Instead, the size of the maze meant he soon felt far away from the others, connected only to the toes of the brown brogues below, on his feet. He was cursing as he followed one promising path after another, only to end up at a dead end, or in a cunning spiral. He could begin to visualize what it was going to be like when the hawthorn had grown, and smelled deeply of the summertime. Almost closing his eyes, he could imagine the sun on his face, as the sounds around him faded away and he felt his way through the high green.

* * *

Gwyneth grinned as she watched the others head off. Well, they pretended to be grown-ups and not concerned, but really, they were just little boys who wanted to play.

And so did she, she thought, counting in her head to twenty.

As she made her way delicately through the streets of cress her thoughts turned to what she would meet at the centre of the maze. Perhaps someone would be waiting there . . . She smiled to herself and hit another dead end – she only just remembered that this maze wasn't real yet, even as she danced along.

* * *

From above, the maze would have looked real, even though the walls were only six inches high (and edible). On the ground, however, people were twisting and turning endlessly through the bright winter sun, the cress glinting green and white with hoarfrost. Howard was enjoying himself. The fresh air was something of a novelty.

* * *

He hadn't come up against a dead end for a while. Arthur was confident he was nearing the middle. Nor had he clapped eyes on a soul for some time. Truly, the maze was enormous. It would work wonderfully, it would. He wondered what would be waiting for him in the middle. He drifted for a second and imagined Gwyneth naked, conveniently forgetting that it was freezing cold and the space was completely open to public view. He spurred himself on.

* * *

I must be getting near, thought Gwyneth. She could feel herself closer to the heart of the maze and began to get excited as to what she might find there. She started to move more quickly, too.

* * *

Rafe had loved building the maze. He'd traced it out endlessly, early in the morning, and couldn't wait to watch the maze man's dream take shape. He'd watered the cress and hoped it wouldn't freeze too much to grow, and here it was. It had taken him a while to decide what to place in the centre, but he'd managed it. Everything was going to be fine.

* * *

Gwyneth's heart was sparkling and her pulse rate high as she realized she had entered the inner sanctum of the maze. It looked like a long room. At the end of it was a figure, turned away.

She ran towards it.

* * *

Arthur almost ran into the middle of the maze, then stopped short as he realized two people were already there, heads bent together. With a sudden drop of his heart, he snapped out of his reverie and looked around him, realizing that he wasn't in a proper maze at all: that he could see for miles around, that the walls weren't real. And that Rafe and Gwyneth were standing very close together in its centre.

* * *

'They're lovely,' Gwyneth stammered. She didn't know why she felt so strange. It was as if she'd been dreaming of being in a real maze – like when she'd seen the model – then it had simply disappeared. But not before she'd seen Rafe. He was crouched down, his strong back towards her, tending the huge bunch of snowdrops he'd been growing in a hole he'd carefully dug right at the centre.

'Thanks!' said Rafe. 'I just thought it would be . . . you know, a nice touch.'

He plucked one of the white flowers and gave it to her. It smelled of distant spring. She smiled at him and he smiled back.

* * *

'Hi!' said Arthur, recovering his composure. 'Hey ho! Here we are!'

They looked around at him, just as Howard crashed through another entrance into the centre.

'Wow!' said Howard. 'That was brilliant! It really felt like being in a real maze!'

'So you'll write a good story?' said Gwyneth, smiling.

Howard shrugged. 'Dunno.'

'What do you think, Arthur?'

Rafe stepped up towards him. Arthur couldn't help smiling at his friend. His own fantasies of Gwyneth in the maze were, of course, only that.

'Okay, Jamie Oliver,' he said. 'It's brilliant.'

'It is brilliant,' said Howard. 'It even smells like – I don't know, hawthorn or something in here.'

Rafe smiled shyly as the centre of the maze started filling up with excited children who'd made their way there too. 'Well, I thought if people could see it, they'd understand what we were trying to do.'

Arthur nodded and glanced at Gwyneth, who was looking back at him, her face unreadable.

* * *

'"Cress disaster in Local Park"?'

Sven held the paper up to the light. 'This doesn't seem much like news to me.'

'Shut up,' said Arthur brusquely. He was sitting with Rafe at one end of the conference table.

Sven read the piece out loud:

261

'"Chapel Fields saw further bureaucratic en-croaches yesterday when it was infested with a cress-like fungus. The park is the site of contro-versial possible development for the European City of Culture (funded from Brussels in Euros). Town planning spokesman Rafe Colemat said, 'This will show them.'"'

'That's not what I said,' said Rafe sulkily.

'"However, park users are being reassured that the growth is 'probably' not poisonous to dogs or small children."'

'Why does everyone think that we're on some big pilgrimage to kill small children?' groaned Arthur. 'Are we? Am I not reading the right memos?'

* * *

'So,' said Arthur to Marcus. 'How's it looking?' He was staring at a pile of financial projections.

'That depends,' said Marcus cautiously.

'What do you mean?'

'Well, it depends on whether or not you manage to throw off all the bad publicity and iron out all the logistics problems and manage to actually win the award.'

'Yes,' said Arthur. 'I rather thought it might.'

'Otherwise of course we'll all lose our jobs and the whole department will probably be eradicated . . . homelessness . . . despair, all that stuff.'

'Okay.' Arthur rested his head on his hands.

'But!' said Sven, leaning over on the back of his chair. 'Did you know we can, technically speaking, get a ferris wheel balanced on top of all this ice?'

'Really?' All the boys huddled round the projection.

'Cool!'

* * *

Gwyneth tried to keep up with Rafe as he strode through the underpass.

'Don't worry about it,' she said. 'I thought your maze was lovely.'

He turned to her. 'I just – you know, I think this is important. This city needs beauty and loyalty and . . .'

'You're a regular knight in shining armour.'

Gwyneth was joking, but realized the double meaning in what she was saying. 'I don't mean . . . not in that way.'

He smiled. 'No, no, It's okay. But I do feel . . . you know,' he kicked a discarded Coke can disconsolately, 'that we should have a *mission* about this place. That we really have to do something.

And you and me and Arthur are the only ones who get it.'

Gwyneth nodded. 'But we're right, though.'

He walked on, then stopped, turned round, picked up the Coke can and put it in the bin. Gwyneth smiled to herself.

'Well, why is it so damn *difficult?*'

* * *

Ross smirked and tapped the newspaper.

'You know, joining the Black Knights was the best thing I ever did,' he mused. 'Apart from you, of course, darling.'

Fay was sitting on his knee, carefully. She half-smiled in response. A couple of weeks in Ross's office and he had finally worn down her resistance. There had been so much shouting, so many whispered threats down the phone to Ross's carefully placed friends in town, so many closeted meetings and private chats with odd-looking men from amusement companies, chocolate concessions . . . She just didn't care any more. She stared at Ross blankly.

'Bloody brilliant, boss,' said Dave. 'We've got those cress-munching bastards.'

'So, what now, darlings?' Ross was wondering whether he could stick his hand up Fay's shirt. Probably.

'Christmas, innit?' said Dave.

'God, so it is. I think we need a celebration – to drink to our very lucrative new year. A proper party, huh, angel?'

'Whatever,' said Fay.

'And see if we can't think up a bit more fun and games for our rivals, eh?' said Ross. 'It's all gone entirely too quiet. Let me see . . . Christmas party. What does he like, Fay-ona?'

Fay slumped her shoulders. 'Well . . .'

* * *

'Um, hi.' Cathy peeped her head round the door.

'Hey,' said Arthur, smiling. 'Come in.'

'I just wondered . . .' she began. Sandwiches came over to say hello. 'Hello, you little sick doggie.'

'Don't worry about him,' said Marcus. 'Worry about Nurse Gunterson here.'

'Ha ha,' said Sven, but it was clear he was still suffering from lack of sleep.

'What is it?' said Arthur.

'Well, I was just speaking to the temp and – well, we usually organize the Christmas party.'

'Really?' said Arthur. 'How long has the temp been here now?'

Everyone shrugged.

'Fifteen years?' said Cathy. 'That's as long as I've been here.'

'Well,' said Arthur. 'Hmm. Christmas party.'

'There's always been a budget for it before.'

'I think we need a party,' said Marcus. 'Although we can't really afford it,' he added rapidly.

'You've *got* to have a Christmas party,' said Cathy reprovingly.

Arthur thought back to the other Christmas parties he'd attended during his time there. They were normally pretty dreary affairs, held in the lobby where people either stood around sadly playing with glasses of warm white wine and wearing party hats in a pathetic manner, or got royally pissed up and started doing shadow boxing on an improvised dance floor. He winced. Fay used to prod him in the back and try and get him to talk to people higher up in the office, and she used to flirt with Ross. Yeugh. That gave him a sticky feeling even now. Then she'd drive him home, berating him for the fact that another year had gone by with . . . well, with nothing. He thought of it with sadness.

'Okay,' he said. 'Cathy, you're right. We have to have a Christmas party. But we're not going to have a crappy one here like we normally do.'

Cathy's face fell. 'But I've got the comedy post-it garlands all ready.'

'Sorry, but that doesn't matter. This year we're

getting out of the foyer and we're going to have fun. Things are different now.'

'Ooh, can we all go to London's West End?' said Cathy hopefully.

'Not that different. But book somewhere nice. Everyone's worked really hard this year, and next year's going to be really important, so . . .'

'Shall I spike the punch again?'

'Yes, I think so. What do you think, Sven? Sven, put that dog down.'

Sven was clinging onto Sandwiches and gently patting his scar. Sandwiches was writhing and snortling and making unappreciative noises.

'You're stifling that dog,' said Cathy.

'I know. But I nearly lost him,' said Sven. 'I don't know what else to do.'

'Not fall in love with your dog,' said Arthur.

'I am NOT!'

Arthur backed away. 'Party! Party! Beer!' he said, holding up conciliatory hands.

Sven sniffed.

'Lots of lovely beer . . .'

'And punch,' said Cathy.

* * *

'What are we doing?' said Gwyneth again.

'We're knocking on doors to see if people will take lights,' said Rafe, looking through his very

267

optimistic artist's illustration of street after street of happy people looking up at their illuminated marvels.

'And sometimes they give us food,' said Sven. Sandwiches backed him up. Man and dog were doing extremely well on this mission. Sandwiches was in danger of getting as fat as his master. Sven was also showing as much enthusiasm for this as anything else so far; Arthur suspected that a corner of his mind truly believed that somewhere, out there, was a naked nymphomaniac waiting for someone – anyone – to come to the door.

Rafe and Gwyneth, on the other hand, were doing slightly less well.

'What if they think we're from some weird religious sect out to kidnap their brains?'

'Tell them you're not.'

'That's exactly what someone from a weird kidnapping religious sect would do.'

An old woman barged up to them in the street with a shopping basket pushed out in front of her. She was tiny and mean-looking. 'Excuse me, are you from the council?'

'Um . . . yes, I suppose so, kind of . . .' said Rafe. Gwyneth shook her head furiously.

'Well, when are you going to do something about my heating?'

'About your what?'

'It's my cats, you see. It's too cold for them.'

'No, actually, we're not from the . . . um, cold cat department.'

'That's what they all say,' she said cryptically.

'We wondered if you might like to put up some lights,' said Rafe. 'To decorate the house next year.'

'What?'

'We're trying to light up the street. Jolly things up a bit.'

'Isn't that what them streetlights are for? And I'll tell you another thing, Mr Bloody Politician, my council tax is an absolute disgrace.'

'So, if we provided you with the lights and the electricity . . .'

'You're going to pay for my electricity?'

'Um, some of it . . .'

The old lady's eyes narrowed. 'Come in and have some tea.'

* * *

'You realize if we promise free electricity to people, our budget is going to overshoot by about fifteen squillion pounds?' Gwyneth pointed out to Rafe as they walked down the old lady's garden path.

'But she was so *lovely*!'

'Yes, because you stroked her cats and told her you were going to give her all the money. Which we're *not*.'

Rafe gave her a puppyish look.

'Don't try that look on me. I've played with the experts: Sandwiches can't get a morsel out of me.'

'But we're doing . . .'

'Good, yes I realize, Sir Lancelot.'

He smiled and bowed deeply. 'And you ma'am . . .'

She laughed. 'Yes, that's exactly the kind of behaviour we need in a suburban street in Coventry.'

Eyes flashing, he dashed off ahead to a puddle and made to take off his coat and lay it on the ground.

'Wrong period entirely.'

'I'd still do it.'

'I'd still ignore it.'

He sighed and picked up his jacket.

'Next house, then?'

'Next house.'

But they bumped into Sven, who'd already sorted it out and was waving a cheery goodbye.

'So you're saying, just for putting on my lights I can pat your dog whenever I like?' said his old lady.

'Yup.'

* * *

Their moods, however, darkened as they went back to the office, looking at the huge pile of paperwork which continued to descend on them daily; endless forms and rules and specifications for the paper-devouring burghers of Brussels.

Arthur was squinting at a brochure through one eye. He smiled wryly.

'Why are you smiling?' said Sven grumpily.

'Nothing. Just something ironic, that's all.'

'Ooh, *ironic*. Very clever. What?'

'You wouldn't understand.'

'I wouldn't *understand*? I will tell you, I am the absolute expert at the ironic quip.'

'Wow. Ironically, in trying to prove how much you understand irony, you've done quite the opposite.'

'I knew that.'

'No you didn't!'

'Dickhead,' said Sven, quietly, leaving Arthur time to get back to his brochure, which had turned up on his desk out of nowhere. It was for an out of town evening attraction called 'Mediaeval KNIGHTS!!!!!' It promised jousting, wenches, ale and large hunks of roasted meats. Arthur looked at it, smiling. He could tell them a thing or two about ancient knights . . . except, of course, he couldn't really. Ever since Lynne's faintly alarming revelation, he'd rather put it to the back of his mind. Suddenly, he wondered where Lynne was. It was hardly fair. Didn't really justify her salary.

'Marcus!' he shouted. 'What do we pay the company therapist?'

'There isn't a company therapist,' said Marcus, without breaking concentration with Rafe.

Of course not. Arthur looked around the office, noticing the charts, maps, diagrams . . . All the way out into the open-plan area there was a general sense of purpose, of people getting on with doing busy things in a useful way. He felt a quiet sense of pride. In the corner, Rafe was arguing with Marcus yet again about the possibility of a small railway system. Marcus's time-honoured automatic 'no' to everything was being steadily worn down, Arthur noticed, by Rafe's boundless and seemingly endless enthusiasm, not to mention the train set that was still running round the room, usually closely followed by Sandwiches. Gwyneth had a studied and serious look on her face as she put together the official bid papers. They'd decided to mostly let her do those, as she had an ability – rare in this office – to handle documents without getting jam on them.

He looked round and noticed Cathy and the temp at the door of the boardroom. They seemed to be arguing with someone. He caught a glimpse of something colourful and wandered over.

* * *

Why were there two jesters in full motley juggling brightly coloured batons over the top of the office?

Everyone had stopped work to watch them.

'Um, what's this?'

One of the jesters stopped immediately and, without blinking, the other caught eight clubs with a flash of his wrist. Arthur shook his head.

'Who are these people?'

'The Wandering Jesters at your service,' said the nearest man, bowing low from the waist until his bells touched the floor.

'Oh God, is it somebody's birthday?' said Arthur, looking around. 'Is this man about to start taking his clothes off?'

'No, no,' said the man. 'We go where we are needed and we hear you have a fair?'

'What?' said Arthur. 'Well, maybe . . . possibly . . . NEXT YEAR!'

Both jesters made elaborate faces of misery. 'But you shall need us again, yes?'

The second jester was looking worriedly behind him. Arthur followed his gaze. Filing in was a long collection of the most oddly dressed people, attired mainly in hessian. On a word from the one at the front, they all brought out strange-looking instruments and, on a count of three, began to play a beguiling tune.

Gwyneth and Sven joined Arthur in the doorway.

'Are those *minstrels*?' said Gwyneth.

'I don't know,' said Arthur. 'Depends whether they melt in your mouth or your hand.'

* * *

'Who do you think they were?' asked Gwyneth, once they'd finally been persuaded to leave (and after an encore of 'Greensleeves').

'New Age travellers, I expect,' said Marcus spiffily. 'They looked absolutely filthy.'

'Don't be . . . oh,' said Gwyneth. 'Yeah, I suppose they would be filthy, eh?'

Arthur, however, was still looking around the office. People were actually coming to him! Word was getting around! With a start, he realized he liked his job.

* * *

Well, they deserved a decent party. And, even if it was only a private joke for him, he reckoned Mediaeval Knights was the kind of place to be. And hopefully Gwyneth would be the only wench for him.

* * *

'Did you send it to them?' Ross asked lazily. Fay nodded.

'Do you think it's the kind of thing they'll go for?'

'He will,' she said firmly. 'He was always complaining about the Christmas party, and why couldn't they go to such and such. Plus, he loves knights and mediaeval things.'

'Great,' said Ross, rubbing his hands together. 'Ooh, I am looking forward to this so much.'

He glanced at the calendar on his wall. 'Let's see – six weeks till presentation day, huh?'

Dave nodded dutifully.

'But Arthur doesn't know that. Howard's done his stuff, right?'

Dave nodded, then shook his head, then nodded again just to be sure.

'Right. This'll rile them. It's psychological warfare, innit?'

'What are you then, some kind of warlord?' said Fay.

Ross leaned over suddenly and thumped the table, hard. 'Yeah!' he said loudly. 'Yeah, I bloody am. This is about territory, darling. This is about land, and money and power, and you either fight for that or you don't. Okay?'

'It seems quite an extreme form of public sector management, that's all.'

Ross narrowed his eyes. 'Are you being funny?'

'No,' said Fay instantly, looking at the floor.

'Good. Dress up. It's about intimidating the

fuck out of them. By the time we're done, they'll be wishing they'd never heard of European City of Culture.'

Chapter Ten

There was a palpable air of excitement in the office. Partly it was because they were closing at four thirty to allow people time to get changed for the evening, partly because a light covering of snow had fallen the previous evening, rendering their world slightly less ugly than it had been before, and partly because Sandwiches was wearing his tuxedo early, because he was so looking forward to the party.

Arthur smiled up at Gwyneth as she walked into the room and she smiled back. She'd been reporting in London and he hadn't had much time to spend with her, but the report was really coming on: they were shaping up to have a strong case. And every time he saw her, his heart skipped a beat like a teenager.

'Hey baby cakes.'

'*Baby* cakes? Who are you, Philip Marlowe?'

'Well, this beautiful broad walked into my office like a ray of sunshine in a deadly tomb . . .'

She smiled and rapped him on the head. 'Thank you. Is this because I'm holding some draft reports in my hand?'

'Aren't you going to ask me if I'd like to investigate a case?'

'Yeah, a briefcase. Here, read these.' She took them off to her desk.

Arthur scrunched his nose up as Sven wandered in. He looked uncharacteristically sheepish as he sidled up to Arthur.

'What's the matter?' said Arthur. 'You've run out of X Men t-shirts?'

Sven made a face. 'Can't you ever be serious?' he said grumpily.

'What are you talking about? You're the one put here on earth to make my life hell!'

Sven stared at the floor.

'Okay, okay. Caring boss mode. What's the matter.'

'Um . . . will there . . . are there going to be girls at this party tonight?'

Arthur stared at him. 'Sven, it's the office party!'

'Yeah, I know . . .'

'So, it'll be full of the women you see around you, *every day*.'

278

'Yeah, but they'll be covered in glitter!'

'Relax. What are you going to wear?'

'Um, my Wolverine t-shirt.'

Gwyneth wandered back over. 'How come Sandwiches gets a tux and you're going to wear a t-shirt?'

'He looks better than me in one.'

'Well, that's true. But still, why don't you tart yourself up a bit? You never know, the temp looks pretty foxy when she's done up.'

Sven squinted. 'Do you think so?'

'Of course! I thought Scandinavian men were meant to be . . .' Gwyneth was casting around for something romantic to say, but she remembered what she meant was, 'really tall and handsome' and there was absolutely no universe in which that applied right at the moment. 'Kind and fascinating,' she finished, patting him on the arm.

'Who are you talking about?' said the temp, who was walking past. 'Nobody like that works here. By the way, Gwyneth, do you know if anyone cute is going to this thing tonight? Maybe from another department or something?'

'Um,' said Gwyneth. Sven sagged slightly.

* * *

The Mediaeval Knights restaurant was in a vast complex off the A250 which also housed a bowling alley and a three-hundred-and-forty screen cinema. Arthur had arranged people carriers to transport everyone, so he didn't have to worry about drink drivers — there was absolutely no other way to arrive. The place had so much flat car park around it, it looked like a massive corrugated shed on the surface of the moon.

'Are you sure about this?' Gwyneth asked Arthur, tucking her hand into his elbow as they fought their way, eyes streaming, across the windscape. Teenagers were taking it in turns to balance on their skateboards and shout obscenities loudly at one another. Some were swigging from enormous bottles of cider, their eyes distracted and aimless.

'Yeah,' said Arthur. 'I think so.'

Round the back of the building, there was a small ditch dug into the ground. A piece of corrugated iron had been placed over the top and, unless his eyes were deceiving him, Arthur noticed there were two of the jugglers he'd had to shoo out of the office the other day, hanging around. They saw them too and bowed low again.

'Well met, sir!' they called out as the party proceeded over the aluminium grate. Arthur smiled back at them.

'There's obviously more jester work around than I thought,' he whispered to Gwyneth.

'I'm not surprised they'd rather work for us than out in this wasteland.'

'We're going to ask them to work in the middle of a river.'

'Yes, well, I suppose . . .'

'What's that smell?' said Sven.

'You know, Sven, if they made a film about your life it would be called "What's that smell?",' said Marcus, who looked extremely neat and tidy in a sharp, shiny suit and immaculately tied bow tie.

'No, no,' said Sven. Sandwiches was snuffling about excitedly. 'I mean it.'

Gwyneth shook her head. 'You lot are such a bunch of city lovers,' she said. 'Although I realize that isn't necessarily a bad thing to be, given our jobs . . . but it's obviously horses. There are big pictures of them all over the brochure!'

'Yes, it is,' said Rafe, bringing up the rear. 'Landlubbers.'

As he spoke, they entered a huge hall lit by enormous braziers. It was so large – and dark – that the corners of the room had completely faded away. There was an enormous roaring fire on one side wall, and they moved towards it instinctively after the cold outside. Two long, rough-hewn tables had been set up near the fire, each laid for a large number of people. At the other end of the hall, was a low wooden wall dividing the dining area from a large space with a dirt floor, covered in straw, like an arena. To the far side was an inn-like bar. Even Arthur was impressed.

'Wow!' said Cathy. 'It's like olden times!'

'Good evening, fine gentlemen and fair ladies!'

A woman appeared in front of them with an extremely highly hoisted bosom bursting out of her loosely laced period dress.

The men goggled at her. The women checked out her underwiring.

'Can I take your coats?' said the wench, without quite so much mediaeval panache. 'Cocktail?'

* * *

Arthur looked around at the faces seated at their long wooden table, made ruddy by the fire and the odd cider ale that was being served as part of the 'Christmas package' as mead, but which tasted rather more like . . . well, flat snakebite. Nobody seemed to be complaining, though. And a smell of roasting meat had overtaken that of the horses, although he suspected the rotating pig in the fireplace was only for show. Well, he hoped that was the case. He suddenly felt a warm feeling of benevolence creep over him. This was his team. Gwyneth was on his left hand, Rafe on his right. Sven and Sandwiches were contentedly chewing their way through the contents of the breadbasket at the other end of the table. Marcus was looking worried and Cathy was being nice to him.

Arthur stood up. 'Friends and colleagues,' he started.

'Good Lord, is he drunk already?' somebody said, but they were quickly shushed.

'I just wanted to say . . .' He looked around, suddenly, suspiciously, then smiled. 'Actually, the last time we all got together for a drink, I got confronted by –'

'Your arch-nemesis?' said Ross, stepping in from the shadows by the bar.

'Aw, fuckit,' said Arthur.

* * *

'What are you doing here?' Arthur asked sullenly. 'Desperate for another punching?'

'Oh, I'm not so worried about that,' said Ross. 'More indulging yourself at the expense of local people, eh? Howard?'

Howard the journalist stepped forward, smiled apologetically and took a big picture of the table with the pig on a spit clearly visible behind them.

'Sorry,' he mugged apologetically. Then, 'Ow! That dog's biting me on the leg again!'

'I would love to say "what a coincidence" at this

point,' said Arthur. 'But it would be pointless, wouldn't it?'

'Just need the right friends, Art,' said Ross, as his party sat at the next long wooden table.

'Oh God, have you been sleeping with people again?' said Gwyneth.

'No!' said Arthur.

Ross picked up a haunch of what could have been venison, and gnawed it roughly.

'Why are you doing this?' asked Gwyneth, shaking her head.

'Oh, I don't know.' Ross sat back in his chair and took a long slug of mead. 'I just can't get over how much I'm looking forward to the day I get to turn up at your offices and tell you you're all out of a job. It pleases me so. It doesn't seem right that I should be the only one who knows what that's like.'

'It was a while ago. So get over it,' said Arthur.

Ross pulled forward Fay, who'd been loitering in the shadows. She looked wan and tired. Arthur was shocked at the sight of her.

'Hey,' he said quietly. She didn't reply, but sat timidly on Ross's knee.

'Yes, we're all *getting over things*,' said Ross. 'Anyway, this isn't about revenge.'

Sven and Sandwiches sniffed at the same time.

'There's only one big troughful of Euro money, my friend, and I'm sure it's going to be ours.'

'What would *you* do with it?' asked Rafe.

'Well, I wouldn't build a fucking tramline,' said Ross.

Rafe looked amazed. 'But that hasn't even . . .' He shook his head. 'That's incredible.'

Ross and Dave Gorman sniggered to themselves.

'So, are you looking forward to the twenty-sixth of January, then?' said Ross, rudely gesturing to the waitress for more drink.

'What happens on January twenty-sixth?' asked Gwyneth, wishing she hadn't had to.

'Ooh, don't you know?' said Dave, sniggering immediately. The group looked at each other.

'Yes we do,' said Sven suddenly, as another waitress came round. 'It's going to be shit. Can I have beef – um, haunch, please? And, do you do onion rings?'

'Shit for you,' said Ross.

Oh, God, thought Arthur. He's probably about to start cleaning his nails with a knife.

Ross picked up the knife. 'Of course, there's whether you think the application presentation date is important at all.'

Only the background of lutes stopped total silence from falling.

'Ignore him,' said Gwyneth. 'He's talking out of his arse.'

'Is he?' said Arthur.

Gwyneth shrugged. 'I just supposed they'd tell

us eventually . . . at the same time.'

Yup, there it goes, thought Arthur, as the knife went under Ross's thumbnail. He's loving this. And: 'Why didn't we know? WHY?'

'You should get your notification in . . . two or three days. Just in time for the Christmas holidays! Such a shame you haven't been able to work on it for a few weeks like us.'

'You've known for *weeks*?' Gwyneth couldn't help it. 'Um, just a salad for me thanks.'

'Not officially, no. In fact, I'd deny that anywhere. Big affair, I believe. Flying all sorts of delegates in from Brussels to hear what you've got to say. *Have* you anything to say?'

'More than you, I bet,' said Rafe. 'Yeah, the chicken, thanks very much.'

'Really? What do you know about our plans, then?'

Arthur's team shuffled and looked at their plates. Oh God, he's going to do a big fake evil laugh, thought Arthur in despair.

'Bwa ha ha!' shouted Ross. 'Oh, this *is* going to be fun. I'll have the chicken too, wench.'

Just as he said this, the lights went down and the show began.

* * *

Fuming, Arthur stared into the gloom. Gwyneth

was whispering frantically at him and trying to take notes in the dark. Suddenly there was a huge yell, an enormous commotion, and two doors at the end of the barn opened up and two horses charged through. The audience gasped.

Seated on the horses were two knights, one wearing black insignia, one in white. They cantered to opposite sides of the arena, then the horses stood stock-still, and on walked people dressed as a king, a queen, and various courtiers. The jugglers were back, joined by a fire-eater, and the jester was dancing around, his bells ringing in the sand. The white knight dismounted and bowed low to the party, but the black knight (who, with his visor closed, did actually look quite frightening) continued to stare straight ahead. Catching on quickly, the crowd booed him loudly.

'Fair ladies and noble gentlemen,' said the king figure.

'I'm glad this isn't going to be really cheesy or anything,' whispered Gwyneth. 'Guys, we need to go and sort out dates. Now!' Arthur agreed.

'But it's our party!' said Cathy, looking stricken.

'And he's the king! Ssh,' said Sven, who looked rapt.

'I can't believe an out-of-work actor dressed up

in tin foil has more authority over Sven than I have,' whispered Arthur crossly.

'Welcome to our humble hall. We trust you are feasting well?'

'Yeah!' the audience roared and cheered.

'Actually, my salad is a bit disappointing,' said Gwyneth.

'That's because you should be here to eat MEAT,' said Sven. 'Like real men.'

'Is this the bit where you say "Hitler was a . . ."'

'Hitler was a vegetarian, you know,' said Sven.

Gwyneth closed her eyes. 'So, there's a causal link between me eating lettuce and invading Poland, is that the point you're trying to make?'

'I'm just saying.'

'You're just saying that I want to commit genocide because I eat tomatoes.'

The white knight was suddenly standing directly in front of their table.

'My lord!' he shouted behind him to the king figure, who had finished welcoming everybody and was settled back, his queen beside him, each on a large gold-sprayed throne. 'I think I have found a talkative shrew, yes?'

Everybody laughed.

'Yes,' said Sven.

'What?' said Gwyneth crossly.

'I will be your liege, milady, if you'll let me.'

Gwyneth looked at Arthur. 'What's he talking about?'

'I think he wants to be your champion,' said Arthur. 'He'll joust for you.'

'I think NOT!' said Gwyneth loudly. Tuts ran around the room. Obviously there were more than a few ladies who would be quite happy for a knight on a white charger to single them out.

The knight, meanwhile, had bowed low and was waiting for an answer.

'What do I have to do? I disapprove of blood sports.'

'It's not to the death,' said Arthur. 'Is it?'

'You have to give him something,' said Rafe. 'A token that he can carry into battle.'

Gwyneth made a face. 'I think I've got my mace in my handbag.'

'Don't you carry a handkerchief?'

'Kleenex?'

'Give him your scarf.' Gwyneth had a stylishly-knotted scarf around her neck.

'Bugger off! This is silk, and I'd rather not have it smelling of horse, thank you.'

Arthur winced. 'Please. Or I think the audience is going to lynch us.'

There was definitely a murmur of discontent coming from the rows of people behind them.

'Okay,' said Gwyneth. She untangled the scarf and handed it over the barrier to the knight, who held it up dramatically, kissed it and tied it securely to his shield.

'Goodbye forever, scarf,' said Gwyneth.

'Splendid,' said the king. 'Now . . .'

''Ang on,' said a loud and unmistakable voice, suddenly. The king looked around, confused.

'If 'e gets to fight for someone and have a bunch of saps cheering him on, we want the black knight.'

'Ooooh!' said a jester. 'Prithee a proper challenge, in faith.'

A mutter ran through the crowd. Someone could distinctly be heard saying, 'God, we're going to be here all night.'

They soon hushed, however, as the black knight began to approach Ross's table. He didn't rush, but walked slowly over. The menace was actually palpable.

He's good, Arthur found himself thinking. The king was looking this way and that, quite perturbed. The black knight stood in front of Ross's party, who were all baying like maniacs. He didn't raise his visor, and stood stock-still.

'Okay,' said Ross. 'Knock out that big pussy and I'll give you a hundred quid. Not some sodding scarf.'

'Um,' said the king, 'I'm not sure we're allowed . . . I mean, I decree that there will be no gaming at this evening of entertainment.'

Ross sneered. 'Okay, forget it,' he said, but winked clearly at the knight.

'Give him your tie, you big poof!'

'Sven, shut it,' said Arthur in a loud whisper. Ross whipped around, looking for where the slur had come from, but quickly refocused on the matter in hand.

'Okay,' he said.

The knight barely nodded his head in response.

'Let's go!' said Ross, turning to his table and raising his arms. They all yelped loudly in response.

* * *

The king raised his hand as the riders got on their horses and retreated to the dark corners of the barn.

'The joust!' he said. 'Who will be unseated in this tournament?'

'I bet,' said Sven carefully, 'it looks like the guy in white is going to lose, but then in the end he grabs the victory back just in the nick of time.'

Gwyneth found her heart was beating quite strongly in her chest. 'Ooh, I'm excited,' she said.

'That's because you're anxious about your champion,' said Rafe.

'No, I'm not. Sven said he's going to be fine and that's good enough for me.'

Sven basked in this unusual appreciation of his powers.

'The knights will joust,' intoned the king, 'and the first man to be thrown three times will be declared the loser and banished . . . from the salad bar!'

The room cheered and looked excited.

The queen stood up and held her handkerchief up high, then, suddenly, dropped it.

The room went completely silent. Then suddenly, the horses started to move, their hooves rumbling over the sand. Every eye was fixed on them, as the riders drew closer and closer together from either end of the vast hangar. The black knight was hunched over on his mount, his hand clasping the lance firmly. The white rider looked calmer, sitting upright in the saddle and urging the horse on with his spurs.

'Go, Whitey!' said Gwyneth. 'Oh God, that sounds really awful, doesn't it?'

'Maybe "Go Honky",' said Arthur.

'I don't think they had equal opportunities in the middle ages,' said Rafe. 'A chance for death for everyone!'

But they were no longer listening to him. The hooves thundered louder and louder and . . .

'FFTHHH!' They could hear the whistle in the wind as, right in front of their table, the two long poles just missed each other. Immediately, the two horses were past each other. The black rider pulled his up with a snort and immediately turned round. The white knight let his canter on for a little, then abruptly turned her round, too. The large white mare whinnied, and reared up.

'Ooh,' murmured the crowd.

The two rode at each other again, this time, it seemed, much more quickly. There was a resounding 'smack' as they met, the clash of the wooden poles on the wooden shields, and suddenly, the black rider had pitched forward in a somersault and landed in the sand, sending up clouds of dust.

'Yay!' shouted Sven. 'In your face, Rossy-boy!'

Ross turned round and for a second looked like he was about to stand up. Sven was giving him the Vs. But he contented himself with sticking up his middle finger, just as the rider got up and started to dust himself off. He growled and shook his fist at the crowd, who excitedly booed him back. He mounted his horse with a toss of his head and galloped back to the end of the arena, then he steadied himself and his horse. Silence fell again.

'This time,' whispered Sven, 'the white rider

will go down. Then he'll go down again. But it'll be all right, he'll stage a triumphant come-back.'

'I think they're waiting for a moody silence,' whispered Arthur.

'Ooh, sorry,' said Sven. Sandwiches was sitting very still on his lap, watching the proceedings with interest.

This time, there was a drum roll from the min-strels, who built up to a crescendo, then watched as the knights launched themselves forward again.

Arthur gnawed on a chicken leg and looked at the scene through half-shut eyes. If he forgot the corrugated iron, and the nasty fake Rolex watches and synthetic fibres at the surrounding tables, there was something soothing to his soul in the smell of the horses, the sound of their hooves and the minstrels, the colours flashing past. It felt very very right, somehow.

'My time,' he said to himself.

'Your what?' said Gwyneth, not taking her eyes off the approaching battle.

'Did I just . . . nothing . . . OOF!' said Arthur, as the black knight thwacked the white knight's shield with an almighty crack. The white knight seemed to fall to the ground in slow motion, bouncing off his armour.

'That's got to hurt,' observed Sven. 'Unless

they're all padded up underneath, like those people who wear fat suits.'

'Ooh, are you wearing a fat suit?' asked Cathy innocently.

'NO!'

Sven appeared to be right, however, as the rider was soon on his feet again. He turned towards Gwyneth and bowed low.

'*Well*,' said Gwyneth. She leaned forward and held out her hand so the knight could raise it and kiss it.

Arthur didn't like this at all.

* * *

As Sven had predicted, the next two rounds ended in a draw – a tumble for each knight. The drum rolls were now growing steadily louder, as the two drew apart to the furthest end of the arena for their final charge and confrontation. The whole audience was banging their pewter tankards on the wooden tables, and the noise was deafening.

'FIGHT! FIGHT! FIGHT! FIGHT!' The chant was started up at Ross's table. The king looked anxiously at them to be quiet, but they drank more mead and did not deign to notice. Even the riders looked nervous – the white knight was tugging at his spur.

The drumming grew to a great crescendo, then,

for the final time, the queen brought down her arm, and the horses reared up.

'GO! GO! GO!' Everyone in the place was screaming their heads off for their favourite. Now they were a hundred feet apart . . . now seventy . . . the horses' hooves were a blur on the dusty floor, the sound of their breathing was heavy in the air, and by the light from the braziers, Arthur could see sweat shining on their flanks.

The noise from the hooves was immense, and Arthur sat back, waiting to engage in a victory whose outcome was already assured.

It didn't come.

From nowhere, a pace or two before the weapons should normally meet, the black rider leaned even further forward in the saddle, and cracked his lance clean across the other rider's helmet.

The white knight was thrown through the air, before landing, motionless, on the ground.

* * *

For a second, everyone in the audience was still, expecting this to be a further part of the entertainment. Then the king threw up his hands and ran forward.

'What the *fuck* just happened?' he shouted, in a remarkably un-regal manner.

* * *

The white knight lay on the ground, out cold. Rafe noticed the black rider and Ross were staring at each other. It was impossible to tell, but it looked as if the dark knight might have been winking.

Without a thought, Rafe threw himself over the barrier between the tables and the arena.

* * *

The whole table stood up.

'What the hell's he doing?' said Arthur. The rest stood there with their mouths open. Rafe ran towards the white horse, grabbed the lance from the ground where it had fallen, and swung himself up and into the saddle like he was born to it.

'Hey!' Gwyneth was staring at Rafe. He pulled back the bridle and turned the horse to the far end of the arena. The crowd was going crazy, stamping their feet and screeching. The king was desperately trying to stop proceedings and stay out of the way of the horses. Meanwhile, the white knight had started to stir, and was carried to the side.

Rafe wheeled the horse round and threw up his hand at the black knight. 'And now me, yes?'

The black knight, no longer sniggering, stared straight back at Rafe. Then, slowly, he raised his lance to his side.

A gasp ran through the crowd – a real one now, not just entering into the fun of watching a show.

'He's crazy,' said Arthur. 'He's not wearing armour or anything. He could get himself killed!'

But it was too late. This time there was no gesture from the queen, but at some unheard signal, both men reared up on their horses and took off towards each other at a gallop.

Gwyneth hid her head in her hands. 'I can't watch.'

'He's *mad*,' Arthur was saying again, standing up. 'STOP!!'

From the side, the white knight struggled to his feet. He held up his shield, then, as Rafe bore down past him in a blur of motion, tossed it towards the huge horse. Amazingly, Rafe reached down a long arm and scooped up the shield, then stood up in the saddle, and extended his lancing arm . . .

There was a cracking noise of wood against wood, and in the jumble of colours and horses in the middle of the arena it was difficult to see what had happened – until, almost in slow motion, and with a strange sort of grace, the black knight slowly tumbled down from his horse, metal scraping against metal as he came to rest on the ground.

Ross let out a chain of expletives that could have turned the white flames blue.

There was a huge storm of cheering. Rafe's face was very red, as if he couldn't quite believe what he had done. Very gently, he patted the horse and slipped down. Then, walking towards the front of the arena, he slipped the scarf from around the shield. Coming closer, he gently and carefully tied it round Gwyneth's neck as she looked up at him.

'My lady,' he said. Then he went even redder, and turned away.

Chapter Eleven

Gwyneth was wandering down by the river, lost in a dream. The frost patterns on the ground were enchanting and, from a primary school down the road, there was the sound of tentatively played Christmas carols. Just now, 'Torches! Torches!' was ringing out with some gusto, along with a little off-time triangle.

It was a sunny morning, and she needed to think. The party had definitely been peculiar. Rafe had been blushing, and so sweet, but Arthur . . . He had been cold and stand-offish to her after the joust, even when everyone else had been celebrating. Could she have been wrong about him? Could he be interested in her after all? Oh God, there was so much work to do; she couldn't waste all this time dithering between a man who could ride, with a very cute tush, and someone – someone she couldn't work out at all. He seemed . . . There was something almost other-worldly about him, sometimes, in the way he looked at her, as if he understood her on some deep level.

Which was rubbish, she thought to herself. Given the chances he's missed already. Grragh! She tried to think of something else. It wasn't easy.

* * *

They had the meeting date, finally. Arthur had spent all day on the phone, apologizing to the Mediaeval Knights company, desperately trying to get the European commission on the phone, and begging Howard not to write a horrible piece for the newspaper (to no avail: Howard had listened carefully to everything Arthur had to say, nodded, agreed with the difficulty of his position and filed 'City of Culture Pretenders Steal Horse, Run Rampage').

Gwyneth smiled to herself, remembering Arthur's expression at that one, and she was pleased she felt tender towards him like that. She moved onwards, not noticing the solitary figure of Fay, meandering along the opposite bank, half sick of shadows and trailing her hands through the willows.

* * *

Lynne blinked. She had reappeared as unpredictably as ever, muttering crossly about something which sounded like 'Mongolian lion-birds', and looking more dishevelled than ever.

'He won a joust?'

'That's bad, isn't it?'

Lynne shook her head. 'No, no. We just see this quite a lot. Some traditions seem to work themselves out through the generations . . . I wouldn't worry about it.'

'But, I mean . . . What's causing it?'

Lynne shrugged. 'Oh, you know – the mystic forces.'

'Oh, *those* mystic forces.'

Arthur chewed the side of his mouth.

'Ah,' said Lynne. 'You're chewing the Gwyneth side of your mouth.'

'I'm *what*?'

'What's troubling you?'

'Nothing. Well, only that I thought we were . . . I thought we were really getting somewhere. But not when someone would MUCH rather give scarves to other people.'

'How were you getting somewhere?'

'I don't know! I put my arm around her for a whole flight!'

'Cool beans,' said Lynne.

'Cool beans? Do you even know what that expression means?'

Lynne looked almost embarrassed. 'We shall forget that instance. I have trouble with this sarcasm standard.'

'No kidding,' said Arthur.

'Indeed, I am not kidding. Have you talked to her?'

'What? What is it with you therapists and talking all the time?'

'I don't know,' said Lynne. She ferreted around on her shelves and finally came up with an enormous, leatherbound hard-backed tome. Blowing the dust off the cover, she slowly opened it. Arthur leaned over until he could see the spine. It was called *Thye Moderne Art and Methode of Psychologie, as Pracktised by Humans*.

'Here,' said Lynne, pointing to page one. In beautiful ornate print it said:

𝔍nstructions on the aforementioned pracktice

𝔓retende to 𝔏isten at all times.

𝔖uggest they talke unto each other.

There was nothing else on the page. Nor, as she turned over, on any of the other pages. The book was totally blank.

'I see,' said Arthur.

'I suggest,' said Lynne, drawing herself up proudly, 'you talk to each other!'

'You utter bloody buggering bastard!' Arthur was screaming into the telephone as Gwyneth walked into the room.

'It's okay!' said Arthur. 'They'd already hung up on me.'

'That *is* okay,' said Marcus. 'Um, what is it?'

'Nothing! Only, *apparently*, the letters of invitation to attend the presentation went out to everyone at the same time, two weeks ago.'

'So how come we didn't get one?'

'Exactly! Do you think there's a mole in here?'

'Just a smelly dog,' said Marcus. 'I wouldn't have thought so. Didn't you have that dodgy newspaperman in?'

'It wouldn't have been him,' said Arthur. 'It was him, wasn't it?'

Sandwiches leaped up from where he'd been sleeping in the corner and sauntered out of the office, a determined cast to his paws.

'Okay, everyone.' Arthur stood up. 'Staff meeting! Three o'clock. And I want us all ready with strategy.'

There was some muttering round the room. Gwyneth sat down quietly.

'OKAY?'

* * *

Everyone sat round the conference table studiously staring at their notepads. Rafe had a livid bruise running down his hand from where he'd slid down his horse. The restaurant management had been very good about it, considering the black rider had resigned on the spot, the queen was having convulsions and even the horses had decided to show their excitement by crapping extensively all over the floor and a little too close to Arthur's chicken for comfort. Bar takings had trebled and Ross and his henchmen had filtered out the back door.

The work was bearing down on them at a rate of knots. It was a week until Christmas, then January twenty-sixth was the date sent to them on the replacement form. The E.C. papers were due to be handed in on Friday. They would have half an hour to present their case in London, as Ross had hinted, rather than Brussels as they'd first imagined; then they had to hang around in case there were supplementary questions, then . . . Well, then they'd find out. And either start the biggest job in the world, or – well, Arthur didn't like to think about the alternative to doing that. He wanted to find a moment to talk to Gwyneth, but there never seemed to be a spare minute. He thought he'd spotted her looking at him, but he didn't really trust his own instincts in that department these days.

'Right, everyone. Okay. We have a big meeting to prepare for.'

'Why? Is something happening? said Sven.

Arthur shot him a look. 'I realize that we're all meant to have an equal voice around this table, but I'm tempted to rescind the privilege.'

'You can try,' said Sven. 'And fai—'

'OKAY,' Arthur repeated loudly. 'Presentation. We only have half an hour. We have to decide what to say and in what order. We're all going except Cathy.'

'Public speaking gives me asthma,' she said, looking as cheery about this fact as she always did about anything else.

'Well, we've got that brilliant maze model,' said Marcus.

'Um,' said Sven.

'Yes, that's a good idea,' said Gwyneth, taking notes. 'It's so beautiful. You can relate to it immediately. Ooh, could we have a model of the town? With the maze as the centrepiece? I know it would be big, but . . .'

'Um,' said Sven again.

'Are you waiting your turn to say something?' said Arthur. 'I approve.'

'No,' said Sven. He looked slightly red. 'The thing is . . .'

'Where *is* the maze model?' said Rafe suddenly.

306

'I thought we usually had it out, in here.'

Sven cricked his neck.

'Okay, what?' said Arthur.

'Sandwiches ate the maze,' said Sven quickly in a small voice.

'*No*,' said Gwyneth. 'That thing was art.'

'And looked like dinner.'

'It looked – and smelled – like a bunch of cardboard HEDGES!'

'I'm sorry, okay?'

'Where is he?' said Gwyneth.

'I think it's probably too late to give him trouble now,' said Arthur.

'Well, he's not stupid. He's not even here. He's probably lurking behind the door.'

'Okay, no maze,' said Arthur. 'That's a shame. A model would have been a good idea, but it would have been difficult to carry to London anyway.'

'What about computer modelling?' said Marcus thoughtfully. 'You know, take some pictures of Coventry, then stick our stuff on top so it looks like a real photograph?'

'Brilliant,' said Arthur. 'I've no idea how that might work, but it sounds good to me.'

'What if they decide that the photographs are good enough on their own and we don't have to build anything?' said Gwyneth. 'Sorry. Silly question.'

'How are we doing on the lighting, Rafe?' asked Arthur.

'Really well!' said Rafe, looking surprised. 'It's mostly old ladies who live on those streets, and do you know, they've all been really nice and friendly to us!'

Cathy and Gwyneth swapped a look.

'Really,' said Arthur. 'That's nice. Well done.'

'I spoke to Johann,' said Sven. 'Everything's going to be fine. No problem. It's all to do with density, you see.'

'What?' said Marcus. 'Like how dense your dog is when he eats the plans?'

The returning Sandwiches's nose had just become visible behind the door. It suddenly disappeared.

'No! It's all hi-tech physics stuff you wouldn't understand.'

'I might understand it,' said Marcus. 'Try me.'

'La la la,' said Sven. 'Arthur, do you think they might like me to sing a Danish song at the presentation?'

'Definitely not,' said Arthur. 'Right. And we've got our jugglers – and doesn't that knight want to set up outdoor jousting with you, Rafe?'

'Probably not on the ice, though, eh?' said Gwyneth.

'No, of course not.'

'In the park,' said Rafe. 'If people want. We could have a whole mediaeval fayre day, get people to dress up. We could raise money for – I don't know, a kidney machine charity or something.'

'I like the sound of that,' said Arthur, making a note. 'I'll tell Howard.'

'Oh, don't speak to him!' said Gwyneth. 'He twists everything.'

'I'm wearing him down by becoming his friend,' said Arthur. 'He'll feel bad about writing horrible stories about us sooner or later.'

'Yes, that's how journalists work,' said Gwyneth.

'Okay, so we'll have the pictures – do you think . . . Hmm. I wonder.'

'What?'

'Do you think we should take the jesters? They could juggle and make music just as . . . you know, entertainment for the judges. It'll make us stand out.'

'As rank amateurs,' said Gwyneth. 'Why not just get Sven to sing his bacon song? It's gimmicky.'

'Yes, but it'll give a flavour of what we're trying to achieve.'

'Yeah. Um, Arthur, this isn't *Pop Idol*.'

'So, you all think we should just go in and be totally boring and give them a boring presentation?' Arthur's feelings were hurt.

'But you don't want them to think we're frivol-ous, do you . . .' offered Cathy tentatively. She was knitting a reindeer jumper.

'Cathy's right,' said Gwyneth. 'We need to go in suited and booted. Dressed to the nines. No smiling. We've got to show them we mean business, that we're not just a bunch of wastrels who like music and can't keep their mugs out of the papers. That's my official consultancy position.'

'They'll never fall for it,' said Arthur. 'You really think they'll be convinced by Sven in a suit?'

'Yeah,' said Sven. 'Plus, a tie constricts my singing voice.'

'I don't care,' said Gwyneth. 'And no dogs.'

Sandwiches's nose had just become visible behind the door. It suddenly disappeared

'So we're trying to pretend we're people we're not,' said Arthur, before Sven could object.

'That's called working in an office.' Gwyneth was clipped. 'It's called being in a job.'

They stared at each other.

Can't she see I worship her? thought Arthur.

Why is he such a WIMP? thought Gwyneth.

'That's crap,' said Arthur intelligently.

'No, it's not!' said Gwyneth. 'If everyone behaved how they wanted to in an office . . . well, we'd all be Sven . . .'

'And the problem is?' said Sven.

'I just don't see why we have to jump through even more hoops than we already do,' grumbled Arthur.

'Really? I thought you loved hoops,' said Gwyneth. And they glared at each other, whilst the rest of the room watched them closely.

* * *

'She's . . . she drives me crazy,' said Arthur to Kay, as they sat enjoying a beer after Christmas dinner at their dad's. 'She is so *annoying*. She has to be right all the time.'

Kay nodded. He was extremely laid-back compared to his nervy half-brother, and was already showing the benefits of the good life in Australia, in particular a tan and paunch combo and an ability to grumble almost endlessly about how rubbish Britain was.

'Well, just phone her up and tell her how you feel. You know, that you love her.'

'I don't love her!'

'Yes, that's why you've stopped talking about her for . . . Not At All since I got here.'

'And, oh yes,' said Arthur, ignoring him, 'just phone her up, blah blah blah, "Hi Gwyneth, here's my innermost feelings, O professional working colleague".'

'You're always like this,' said Kay. 'A complete coward. And ponce.'

'I am *not*.'

'Yes, you are. Fay was exactly the same. Had to do all the running because poor little Arthur didn't want to talk about it.'

'That's bollocks! Just cos I don't want to go on *Trisha* about it and use lots of Kleenex about relationships. It's pathetic.'

'I'm telling you, mate. Girls dig that kind of stuff.'

'Do they?' said Arthur, glumly. He changed the subject. 'Kay, when I was a kid, right – was there anything funny about me?'

'What do you mean? All of you. You were a complete nutter.'

'I don't mean like that. I mean . . . anything that made me stand out from other kids?'

'Yeah,' said Kay.

'What?' said Arthur, leaning forward.

'You were a complete dick.'

* * *

'Well, dear,' said her mum, efficiently drying up straight after dinner. Gwyneth was nominally helping, but actually taking a chance for a quick heart to heart without her four brothers and sisters bursting in.

'What are you looking for really? He sounds lovely.'

'He *is*.'

'So?' Her mum kept drying up. She worried about her fiercely independent daughter sometimes. She had a wilful, cutting streak that made it hard to compromise and settle down. Seemed to come with the territory of being a perfectionist.

'Mmm,' said Gwyneth. 'I'm just not sure it's right, you know? It's not professional. Plus, there's this other guy.'

'You always hide behind "professional" when you don't want to do something,' pointed out her mother. 'And there'll always be another guy.'

'Mmm. Grrr!'

'So what's wrong with him?'

'Nothing, really. In fact . . .' And her face softened. 'Did I tell you he killed a wolf?'

'You told everyone,' said her mother. 'But I actually believed you.'

'And he has such a sweet smile, and . . .'

'There you go,' said her mother. 'Why don't you call him?'

Gwyneth winced. 'I hate calling guys.'

'Happy Single Christmas,' said her mother.

* * *

'Hey,' she said on the phone. 'Alright?'

Arthur couldn't have expressed how pleased he was to hear her voice.

They met at hers, in the eyrie of the old house. There wasn't much talking.

'We should talk,' said Arthur.

'Let's not,' said Gwyneth.

And she walked over to him, the house so cold they could see their breath in front of their faces.

'Let me . . .' she breathed.

'No . . .' He scarcely knew what he was saying, as he took in the feel of her, the smell of her, the way her lips felt on his. He was overwhelmed; transported.

'Is riding a horse as much fun as that?' he said afterwards.

'Not since I was thirteen,' she said. 'No. Of course not.'

He laughed and pulled her close.

* * *

'Good Christmas? Good Christmas?' Cathy was asking everyone cheerily as they filed back into the office. Outside the weather was a steel grey, and the motorway and the sky had blended to the same colour, so the cars looked like they were flying over the bypass. It was bitterly cold, but the offices were terribly overheated, meaning everyone permanently looked a bit dry and crispy round the edges.

'How was your Christmas, Cathy?' asked Rafe, breezing in, tanned and healthy-looking from skiing. He looked edible.

'It was fantastic,' said Cathy. 'The boys got lots of computer games and Peter got to go to the pub a lot, so I think it worked out really well all round.'

'Excellent. What about you, tempy?'

'I threw up fifteen times and copped off fourteen times.'

'Great! What a shame for the last guy, missing out on all the vomit . . .'

Sven and Sandwiches wandered in.

'Good Christmas?'

'It was good,' said Sven. 'Although a lot of tinsel disappeared for some reason.'

Sandwiches burped loudly.

'I wonder how the happy couple got on?' said Marcus slyly. The others looked at each other. The obvious – that Arthur and Gwyneth appeared to be having some kind of relationship – had never been mentioned before.

Rafe went quiet. 'None of our business, I expect.'

'Ooh, I think it's lovely,' said Cathy.

'*Lovely*,' said Sven, snorting. 'You won't be saying that when there's unidentified stains all over your stationery cupboard.'

'Don't be nasty,' said Cathy.

'Yeah,' said the temp. 'Lots of us get stains on

things. Plus you just can't believe someone might be getting laid.'

'That's not true!' said Sven. 'Marcus hasn't got a girlfriend, either.'

'That's because I've had a boyfriend for the last four years,' said Marcus. 'Tosser. You I mean, not him.'

Sven looked grumpy. 'Well, I just hope they won't be at it all over the office, that's all. It's disgusting and it's bad for morale. What if they break up and start fighting all the time?'

Arthur and Gwyneth walked in together, gazing into each other's eyes. They were practically holding hands.

'Oh . . . Welcome back, everyone,' said Arthur. 'What have you all gone so quiet for?'

'Nothing,' they said at once.

'Um . . . we're not on the cover of the newspaper,' said Marcus. 'You might want to get onto Howard. Ooh, and I was at my – ehem, my friend's at Christmas time. He lives in Slough. I'm sorry, seeing as you're just back and everything, but he showed me this . . .'

Marcus pulled out the *Slough Daily*. There was a huge picture of Ross and Fay on the front: '**Slough looks Definitely Set for Glorious Triumph in European Challenge**' read the headline. 'Exclusive by Howard Phillips'.

'Oh crap,' said Arthur. 'Happy New Year.'

* * *

The train to London was dirty, smelly and packed. January torpor and a smell of wet blazers had settled over all the inhabitants.

The three weeks since Christmas had been a blur of activity; of trying to tie their presentation together in a way that made it coherent, practical, legal, pragmatic and not completely barking.

Arthur and Gwyneth had tried to fit in as much time together as possible, but it wasn't easy. At the very least, there would be three other people walking in, calling their mobiles, and the sheer weight of work meant that a few late snatched meals were as much as they could manage.

For Arthur, though, these were everything. He couldn't get enough of this girl. She was everything to him. He had to find a way to tell her how he felt: more than sex, more than spending time with her.

Gwyneth was enjoying it – much more than she'd expected. For someone with such a lanky frame and awkward manner, he was surprisingly commanding in bed. But he hadn't indicated where this was going at all. Sometimes, even lying in his arms, she couldn't read what was going on in his head. She worried then that this was just a 'thing' to him; a passing affair, even on the rebound. Well, she certainly wasn't going to force the issue. She wasn't one of those clingy, insecure women. She was a consultant!

Marcus had spent night after night tweaking Excel sheets, juggling numbers and budgets to come up with a sum that was going to be acceptable to the burghers of Brussels. Sven had spent long hours arguing about ice (at least, they assumed that was what he was arguing about) with Johann on the phone and pretending to do long calculations whilst in fact entirely trusting in the professionals. His graphs of expected people flow were slightly more reliable, based on years of research done by other people. Traffic, however, was still causing a headache. Like all towns run on cars, Coventry had been overstuffed with them for years. There weren't many easy ways to accommodate more, and especially not with Rafe popping up and whispering, 'Light Railway! Trams!' every hour on the hour, when he wasn't filling in the hundreds of official plans required for the siting of a maze, subsection (d) Points 1.1 through 6.4 in the official 'Maze Siting' portion of the council's extraordinary forms department. Occasionally Rafe wondered whether there really was an entire department devoted to maze siting, but he was too busy between the maze and haggling with electricity suppliers to worry about it too much.

The lights part of the festival should, if it came together, be entirely spectacular. There wouldn't just be patterns visible from the sky: forests of lamp-posts would be put up, sponsored by local businesses; tall buildings would have rotating patterns set up in the windows; Coventry would become – hopefully – a living, breathing light bulb.

'As long as we have fireworks, too?' asked Gwyneth

'Of course, my love.'

'And perhaps just a Very Small tram,' ventured Rafe.

'No!' said Arthur.

* * *

Now they were all tense, sitting on the train surrounded by other people hollering into phones, or listening to insanely irritating buzzes coming from loud Walkmans.

'I used to do this every day,' whispered Gwyneth.

'What – swallow the urge to kill?' said Arthur.

'Yeah. Pretty much. Commute, I mean.'

'How did you manage?' asked Sven in wonder.

'Lots of people do it, you know, Sven,' said Gwyneth. 'It's not exactly like being tortured.'

'It feels exactly like being tortured,' said Sven. 'Don't you think, Sandwiches?'

Sandwiches poked his head through the luggage rack, where he had been ignominiously dumped by station staff.

'Hnrgh,' he said.

'I thought he'd have been happier in the guard's van,' said Marcus.

'Actually he quite likes being up high,' said Sven. 'Gives him a certain lofty sense of satisfaction.'

'When did you stop commuting?' asked Arthur with interest.

'Only when I came to you,' said Gwyneth. 'Oh, gosh, that's odd – that must have been around about the same time my nervous rash cleared up.'

A man in a striped shirt sitting in front of them abruptly stopped scratching the back of his neck.

'And about the time I managed to remember how to get myself a decent night's sleep.'

Another man, wrapped up in his overcoat, snorted and jerked awake, his eyes bright red and rheumy.

Gwyneth shook her head. 'You know, I once really thought I missed London.'

The train drew to a halt and sat there for no reason for forty-five minutes.

'But actually, maybe the sticks aren't so bad after all.'

* * *

The city was heaving with smartly dressed men and women rushing everywhere down ancient streets in some great hurry. Arthur was conscious that in his best suit, a navy wool M&S job, he actually looked like shit in comparison to all these men with their handmade pinstripes and fat bottoms.

'All of these guys have back ends like Sandwiches,' said Sven loudly. Sven was wearing a black t-shirt with 'Anthrax' written on it, and a dinner jacket of entirely uncertain origin. Gwyneth was trying to get him to button the jacket to hide the slogan, but it was an ongoing battle.

'And lots and lots of money,' said Marcus gloomily. 'I'd take the arse.'

They drew closer to the address, laden down with flipcharts and slides. They'd drilled and gone over the speech so many times, Arthur knew it in his sleep, not that he'd had any.

'Do ray me fa so la . . .'

Marcus kicked Sven sharply on the ankle. 'Arthur! Sven's singing!'

'He kicked me!'

'Stop it, you two,' said Arthur in anguish. 'You just need to behave for one day, okay? Is that too much to ask?'

They both shrugged. They had reached the

building named in the letter. It wasn't any old building, though – it was a cathedral. A huge, pink, pointed, jagged structure that looked like a church, but worshipped money, politics, power . . . It towered thirty storeys off the ground, the shards of windows glistening in the light.

'Bloody hell,' said Rafe. 'That is *not* a friendly place.'

'You don't think it has dungeons, do you?' said Sven anxiously.

'No, but there's probably a speedy exit chute for those of us who don't make the grade.'

They all gazed at the façade, which glistened like one of Johann's ice palaces in the early morning sunlight.

'Well, nothing ventured . . .' said Arthur. 'There's no moat, after all . . .'

'Good afternoon, sir,' said the doorman. 'Can I see your passes, please?'

Arthur looked at him. 'Um, we're here for the European Culture meeting.'

'Yes, sir. I need to see your special author-ization.'

'Special authorization? I have a letter here . . .'

'No, sir, I think I'm going to have to talk to my superior.'

Arthur turned to the others, who were eyeing him suspiciously. '*No*, there wasn't anything else in the envelope we were sent. Unless somebody has been secretly opening the post and eating the contents.'

Sandwiches gave his most innocent look.

Suddenly Gwyneth caught sight of someone getting into the lifts at the far side of the lobby.

'Oh crap – look,' she said.

Ross waved at them as the doors of the lift started to close. 'I'm sure you're not carrying any hazardous materials,' he said, 'but I thought I'd better warn the staff just in case.'

The doorman's supervisor, who looked to be about six foot five, was on his way over.

* * *

One hour later, slightly uncomfortable after a fairly thorough search, the five made it up to the waiting room. Ross and Dave sat killing themselves laughing in a slightly over the top fashion.

'You pigs,' said Rafe.

'Leave them,' said Arthur. 'They're not worth it.'

'All's fair in love and business, mate,' yelled Ross.

'This isn't business!' said Arthur. 'This is service. There's a difference.'

Ross leaned forward. 'What? What are you

talking about? What century are you living in? You take this money from whatever you like, boyo, but it's still about getting the punters through the doors, to look at whatever their plebby little hearts want to see. It's about money in and that's all. And if you can't see that, you're a bloody idiot.'

The two men stared at each other, colour running high. Finally Arthur sat back and shook his head.

'I feel sorry for you,' he said simply.

'You won't,' snarled Ross. 'When I'm waving at you queuing in the job centre, scratching your scabies and wondering if you could afford one Viagra tablet to remember what an erection felt like.'

'Mr Maudrin?' said a young receptionist. 'They're ready for the Slough delegation.'

'Right, love,' said Ross. He got up, and, suddenly, winked at Gwyneth. 'I'm sure we could find some room for you though, darlin'.'

* * *

The Coventry group sat, bored and adrenalin-fuelled at the same time, in the large waiting area on the thirty-fifth floor. Alongside them there was a German party, who were still having a sensible, reasoned conversation about – well, Arthur couldn't tell, but certainly no-one was slagging off anyone else's dog's behaviour, or attempting to sleep with people. Likewise the Italians, who seemed entirely and hopelessly nonchalant about the whole thing. In his head, Arthur compared Coventry to Verona in a cultural competition. The results, even in the head, did not really bode well. Meanwhile, Marcus and Sven were arguing again about whether or not it would be possible or tasteful to have giant truck wars on the ice. Rafe and Gwyneth had their heads together, deep in conversation. Arthur thought he wouldn't have to get much closer to hear the phrase 'light railway'.

Custard creams, small unpleasant mints in glass jars, lime and orange cordial – all were consumed, refilled. Mouths felt gritty, heads stuffy with the air conditioning and the knowledge of the ordeal to come. Sandwiches snoozed happily on the fake fibre carpet. If the Slough party – the only other British attendees – had come out, they had done it a different way. Now a crowd of insultingly tall and attractive Scandinavians were filing in, speaking loudly and confidently. Arthur ran over his speech for the eleventh time. Perhaps just as well, he thought, not to have gone with the jesters and minstrels. Might not have gone down so well here, in a world of quietly whispered petitions and hushed corridors, where unimaginable amounts of money, for unimaginable purposes, were whisked back and forth, invisible. Perhaps, Arthur thought unhappily, perhaps Ross was right after all. These were money people; grant givers, life changers. Nothing idealistic was going to impress them. Hard-headed, EU PLC . . . oh God. Maybe they'd got everything wrong, at every step.

* * *

'The Canterbury panel, please?' said the young receptionist. They sat there, until she coughed and said, 'Sorry – I mean, Coventry.'

'Well, that's a good start,' said Arthur.

He moved to the door.

'Sir, you can't take that dog in there,' a receptionist was saying to Sven.

'He's my guide dog,' said Sven. 'I have no sense of smell.'

The receptionist breathed in deeply. 'Well, that's obviously true,' she said.

Sandwiches concentrated very hard on being well behaved.

'All right, then.'

And she shepherded them down the corridor and into the main boardroom . . .

* * *

Walking through the door was an extraordinary experience. Everyone hesitated and blinked. The people in the room were obviously expecting this reaction and smiled patronizingly. Outside, they had been sitting in a bland corporate reception, with basic leather sofas, beige carpet and floor-to-ceiling windows.

They had just stepped into a Georgian drawing room.

Sash windows were gently lit by wall lamps. The walls were moulded plaster, painted soft shades of white and eau de nil. A huge wooden fireplace dominated the far end of the room, its beautiful proportions framing the perspective. A fire burned in the grate.

Oil paintings hung on gold chains from the picture rail, and in front of them was a seemingly endless table, polished so sharply it looked like a mirror. Someone had obviously gone to a lot of trouble and a lot of expense to bring this here, and wanted you to know it.

Standing on the threshold between what felt like the new world and the old, Arthur felt caught, like a child in front of the headmaster. He squeezed his eyes shut. What would his slightly more famous ancestor have done in the circumstances?

Slain a dragon, he expected, smiling ruefully to himself. He stepped forward, first out of the group.

'Good afternoon,' said the man at the centre of the panel on the far end of the skating-rink table. 'I'm Jean-Luc d'Aragon.'

* * *

Afterwards, Arthur could only shake his head whenever he thought about it. It was such a stupid coincidence, he nearly laughed out loud. Again there were three figures seated at the end of the table. But these ones didn't talk, or rudely ask what he was doing. They didn't seem to react at all to anything, but sat calmly, unhurriedly, waiting for Arthur's motley band to organize themselves.

'Hello,' said Arthur, finally. He introduced himself. 'I'm leading this project . . . with Gwyneth Morgan.'

D'Aragon looked at them. A tall, saturnine Frenchman, he had very fine features; it looked like the planes of his face were pulled back from his nose, which was pointed. He looked at them as if there was nobody there.

'Welcome then,' he said. 'I'm chairman of this panel, I am from Brussels,' – his accent was so faint as to be almost undetectable – 'and these are my colleagues, Miss Hauns and Mr Obute.'

Both nodded slowly.

'If they ask us three riddles I am *so* out of here,'

said Gwyneth. Arthur was suddenly thinking the same thing.

'Well, maybe *this* time they'll ask some proper algebra,' said Marcus.

But they didn't. That was the curious thing. They sat and watched – not even taking notes – as Arthur fumbled with the overhead projector; as Marcus set out clearly their financial implications and projections; as Sven tried to convey just how necessary to life was a good ice-maker; as Rafe waxed lyrical over his admittedly beautiful, if entirely fictitious photographs of what Coventry would look like if it was turned into a city of light. There were statistics of people input, parties, festivals, fireworks – the maze was shown, and Rafe even had a video of people running through his cress fascimile, which had eventually – but after a remarkably long lifespan for underfoot cress – succumbed to frost.

Gwyneth spoke of the city; Le Corbusier and Walter Moses; the post-war rape of the town that many considered worse than what the Luftwaffe had done. The renown for ugliness and the longing for improvement. She talked about public art and the Angel of the North, La Defence, the failures of the London dome, and the strength of the community. She was magnificent. Arthur looked at her, full of pride and love.

'And,' she finished, 'it's just an addendum, but we would love to provide some sort of alternative to driving to these attractions. Something along the lines of a light railway.'

Arthur was so surprised he nearly contradicted her there and then. Rafe beamed. None of the judges so much as indicated they had heard.

Arthur stepped up to the lectern, feeling quietly confident. 'Thank you for listening,' he started, tentatively. 'I think you can see from this . . . We're a really committed team, and we know exactly what we want to do in Coventry. I don't want to repeat what my – ahem – colleague has said, but, if you look at Glasgow . . . and, erm . . .'

Suddenly, it was as if a cold wind blew through him. He started, put off his stride completely. His words had run out. What had seemed so clear and passionate in his mind about what he wanted to say had deserted him. The others were still looking at him expectantly.

D'Aragon was staring straight at him, with a disapproving look. Arthur felt his mouth grow thick and sticky. This couldn't be happening. This was *not* the time to get stage fright. He had things to say, goddammit. People's jobs were depending on this. His bloody town was depending on this. And these . . . these people, that bloody dragon man, whoever the hell he thought he was, just sitting there . . . and he was supposed to be impressing him. But maybe he couldn't impress him! Maybe he wasn't the leader after all! Maybe he wasn't destined to do this. Because if he was, he wouldn't be making such a bloody hash of it now, would he?

This flashed through his mind in seconds, although it felt like hours. The others started to look at him with some concern. The judges showed no change of expression whatsoever.

Arthur desperately tried to swallow his panic. He didn't feel as if he could tear his eyes away from d'Aragon's face.

'So what I'm trying to say is . . .'

What was he trying to say? It seemed confused in his head; or a silly thing to want to do, or a waste of time, or a pointless lie, or, or . . .

The silence was definitely lengthening now. Somebody cleared their throat quietly. Arthur felt so *stupid*. The tension levels in the room were sky-high. Transfixed by the judge's eyes, he could still feel the others' gaze upon him, concerned and frightened. He was frightened. What was the matter with him? Why couldn't he catch his own tongue and . . .

God, he remembered Lynne saying something: not to worry about the dragon. Well, she was bloody wrong, wasn't she? Here he was, making a Big Idiot out of himself, and his entire department, and . . . the sweat was bursting out of his forehead . . . He thought of Lynne suddenly. She would be so disappointed in him. He tried to remember what she had said – that these men were neutral, that was all.

Suddenly, out of nowhere, there came a very soft sound, almost inaudible. Sandwiches' head whipped up and he looked towards the door. D'Aragon's eyes briefly flickered in that direction. It was only for a millisecond, but his hold on Arthur was broken at last.

Arthur staggered backwards, as if he had been hit. What did he think he was doing? He was only giving a speech, for goodness' sake. He'd done it a hundred times before – albeit for less lofty aims – and he'd do it again, and he really had to get over himself. He almost laughed in disbelief.

The sound grew louder, though it still wasn't loud. It was now, clearly, the faint timbre of a lute playing. The minstrels must have got in after all, thought Arthur, shaking his head. They must have found out about the meeting and decided that they were required to accompany the speeches. Well, they were right.

He cleared his throat and stepped forward once again.

'Look,' he said. 'Anyone who doesn't want to be part of this project – the biggest, the most important thing that has ever happened to our town – they can go. I include everyone,' he nodded at the judges. 'But I want to be able to tell my children that one year I was there at the best thing that ever happened to Coventry, that made people believe in it in a way they couldn't have imagined. And that it wasn't the easiest thing we ever did. But I feel sorry for every Coventry man and woman that won't be doing it with us.'

The music began to swell to a crescendo, and he raised his voice.

'I want, every year that goes by, for people to remember Coventry and what it meant to us. There aren't many of us, but we will struggle, and work, and create something to remember, so that in one year – when our names are forgotten and every-thing is past – it won't be forgotten that Coventry did something and it meant something, and it was all because of you and it started today.'

Arthur found he was pounding his fist on the lectern, and that he was faintly out of breath.

The music faded away as quickly as it had begun. Unbelievably, the others applauded quickly. Then stopped abruptly and looked round, faintly embar-rassed.

'Yeah,' said Arthur. 'Well, um, thanks.'

'Sorry about the musicians,' said Arthur to the young receptionist.

She looked up at him in confusion.

'What musicians?'

* * *

They were directed to a large room at the top of the building, where all the prospective teams were waiting to hear if they would be called back. A faint aura of anxious sweat was overlying the carefully applied deodorant, the new shirts and expensive aftershave. One of the teams — Arthur couldn't tell where from — Turkey perhaps? — was going through their entire presentation all over again, with one obvious boss character haranguing them at every stage.

Rafe sat next to him with his eleventh cup of coffee of the day. 'I thought . . . it was all right, wasn't it?' he asked keenly.

'Yes,' said Arthur. 'I think it was . . . all right. Good enough is another matter.'

Gwyneth came over. 'My two favourite boys!' she said. 'I am SO pleased that is over with. What happened to you?' she nudged Arthur playfully.

'Stage fright, I expect. Didn't you think there was something weird about that d'Aragon bloke?'

'Apart from the fact that he was named after a terrifying mythical beast?'

'God, yeah.'

Gwyneth shrugged. 'No weirder than all the other complete weirdos I've met since I started this project.'

'Yeah,' said Arthur again. 'Hmm.'

Ross and his posse passed by their sofa. Immediately Ross nudged Dave in the ribs, who shouted, 'God, we were GREAT in there,' and the whole team gave an enthusiastic round of applause.

'You laid it in right. High cash, high profits, fast cars, fast food . . .'

'Nothing like it,' said Dave. 'I've never seen a panel spontaneously clap before.'

'Go bite him, Sandwiches,' said Sven. 'Fast food.'

'Oh, sorry,' said Ross, turning round with exaggerated slowness. 'Didn't see you lot there. Don't you have a train to catch back to the sticks?'

'As opposed to the buzzing metropolis of Sluff?' said Marcus.

'Soon will be, mate. Soon will be. Had them eating out of our hands in there. And D'Aragon tipped us the wink.'

Are you sure he didn't just hold you in his hypnogaze? thought Arthur, but he kept it to himself. He didn't want to talk to this crowd, but he couldn't stop himself asking, 'Where's Fay?'

'Sorry mate, tired her out!' Ross laughed, until he saw the appalled faces of even some members of his own group, in particular a large snotty woman called Niamh, who sneered at everything. 'She ain't been too well.'

'What's the matter with her?'

'What's it to you?'

'I don't know. She's a human being who's accidentally taken up with a big fat rat. Why wouldn't I be worried?'

Ross shrugged his shoulders. 'Well, I don't know what's the matter with her. She just keeps mooning around.'

'How would anyone notice any difference?' said Gwyneth under her breath.

'Has she seen a doctor?'

Ross looked at Arthur full on. 'Keep out of this. In fact, you should just keep out of all of THIS,' he swept his arm around the room, 'if you've got any sense. Unlikely.'

Arthur thought he'd never hated another man more than he did at that moment. 'It's in the laps of the gods now, Ross. Nothing to do with you or me.'

'That's right, sunshine,' said Ross, turning away suddenly. 'You believe that.' A camera flashed, and Ross flashed a grin to reach it.

'Thanks Ross!' said the voice. 'That'll go down great on the front page! Well done!'

'Howard,' said Arthur, with resignation in his voice.

'Oh, hello, Arthur. How are you? You're looking well. Um, sorry I can't take your photo. Unless you want to look really sad, you know, like you've just been defeated.'

'No,' said Arthur. 'No, I won't do that.'

By six o'clock, the mood in the room was poisonous. Except to Rafe, who was stretched out fast asleep. Sandwiches was watching Howard's every move and growling almost imperceptibly every time he as much as twitched. Howard had been desperate to go to the toilet for nearly ninety minutes, and was trapped in a tight and encircling hell of his own.

Finally, at twenty past six, the receptionist entered the room. The air immediately sparked with tension. Rafe woke up and accidentally rolled off the sofa.

'Sorry,' he said, but no-one was paying him any attention.

The receptionist looked around. 'Could the Helsinki team report upstairs, please.'

There was no inflection, no emotion in her voice at all. It wasn't clear what she meant – was this it? Were the rest of them all just to go home?

The tall Scandinavians stood up, brushing themselves down and looking as puzzled as everyone
else.

'Fuck,' said Gwyneth sharply under her breath.
Arthur stilled her.

'Don't . . . we have no idea why they've just
been called.'

'Because they're Finns,' said Sven. 'Prejudiced
bloody panel.'

'How could they possibly be prejudiced towards
Finns?'

'Well known fact. Everyone is,' said Sven, and
stuck out his bottom lip.

'Well, don't panic. Yet,' said Arthur. 'You never
know – it could be like *Big Brother* and they call
them out in reverse.'

'Yes, because the panel looked like the fun,
game-playing types.'

Nothing else happened. No-one had told the rest
of the teams to leave, and no-one had wanted to ask
if they were dismissed, in case it showed a defeatist
attitude. So the groups sat stock-still, heavy of
shoulder, shadows gathering under reddening eyes.

After another twenty minutes, the receptionist
appeared at the door again. Once more, faces popped
up eagerly, like hungry dogs at six o'clock.

The receptionist cleared her throat. 'Could the
Bonn team . . .'

No-one heard what she said after that; the exhalation of relief — or anger, from the German contingent — was so strong.

The teams trooped out one by one, their attempts to look stalwart belied by the pricking ears and tilted heads trying to pick up the rap of the receptionist's heels on the long corridor each time she returned. Cleaners came in, worked around them and disappeared again, and however well soundproofed the offices may have been, there fell on the building the undoubted sense of a place uninhabited; they were intruding into the world of the office at night, when computers hummed and backed up, and complied, and janitors polished floors, and phone lines picked up information and messages from the side of the world still bathed in sunshine.

Ten o'clock came, eleven. It was after midnight. They were all exhausted. At eleven thirty precisely, the receptionist had appeared, framed in the doorway, to remove one of three remaining teams. It had been the Italians, the team from beautiful Verona. Perhaps, Arthur thought, Verona didn't need any money to make it beautiful, to make it cultured. Verona was fine as it was, and people loved it. Coventry wasn't fine. It wasn't loved. It needed them.

He snuck a glance at Ross. And now there were

two. Slough was the only other team left. Ross's people were slumped in a corner. Some of them were asleep already, but he couldn't make out Ross's eyes, hidden in the moonlight.

Arthur crept to the high window and peeked out over London. The lights of the London Eye were glowing, and Tower Bridge could be seen, raised, and letting through a great ship. It was beautiful. Arthur smiled ruefully. Okay, so Coventry wasn't so hot on the great bridges and towers and wheels stake. But still . . .

He thought of the cathedral he was standing in, and closed his eyes for a second. Suddenly, briefly – later, he realized he must have drifted off for a second – he was on the horse again. But alone this time. He was riding like the wind down the passageways of this pink monument, scattering papers behind him like a blizzard, vaulting the reception desk, pursued by . . . he couldn't tell, but he was definitely being pursued. He found himself pounding into the Georgian state room, and the white mare effortlessly, gloriously vaulting the shining table, which was now made of ice, and as cold and as sharp as steel.

He could see the dragon veer up now, and join in the chase. But he was too far behind. The horse galloped over desks, over photocopiers. It wasn't just this office now, it was Coventry too, and many other places where he'd sweated and worked and poured years and centuries and . . .

The horse spilled coffee over desks but did not stop. Printer toner exploded over everything but they went on without stopping. Computer disks, ring binders, hanging files, desktop toys, calendars, reminders, circulars, memos, staplers, pagers, ties, vouchers; all went whirling into the great maelstrom of the horse's wake, chaos erupting behind them, until they reached the great window and Arthur realized there was no stopping them now, and they broke clean through the glass and were soaring, high, shadowed against the cold, bright, clear stars and the wild empty night, over the land, the motorway, the delays, the accidents, the stalled train sulking in a siding, the lone hitchhiker, the greasy, overlit service station, the hurtfully orange sodium bulbs, and only a small child, tucked up in the back of the car, tiny on the great road, and supposed to be sleeping whilst his parents made an absurdly early start in an ever-defeating attempt to beat the traffic – the perpetual, endless traffic – saw them as they flew and pointed his finger and gleefully cried out, 'horsie' as his parents sighed and bickered as to whose turn it was to get him back to sleep.

'Well, well,' said the quiet voice.

Arthur immediately snapped back, to find himself leaning on the window ledge, his nose practically pressed against the glass to the city below.

Just as he noticed Ross standing beside him and staring out at the view, a soft tongue licked at his hand. Silently, Sandwiches had left Sven's lap and come over to stand next to Arthur. Arthur felt ridiculously grateful and scratched the dog's head under his hand.

'More of a cat man myself,' said Ross.

'Yes, you would be.'

Ross sniffed, then glanced behind him. 'It's all right, they're all asleep.'

Arthur looked at him strangely. 'What do you want?'

Ross shrugged. 'Nothing, really. I just thought, you know. Here we are, still. Just the two of us. You must be doing something right.'

'And your point is?'

'I don't know. Just, you know, maybe we shouldn't always be working apart.'

'Yes, well, you started it by trying to fight me and calling me a tosspot.'

Ross shrugged again. 'Yeah, whatever. I was just thinking, you know, maybe turn things into a joint operation . . .'

'I know what you're thinking,' said Arthur, speaking as quietly as he could through his anger.

'You think we're going to win and you want a piece of the pie. Great. Actually, that makes me feel really good.'

'I don't think that at all,' spat Ross. 'I was trying to do you a favour. Help you out.'

'What *are* you getting at?' Arthur stared at him in the darkened room.

'Well, you know . . . might be able to find a place for some of your staff when you lose this competition.'

Arthur blinked rapidly. 'Christ, Maudrin, you are absolutely unbelievable.'

'What? It's reasonable.'

'You want Gwyneth.'

'She's the only one with half a brain in your lot.'

'Unbelievable! Just when I think you couldn't possibly slime any lower, you surprise me.'

Ross shrugged. 'Fair enough, mate. It's not like I have any trouble sorting out your birds.'

'Excuse me? You picking up my leftovers, you mean.'

'I don't think she'd go back to you, mate.'

'Well, you stay away from Gwyneth. She's mine.'

'And she knows that, does she? That she belongs to you?'

'Just bloody keep your hands away from my stuff!'

343

Arthur couldn't remember being so angry.

Ross put up his hands.

'Wow, calm down, mate.'

'Yes, perhaps you should calm down,' said Gwyneth.

Arthur turned round, his heart draining down through his boots.

'You weren't talking about me,' she said. Arthur couldn't tell if it was a statement or a question.

'Er . . .'

'I didn't know you "belonged" to him,' said Ross with a sneer. 'Don't want to dabble in anyone else's property.'

Gwyneth stared straight at Arthur as Ross slouched off.

Arthur closed his eyes. Crap, crap, crap. This was all he needed. He couldn't believe it. 'I'm so sorry,' he started.

'Forget the macho bullshit,' she said. 'Believe me, in this job I've got used to that.'

He looked at her. 'But . . .'

'What did you mean, Arthur? What am I to you? I wish I had one fucking sign, one tiny idea. I mean, I'm sleeping with you, so I'm your property? Is that what you mean?'

Arthur stared at her, caught completely off guard. It had never even occurred to him that his adoration wasn't clear and absolute. He opened his mouth to speak, when he felt Sandwiches push him to face the door. There, looking as perfectly made up and set as she had done sixteen hours earlier, stood the young receptionist.

Chapter Twelve

Immediately everyone stood up and started patting themselves down, but in the midst of all the confusion, Gwyneth didn't take her eyes off Arthur for a second. What was . . . he was . . .

She realized, watching Arthur stare at her, that he had truly no idea, no awareness of his inability to communicate with her – God, maybe with Fay, maybe with all women. Why was it so hard for him to make even the tiniest gesture towards her, when he was quite happy to get involved in some macho pissing contest with a short-arsed tosspot from Slough? The *jerk*.

Arthur could feel his blood galloping through his veins. He strained forward to hear the receptionist, even though she hadn't started speaking. She waited until everyone was up, dazed. Rafe had a big chunk of hair sticking up from his head.

The entire room was completely quiet, apart from Howard hopping from foot to foot, still trying not to go to the toilet.

The receptionist stared at them blankly. Arthur could feel sweat breaking out on his forehead. Oh, God.

'You are all required upstairs,' said the receptionist. Then she closed her mouth and walked out.

At first there was silence, as people tried to take in what she'd just said. Then pandemonium, as everyone tried to scramble to the door to follow her.

'If they're going to make us work together, I'm going to get Sandwiches to bite off the bollocks off every single one of you,' said Sven loudly to Ross's team as they left the room.

* * *

The room looked exactly as they'd left it. Again, the three judges sat at the far end of the table, with only d'Aragon rising to greet them. He smiled an unpleasantly tight smile, like a crocodile.

'Welcome back,' he said.

Arthur looked at Ross, who was looking at him. Then he moved his glance to Gwyneth, who looked away.

D'Aragon briefly looked at his notes. 'We have considered all of the proposals,' he said. 'And we have explained to the other teams why we will not be proceeding with their applications.'

They weren't going to appoint two cities, were they? No, that would be impossible – far too expensive. It was much more likely they were going to have to share – some kind of Midlands/South festival thing. Oh, boy, that was going to be terrible. How was he going to work with that man?

He realized d'Aragon was talking again.

'We were impressed by both of your . . . very different applications. After much discussion –' He paused. Neither of the other two judges did as much as look up. 'We have decided that we need to see a bit more before we choose between you.'

Arthur breathed a huge sigh of relief inside. At least they hadn't lost outright. Deep down he had been really worried that this was a particularly cruel way of awarding the contract to Ross whilst they had to watch. On the other hand, he had also hoped that it might have been going their way . . . and now there were more hoops to jump through.

'We've decided to see – we need to see what you're made of. This is a huge contract, and it's worth millions of pounds to your cities. We need to know it's in safe hands.'

Arthur blinked, trying to get a grip on what was coming.

'We're sending you both off on a management training exercise. In Wales. You'll both have an objective, and you'll be playing against each other. It'll be specially designed to be mentally and physically tough, and at the end of it we'll know what kind of teams we're dealing with. And that will decide it.'

The room was quiet as both sides digested this. Then Ross thumped Dave's massive arm. 'Great!' he said.

'Absolutely,' said Arthur stoutly. 'That sounds like a great idea.'

'Will there be running?' said Sven.

'There will be running, finding your own food and shelter, solving problems, and you'll have to fight each other . . . with paintballs, of course.'

'Shouldn't be a problem,' said Ross levelly.

'Absolutely not,' said Arthur.

Sven and Sandwiches gulped.

'Excellent. Would your two leaders like to shake on it?'

Arthur put his hand out. Ross grasped it, reluctantly.

'Let battle be joined,' said d'Aragon, mildly.

* * *

Arthur took a deep breath. It was now or never. Lynne, he thought ruefully, would be proud of him. He walked up to Gwyneth.

'I'm so sorry,' he said, off the bat.

'Don't worry about it,' said Gwyneth. Arthur was vividly reminded of the tight ice queen who'd first walked into his office.

They looked at each other.

'Is that all?' said Gwyneth. She gathered up some files and prepared to leave the room.

'You mean so much to me, I can't tell you.'

She looked up, her heart beating unsteadily. 'Well,' she said. 'Really?'

Arthur took another deep breath. 'I'm in love with you, Gwyneth. I love you. I do.'

Gwyneth froze. Even though she'd thought about it – a lot – she hadn't been expecting this. This was . . . this was more than anything.

'You what?'

'I know. It's a lot.'

'It's a *lot*? You've gone from nothing to a million miles an hour!'

'Yeah . . .'

'I mean, couldn't you have started with a flirtatious text message and worked your way up?'

Arthur couldn't think of anything else to do but stare at her with a mute appeal. Her shock was making her sarcastic, and she was well aware of this.

'I mean, Christ, Arthur – what have you been doing?'

'But . . . I didn't want to make it really horribly

350

obvious . . . and I didn't know and . . . Oh, God.'

'Oh, God,' repeated Gwyneth.

'Please,' said Arthur. 'I mean, I thought it was obvious.'

'You assumed,' said Gwyneth. 'And now I don't know what to think.'

'*Please*,' said Arthur. 'Come to Wales. That'll be great. We'll get a chance to be together. It'll be really good . . .'

'I'm not sure I should be under canvas with you right at the moment,' said Gwyneth.

Arthur looked at her, his face creased with disappointment. 'But the team needs you . . . I need you . . .'

Gwyneth backed out of the room. 'Yes . . . yeah . . . let me . . .'

Words failing her, she fled.

Arthur stared after her. Maybe, it occurred to him, he didn't really understand women.

Chapter Thirteen

Mixing a man deep in thought with a dirty Landrover and several hours' driving in the pitch dark into completely unknown territory was, Marcus thought, a terrible idea, as the vehicle hit another seemingly enormous puddle in the road and bounced the occupants of the back seat up and down. Sandwiches yelped under his yellow mackintosh.

'*How*,' said Marcus, 'is that dog going to get up Welsh mountains? He's got legs the size of a chicken's.'

'Just like the rest of us,' said Sven. 'Very, very slowly.'

Arthur was clenched over the wheel in front, cursing the driving rain that was throwing itself against the windscreen. It might have been February, but the weather showed no sign of granting them any mercy at all. He was struggling to remember what it was to have a sunny day.

'Bugger it!' he shouted into the windscreen. 'It's all mud. I can't see a damn thing.'

They had graduated from the motorway to A roads, and now they were trying to make their way along various strands of mud in the pouring rain through Wales, where none of them had ever been – except Gwyneth of course, and she wasn't there. She'd taken the day off, for God's sake. She'd told him she'd ring to say whether she was coming, but she never did. And then when it had been time to go, Rafe had disappeared on another of his mysterious errands, shouting that he'd follow them in his own car later on.

They'd left the office at five – this was to be a weekend event and it was important, the very strict letter that had arrived had said, that they spent a typical week at work beforehand, as the programme would 'push their mental and physical strength to the limit'.

Arthur fully suspected Ross's gang would have been at a health farm all week. He was feeling perilously close to his emotional limit as it was, but he gritted his teeth and pushed his face even closer to the windscreen, splashing the car through the great holes in the road and trying not to knock over any sheep.

The mood in the back of the Landrover wasn't

much more cheerful, as everyone thought about what lay before them. Only Marcus, it had turned out, took any regular exercise whatsoever, and Arthur wasn't convinced that trainspotting counted as exercise anyway. Rafe was fit of course, but Rafe was mysteriously not with them, and without his jolly demeanor and optimistic attitude, the rest of them were feeling very flat and full of trepidation about whatever lay ahead. Arthur, in particular, realized how much he'd come to rely on Rafe to buoy up his own moods. The brochure which had arrived, and been passed around many times, was fairly clear about what was required – 'EXCELLENCE in team building and FIRMNESS in its goals' – without exactly saying what was about to happen to them. There were lots of pictures of stern-jawed men climbing hills and achieving things. They were all worried about it.

Cathy had been particularly downcast. Even now, she was sitting mute in the van with a pair of trainers on. Arthur hoped these weren't the closest thing she had to hiking boots.

'CHALLENGE your DEEPEST FEARS and GROW to a higher PLANE!' the brochure had said. It made it appear suspiciously like a cult.

'By doing what?' Sven had said worriedly. 'I don't like vegetables very much. Do you think that will come up?'

'Could be almost anything,' said Marcus, studying the brochure. 'This thing is a masterpiece of doublespeak. Now I must get back to re-tabulating the commercial projection analysis.'

'It says, "Bring lots of clothes you don't mind getting wet,"' said Sven unhappily. 'I've just bought Sandwiches that duffel coat.'

'Yeah, well, it makes him look like Paddington Bear with long ears,' said Gwyneth who was passing. 'It's not a good look. You should have stuck with the Burberry.'

'Every poodle, basset and badger has *Burberry*,' Sven had said. He himself was wearing an ACDC t-shirt, a Hawaiian shirt and some suspiciously out of season shorts.

'Marcus! Map read!' shouted Arthur now.

'I told you before,' said Marcus. 'You need a fixed position to map read from. If you've no idea where you are, you can't work out how to get somewhere else.'

Arthur cursed again and drew up at a pub. Then he looked at the mutinous eyes of his colleagues and drew away again, to a howl of disappointment.

'No!' he said. 'We stop there and we will never leave. Listen, I think this is shit as much as the next man, but we're doing it, and not only are we doing it, we're going to win.'

'Yur . . .' said the back seat.

'So, we're going to have to get a positive mental attitude about this.'

'He's been reading the brochure again,' said Sven.

'We've got to get there by ten o'clock and it's . . . well, it's quarter past ten, so this is not going well, okay? We *have* to win this.'

'If only we could win it by watching *Friends* and eating pizza,' said Cathy dreamily. 'I'd be great at it.'

* * *

It had been an unusually blue and unclouded day for February. As usual, Gwyneth was hoping that the river might help her. Her mind was in tumult. After all, she'd thought they were just starting out, or worse, that it was just a brief affair . . . Memories of other brief office affairs she'd had came back to her, nastily, and she squirmed.

But suddenly, everything had jumped forward. And now . . . how did she feel? A smile played about her lips as she remembered the way he had come out with it . . . how he looked asleep . . . the trip to Denmark . . . and if she wanted to go to Wales, it was probably too late . . .

Suddenly, someone loomed up ahead of her. She couldn't see him as the sun came dazzling through the leaves.

'Hey hey!' he shouted.

Gwyneth put her hands over her eyes. 'Yes?'

'It's me,' said Rafe, grinning like a naughty schoolboy.

'You normally run around parks shouting "hey hey"?' said Gwyneth incredulously.

'Nope, only today! What are you up to?'

'Now?'

'Yes.'

Gwyneth shrugged. 'Having life debates with myself, I suppose.'

'Forget that,' said Rafe. 'You have to come with me. Just for a minute. I've got something you'll really like to see, I promise.'

'Um . . .'

'Look, I'm on my way and I see you. It's fate. You have to come. Like – hey hey!'

'That great, huh?'

'Hey hey!'

* * *

Gwyneth followed him out over the common, shaking her head and smiling. His enthusiasm was contagious.

They headed down a maze of backstreets into rundown areas along the railway track that Gwyneth had never seen before.

'Where *are* we going?'

They ended up in some kind of goods yard filled with tumbledown sheds.

'Spooky, isn't it?' said Rafe.

'I'll say. What the hell are we doing here?'

'Follow me,' he said, delving into his pocket and taking out a strong torch.

* * *

'Oh my God!' said Gwyneth. 'It's . . . it's FABU-LOUS!'

'I know,' said Rafe, his smile cracking open his face. 'Sorry. I can't be modest about this. Aren't they fantastic?'

'So this is where you've been sneaking off to all this time?'

'No, sometimes I was sneaking off to build the cress maze.'

'Oh, yeah,' said Gwyneth.

'But mostly this.'

'Well, congratulations. You've done . . . I mean, are they going to work?'

Gwyneth had tentatively – and with some eye to her heels – followed Rafe into one of the warehouses. There, Rafe had lit some large oil lanterns and the light had fallen on what he'd been building.

'They were just rotting away in here. Can you believe that?'

Three ancient shapes loomed out of the gloom. They were original trams, with the railings intact on the front and old advertisements for long-dead products visible on the sides. Except, as you looked at them closely, you could see that the wood had been highly polished, and they had recently been painted a rich dark hunting green. The brass bell at each tram's back had been buffed up and the dull metal shone. They even smelled new – of varnish and leather.

'Can I jump up?'

'Be my guest.' And Rafe held up the lamps.

Inside, the trams felt brand-new. Gwyneth sat on one of the red leather seats and felt a broad grin crossing her face.

'They're . . . it's . . .'

'You like?'

'Can they go?'

'Sure,' said Rafe. 'Get the lines back up and running for a few thousand quid, have a tricky conversation with the road department, and Bob's your uncle.'

Gwyneth ran up to the open-topped roof. 'I LOVE them!'

Rafe grinned back at her. 'They're just finished. I bought them off some geezer. I thought they might work for us.'

'Oh, yes,' said Gwyneth. 'I'm sure they will. I

want a shot in this one right now.'

'Not possible, I'm afraid,' said Rafe, looking at his watch. 'We need to get on the road.'

Gwyneth leaned over the top railing, looking down on him. 'Oh. Oh, yeah.'

'You are coming, aren't you?'

She closed her eyes for a second. 'Yes,' she said.

They looked at each other. Gwyneth rubbed the barrier under her hands. They were both thinking of how much of a hope they were going to have out there.

'It'll be fine,' she ventured.

'I know!' said Rafe. 'Come on, then. If we're too late, they'll sneer.'

'The office runs on sneer,' said Gwyneth. 'It'll help. Look.' She indicated a wing mirror. 'That mirror's cracked,' she said.

'Can't finish everything,' said Rafe. 'And we have to go.'

What is fate, anyway? wondered Gwyneth, following him out.

* * *

'Are we there?' said Sven as the Landrover slowed from a crawl to a waddle.

'No,' said Arthur. 'The fact that this is the sole point of light in the last seventy miles is a mere coincidence.'

'Alright, alright,' said Sven, rubbing his dog's ears. 'No need to get grumpy just because we're stuck in the pissing rain in the middle of nowhere and we're three hours late for a competition we probably can't win.'

Arthur closed his eyes tight in exhaustion, but opened them again and parked next to the low bothy-style wooden building.

'This is the place,' he said. 'Now, get your stuff and march in, and at least *try* and look cheerful.'

'We'll follow your lead, then,' said Marcus.

Arthur stretched his neck and cricked it. 'Oh, yes,' he said. Then he pasted a huge smile on his face. 'Come on, everyone! This is going to be the most fun of our lives!'

* * *

The bothy was tiny and looked completely functional – like a wigwam made out of wood. The darkness was the type that's never seen in the city; as soon as the car's headlights were turned off, the world receded into complete blackness, barring a solitary oil lamp. One had the sense of hills, of infinite blackness somewhere out there, and no sense at all that there was civilization remaining somewhere far, far behind them.

Arthur pushed open the wooden door cautiously.

He could hear voices. As they entered the room, the voices stilled and all heads turned round.

The room was as unprepossessing inside as one might have guessed from the outside. Straw had been strewn on the floor, and round the top of the teepee shape was a platform that could presumably be used for sleeping on. The sweet smell of the wood and the straw mixed uncomfortably with the scent of generations of smelly hiker. Cheeringly, however, a fire burned brightly in the grate.

'Oh, how kind of you to join us!' said Ross. He was dressed in all-new Alpine outdoor gear in purple, black and green, with brand-new boots and rucksack. He looked a dick.

'Good evening, Dick,' said Arthur. 'I mean, Ross.'

'Good evening,' said another voice. D'Aragon. He was dressed in an understated grey fleece. Hard, thought Arthur, to make fleece menacing, but he'd somehow mastered it.

'This is your team?' he asked, with a hint of disbelief as the others slunk in. Cathy was wearing several brightly coloured mohair sweaters, one on top of another.

'I only count four of you. The notes specify five. I'm afraid the dog cannot be accepted as a team member.'

'He's got more brains than most of them,' said Ross. 'You should let him in.'

Sandwiches tried to growl menacingly, but let himself down by trying to eat some straw at the same time.

'No,' said Arthur. 'One of our team-mates has been delayed. He'll be with us shortly.'

He fervently hoped this was true.

D'Aragon blinked. 'Very well. But I shall have to outline the rules now, and you will be responsible for making sure he understands later.'

Sven and Marcus struggled to see who could be the first to programme the right recording facility on their palm pilots.

'Okay,' said Arthur.

* * *

D'Aragon unfolded a huge Ordnance Survey map.

'As you should already recognize, this is a map of our surrounding area.'

Arthur's team leaned over and nodded knowledgeably, as if it meant something to any of them.

'Here is the bothy.' The bothy looked very very small in the vast undulations of the Welsh mountainside. He indicated two crosses equidistant – and both far – from the building. 'These are going to be your camps. You will be making your way to them at first light tomorrow morning.'

Arthur thought about it. That was about five thirty. It was after midnight now.

'There are several things hidden you have to pick up on the way – there are clues to what these things might be and where you might find them in these envelopes here.' He handed huge cardboard folders to Ross and Arthur. 'Once – and only once – you have everything, you, Maudrin, are setting up camp *here* and Pendleton, you're over here. Both settlements are in sight of this point here.' He pointed to a small sign on the top of a hill. Arthur craned in to see. 'That is the castle. The following morning you will fight your way in there with the paint guns you'll find at your campsites and rescue the treasure from within. Then,' he stood back, 'then it will be over.'

There was a silence.

'Not that I mind,' said Arthur, 'but did you say, "guns"'?

'Paintball! Yes!' said Ross.

'Uh huh,' said Arthur. 'It's a shame they didn't throw in ten pin bowling and an Imax cinema, then you could have had the full out of town leisure complex experience.'

'What!?' said Ross, his face lighting up. 'You mean you've never done it?'

'Yeah, nor paintball neither,' said Dave, sniggering to himself. It was obvious that their team could not contain their glee.

Sven turned puce.

'Oh, God,' said Cathy. 'This is just *awful.*'

D'Aragon fixed them with a look. 'And if any team wishes to withdraw at this point, thus forfeiting . . .'

'No!' said Arthur. 'We'll be fine.'

'Very well, then. I suggest you get some sleep. You have a busy couple of days. Remember: five people per team. Oh, and if you were thinking of getting help, your mobiles won't work up here.'

And with that he left the room and was gone. Arthur listened for a car, but didn't hear one. And then, by the time he'd turned round, he realized that Ross's team had already colonized the sleeping platform that ran, warm and dry, entirely around the upper area of the bothy.

'Goodnight you lot!' giggled one particularly obnoxious older woman from her sleeping bag.

They looked at each other.

'No way,' said Sven. He lifted Sandwiches up in the air. Sandwiches immediately ran to the nearest sleeping bag and made to cock his leg. The man let out a yelp.

'Get this beast away from me immediately.'

'Sorry!' said Sven innocently. 'Unfortunately, due to a medical condition, Sandwiches always has to pee up high.'

Sandwiches grimaced, trying to look as though he was about to do an enormous crap.

'Get that filthy dog down at once,' said Ross.

'You're more than welcome to try and hold onto him mid-crap if you like,' said Sven. 'I'm not.'

There was a moment of flurry, which Sven watched very carefully in case anyone laid a finger on his dog, in which case they would have to die and the team competition would be over as soon as it began, until, grudgingly, the man slipped down the ladder.

'Okay,' said Arthur. 'Why don't we say that the women get to sleep up there and the menfolks sleep down here?'

'Normally I would say that was sexist,' said Naimh, the nasty-looking woman on Ross's team, 'but tonight I'm very grateful.'

'I'm not trying to be sexist,' said Arthur. 'I'm trying to share without blood being spilled.'

'That'll do for me,' said Cathy, hopping up the steps.

'But what about that dog?' said Naimh.

'Hup!' said Sven, and Sandwiches gracefully launched himself over the platform and into Sven's

366

arms. 'I'll just take him outside . . .'

Ross swore briefly, but unrolled his sleeping bag on the ground, right next to the fire. 'I think I'll save our fights for the next couple of days, eh team?' he shouted.

'Yay!' they shouted.

Marcus looked at Arthur. 'Have we got anything for dinner?'

Arthur had already thought of this, with growing alarm at his abilities to lead a patrol out in the mountains. 'No!

'Right,' said Marcus. 'Well, I'm sure we were doing the right thing, passing that pub and not going in.'

Arthur lay down on the hard ground, thinking about sleep, but knowing for a fact he wasn't going to get any.

* * *

The wind was getting up. Gwyneth huddled down in the bucket seat of Rafe's car as they sped along an almost deserted motorway, hopefully in the right direction.

'Maybe this wasn't such a great idea,' she said. 'There isn't going to be a lovely country hotel at the end of this, is there?'

'Nope,' said Rafe, 'And I wouldn't hold your breath for pizza delivery, either.'

Gwyneth stared out of the window. Where was Arthur? What was he thinking?

* * *

The elements weren't on their side as they drew deeper and deeper into Wales. The rain was now driving against the window and visibility was extremely poor. Rafe was pushed forward in his seat, struggling to make out the number of the road ahead.

'I thought you were Welsh,' he said to Gwyneth, who was poring over the map.

'And that means I should have memorized all the roads, does it?'

It was now after two o'clock in the morning; they had been lost six times, and they were finding it very hard going.

'Look, we'll just . . . I mean, either we can stop . . .'

'And sleep by the side of the road? Isn't that how you get yourself murdered? Haven't you ever heard any urban myths?'

'I'm sure we could find a hotel.'

'You've never been to rural Wales late at night, have you?'

'Hmm. Anyway,' said Rafe, 'we don't know what time they're setting off in the morning. We might miss them altogether.'

'And *then* we could find a hotel, having tried

our best!' said Gwyneth. 'Ooh, we could go to Portmeirion.'

Rafe shot her a look and they continued onwards into the night.

* * *

Marcus found himself contorted into an unlikely angle, freezing cold and desperate for the toilet, on cold stone ground in the pitch darkness. At first he had no idea where he might be, or why. It didn't feel like the kind of place he'd choose to wake up.

'Get up!' a voice was screeching. There was groaning and cursing coming from all around him. Perhaps, he mused, he'd died in the night and awoken in the pits of hell. Blinking, he attempted to sit up without removing his arms from his sleeping bag. In the dim light, in various degrees of disarray, the men of his team and Ross's were sprawled all over the floor. The fire had long gone out, and the straw had proved to be pretty much decorative.

'Get ready!' screamed the voice again. Marcus blinked up at the door. There stood a man who appeared to fill the doorway. Next to him was d'Aragon, again looking natty, this time in a slate-coloured anorak.

'This is your unit commander,' said d'Aragon.

'You can call him Sergeant. You do as he says at ALL times. This course may be tough, but we don't want anybody dead. Well, not literally.' His mouth curled in a faint smile.

'Out to the stream and get ready!' screamed the man again. The men immediately made a burst for the door.

Outside made inside feel like a sauna. It was shockingly cold; it penetrated to their very marrows. It was dark still, with the stars freezing in the sky above them, and one faint line of grey at the edge of the hills to the east.

'Hey,' said Arthur, as they both ran round the side of the gate to have a slash. 'Bet you didn't think things could get this great when you went to accountancy school, huh?'

Marcus didn't answer, as they both concentrated on emptying their bladders without snapping off their penises in the cold.

'I'm worried about food,' he said eventually, as they knelt by the stream and threw water over their faces, wincing.

'Yes,' said Arthur. 'I think I'll go through the Landrover, see if any other intrepid explorers have left some muesli or something behind.'

From behind them came the unmistakable smell of bacon frying.

'Oh, they're such bastards,' said Arthur.

Marcus raised an eyebrow.

'Okay, that wasn't being a bastard, that was just us being stupid,' he conceded. 'But still, I thought these outward bound things were organized by companies. I didn't think you'd have to bring *everything*. I was amazed we managed to round up the sleeping bags.'

Suddenly Cathy crept out of the building and wandered over to them shyly. 'Um, if you want it,' she said.

'What?'

She opened the bag in her hand to reveal two bars of Toblerone, a Snickers and a large packet of chocolate buttons.

'Cathy! You're a genius!' said Arthur. 'Where did you get these?'

'You don't think I wear the "I'm A Chocoholic" badge for nothing, do you?' said Cathy, smiling.

'I thought you were doing it to be twee,' said Marcus. 'I mean, I hadn't noticed.'

'And how do you think I got this lovely figure?'

'I hadn't noticed,' said Arthur. 'Er, I mean, you look great!'

They gratefully took the chocolate and split a bar between them.

'Better hold on to it,' said Arthur. 'This might be all we have to last us. And please, somebody, tell me Rafe and Gwyneth arrived in the night . . . the earlier night.'

Marcus and Cathy looked at each other and shook their heads.

'Well,' said Arthur stoutly. 'More chocolate to go around, I guess.'

They stared at their small triangles of breakfast, as rich and unpalatable at this time of the morning as a glass of red wine.

* * *

'ATTENTION!' screamed the sergeant from the door of the hut, so loudly that several neighbouring sheep wandered over to take a peek. Sandwiches eyed them warily.

'If that poxy dog chases the sheep, they'll get instantly disqualified, won't they?' said Naimh.

'He's not a member of the team, it doesn't count,' said Arthur.

'He'll get shot,' said Ross.

'He is a member of the team and he's not getting shot,' said Sven. 'Don't try to teach my dog about sheep.'

And they watched as Sven picked up Sandwiches and carried him over to the nearest inquisitive sheep. As they grew closer, the dog wagged his stubby tail more and more excitedly and, bizarrely, the sheep started to do the same thing with his hindquarters. It was an extremely odd sight. Then, as they came nose to nose, Sandwiches started licking the sheep's face with his long rough tongue, and the sheep did the same to him in return.

'Well, that's that,' said the sergeant, as the others stood around in awe. 'Your dog is gay.'

'He's not gay!' said Sven.

'He's a friend of Dolly's. Everyone shut up and gather round.'

'Excuse me,' said Marcus, 'but one of our team isn't here.'

'Well, let's hope he's an Indian trail follower,' said the sergeant, 'because that's the only way he's gonna track you down.'

There was a silence.

'He's not, no.'

* * *

Gwyneth woke up against Rafe's neck. The sweet, hay-like smell of his young body was delicious and she sighed pleasurably, before realizing she was in a parked car on a B road in Wales feeling horribly icky and in the middle of absolutely nowhere.

'Wake up!' she yelped. 'There might be a maniac on the roof banging your severed head . . . or something.'

Rafe blinked awake like a newly born puppy.

'What . . . ? Oh, hello.' He smiled at her. 'Where are we?'

'That's what we're going to find out this morning. You know, we've only been asleep for a couple of hours.'

They had searched the B roads and byways until half past three in the freezing rain – bloody mobile reception – until finally Rafe had called it quits, rubbing his red eyes. They'd bedded down in a lay-by off an ancient grey road the width of one vehicle, and made themselves as comfortable as they could. Now the road was beginning to brighten up a little, and a car had swished noisily through the gravel next to them, waking them.

'Crap – we *so* need to find them!' said Gwyneth suddenly. 'What if it started last night and they've gone without us?'

'Don't worry,' said Rafe. 'And hand me that map – we ought to be able to see properly now.' He studied it closely. 'Ah,' he said. 'Well, those hills – just over there, slightly to the east – and a double stile . . . one small stream . . .' He scratched his head, then climbed out of the car and walked ten feet across the road.

'Yuh,' he said, peering over the old stone wall to the partially hidden bothy, the last remains of the smoke drifting into the early morning air.

'I'll leave him a note telling him where we're going,' Arthur had said half an hour before.

'You will not,' said the sergeant, overhearing. 'I don't know who you'll have turning up with additional supplies and a GPS, but they're not playing in my game, sunshine.'

'That is so unfair,' said Cathy, who instantly shrank back as the sergeant fixed his beady eyes on her.

'Unfair! Unfair! He gets a good night's sleep on a soft feather bed at his mummy's house, no doubt! There's no room for that in my ar – outward bound team! Now, get on it! Now! Go!'

* * *

Thank God they had Marcus, who at least knew the right way up to hold a map. Apparently the sergeant and the dragon were going to shadow each team and make sure one didn't stray too far into the other's territory. And, Arthur assumed, rubbing his knuckles together in the paralysing early-morning cold, rescue them from hypothermia. Although he wouldn't put money on the last bit.

'If we don't go exactly the right way we get penalized, apparently,' said Marcus, peering closely at the paper. 'And it looks like we have to ford a big river.'

'What!' said Arthur.

'Bloody hell!' said Sven. 'I hate getting wet. And cold. And being outside.'

'But . . . I mean, there must be another way across,' said Cathy, looking pale. 'Do you think they'd notice if we looked for another route? We don't want to wade into the middle of a river.'

'Yeah, I mean, how do they know what we do?' said Sven.

They had come to a halt, and all that could be heard was the whipping of the steely breeze through the copse.

'I mean, it's not like anyone is behind us,' he went on.

'Mnrgh! Mnrgh! Mnrgh!' said Sandwiches suddenly.

'What is it?' Sven crouched down and looked at his dog.

'Mnrgh! Mnrgh! Mnrgh!' repeated Sandwiches.

'Oh, look at that!' said Cathy, pointing over the crest of a distant hill. A magnificent hot air balloon, painted entirely black, had gently risen over the top of it. 'Isn't it lovely!'

'Who goes ballooning in February?' said Arthur.

'MNRGH!' said Sandwiches.

'Are they looking for us?' said Marcus, his nose still deep in the map.

'No, don't be daft,' said Arthur. The balloon changed direction and started heading straight for them.

'Unless this is a very very slow version of *North by Northwest*.'

'A black balloon,' said Marcus, glancing up. 'That's rare. Next thing you know it'll have mounted machine guns.'

The beautiful, menacing thing floated even closer.

'What are those big metal things attached to the side of the basket?' said Cathy.

Arthur giggled nervously. 'Um, don't be ridiculous.'

There was an uncertain silence.

'Er – there's the river over there,' said Marcus. 'Shall we – you know – just ford it anyway?'

'Yeah!' said everyone, and started making swift headway in that direction. The balloon drifted to the east and soon disappeared.

'There you go – just a coincidence,' said Arthur.

'We're going to be cold, wet, cold and outside,' said Sven sadly, unbuttoning his shirt.

* * *

In fact, fording the river was clearly considered to be far too easy. As they came out on the banks, the first things they saw were a large yellow envelope attached to a fence post and several long pieces of wood.

The river itself was much wider than Arthur had been expecting – he'd been hoping he'd get something he could actually jump across – and looked deep, clear and icy as it flowed over the brown pebbles.

'Do you think these things are for us?' asked Cathy mildly.

'We're in exactly the right spot,' said Marcus proudly.

'Just take it as read that we know you're a terrific map reader, Marcus,' said Arthur. 'Well done.' He stepped forward and picked up the envelope.

* * *

'Well, this should be interesting,' said Gwyneth, looking at the remains of the camp. 'Did anyone leave a handy sheet of paper saying "we're all heading in this direction"?'

'I don't think so,' said Rafe. He was outside, padding around. 'I can't believe Arthur didn't leave us *something*.'

'Maybe he thought we weren't coming.' Gwyneth swung by her arms on the doorframe.

Rafe looked up. Instantly she could see the hurt in his eyes.

'But we told him we were coming.'

'I didn't mean it like that. Maybe he just thought . . .'

'He thought I'd let him down,' said Rafe. 'I would never let him down.'

'I'm sure he didn't.'

'Maybe I did. Maybe I have already.'

Gwyneth went up and took his arm. 'Of course you haven't. You've done everything. We depend on you. And the trams are going to be . . . they're going to be the absolute best thing.'

Rafe's face didn't soften. 'Yes,' he said.

'Look at that!' Gwyneth said suddenly, not letting go of his arm, but pointing with her other hand. 'Look at that balloon in the distance.'

Rafe squinted. 'It's entirely black.'

'That must be where they are.'

'What makes you say that?'

'Because I know Wales and there is FUCK all else out here except other outward bound teams. At the very worst we'll get rescued by a scout brigade. Come on.'

'If there's any point,' said Rafe.

'I slept in a car and missed *Frasier* for this,' said Gwyneth. 'We're going.'

* * *

Build a way of crossing the river using ONLY the materials provided. If you do not complete the task

*within forty-five minutes you will not reach the camp
ground before nightfall and thus will fail the challenge.
It is not recommended that you try to cross the river by
other means. At this time of year the temperature will
bring early onset hypothermia and death is likely.*

Arthur read the note aloud.

'It's amazing, isn't it,' said Cathy, after a while
when nobody spoke, 'the way they make things
seem realistically dangerous.'

'Yes,' said Arthur, slowly. Marcus, meanwhile,
was carefully unstrapping his watch.

There were four planks of wood and four stumps.
Obviously they were not wide enough to form a
bridge over the river on their own.

'I wish this was the problem about the farmer
and the fox that eats the chicken and the corn,'
said Marcus. 'I'm brilliant with things like that.'

'You're the engineer,' said Arthur to Sven. 'You
must be able to sort it out, surely.'

Sven made the kind of face usually seen at
garages when you don't know what's wrong with
your car. 'Ah,' he said. 'Well, you know, if it was
ice, I could probably help you.'

'Yes, we could walk across it,' said Arthur, a tad
sharply.

'Forty-two minutes,' said Marcus.

'You're not going to start doing that,' said
Arthur.

380

They stared at the river and again at the pieces of wood.

'Maybe you're supposed to build an enormous catapult and propel yourself over,' said Sven.

'And you wonder why we didn't make the finals of Scrapheap Challenge,' hissed Marcus.

'Shut up,' said Sven. 'I would have done if it hadn't been for your inferior robotic ability.'

Arthur decided not to enquire into this any further. 'Could we build a bridge as we go?' he said. 'Plant the logs and pick the planks up behind us as we go?'

They considered this.

'You'd need to be very bendy,' said Sven, contemplating his toes, which he could only just see underneath his belly.

'And steady on your feet,' said Cathy in a slightly trembling voice.

'Thirty-nine minutes,' said Marcus.

'Well, come on, then,' said Arthur, and stalked towards the water's edge.

* * *

Four of them – plus Sandwiches, who had adopted his playing dead position around Sven's neck, thus giving Sven the aura of a man wearing a Megadeath t-shirt and a very expensive stole – were perched on a plank a quarter of the way out into the river, having rather belatedly realized the obvious.

'Maybe if I threw the next log . . . it might land the right way up and we could balance the next plank,' suggested Arthur.

'We don't know how deep it's going to be,' said Marcus. 'My guess is it's too deep.'

'Yeah,' said Arthur, shamefaced. 'I'm sorry. I don't suppose Sandwiches can swim, can he, Sven? He could take the logs and . . .' His voice tailed off as Sandwiches lay stock-still, not even twitching when his name was mentioned.

'Okay, I guess that idea's out.'

'Shall we go back?' said Marcus. 'I don't want to sound like a coward, but we're standing on a fragile plank in the middle of a freezing river.'

* * *

They managed to retrieve both logs by dint of Arthur getting wet to the knees and leaning over a very long way, and reassembled on the bank. Marcus was concentrating very hard on not looking at his watch.

'I didn't want to say before,' said Cathy, 'but I don't suppose you could join the planks together . . . this is stupid, really . . . and make some kind of a raft . . .'

The others looked at her, stupefied.

382

'Why . . . *why* didn't you think to mention it before?' said Arthur finally.

'Oh, I didn't want to be a bother, you know.'

Arthur shook his head. 'Cathy, you are – you are the exact opposite of a bother.'

Cathy smiled and flushed. 'Gosh! I don't know what to say!'

'Yeah, what would you do if he paid you a real compliment?' said Sven – but he was already on his hands and knees, pulling up long reeds that seemed strong enough to tie the logs together.

* * *

It wasn't the best raft in the world. It wasn't even the best raft within an eight mile radius. And by the time they'd loaded Sven on, it didn't even sit above the waterline. But as long as they paddled like fury – starting off with branches, but moving on to hands and paws – and ignored the feeling of the icy water and the speed of the current (already it was clear they were going to land far downstream on the opposite bank) then it would get them across.

'More starboard!' shouted Sven, as they paddled away.

'Er?'

'Which the hell's that?' said Arthur, having to shout above the sound of the roaring water.

383

'Right!' shouted Marcus. 'Hey, Sven, in life or death water situations, maybe keep your smart-alecky Viking terms to yourself?'

* * *

'I'm not sure trekking towards God knows where is the ideal pastime for the Welsh mountains in February,' said Gwyneth, as they clambered over a five-bar gate.

'Nonsense,' said Rafe. 'I haven't felt this good in ages.'

His face had gone ruddy and his eyes clear with the wind and bright cold sky. Gwyneth smiled, and enjoyed how beautiful and at home he looked.

'It's true,' she said. 'I'm really enjoying it as well, actually.' She cunningly circumnavigated an enormous pile of dung. 'I forgot how much I love the countryside.'

'It's beautiful,' said Rafe, but he was looking at Gwyneth.

* * *

'There's poo *everywhere*,' Marcus was saying, hopping from foot to foot to keep warm.

'Yes, we know you hate the country,' said Arthur. 'But can you get the map out?' He looked up to the sky. 'Those clouds look like they're rolling in.'

'Oooh, hope it rains again,' said Sven with feeling.

Marcus held the map up. 'Okay, it's marked – there's a funny sort of hill thing.'

'What do you mean, "funny"?' said Arthur. 'That doesn't sound good.'

'I can't . . . it just looks strange, that's all.' Marcus set off towards the west. 'Well, better go check it out.'

And they followed him over the rolling green hillocks and bumpy stone walls.

* * *

The clouds were indeed rolling in, and the going very quickly became much harder than Arthur had imagined. They were headed almost entirely uphill, and the marks on the map seemed to lead them through the boggiest, rockiest parts of the entire county. All of them were exhausted – Sven was sweating in quite an alarming fashion – but Arthur felt compelled to keep up the lead. Every muscle in his body was screaming at him, and all thoughts had been driven out of his head apart from the gut sense of putting one foot in front of another. It occurred to him that he had no idea how or why people climbed Everest.

'How much further?' Cathy asked plaintively.

Marcus squinted at the map – under the dark sky

it was quite difficult to see anything. Arthur had thought earlier he had caught a glimpse again of the black hot air balloon, concealed within the dark clouds, but hadn't mentioned it to the others.

'It's a long way,' said Marcus finally. 'We're about halfway there.'

It was two thirty in the afternoon. Not that long until darkness, and all of them were tired to the bone. Cathy handed round the rest of the chocolate, and they drank from a stream.

'There'll be food for us at the campsite tonight, won't there?' she asked anxiously.

'I'm sure there will,' said Arthur, not sure at all. 'After all, it's not like any of us can catch rabbits.'

Sandwiches whined.

'Come on,' said Marcus. 'If we don't keep moving, that's it. We'll be disqualified by nightfall.'

Arthur stretched out his arms. 'That is *not* going to happen.'

The others looked at him.

'Of course not,' they said, marching on.

* * *

'Hmm,' said Rafe, looking at the bounding river.

'So much for the balloon guidance,' said Gwyneth.

'And the Toblerone wrapper!' said Rafe. 'That *had* to be them.'

'True,' said Gwyneth. 'And we must be much faster than they are. I can't imagine Sven being much of a hill walker.'

They sniggered at the thought of it.

'Look!' Gwyneth pointed. Downstream, washed up on their side of the shore, was the remains of what must have been their raft.

'Great!' said Rafe. He headed down to fetch it and dragged it back up. 'We're on the right track.'

'The water is *freezing*,' he said.

'And they made it across . . . on *that?*'

Gwyneth had a point. The loosely bound logs weren't the picture of seaworthiness.

'They've got more balls than I gave them credit for.'

Rafe gave her a look. 'Well?'

'Well, if *they* can do it . . .'

Rafe held the raft steady as Gwyneth knelt on it. Cold water came running over the top.

'Ooh CHRIST!' she said. 'How come this water doesn't freeze?'

'It moves,' said Rafe. 'What we need are those artificial ice people.'

For a moment, Gwyneth thought about their trip to Denmark and she remembered the old man's house. But the shock of the cold water as they started to paddle put everything out of her mind.

The current became stronger as they neared the middle of the river, and the going was harder with only two people. The wind was stronger now, too, with the clouds blowing across the sky.

Gwyneth looked at Rafe and managed a grin. 'Oh God, I hope we're not going to turn into one of those sad folk songs about people who get drowned crossing rivers . . .'

But Rafe wasn't looking back at her. 'WATCH OUT! THE ROCK!'

* * *

A maelstrom of water broke over the raft. Gwyneth, not even consciously thinking, grabbed hold of one corner so tightly she drove splinters into her skin. Everything went black and cold as the piece of wood tipped over, and she felt herself being swept along. Then, as quickly as it had flipped over, the raft righted itself again. It barged into the far bank, and she realized she'd made it, wet, still holding on, but alone. She stumbled up the weeds and pulled herself onto the bank.

'RAFE!!!' she screamed out into the wilderness, terror grabbing at her heart. 'RAFE!!!!'

And the raft dislodged itself from the bank

and bounced off down the river, turning over and over again.

* * *

It was near nightfall by the time the main party stopped at the foot of the mountain. Every bit of them wanted to lie down and sleep, but they had carried on, through the dark day, with its sporadic rainfall and gusts of wind from which only Sandwiches, with his low centre of gravity, had been immune.

Marcus craned his neck to look at the towering edifice above his head. 'It's these weird shapes on the map,' he said. 'I don't understand it.'

'Um . . .' said Cathy. And she held up another large yellow envelope. 'I think that may be deliberate.'

* * *

Gwyneth ran along the bank the way they had come, desperately scanning the roiled up surface of the water.

'RAFE!! RAFE!!'

There, some yards away, she saw it. If she hadn't seen it before in her life, she wouldn't have known what it was, but she had seen it before, on a dark dawn in November. She recognized straightaway that the bone-white shape, outstretched, pushing through the reeds, reaching up from the tumultuous water, was a hand.

* * *

The last of the weak sunlight was sinking behind the horizon as they sat on the ground and tried to figure out the latest set of instructions. Inside the yellow pouch was a single, tiny, but surprisingly powerful, torch and a piece of paper with further instructions.

'*It should now be dark,*' the instructions read.

'Genius,' murmured Sven.

'*The Welsh Mountain Service does not recommend anyone climbing outside of daylight hours and* cannot *guarantee their safety.*'

'Owwwwooo,' said Sandwiches.

'*Inside you will find a single flashlight. You will presumably have already noticed the series of carved ledges going into the hillside.*'

'So that's what they are,' said Marcus.

'*Please climb these and cross at the top. You should be able to see the campsite.*'

'Well, that doesn't sound too difficult,' said Arthur.

* * *

Gwyneth waded in waist-deep, the water so cold she couldn't stop herself yelping from the shock.

She shut her eyes briefly, and waded on to where she'd seen the hand break the surface.

'RAFE!!' she shrieked again, her words disappearing, carried downriver by the barrelling wind.

Nothing. Silence. She couldn't go any further; the water was up to her chest. She took a deep breath and, swallowing hard, pushed her face underneath the water. At first the cascade of bubbles and reeds made it impossible to see anything. Then she caught sight of a white — very white — shape, scrabbling about in front of her. She reached out her arms and grabbed the first thing that came to her.

* * *

They burst above the surface at exactly the same moment, coughing and spluttering up into the break between the water and air. How Gwyneth dragged them both to the side of the river, she could never afterwards have said. Rafe was as white as a sheet and staring straight ahead.

'RAFE!' She seemed to scream his name a hundred times as he lay on the bank, water seeping from his mouth. As she leaned over to attempt CPR — she'd seen it on TV a lot, so she supposed she knew what to do — he coughed suddenly, his neck jerking up from the ground. Caught off guard, Gwyneth jumped back.

'Are you . . . are you . . .'

He blinked slowly, then coughed a flood of water onto the ground. Eventually he managed to raise his head a little.

'I'm so cold,' he said.

* * *

'How . . . Who would do this?' said Arthur, as they inched their way sideways across the ledges, foot to foot like some bizarre line-dancing movement.

'It's too sheer to climb,' said Marcus, grunting, slightly further on. He was using the flashlight to discover the next ledge – they sometimes doubled back on themselves, or meandered around the hill. They were like some crazed giant's staircase.

'So *this* makes sense.'

'I can't see the ground.'

'That's because your stomach's in the way, Sven,' said Arthur.

'No, it's because it's getting dark. And we're really high up. And by the way, shouldn't we have protective ropes?'

'I definitely think a word with the health and safety authorities about this outward bound company wouldn't be *entirely* amiss,' murmured Marcus.

'Cathy? Are you all right?' called Arthur, suddenly conscious that they hadn't heard from her since the long climb had begun.

'Uh-*huh*!' squeaked a tremulous, extremely high voice. Arthur stopped and looked back for her.

'Are you all right?'

Marcus flicked the flashlight backwards. Cathy, at the rear of the group, was inching along, eyes tightly shut, clinging to Sandwiches's tail.

'I don't really like heights,' she squeaked.

'No kidding,' said Arthur, looking at her frozen stance. 'Why didn't you tell us? You can at least walk in the middle, and hold onto us.'

Sandwiches looked somewhat aggrieved.

'I didn't . . . I didn't want to . . .'

'Cathy, come your next performance review, remind us to have a quick session on what precisely constitutes a "fuss" or a "bother".'

'Okay, Mr Pendleton.'

'Do you want to come to the middle now?'

Cathy shook her head frantically.

'Well, what about if I come back there and take up the rear?'

'Heh, heh,' said Sven.

'No, thank you!' said Cathy. 'I don't want anyone going past me on the ledge!'

'Okay, then if we just slow down a little?'

'YES PLEASE!'

'Right,' said Arthur, trying to will away the tiredness in his bones and his desperation to reach the top and see the campsite.

'Onwards, then.'

* * *

She knew what they had to do from numerous public information films, but it didn't make the process any less embarrassing. Gwyneth found an overhanging rock which provided some shelter from the wind, and unpacked the sleeping bag from Rafe's rucksack. He was still panting, and his skin was grey. Gwyneth herself was shivering so much she found it difficult to undo the knots, but hadn't had anything like the dunking Rafe had endured, and had torn off her wet clothes as soon as she could.

The raft was no longer anywhere to be seen, and by some instinct, Gwyneth had headed for the far bank, which meant they were cut off from any route back and a very long way from home.

Gwyneth undressed Rafe methodically, trying not to think about what she was doing, even as she peeled the plaid shirt and white t-shirt from his hairless chest. She must concentrate on helping a possibly endangered human being.

Lying naked, like spoons, in both sleeping bags, sheltered by the hanging rock, she encircled his chest with her arms, and pressed herself to him, closer and closer, willing her warmth into him. He hadn't said a word since the first mutterings when she had pulled him from the river, and he felt terribly, dreadfully cold.

* * *

There was only the moon to see by when they finally, exhausted, scrambled up the last footstep to the top of the hill.

'The camp *must* be here,' Sven was saying. 'They knew it was going to be dark when we got here.'

Arthur leaned down and lifted Cathy up the last little way.

'Did you do that whole thing with your eyes shut?' he asked her.

'Well, I was holding on to Sandwiches,' she said, still quavering a little.

'Yeah, but I think Sandwiches had his eyes shut, too,' said Sven, leaning over to check on his dog.

'They are *bastards*,' said Marcus, straightening up and seeing what was in front of him. 'One hundred per cent diamond carat, A1 solid *bastards*.'

* * *

It was, finally, warm inside the sleeping bags. Outside, the wind was buffeting the earth relentlessly, but inside, the absurdity of the situation felt far away and slightly dreamlike to Gwyneth, who could do nothing but focus on radiating warmth over the huge, buff body in her arms.

Gradually, slowly, she felt him stir. His hands moved, and a huge shiver passed all the way up and down his body. Then, after a pause, he gently took her small hands in his large ones, and slowly, slowly, began to turn round to face her.

He still wasn't saying anything, but she saw by his eyes that he was awake and fully concentrating on her. He put his hand up to her face and stroked it softly.

'Rafe,' she said, but whispered this time, feeling a lump in her throat that wouldn't dissolve.

'Ssh,' he said. He stroked her face again. 'You know, the Chinese say that if you save the life of a man, he is yours forever.'

And he pulled her towards him as gently as the sky outside was wild.

* * *

The five of them stood, high above Wales, staring straight ahead. In the distance could be seen a camp fire. This was undoubtedly their camp. It was, however, on the peak of the next hill. It wasn't far away, but you'd still have to crawl down the valley and up again.

But linking the two hills was an odd triangular

wire construction. There was one wire at the bottom, and two strands at waist height, attached to the bottom wire with zig-zags. It looked like a bridge, but a bridge with nothing to walk across.

'Shit,' said Arthur. 'Shit shit shit shit!'

The others, bar Cathy, gradually drew closer to the structure.

'What the *hell* are you meant to do?' said Sven.

'I think — well, you hang onto to the top wires and walk along the bottom,' said Marcus.

'They must be joking.'

'They must have left safety ropes around here somewhere,' said Arthur, dropping to his hands and knees with the flashlight. But there was nothing to be found.

Marcus turned round 360 degrees. There was absolutely no sign of human habitation anywhere, except in the winking light of the campfire. As it had grown dark, the cold had reasserted itself, and he thought he could feel drops of rain in the wind.

'Oh God,' he said.

'I'm not sure Sandwiches can walk across a wire,' said Sven pensively. 'He's got twice the appropriate number of legs.'

'So have I,' said Arthur, 'by virtue of not being a monorail.'

Marcus gingerly took hold of the wires and

stepped bravely out, keeping one foot firmly on land. The whole structure wobbled alarmingly. Swallowing audibly, Marcus tentatively lifted his other foot on. He closed his eyes for a moment. When he opened them, he was still there.

'Well done, Marcus.' Arthur found he was smiling, even in the middle of their predicament. The idea of Marcus volunteering to climb a high wire up a windy mountain in Wales in mid-winter was not one he had ever dreamed of, and he was proud of him.

'Well done!'

Cathy was standing in the dead centre of the hilltop, shaking like a leaf. Arthur went to her, while Sven lit the way for Marcus, who was tentatively moving forward now. Sven wondered aloud if Sandwiches could jump that far (it was at least thirty feet).

'Hey,' Arthur said.

'I'm not doing it,' said Cathy. 'I can't. There's just no way.'

'I know,' said Arthur.

'So you can't try and talk me out of it, or anything.'

'God, no. Wouldn't dream of it.'

'I shouldn't even have come here. It was meant to be Rafe, not me. I'm only good at being in the office.'

'You're very good at being in the office.'

She looked up at him. 'I don't want to . . . I know it sounds silly, but I feel like someone could *die* out here.'

'Don't worry,' said Arthur. 'No one's going to die.'

Cathy looked around into the wild night. 'It's ridiculous. I'm imagining I can hear wolves howling.'

Arthur stiffened.

'Can you?'

'No, no of course not. It's just Sven farting, most likely.'

They stood there for a while, looking into the gloomy blackness. Stars were coming out overhead, but there was nothing in the countryside around them to illuminate.

Arthur suddenly thought of Ross's team. He imagined them tucked up right now in their cosy camp beds, gloating and planning their tactics for tomorrow, and here they were, stranded on the top of a hill, half the team missing . . .

He shook his head. 'Cathy,' he said.

She looked at him. 'You're going to ask me to do this, aren't you?' she said.

'Cathy, we're on the top of a mountain.'

She nodded. 'Can't you get me a helicopter?'

'I forgot my RAC card.'

Some way in front of them, they could just make out Marcus. He was about halfway across, and Sven was shouting encouragement.

'Look how well Marcus is doing,' said Arthur. 'We could have it all over and done with that quickly.'

Cathy looked up at him, her eyes suddenly large in her chubby face. 'What are you most frightened of?'

Arthur blinked at the question. 'What do you mean?'

'I *mean*,' said Cathy, her voice rising slightly in panic, 'that I want you to know what being up here is like for me. That's all.'

'Well,' said Arthur. He turned round and stared into the thick velvet blackness, thinking as he did so of the streetlights in his cul-de-sac and how he never saw the dark; not really. There was always an electric sheen rising off wherever he went, wherever he was.

'I just want . . . I just want not to cock things up, really. I feel . . . this is going to sound silly, but I feel I've got this destiny that I'm meant to live up to and it's really important that I do things properly. And I've failed and failed a lot up until now, but things have been – are going – the right way, and I'm worried about letting myself down . . .'

Cathy was looking at him.

'And wolves. And snakes. And religious fundamentalists. And I don't like that chemical stuff at the bottom of crisp packets.'

Cathy came forward. 'You know, everyone feels that way, about missing their destiny, about what they're supposed to be.'

'Yes, but mine is a real destiny,' said Arthur.

'Mine too,' said Cathy.

'Really? Does everyone think that way?' Arthur grimaced. 'I thought I'd been chosen specially.'

'Uh huh,' said Cathy.

'Well,' said Arthur. 'This is yours.'

Marcus was waving frantically from the middle of the bridge.

'It's okay!' he was yelling, his voice almost lost in the wind. 'Come on! It's okay!'

* * *

They stood around Cathy and gave her a huge hug. Ordinarily, this would have elicited loud snorts from Sven, thought Arthur, but here on top of this mountain, when they felt like the only people in the world, it seemed like the right thing to do.

'You can do it,' said Sven. 'If, you know, I'm not so fat I break the whole wire.'

'You're not so fat,' said Cathy. Sven actually smiled.

'Go between Marcus,' – Marcus was now hopping up and down the wire as if he'd been born to it; Arthur was worried he was going to start doing tricks – 'and me. We'll let Sven bring up the rear just in case . . .'

'Thanks for spoiling a nice moment,' said Sven. 'But aren't we forgetting someone?'

Sandwiches was looking at the gently swaying wire bridge with a very disconsolate expression.

Arthur asked Marcus, who was coming back to help, 'Can you take him in the rucksack?'

Marcus screwed up his face to complain, then smiled instead. 'Of course,' he said. 'He can join Marcus's official high wire act.'

* * *

But of course it didn't feel quite as comical once they were all finally on the bridge. Marcus, with Sandwiches peering out the back of his rucksack with complete equanimity, wobbled over first. Then they cuddled and cajoled Cathy onto the wire.

'I'm keeping my eyes closed,' she warned them.

'That's the way! Well done!' shouted Arthur. Not at all it was the way, as the wind swayed the bridge alarmingly. After a tense moment halfway across when she froze completely – until the other three started up a rousing chant of 'CATH-EE!

CATH-EE!' – she finally, painfully, made it to the other side and fell into Marcus's arms. Arthur felt an amazing burst of energy.

'Whoo hoo!' he screamed over the gap. 'You did it!'

Cathy waved back, smiling hugely. 'I KNOW!!!!'

He realized the full extent of her bravery as he wobbled across himself, trying not to peer into the abyss beneath his feet. Yet somehow, on top of the wire, balanced in mid-air in the middle of nowhere, muscles aching with weariness, he felt a sense of being as alive under the stars as he had ever known.

* * *

The campsite was a rough affair: two tents and a fire, nothing more. They literally collapsed in front of it, legs dropping underneath them. Next to the fire were four packets of soup.

'*Soup*!' said Marcus. 'We do all that bollocks and all we get is *soup*?'

'This is starvation rations,' said Arthur, nervously.

Sven ponderously opened up his rucksack.

'Don't tell me you've got food in there,' said Cathy. The Toblerone was long gone.

'Yes,' said Sven. The others jumped up. 'Unfortunately,' he added, 'it's not for us.' And he deposited two cans of Pedigree Chum on the ground.

'Sven!' said Arthur.

'Well, I didn't know, did I? I assumed they'd feed us.'

'They have,' said Marcus. 'Soup.'

'Well, look on the bright side,' said Cathy comfortingly. 'They're not trying to kill us quite as much now.'

They stared at the Pedigree Chum, all thinking the same thing.

'I'm so hungry,' said Marcus.

'We couldn't,' said Cathy.

'And you're not going to!' said Sven. 'Sandwiches!'

Sandwiches had wandered off.

'That's all we need – a lost dog,' said Arthur.

'My dog does not get *lost*. He goes out on *business*.'

'*Okay.*'

After fifteen minutes, as they huddled round the fire trying not to think about the consequences of the disappearance of Sandwiches, he returned with something in his mouth, looking rather smug.

'Euk!' Cathy jumped up and screamed when she saw what it was. 'Rabbits!'

'Rabbits!' said Sven, in an entirely different tone of voice.

Arthur watched in amazement as Sven bent down and took the gift from the dog's mouth.

'Don't tell me you know what to do with those,' he said.

'Don't tell me you've never skinned a rabbit,' said Sven.

'Of course I've never skinned a rabbit! I'm a town planner, for Christ's sake!'

Sven pulled out a knife from his rucksack. 'In Denmark, we would call you a *fejghed*,' he said.

'What does that mean? Completely normal person who for completely normal reasons doesn't like ripping the guts out of furry animals?'

'Yes, you think that,' said Sven, getting stuck in.

* * *

Rabbit cooked in soup, followed by Maltesers, washed down by water that tasted suspiciously of sheep dip wouldn't have been Arthur's usual top choice, but he was surprised how wonderful things tasted when you were starving hungry. As the others rolled away towards the tents – and fell asleep instantly, he could tell, completely worn out by the fresh air and the exercise – he stayed by the fire, looking into the embers and letting his thoughts drift – to tomorrow, to Gwyneth, to what would happen after this was over; to finally, and almost for the first time, thinking what it might be like to win this competition. He couldn't tell how much time had passed in his reverie or whether he had even come out of it when, with a complete lack of surprise, he glanced up to find Lynne sitting beside him.

Chapter Fourteen

'Hello!' he said cheerfully.

'Ssh! The others are asleep.'

'Oh yes, and I'm not. Right. Uh huh. Yeah.'

He looked at her. She appeared to be wearing some kind of pheasant on her head, and was wrapped in several layers of tweed.

'It's so good to see you. Where have you been?'

'Oh, here and there, tossed on the wind. Well, actually, I had a spot of twin trouble. Nothing to worry about.'

'Really?'

'Yes. Both dead of course. Mad as eggs.'

Arthur didn't quite know what to say to this, so he turned back to stare into the fire.

Lynne looked at him, noting that he looked tired around the eyes and somehow . . . different to when she had seen him last. Firmer, somehow. There was a set to his jaw that hadn't been there before. She sensed determination.

'How goes it?' she asked him gently.

'It's crazy,' said Arthur. 'Is that why you're here? To ask how things are going on this ridiculous exercise?' He plucked at the grass beside him.

'No.'

'I didn't think so.'

She turned to him. 'Arthur.'

His face when he turned towards her was stricken.

'I'm here to warn you. Tomorrow is going to be . . . difficult, beyond, I think, your imagining.'

He stood up. 'I thought it might be something like that. You're always asking me to do things . . .'

'Yes, well, that's part of the – what is it I'm meant to be again?'

'A psychotherapist.'

'Yes, that. Come, walk with me a while.'

They strode away from the fire, to the edge of the cliff, and wandered along it.

'Have you . . . come to help me?' said Arthur, realizing as he spoke that he sounded weak.

Lynne shook her head. 'No. But to prepare you a little.'

'What do you know?' said Arthur. 'Been sneaking into the plans? No, no, destiny, blah blah, yes. You said.'

'You're being very touchy.'

'Well, you just turned up to tell me that something horrible's about to happen.'

'Oh yes. Sorry!'

They looked out at the stars.

'You are going to have to make a choice tomorrow.'

Arthur hardly dared to breathe in case he missed anything.

'It will be very important. Very.'

'Okay. What do I do?'

Lynne looked at him.

'You're not going to tell me, are you?'

'Destiny's rubbish like that.'

'Well, how am I going to know?'

She put her hand on his arm, and he realized it was the first time they had ever touched.

'You just have to be aware. And be ready. It's very important.'

'This isn't going to be between the continental and the cooked breakfast, is it?'

She shook her head and looked at him sadly.

'Okay,' said Arthur.

'You're doing well,' she said.

'Do you really think so?' said Arthur, moving

back to the heat of the fire. But of course, when he turned around, she'd gone.

* * *

Sven wasn't usually an early riser. In fact, before Sven had been allowed to bring him into work, Sandwiches had been a bit of a latchkey dog. This morning, however, Sven found himself squashed up against the door of the tent the men were sharing just before the sun came over the horizon. He got up to relieve himself and, in the early morning chill, was pleasantly surprised by the beauty of the surroundings. Sandwiches came bounding up joyfully – Arthur had thrown him out of the tent four times for threatening to asphyxiate the company – and man and dog walked on a little. The sky had cleared and was turning a watery blue. Sven thought it might be the first day of the year they could see the sun.

From where the tents were pitched on the side of the cliff, the vista was breathtaking. The next hill – from where they'd crossed on the wire – rose on his left, crumbling away to chalk in steps that had been cut away from the side. Down in the valley, so far it could hardly be seen, was the river they had crossed. At this distance it looked like a calm silver thread, not the torrent he remembered. Then he turned round and for the first time saw what was above him. He gasped. Perched several hundred feet higher up was a small ruined castle that had obviously been invisible from below the cliff the night before. It had no roof and ivy climbed in and out of the empty windows. Sven stared at it for a long time, rubbing his sore muscles from yesterday. In his mind, he knew that was where they would be going today. For a reason he couldn't quite put his finger on, it gave him a terrible sense of foreboding – well, it was a spooky ruined castle, he supposed.

He scratched Sandwiches affectionately and decided to head back to find a can of dog food. All of a sudden he heard his name being called.

'Sven! Sven!!!'

He looked around to find the source of the noise. It was coming from just under the lip of the hill. As he moved towards it, Gwyneth's blonde head popped over the ridge.

'Sven!'

'Fuck a duck!' said Sven. Gwyneth, normally so immaculate, was absolutely filthy. Her jeans were torn and dirty, her fleece and puffa jacket in a terrible state. She sounded perky, though. Behind her was Rafe. He too was dirty, and had big dark shadows underneath his eyes and a slightly haunted expression on his face.

'Where did you two just spring from?'

Rafe and Gwyneth glanced at each other, just for a split second, as Arthur came out of the tent to see what all the commotion was about. His hair was sticking up all round his head, and he was yawning hugely. Despite the uncomfortable ground and awkward proximity of the other men, he couldn't remember the last time he'd slept so deeply.

'Fuck a duck!' he said. 'What are you two doing here?' He paused. 'Did Sven just say that?'

* * *

Over tea – blessed tea, which Rafe had brought with him – they haltingly explained a little – not all – of what had happened.

'I'm *so* glad you're here!' said Cathy, beaming.

'Thanks, Cathy,' said Gwyneth. She'd never particularly gone out of her way to be nice to the woman, and was touched by the show of support.

'I won't have to do today now, will I Arthur?' Cathy went on.

'Well, no, I guess you won't,' he said, blinking in surprise. They were even more surprised however, when, seconds later, the black balloon appeared over the lip of the hill, behind the castle.

'Bloody hell,' said Gwyneth, 'That thing's weird.'

They watched it as it came towards them, like something from *The Prisoner*. As it drifted, fifty feet or so over the campsite, a ladder was thrown over the side and a small figure hopped onto it. With complete agility, it romped down the steps, swaying wildly in the wind. As it grew closer, Arthur realized it was the sergeant. The rope ran out about eight or nine feet above the ground, and he jumped down like a cat. The ladder disappeared almost immediately and the balloon headed towards the next peak and was soon out of view.

'Morning,' said the sergeant cursorily, standing in front of their fire.

* * *

Gwyneth glanced at Rafe as the balloon came in. His face was stricken.

'I can't believe . . . I feel awful,' he said, looking at Arthur, who had gone over to talk to the sergeant.

'You nearly drowned,' said Gwyneth. She had a horrible feeling in the pit of her stomach, and tried to cover it up by being terse.

'He's my friend,' said Rafe, looking wounded. Gwyneth gave his hand a quick squeeze.

'I know,' she said. 'I know.'

* * *

The sergeant looked around at them. 'Busy day

413

today,' he said. 'Can't believe you all made it in one piece.'

Cathy smiled broadly.

He glanced at the new arrivals.

'But it's still looking a bit *too* busy round here.'

Gwyneth cleared her throat. 'Um . . . hello . . . nice to meet you . . .'

The sergeant completely ignored her and turned back to Arthur. 'There's too many people in your team. I can't allow it.'

'No,' said Arthur. 'Well, Cathy here has volunteered to withdraw.'

'Uh huh. Who's going to accompany her down the mountain?'

Cathy looked like she was about to say she was fine, then remembered how much she hated mountains and decided to keep her mouth shut. The rest of the team looked at each other, then, as one, at Marcus.

'What? Don't look at me? Am I the only one having a good time?' said Marcus.

'Yes,' said Sven.

'You'll need me and my analytical brain! Won't you, Arthur?'

'Well . . .' said Arthur. 'I thought you'd be glad to be finished.'

'No, I wouldn't.'

They stood silently.

414

'Let me take her,' said Rafe suddenly.

'But we've just got here!' said Gwyneth.

'I had a really tough day yesterday.'

'You can't go,' said Arthur. 'I need you. This is going to be the hardest day.'

Rafe and Arthur looked each other in the eye.

'I'm sorry,' said Rafe.

'Don't go, then,' said Arthur. 'Sven'll take her.'

'No, I mean, I can't . . .'

He plucked nervously at his neck suddenly.

'What's that?' said Arthur. He peered closer. Round his neck, Rafe was wearing the white scarf Gwyneth had given the white knight at Christmas time.

'Is that Gwyneth's scarf?' he said, starting forward.

'No,' said Gwyneth.

'Yes,' said Rafe, staring at the ground.

'It was a joke,' said Gwyneth.

'I'm sorry,' said Rafe again.

Arthur looked at them both solidly for a long moment. Gwyneth, suddenly, felt the full force of his love; understood exactly what he felt for her simply by the look on his face. It had been real. He hadn't been able to tell her – well, he was a man. But it had been there, and it had been real, and she had thrown it all away. Inside she turned to ice, and realized, too late, how much she wanted him.

Inside, Arthur was crumpling in despair. All his hopes and . . . All he could do was curse himself for being too late; for hesitating, for holding back, for never having the courage to go for what he wanted. This wasn't how a king would have behaved. He hated himself.

He looked at Rafe, who was clearly in agony, too.

'Maybe you should go,' he said finally, swallowing hard. Rafe's normally mobile face was a picture of misery.

'I wanted to be there for you, Arthur.'

'I rather think you already have been,' said Arthur, forcing a tight little smile. He turned to Gwyneth. 'Maybe you should go, too.'

'No,' she choked. 'No!'

'Why not?'

They were both finding it difficult to speak. She pulled her eyes away first. 'For the team,' she said simply.

Arthur merely nodded and turned away. The pain sliced through him like a sword.

'As you wish.'

* * *

'Come *on*,' said the sergeant. 'Move it along! Move it! Move it!'

* * *

After Cathy and Rafe had packed up their things – Cathy, oblivious to the atmosphere, was rabbiting away about how she thought she'd almost lost her fear of heights – they began to trudge down the hill, Rafe shepherding her down carefully. Gwyneth was unable to stop herself glancing at him as he went; Arthur was unable to miss her doing this or to hide the sadness in his eyes.

The sergeant unpacked his rucksack and spread its contents on the ground in front of them. There were four paint guns. These were attached to odd-looking canisters designed to go on your back, filled with what looked like bath spheres. The equipment was terribly splattered with red and yellow paint. There were also four pairs of red armbands, four capes in camouflage colours, one camouflaged handkerchief, which Sandwiches correctly surmised was for him, and four pairs of goggles.

'The enemy . . .' he began, clearly trying to put a threatening spin on things. This was completely unnecessary – none of them had any doubt that Ross and his cronies were very much their enemies. '. . . the enemy is on the far side of the hill. They are well fed and well rested.'

'Bet they're not,' said Sven. 'Bet Ross was crying.'

'*Quiet*, soldier.'

417

Sven rolled his eyes but held his tongue.

'From this point onwards . . .' The sergeant unrolled the map. 'Anywhere higher than this point is the fighting field. I think the goal is fairly obvious.'

They looked at the castle, looming above them in the chilly morning light.

'These are the rules, ladies and gentlemen. Shoot your opponents before they shoot you, and storm the castle. Do not go below this point. Tactics are up to you.'

'*Tactics?*' Sven mouthed to Marcus, who looked equally nervous.

'If you are shot by the enemy — their paint is yellow, incidentally, yours is red — you are out and must sit on the sidelines. If you are shot by a member of your own side, you are also out and must sit on the sidelines. We *will* spot you. If you continue to play once hit, your entire team will forfeit this game. Do you understand?'

'*Yes*,' said Sven.

'Yes,' said Arthur, too wrapped up in himself for sarcasm.

The sergeant looked them up and down. 'And don't shoot them in people's faces.' He sounded disappointed to have to give any safety information. 'They can be dangerous.'

'They're *guns*!' said Sven.

'Well, get kitted up. I'll show you how to shoot these things, then we'll get started.'

* * *

Gwyneth walked over to Arthur as they were putting on their masks and strapping on the canisters. If there was any chance at all . . .

'Arthur . . .'

'Not now, Gwyneth.'

She looked at him fearfully. 'But I want to explain.' She did. To tell him how his holding back . . . her insecurity . . . what might have been great had all gone so wrong.

'Not now.'

And Arthur clamped his mask over his face and lifted up his gun.

* * *

At ten a.m. precisely, a starter pistol sounded. It echoed off the hills, startling a crowd of birds, who rose dramatically into the sky with a great squawking. The team members looked at each other. They each wore red insignia on their arms so they wouldn't shoot their own side if at all possible. They had had a quick huddle before they started. Sven had pointed out a pile of rocks right at the top of the headland, and their plan was to get up there before the other team could reach it, dig in and hopefully pick off Ross's little gang as they came up.

They hadn't really reckoned, however, on how hard it is to run up a steep hill, particularly if you're an extremely overweight man pulling a dog, and that plan had to be abandoned before they'd made it fifty yards.

'What about . . . if we still do it that way, but slowly?' panted Marcus.

Gwyneth was looking all around, anxiously. 'They'll pounce on us,' she said.

'What about crawling through the undergrowth like those slinky action men?'

'It'll take us nine hours to get up there,' said Arthur. He looked around, too. The hillside was woefully exposed – there were no trees or shelter anywhere. The best they could do was try to scamper from one small rock formation to another. Arthur craned to see if anyone was coming over the horizon. Part of him hardly cared.

Their patchy rhythm wasn't helped by Sandwiches settling down to take a long and relaxed dump in the middle of the open hillside.

'Oh, for goodness' sake,' said Gwyneth. 'Do we all have to stand around and watch?'

'Yeah, how would you like it?' said Sven. 'And, normally, he likes the *Daily Telegraph*.'

'I meant, can't we hide?' said Gwyneth. 'And I

hope you're going to pick that up?'

'What do you think the *Daily Telegraph* is for? And no, I'm not going to pick it up here, thank you. If you might like to examine the ground for a moment, anything five foot deep in sheep crap can take a little bit of ex Pedigree Chum.'

'Okay, okay,' said Arthur. 'Let's keep moving. I'm sure he'll catch us up once he's . . . finished his business.'

'I'm not leaving him out here unprotected,' said Sven, stubbornly.

'Very good, soldier,' said Marcus, rolling his eyes.

* * *

They had reached the rocks, and the party let out a sigh of relief. There had still been no sign of Ross's troops, who must be further down the hill; and they arranged themselves so they could see in every direction below. For five minutes they watched; ten, fifteen.

'I don't like this,' said Arthur.

'They can't be *that* much slower than us,' said Marcus. 'We got . . . held up.'

'It's too quiet,' said Sven. 'Ooh, I've always wanted to say that.'

Arthur turned and looked up at the castle. He stared fiercely at it.

'Bloody hell,' he said finally. 'Look carefully, but I think I just saw something move.'

Gwyneth focused on the pointed direction. At first she thought he was just imagining things, the wind moving in the rushes. Her heart was thumping. She forced herself to concentrate, and suddenly she did see it – someone was pushing through the undergrowth, coming up round the castle's other side.

'I see it!' she yelped, quietly.

'Dirty buggers,' said Sven. 'I hope they crawled through Sandwiches's poo.'

'Dammit, they've avoided us completely,' said Arthur. 'We should have thought of that way. And they're a hell of a lot closer to the castle than we are.'

'Can we run up behind them and mow them down like dogs – I mean, like badgers,' coughed Marcus.

'Okay, everyone. We're going to make for my right, there. If they're together, we should be able to get immediately behind them.'

'Won't they see us running?'

'No – we're below them, heading the other way, and they've got their noses in the dirt.'

'What if they've got someone covering their rears?' asked Marcus.

'Good question. We're completely fucked.'

'Okay.'

'Right . . . on my shout.'

* * *

It wasn't a bad plan, as plans go. They made a huge right angle under the crest of the hill and crawled back up the other side, behind the other team. Now they had to run as quietly as possible, with even Sandwiches taking care not to let his claws bounce off rock, and crept up to the rear of the enemy's slowly snaking line, leaving Sven at the back to keep watch.

The person at the rear of Ross's line, Naimh, took a routine look round just as they were coming upon her, and screamed so hard it echoed round the mountains.

Arthur picked up his gun to fire it, but before he could do so, there was an almighty WHUMP and a ball of red exploded onto her newly exposed chest.

Naimh lurched backwards in shock, clutching her heart as if she'd been shot by a bullet. Arthur and Sven stared in amazement, Arthur shocked out of his torpor.

'Ah – good recoil,' said Marcus, blowing calmly on the nozzle of his gun.

But . . .

'GET DOWN!' screamed Sven, and they hit the

floor as the other three men came cascading round the corner of the castle.

'Those bloody bastards SHOT me!' screamed Naimh, as if this was the most ridiculous thing one could imagine in the middle of a paintball game.

'Wipe it off,' said Ross immediately.

'You're not allowed to wipe it off!' shouted Marcus. 'Oh bugger – I've just given away my position, haven't I?'

'Get 'em!' shouted Naimh hysterically. Ross, Dave, and another of Ross's colleagues, big Al, surveyed the ground in front of them, and Arthur couldn't believe the camouflage was actually working long enough for him to squeeze the trigger and see an enormous red splodge whistle past Dave's ear and splash-land on the castle wall.

'Bugger it!' said Dave. 'Quick!'

And the three men disappeared round the wall again to safety, leaving Naimh crying uncontrollably and stamping her feet on the grass.

'It's not FAIR! Stupid GAME!'

Until finally, she stomped off in the direction she'd started in.

* * *

Immediately everyone jumped up and threw themselves at the opposite wall. The base of the castle was larger than it looked from further down the hill, and lush green grass covered what had clearly once been a moat. They headed carefully around, anti-clockwise, Sven bringing up the rear again walking backwards, Arthur carefully peering round corners and between stones. They didn't know which side of the octagonal structure the entrance was on – it wasn't the side they'd come up. Now they just had to hope they stumbled on it before the other team made it round the other side . . .

Looking out across the wide landscape, Arthur suddenly felt a pull. It was beautiful up there, clear and wild. He imagined what it would be like if he was *really* attacking this castle, then he remembered that, of course, he was. The fact that the rest of his life was rapidly turning to shit seemed, briefly, less important.

Round the following bend, he spotted out of the corner of his eye what he had been looking for – a dark break in the stone that must be the entrance.

'Okay, there it is,' he whispered down the line.

'What are we going to do?' said Marcus. 'Are they there?'

'No – but they can't be far away,' said Arthur. 'We're going to have to go NOW, before they get round the outside way.'

Marcus passed the news back, and they all nodded solemnly.

'Okay, on my count, we're going to run for the door and then stand with our backs against it to defend . . . oh shit, I think I just saw a flash of yellow – GOOOO!'

They dashed out from behind the cover of the wall and plunged around to the front, Sandwiches barking madly, just as the yellow armbands were trying to prime their weapons on the opposite side. The first sludge hit the wall behind them.

'DOWN! DOWN!' screamed Arthur. 'And FIRE!'

The red balls went whistling through the sky with a surprising velocity.

'And again!'

Ross's team, cursing and outnumbered, had retreated to the cover of some nearby trees, and were digging themselves in and watching the others closely.

'Arthur,' said Marcus, who had turned round to open the door. 'Small problem.'

* * *

Arthur made sure Sven and Gwyneth were in guarding positions, checked none of the team in the trees was creeping forward or trying to flank, then tried to give his undivided attention to Marcus.

The door was, in fact, a portcullis, truly and

firmly down. You could tell just by looking at it there was no point in trying to budge it – this was ancient and solid metal and would neither give nor be lifted. Down on the right-hand side were three levers: one red, one blue and one green.

On the red lever it said, 'I open this door'. The blue lever said, 'I do not open this door.' The green lever said, 'The blue lever does not open this door'.

'Great!' said Arthur, the adrenalin in his body working properly now. 'Pull the red lever. That's nice of them.'

'Hang on!' said Marcus. His voice was shaky with excitement. Underneath the levers, there was a now familiar yellow folder. Inside it said, 'One of these statements is true. One is false. One is either true or false. You have one chance at pulling a lever.'

'Oh crap!' said Arthur. 'We don't have much time. They're not going to stay in that bloody wood all day.'

'Quiet,' said Marcus, drawing himself up to his full five foot six. 'This, I believe, is a logical problem.' He beamed. 'My moment has come.'

* * *

All was silence except for Sandwiches, who was capering about, barking madly.

'That's not bloody fair, having an extra bloody dog,' could be heard emanating from the undergrowth.

'Cowards!' shouted Sven.

'Sh,' whispered Arthur. 'Otherwise someone is going to say, "Come over here and say that," and this whole thing is going to turn into a paint bath.'

'Come over here and say that!' came the growling voice from the undergrowth. Arthur shook his head at Sven frantically.

'It's the green lever,' said Marcus, straightening up and announcing solemnly.

'What about the red lever that says it's the lever?' Arthur was sceptical and reckoned on a double bluff.

'One's true and one's false, right?' said Marcus. 'So the red lever can't be true because then they'd all be true. And the blue lever can't be true because then they'd all be false.'

'My arm hurts,' said Gwyneth, who was holding her gun high, trained on the undergrowth, 'and now my head hurts, too.'

'Trust me,' said Marcus.

Arthur smiled at him. 'You're the only one that could have worked that out.'

'Neh,' said Marcus.

'Yeah, I could have done it,' said Sven. 'Probably.'

'Hang on,' said Gwyneth. 'What if it's the wrong one and he gets electrocuted or something?'

'Good point,' said Arthur. Then he swallowed, thought about it for a second and finally said, 'Would you like me to pull the lever?'

'Nope,' said Marcus. 'Logic never lies. Has no moral imperative. It's right. Don't worry.'

And he stepped forward proudly, brought his hand calmly onto the lever and pulled it down.

* * *

Simultaneously there was a huge creaking noise as the giant portcullis began to lift, and an ominous, horrifying splattering noise.

'Marcus!' Gwyneth's voice arced slowly over the air, as Marcus, his hand the last thing to leave the wall, was thrown back several feet by the paintball bullet. Sven immediately started pumping his gun into the trees, but it was too late; the damage was done.

Marcus, all seven stone of him, had been thrown onto the ground by the force of the close-range shot.

'Are you all right?' Arthur knelt beside him, aiming to pull him to safety under the opening of the gate.

'I'm fine,' said Marcus, breathless and winded. 'You'll have to go on without me.'

'We can't leave you here!'

'After all you've done.' Gwyneth knelt down beside him. Sven was making Rambo-style terror noises out in front, shooting repeatedly.

'GO I tell you! If you fail now I'll never forgive myself. Go, and leave me here. DO IT.'

Arthur looked at him with more respect. 'You've . . .'

'It's all right,' said Marcus, settling back and beginning to close his eyes. 'You don't need to tell me. I know.'

Arthur clapped him on the shoulder and Marcus grabbed his arm and clasped it one last time.

'Thank you,' said Arthur softly. 'Sven! Sven! Come ON! We've got to get inside and close this bloody gate.'

Sven was dancing between splashing yellow bullets. 'Come on, you WANKERS.'

Gwyneth jumped up and dragged the back of his collar. 'QUICK! IN!'

On the other side, underneath the dark arch, thankfully, there was only one lever to pull. Arthur did so immediately, and the portcullis began to come down quickly. For some reason, he got a lump in his throat watching Marcus there on the other side of it, patient where he had fallen.

'SANDWICHES!' screamed Sven suddenly. 'He's not going to make it!'

430

The game little dog had been hurtling himself about and nipping and yapping at the enemy's ankles as they had emerged from their tree hideout and even now were running towards the gate.

'I have to go . . .'

'You CAN'T,' said Arthur, pulling him further into the safe recesses of the wall.

'You'll get shot immediately. I can't do without you.'

'So you'll leave him like you left Marcus? Sandwiches!'

And Sven leaped out again, putting himself into the range of fire.

'I'm NOT stopping it,' said Arthur. Ross's mob were thirty feet away . . . fifteen . . . ten . . . and the portcullis was five foot . . . four foot . . . three . . .

'SANDWICHES!'

Now there was less than a foot to go, and the other side were nearly on it. Realizing he wasn't going to fit his fat bottom underneath the gate, Ross had reloaded his gun and was standing full square in front of the entrance.

For the second time, Gwyneth grabbed the full weight of Sven and pulled him, and they both went flying backwards into a small alcove, just as a tiny flash of white, brown and black squeezed itself under the tiniest gap between the closing gate and the ground, and catapulted itself into Sven's arms.

The three of them landed in a heap, watched by an incredulous Arthur, shaking his head.

'Unbelievable,' he said. And, 'Great!' when he saw that what he'd taken for an alcove in fact led to a dark passageway.

* * *

Arthur unpacked the torch Rafe had passed onto them and gingerly pointed it upwards. The staircase curled round the inner wall of the castle. Other walls were long gone, and tangled weeds and wild undergrowth furled up between the rocks across the floor. Holes in the roof let through light from the sky, but mostly it had held, and as they moved further away from the portcullis and the central courtyard, it became more and more difficult to see where they were going.

'Who do you think used to live here?' said Gwyneth in wonderment. 'It's a proper castle. I feel like I should be wearing a wimple.'

Or a chastity belt, Arthur found himself thinking sadly.

They clung to the wall and wound up and around the inside stairs. Water dripped down the sides of it, and moss grew. It didn't feel like anyone had been there for hundreds of years.

'I wonder what the last person to leave thought?' said Gwyneth dreamily, envisaging a world full of princesses and marriages and – oh, things that could never happen now. She swallowed hard.

'Probably, "Oh no, I've just been horribly killed by marauding hordes,"' said Sven.

Ahead, in the torchlight, at the top of the stairs, Arthur suddenly caught sight of a door. His heart jumped.

'Ssh!' he said, and pointed ahead. The door was made of an ancient heavy wood, studded with massive iron bolts, with a large black knocker in the middle. 'That's got to be it,' he whispered.

All of them stood stock-still in trepidation.

'Well,' said Gwyneth. 'I guess that's where we're headed.' Still none of them moved.

'What do you think's behind the door?' said Sven, voicing their fears.

'Oh, come on, what can it be?' said Gwyneth stoutly. 'You'd never get a . . . ehem . . . twenty-foot python up these stairs. Or a shark, say.'

'Yeah,' said Sven. 'Right. They still haven't cloned Hitler, have they?'

'Don't talk nonsense,' said Arthur. 'It'll probably just be another problem solving thing.'

'Well, that's handy now Marcus is dead,' said Sven.

'Marcus is not *dead*,' said Arthur. 'Come on. It's the last hurdle now. We've done brilliantly. Just a few more steps. Let's keep moving.'

He took one more step, and the castle exploded.

* * *

Gwyneth screamed as what felt like black shrapnel came towards her. A flurry and a dreadful roaring, flapping sound filled her entire field of sensation.

'ARTHUR!' she screamed.

But Arthur too was engulfed. He pushed out his arm in front of his eyes, and forced his back against the wall. Sandwiches, however, was leaping and throwing his body in the air, desperately trying to push himself upwards.

'*Flagermus*!' shouted Sven. 'Bugger it!'

'*What?*' yelled Arthur, trying to fight off the whirring torment.

'Bats!' said Sven. 'Bloody bats!'

'They're in my hair,' yelped Gwyneth. 'Urgh! Get off!'

Arthur tentatively opened his eyes and saw that Sven was right – but it wasn't just a few bats. There were literally hundreds of them, maybe thousands, streaming through the passage like an oil spill.

'They're biting me!' said Gwyneth.

'They won't bite you,' said Sven.

'No?' She flailed desperately at her head. 'Why do they call them *vampire* bats, then? Why not the friendly bats? VEGETARIAN bats?'

'Keep quiet,' said Arthur. 'They get about by

radar, don't they? We must have been making too much noise.'

'Yes, that's because BATS ARE FLYING IN MY EYES,' said Gwyneth, as the cloud circled and squawked.

Arthur pulled out his gun. 'Oh God,' he said, and put his finger on the trigger.

'You can't shoot the bats!' said Sven. 'They're a protected species!'

'Yes, and I AM NOT!' shouted Gwyneth. 'Shoot the fucking bastards!'

'I'm not going to shoot them, only splat them.'

'They're only small. You'll kill them.'

Arthur heaved a sigh. 'Okay.'

He held the butt of the gun and started flailing it about in front of him.

'What's he doing?' said Gwyneth, who now had her jacket covering her entire head.

'Flailing around,' said Sven.

'I'm using my gun as a sword to cut a way through here, *actually*,' said Arthur.

'Okay. Let me know when they've all got tired and gone home,' said Gwyneth, slumping with her back against the wall. 'Eurgh. There's bat crap everywhere.'

Sandwiches came and put his head in her lap.

'Sandwiches and I don't like it up here. It's yucky and frightening.'

Arthur was antagonizing the bats, which were swirling in rapid concentric circles. 'Ha!' he shouted, cutting a rather elegant swathe through with the heel of his gun.

Amazingly, the strategy began to work; the more Arthur lunged at them, the further away the strange creatures were moving. Finally, they started to swoop out and under the eaves, across the dark spaces and into the further reaches of the castle, as if they had checked the visitors over thoroughly and found them wanting.

'Phew,' said Arthur, brushing the last few away. Then, with some reverence, he cleaned his sword – gun, and thrust it back into the scabbard – holster, round his waist. 'Thank God we're through that.'

'Yeah,' Sven agreed, brushing himself down. 'How the hell do you think the outward bound team got them all up here? That's amazing.'

* * *

Once they'd checked everyone was all right, and made absolutely sure there weren't any bats accidentally still tangled up in Gwyneth's hair, Arthur tentatively set forward once again. No one had come out from the room ahead of them at the commotion, and he couldn't imagine what lay beyond. He put his hand on the heavy bolted door.

Chapter Fifteen

The door swung open at the lightest touch. It wasn't locked after all.

Daylight streamed in. The room was octagonal, like the castle itself, and had windows – well, not glass windows of course, holes cut into the walls – on all sides. The room was cold, but bright; with heavy stone walls and great, crumbling flagstones on the floor.

There was only one object in the room, and all of them crept in and stared at it.

* * *

'But that's . . .'

Arthur nodded slowly, grimly. 'This is . . . this is absolutely impossible.'

Sven leaned forward. 'Why is she . . .'

'I don't know.'

Arthur's face had gone white, staring straight ahead, as cold as ice. 'What the hell are they doing to me?' he said, almost to himself.

* * *

Fay didn't stir. It really was impossible to tell, as she lay on the surface of the stone table, whether she was asleep or even alive, although when you looked closely you could see her chest lightly rise and fall.

She was dressed in a simple long grey shift, belted loosely around her hips. Her hair, normally pulled back with cheap scrunchies in untidy pony-tails, had been brushed around her shoulders, and her cheeks were pink in the cold.

None of the three could approach her. It was as if they were rooted to the spot by some deep sense of uneasiness, of an enchantment sensed in her peaceful face.

'I've seen this before,' said Gwyneth, nodding. 'It's very clever. You take someone out of one of the teams to be what you have to find. Woman in jeopardy and all that. This is a good company.'

Arthur looked at her. 'You have . . . you have *no* idea.'

Gwyneth looked at his stricken face.

He took a step backwards, and looked from one to the other, his head spinning. This must have been what – no, it couldn't. Could this have been what Lynne had been talking about? Nothing made any sense.

'Do you think she's wired to a bomb?' said Sven.

Arthur staggered back. 'You're right. It's just a trick. It's just something they're doing as part of the game. That's all it is.'

'Has he gone bonkers?' said Sven to Gwyneth. But she didn't answer. She had some idea of what he was thinking. She swallowed hard, and looked at him.

Arthur was looking at Fay, then turned to look straight at Gwyneth.

Gwyneth looked at Fay, then back at Arthur, and for a very long moment, neither of them could speak.

* * *

'You were . . .'

He couldn't finish the sentence. 'You would have been my queen.' He smiled ruefully.

Gwyneth stepped towards him. He automatically stepped one pace backwards. 'I – can't I?' said Gwyneth. Her eyes, suddenly, were filling with tears.

Arthur couldn't speak, just stared back at her.

'What are we doing?' said Sven, suddenly. 'I

mean, call me crazy, but don't we have a plan to carry out? It's almost like there's some kind of atmosphere between you two.'

Gwyneth and Arthur couldn't tear their eyes away from each other.

'Don't,' said Arthur to Sven. 'It might be dangerous.'

'Everything's dangerous,' said Gwyneth.

'No, playing with fire is dangerous,' he shot back.

'La la la la,' said Sven. 'Come *on*. Let's move!'

'Don't,' said Arthur again. 'You could get hurt. We'll have to figure this out together. I don't trust the people running this for a second, and neither should you.'

There was silence in the room.

'I . . .' she started, stuttering. 'Well, I mean, *she*'s here. It's almost like a sign.'

'She was true,' said Arthur.

'Yes, apart from when she slept with Ross and fucked you out of our info!' said Gwyneth, outraged.

'But you were . . .' Arthur shook his head.

'Whatever you thought,' she said, 'maybe I just wasn't. Maybe I was just what you wanted me to be.'

'No,' said Arthur. 'You were.'

'Well, then,' said Gwyneth, suddenly furious. If

men wanted her and couldn't talk to her, was it her fault? Her problem? 'You couldn't talk to her – you couldn't talk to me. Choose.'

* * *

'Oh God,' said Sven suddenly. 'Well, seeing as I'm the virgin round here, I think I'm going to have to kiss the princess. Or get the grail. Or whatever the consolation prize is in amongst everyone else's sexual tension, because I am Very Brave.'

Neither of them heard. Arthur was staring at Gwyneth, with absolute sadness in his eyes, as if he couldn't tear his gaze away.

And before either of the others could turn round, Sven strode across the room, and gently, passionately and firmly, kissed Fay's still body on the mouth.

* * *

It happened so quickly and so slowly at the same time, Arthur could never put it together again in his memory, not in any coherent order. But when it came, he had not hesitated, and he was not afraid.

In fact, his face was already turning towards Fay; already moving away from Gwyneth, just as Sven started to move. Then, the face at the octagonal window – that was first. Then, the gentle fluttering of Fay's eyelids as she woke up. Then, the huge noise, ricocheting in the heavy walled room, louder than he could believe. Then – was it then? – he was flying, flying straight without a doubt in his mind towards Fay, pushing her out of the way, down onto the floor. Then the enormous burst of yellow, such a garish colour at such close range. Then the red, and Arthur wondering why they would have red paintballs as well as yellow. And then, infinitely slowly, a white flower dropping from Gwyneth's grip, and Sven slowly sliding off the stone table and onto the floor and not moving.

Chapter Sixteen

Later, Arthur would remember odd fragments, like Howard. Everything else, this huge shadow, this whole wall of oblivion and grief, was tempered by a niggling annoyance with this man beside him, who had been following Ross's party to make a victory record. And that terrible ladder of course; the dreadful rickety construction the opposing team had managed to put together and push up the tower in an attempt at a final confrontation. It had collapsed immediately after the accidental discharge of Ross's gun, just as he had grabbed the inside of the window sill in triumph. Ross had dropped straight to the ground and had been lucky to get away with a broken leg and a sprained wrist.

The balloon had arrived in moments of course, and within minutes a helicopter was over the horizon, reminding Arthur that however far he might have felt from civilization, it had never gone away at all. But the minutes had seemed like hours, and worthless, worthless hours when the mountain ambulance man simply shook his head, confirmed that a paintball had entered Sven's left eye – they had all of course taken off their masks once they were inside – with enough force to puncture a hole in his brain. He may as well have been shot by a real bullet. It would have been very quick.

Gwyneth went outside and promptly threw up by a wall. Arthur was dimly aware of Fay awake, there, standing with her, finding this confusing but unable to make sense of it. There were many people here now – time had passed without his being aware of it somehow; police in bright yellow raincoats, who were talking deeply and intently to Mr d'Aragon and the sergeant, neither of whom, now, in the light of day, looked in the least bit intimidating. Vaguely, Arthur was aware that they were loading something onto the helicopter, and in his head he supposed it used to be Sven. He stumbled around the castle, alarmingly unaware of his surroundings.

Ross was lying on the ground, yelping in pain as the police and ambulance crew competed to take information from him.

'I didn't mean it, Arthur!' he screamed, as

Arthur floated past him. 'I didn't mean it!'

The noise, with people shouting and the flap flap flap of the helicopter's rotors, was immense.

But Arthur was looking for something, and he couldn't think what. He was aware of his body moving, but couldn't possibly have said why. It did a tour of the area outside the castle, then headed back in again.

'I'm afraid you can't go up there, sir,' said the policeman. 'We've sealed it off for now. Might be a crime scene.'

'I'm sorry,' said Arthur, again aware of his voice speaking the words, but not knowing how they were coming out of his mouth. 'I must. It is my will.'

And the policeman stood aside.

* * *

He was back in the octagonal room again, empty now except for the ghastly, livid red and yellow cascading down the walls.

He walked round the room three times, quite unable to articulate what he was doing there. Finally, on his fourth repetition, he saw it.

* * *

If you hadn't looked very closely, you wouldn't have seen it at all. There was simply a snip; a smidgeon of black peeping out from the corner, underneath the slab table where Fay had lain.

Arthur knelt down on his hands and knees and pushed out his hand.

'Sshhhh,' he whispered. 'Sssshhhh.'

Although, of course, Sandwiches wasn't making any noise at all.

Arthur gently touched the dog on the neck, not entirely sure he wouldn't get bitten. On one level he would have welcomed that; something to break through the terrible numbness that seemed to have taken hold of his body.

But Sandwiches didn't bite him. Instead, he nuzzled his nose forward and looked straight into Arthur's eyes, as if trusting him to help him understand exactly what had just happened.

'Oh,' said Arthur. 'Oh, Sandwiches. Oh, Sandwiches.'

And he began to weep, big tearing sobs that ripped through his whole body and caused his upper half to shake and convulse.

Sandwiches shuffled himself forward just enough, and put his head in Arthur's lap.

* * *

Arthur couldn't go home. The others had, Cathy and Rafe as shocked and disbelieving – almost more so, for they had seen the helicopters but had

446

no idea what had taken place — as they were. Ross had been taken to hospital; there would of course be no charges. This was undoubtedly an accident, not even, Arthur was stunned to find out, a massively uncommon one. And if he hadn't got Fay out of the way, it could have been worse.

It wasn't easy to track down Sven's parents. The Danish embassy were on to it, but in the meantime Arthur had to identify the body, sign the paperwork and liaise with Mountain Rescue to take the body to London, where it would be shipped on to Copenhagen.

It didn't help that he was getting no sleep; partly from the horror, and partly from having Sandwiches in the room at the local inn. The little dog was refusing to sleep at all, and paced in front of the door the entire night, waiting for his master to come home, his nails click-clacking on the cheap linoleum. At every car's headlights which passed through on the road he would immediately stiffen and hold himself to attention; every door closing, every toilet flushing. It was driving them both crazy.

He wouldn't eat either, although Arthur couldn't blame him for that; nor was Arthur. He could barely think; get up, move around. His concentration was shot and he completely ignored the messages that were piling up around him.

The kind landlady tried to go out of her way to make palatable meals, to look after this heartbroken-looking man. She also gave him the newspapers which had been sent from Coventry, and he glanced at them. On the cover of the Coventry *Herald* was Howard's exclusive, with an exceptionally flattering picture of Sven and Sandwiches taken at least five years ago – Sven's beer gut was less than the size of a space hopper, and Sandwiches was only a pup. Looking closely, Arthur realized it was his graduation photograph. Sven hadn't even been thirty when he died.

'**Brave Coventry Man Dies in Tragic Accident Trying to Save Town**' ran the all-new headline.

A member of the planning committee for the European City of Culture bid for Coventry has been killed in a tragic accident on an outward bound course.

There were details, then the leader column, right on the next page.

Sven Gunterson loved this city. A foreign national, he came from far away, but settled here and proceeded to dedicate his life to improving it for all its residents. We owe him our deepest debt of gratitude, from his wonderful plans for an ice festival imported from his native Denmark, to his support of the maze currently in the planning stages for Chapel Fields.

His loss is a tragic one for Coventry, but must not deter us from our aim. This paper has always supported the application. But now we go one further; we at the *Herald* say we WILL be the European City of Culture. And we will do it for Sven.

Arthur read this and almost smiled to himself. Of course, the paper wouldn't realize it was over. All was lost, surely. They couldn't possibly consider continuing to put themselves forward. It had all been for nothing. Less than nothing; much, much worse than nothing.

* * *

He walked out onto the tiny airstrip, which was barely more than some concrete plonked in a field. In the helicopter was the coffin containing Sven's body, which Arthur was accompanying to London, where Sven's parents were now waiting to take their son home for the last time. He couldn't bear to think what he would say to them. After all, he was Sven's boss and this had happened on his watch. He had been in charge; he had told Sven not to touch Fay, but he obviously hadn't told him strictly enough . . . The guilt bit deeply. He stepped up into the side of the helicopter, carrying Sandwiches, who was noticably thinner and quiet as a lamb. He probably thought they were going where Sven was.

Arthur prayed that no canine intuition was going to come into it, but he was thwarted – Sandwiches immediately climbed onto the coffin, lay down and started moaning. Arthur had never heard a dog moan, and this low crooning disturbed him immensely.

The nice man from the police liaison unit looked enquiringly at them both, but Arthur shook his head, and put his arm over the dog in lieu of a seat belt.

'It'll be about an hour into Heathrow,' said the pilot; there was no separating curtain in the tiny aircraft. Arthur nodded numbly. Normally he would have been thrilled to be taking his first trip in a helicopter, but under these circumstances . . .

He sat as the bird lifted, the noise immense, rumbling right through him, and kept a close eye on Sandwiches, who seemed immune to the noise, mourning his dead master on a ride through the night sky.

Arthur watched the stars coming out, thinking of the horse he had once seen riding across the constellations, leaving destruction in its wake. He wondered if this was the horse.

Suddenly there was an exclamation from the pilot. 'Fucking hell!'

Even in his state of shock, Arthur still registered that the one thing you never want to hear a pilot exclaim is 'fucking hell'.

'What is it?' said the policeman.

'Look at that!' said the pilot, pointing downwards.

Below, beneath the clouds, was darkness, punctuated by motorway lights and the occasional fairy-tale cluster which marked a town or village.

This wasn't a town, or a village, however. At first glance it might have been an airport.

'I've never seen anything like it,' said the pilot.

Arthur craned his eyes. They were flying over what looked like, but couldn't be – the scale was such it was extremely difficult to get his head around it – an enormous star.

The rows of lights went on for miles, tiny house lights and large streetlamps all turned on together by the people of the town below, spontaneously spelling out a great, shining star on the ground, a reproachful reflection of those above.

'What the hell are they doing down there?' said the policeman. 'That's amazing. It's great. People are going to love it, flying over that at night.'

The pilot nodded. 'I've never seen anything like it,' he repeated.

They were moving away from it now, and it was twinkling, huge and beautiful, in the distance.

'Where are we, anyway?' asked the policeman. The pilot briefly checked his co-ordinates.

'That was Coventry,' he said, although of course Arthur already knew.

Chapter Seventeen

It was such a beautiful morning, and there was a lot to do. Arthur couldn't stay in bed another second. It was too warm to wear a suit and tie — the weather was fantastic, even for July — but he did anyway, and headed outside.

There was so much to look at. Every day all year the town had been a hive of activity, after they'd won. Builders were everywhere, driving people crazy by digging up the main street to put the tramline back down that they'd only pulled up thirty years before. Every week different lighting schemes came in and were turned around, so that one night there might be a flower on the insurance building, or an arrow by the railway station; or all the lights down one street would be red. People's desire to join in never ceased to amaze him, and he never failed to smile at their ingenuity. Flowers raged everywhere that could be seen. All the leftover monies — sponsorship and donations — that came flooding in once they had officially won the competition — they'd used to carpet the town. It had been Cathy's idea to cover the roofs of the many, many low-level industrial buildings, warehouses and discount carpet stores in flowers. They looked like they were huddling under a huge colourful canopy, which could be seen from the bypass and motorways, poppies, dahlias, daisies and daffodils sailing away as far as the eye could see. That, and they'd made a hefty donation to the local renal unit.

He turned into Station Road, heading towards Chapel Fields.

Weeks he'd spent indoors, wondering over and over again what he had done to cause, or at least be there for a death; whether his absolute desire to take over this quest hadn't . . . Part of him knew it was an accident, part of him couldn't square it, not yet.

But the application had gone ahead. They had got the official confirmation from Brussels soon after Sven's funeral. Arthur was amazed they had done it, but it seemed there had been little discussion; this would certainly be the last time it would be decided this way, but decided it had to be, and it would be Coventry. Arthur hadn't known how he would take this news, but when it came he was very pleased. It felt in some way as though everything wasn't a complete waste of time.

Of course, there was to be an enquiry into the methods of how the award was given, but that didn't detract from this result; just closed down an outward bound company. The award had been so overwhelming, coming as it had in the depths of his grief, and Arthur had reached out to it – and the endless meetings; the paperwork, the administration; the fourteen-hour days; the hordes of new staff; the constant publicity   he'd even been on *Newsnight* – like a drowning man clinging to a life raft. Everything was work, and that kept him sane.

And now, it was five months on and here he was, walking to the park to open the maze. Finally. It was hard to believe it was here, that it would be even larger than the Sandwiches-savaged model.

The size of the thing, as he came to it over the path, completely threw him; it had been imported nearly full grown, and the rosebushes were taller than he was. The sides stretched away, further than the eye could see.

The maze man was there too, and like before he bowed gravely. 'You are happy?' he asked Arthur.

'It's beautiful,' said Arthur, not answering the question.

'Well, watch out for the thorns.' The man looked at him. 'But you know all about thorns, don't you?'

'Yes,' said Arthur.

A crowd had gathered – it had been well publicized in the press – and a small podium with a microphone had been set up. Sir Eglamore was positively beaming.

Arthur looked at the crowd that had gathered and coughed slightly.

'I just wanted to say . . . thank you so much to everyone who's here.'

Howard stepped forward and took a photograph.

'Yes . . . thank you. The support that's been shown to us in this town over the last few months, if not before . . .' He thought about it. 'Well, not before, but definitely since then, has been overwhelming. We . . .'

And Arthur surveyed the crowd to see who was there.

In fact, since they'd got back, there'd been a general diaspora of the office, even after the official awarding of their status.

Gwyneth had returned to her office in London almost straight away. They had barely spoken. He couldn't bring himself to talk to her.

But there she was today, shyly standing at the

back of the crowd. Her hair was a little longer. It suited her. Also in the crowd was Rafe. He had left the office too; he was off to pursue a PhD in international poverty and relations in Nairobi. Arthur had high hopes for it. He couldn't tell if they'd noticed each other yet – but that was ridiculous; they must have. There was Cathy, already going up to Gwyneth, wearing her broad smile. Since they'd got back, she'd practically been a different person. She'd stood up for herself more and more around the office, refusing to take any shit – and, from the way she told it, taking less and less at home, too. She had confided in Arthur that conquering her fear of heights had made her think about what other fears in her life were holding her back for no good reason – and she had found more than a few.

Marcus had come back for two weeks, then, completely out of the blue, handed in his notice. He had returned to Wales with his boyfriend and started working for an outward bound company – not the same one – and, in the one brief postcard Arthur had had from him, was having a fabulous time, outdoors in all weathers getting cold and wet and helping people climb hills for no reason.

And Arthur had finally turned up one morning and given the temp an official certificate of permanent employment. Overwhelmed, she had broken down into tears and insisted on telling him her name. Since then she had been late or absent eighty-six times.

'We – from the planning department – we put a lot into this maze; into this city. And it took a lot out of us. So we just hope that you enjoy this . . .'

He swallowed suddenly.

'There's someone who can't be here, but who would have loved it very much. Well, he would have complained that it was boring and he couldn't be bothered to walk round it. But underneath he would have liked it. Maybe. So, I'd like to welcome you all to the Sven Gunterson Memorial Maze.'

Everyone clapped loudly as he cut the ribbon, Howard took another photograph, and then the crowd surged forward, chattering excitedly.

Within moments, it seemed, everyone had disappeared into the maze, and he was left outside alone. The high walls muffled the noise, and it felt as if he was the only person in the park, except for the maze man standing there with him.

'Aren't you going to try it?' he asked.

'Yes,' said Arthur. 'It's just, last time, it seemed to have a rather strange effect . . .'

'It's a well-sited maze,' said the man. 'You should try it.'

* * *

The dark yew and rosebushes kept off the heat of

the sun; it was pleasantly cool inside and ridiculously quiet. Fifty people must have disappeared inside here, thought Arthur. Where had they all gone? Occasionally he caught a high-pitched giggle, or a light footfall, but whenever he whipped round to spot where it had come from, there was nothing there.

He didn't plan which way to go, but meandered, enjoying the scent of the bushes, the occasional buzzing of bees, the coolness of the deep green. His heart felt lighter than it had in many many months. He was surprised to suddenly turn a corner and find himself in the heart, the centre of the maze.

A small fountain tinkled there. A cherub stood in the centre, next to an elaborately carved bench, and white flowers carpeted the ground. Arthur went and sat on the bench to wait for her.

* * *

She was looking a lot less drawn, he noticed. In fact, she was looking well. As well as when they'd first met, at that personnel conference, six years ago.

'Hey,' she said softly.

'Hello.'

Arthur stood up and walked towards her, and suddenly they found themselves hugging.

'Oh, Fay,' said Arthur. 'I'm so sorry.'

* * *

They were both on the edge of tears.

'Well, you saved my life,' said Fay, as they pulled apart.

'Yes, but . . .' He forced himself to talk and not change the subject. 'I'm sorry.'

'Why?'

'Because we were in love . . . once. And I was . . . lazy. Complacent. I wouldn't talk to you. And I pissed it up against the wall.'

'Well, I was no barrel of monkeys. Wait, is that right? Well, you know what I mean. Maybe I *was* a barrel of monkeys. Hairy and hard to control.'

'Well, a bit. But I – I should have fought for it.'

'Seems like you do plenty of fighting.'

'God, yes, it does, rather.'

She shrugged. 'It suits you, taking the initiative.'

He grimaced, and there was a pause.

Fay sat on the bench. 'Well, I did some pretty awful things too.'

'You weren't yourself.'

She raised her eyebrows. 'I wasn't, you know. You – you split my heart right down the middle. For nothing, Arthur. For some excitement, and some blonde bitch and . . .'

He raised his hands. 'Again, already I know.'

Fay shook herself. 'And I made myself a victim,

too. But, it's in the past. And, when it was really important, you came through for me.'

He looked at her, and remembered her as the girl she had been, not the shrew he'd pictured her as in the last couple of years. He pushed a stray strand of her hair, an oddly affectionate gesture. She looked up at him.

'You know, when Sven kissed me . . . it was like he really did wake me up.'

Arthur kept looking at her.

'Like I'd been asleep since I left you . . . like I had no idea what was happening . . .'

He smiled. 'And yet you still went back to . . .'

'I know,' she said, thinking of all that had happened since.

'How's Sandwiches?' she asked, quickly.

'Not bad,' said Arthur. 'He ate a tablecloth the other day. Gives one cause to hope, you know? That he's eating at all.'

Fay nodded.

'How's Ross?'

'Not bad,' said Fay. 'Much better, in fact. You really put the fear of God into him. He's a changed man. Six weeks in bed was quite useful, too.'

'Really?'

'Yes, he's had to take up yoga and changed into a much more spiritual person. Practically a conversion. He's discovered a lot of inner calm. In

461

fact, he's opening a chain of yoga centres called "Yogotit".'

'Well, that sounds great,' said Arthur, trying to sound sincere.

'Reckons we'll make a fortune.'

'Great!'

'And . . .'

She coyly rubbed her stomach. It took him a second to realize what she meant.

'You're not?'

He was genuinely delighted, if fairly desperate that it would take after its mother.

'Looks like it.'

'Oh my God! Congratulations.'

She smiled.

'If it's a boy we thought we'd call it Sven. The hygiene issue is a worry of course . . .'

Arthur smiled and hugged her again.

* * *

They left the heart of the maze by one exit, just as Gwyneth entered by another, too late to see them, Rafe by another.

'It's okay,' said Rafe, quietly. And they came together in the summer light, soft on Gwyneth's golden hair and Rafe's long eyelashes, soft on the rippling water and the gentle perfume of the roses, where they kissed in secret as long as the summer afternoon, and the white flowers blew in the breeze, and no-one else found the heart of the maze at all.

* * *

'Not this way,' said Fay, only half-joking.

'That'll take us to the exit, won't it?' said Arthur.

'No, definitely not!'

They looked at each other and smiled.

'Well, why don't you go *this* way and I'll go *this* way?' said Fay, smiling.

'I wish it could have been that simple last time,' grumbled Arthur, but he too was smiling. And he embraced her one last time, and they separated.

* * *

At first, he scarcely noticed it getting colder. It was so pleasant, after the heat of the day, to feel a cool breeze through his shirt.

But it was definitely feeling cooler. Practically chilly. Arthur shivered in his shirt. It was late July – why so chilled? He looked overhead, and the bright blue sky of the morning was rapidly darkening. Even the green on the walls, and the trees of the park he could see up above him looked oddly different – with a start he realized they were turning brown.

This couldn't be right. But it was properly cold now; there was a frost in the air, and the grass was crackling beneath his feet. He started to move faster, breaking twigs. The cold air froze in his lungs.

It started to snow.

* * *

This was ridiculous. It must be one of those freak storm things that blow in from Greenland: El Niño, something like that. In the meantime, he would have to get somewhere warm or put some more clothes on. He worried about the other people trapped in the maze, but he couldn't see or hear any signs of anyone at all – maybe they'd already left.

He wasn't sure for how long he tried to struggle through the maze, but the snow came down harder and harder, and he held his thin shirtsleeve over his face to try and make out a way ahead.

Finally – and it was, very quickly, becoming dark – he stumbled through a gap in the hedge and into a part of the park he hadn't visited before.

* * *

'God, there you are,' said the familiar voice. 'That took you bloody well forever. I've watched frog-spawn evolve into monkeys in the time that just took you.'

Arthur looked up crossly. 'Yes, well, your concept of time wasn't the best to begin with.'

'Nonsense.' Lynne took out a heavy pocket watch, and tapped it twice. 'It is absolutely and immutably, two thousand years past four. And we are late!'

'Late for what?' said Arthur. 'And why is it so cold?'

'Just . . . um, freak storm,' said Lynne. 'El Niño?'

She handed him a large fur.

'Is that real fur?' said Arthur.

'I don't know, is that real pleurisy?'

Arthur would have worn the still beating hide of a Disney fawn at this point, so didn't argue, threw it on – it was wonderfully warm – and followed Lynne as she hurried across the fields.

'Where are we going?' he said, more than once. Lynne shushed him.

'How are you feeling?' she asked. 'As your therapist, I mean.'

'Not bad,' said Arthur. 'Things are – well, you know.'

'Do you miss Sven?'

'Yes, but . . . more . . . I just can't believe . . . how could he be there and then not?'

Lynne's voice softened. 'You made the right choice, Arthur.'

'But still,' said Arthur, shaking his head. 'It just . . . it means it wasn't worth it.'

Lynne reached the end of the clearing, and they pushed their way through some trees which were covered and frosted with snow.

'Now,' she said. 'Where were we?'

* * *

In front of them was the river; great, wide and, to Arthur's stupefaction, completely frozen.

All up and down it, as far as the eye could see, were people, stalls, colour, and light. Braziers from which people were selling chestnuts were actually lit on the ice. Children skated, screeching and laughing, in and out of the crowd.

Lynne stepped out onto the ice. 'Don't fall over,' she said to Arthur, who immediately did so. She hauled him up with remarkable strength as he found his ice legs.

They wandered carefully through the crowds, Arthur marvelling at the different things there were to buy: not only that, but the ferris wheel was up and running. He couldn't imagine who would dare to go on that, but it was full.

More than that, dancers on ice were circling on a makeshift stage marked out with braziers, as musicians played, and jesters roamed, and one of the jesters tried (badly) to juggle with fire brands.

It was exactly as he had pictured it, and everything he could have wished for.

Down the bank, Arthur saw a group of bright lights heralding the tram station. The colours, noises and smells on all sides overwhelmed him.

'I don't . . . I don't believe it.'

He waved wildly to the jester, who looked straight through him.

'Keep moving,' said Lynne. 'Don't try to talk to anyone. For . . . um, no reason.'

'This is great . . . it's *great*,' he said.

'Well, pat yourself on the back.'

A hectic game of ice tag came between them. Arthur looked at the joyous children and shook his head. 'But still . . . was it worth losing Sven, though?'

'Remember those kids underneath the embankment that day?' said Lynne

'Yes.'

'That's those kids playing tag.'

She smiled at him. 'It was worth it. This city could have taken more than losing Sven, I promise.'

Arthur stood stock still, trying to take in all the scene at once.

'Come on, come on, we can't stay.'

'*Why*? I want to stay.'

'Well, you can't.'

Gradually, the lights of the ice carnival had tapered out and the noise was fading behind them. They were approaching the far bank of the river. Looking up, for an instant, Arthur thought he saw something move through the trees.

'What's that?'

'That's where we're going.'

The fair was well behind them now, and everything was quiet, just the crackle of the ice beneath their feet. Arthur peered, with only the moonlight to guide him, at the white shape moving between the trees.

Eventually it resolved itself.

* * *

'Oh my God,' said Arthur. 'It's the horse! The horse that was in my dream!'

It was. The beautiful mare stood at least seventeen hands high, and was snorting cold air through her nostrils. Lynne stalked towards it.

Arthur turned around and took one, last regretful look behind him at the town; glowing, with light and colour, and even in this sudden, suspicious chill, with warmth and fun and glee. As he watched, fireworks exploded over the river and lit up the sky. Lynne was untethering the horse.

Suddenly, he felt something under his hand. Starting and looking down, he saw that it was

Sandwiches, or, more specifically, Sandwiches's tongue, giving him a friendly lick.

He smiled in pleasure and knelt down in the cold to scratch the little dog.

'Come on!' said Lynne sternly. 'It's time you learned to ride. There's a Commonwealth games going begging in Barnsley.'

'God,' said Arthur to Sandwiches, as both man and dog looked at Lynne, then straightened and followed her into the trees. 'You have no idea how glad I am you're here.'